THE SECRETS OF ONE MARLBOROUGH COLLEGE GIRL

BY E.L.GOGH

First published in Great Britain in 2016 by E.L.Gogh

Copyright © 2016 E.L.Gogh. All rights reserved.

No part of this publication may be reproduced, stored in retrieval system or transmitted in any form or by any means, electronic, mechanical, photocopying, recording or otherwise without the prior permission of the author.

This is a work of fiction. Names, characters, businesses, places, events and incidents are either the products of the author's imagination or used in a fictitious manner. Any resemblance to actual persons, living or dead, or actual events is purely coincidental.

The moral rights of the author, E.L. Gogh have been asserted.

To my beautiful mum

Acknowledgements

I'd like to thank my editor, Alice McVeigh, for all her help and encouragement and Stephanie Parcus for designing the cover.

CONTENTS

CHAPTER 1	7
CHAPTER 2	21
CHAPTER 3	27
CHAPTER 4	35
CHAPTER 5	43
CHAPTER 6	49
CHAPTER 7	55
CHAPTER 8	63
CHAPTER 9	69
CHAPTER 10	75
CHAPTER 11	83
CHAPTER 12	97
CHAPTER 13	103
CHAPTER 14	113
CHAPTER 15	123
CHAPTER 16	143
CHAPTER 17	151
CHAPTER 18	165
CHAPTER 19	173
CHAPTER 20	189

CHAPTER 21	197
CHAPTER 22	203
CHAPTER 23	213
CHAPTER 24	229
CHAPTER 25	235
CHAPTER 26	251
CHAPTER 27	263
CHAPTER 28	275
CHAPTER 29	285
CHAPTER 30	293
CHAPTER 31	301
CHAPTER 32	311
CHAPTER 33	317
CHAPTER 34	325
CHAPTER 35	331
CHAPTER 36	345
CHAPTER 37	351
CHAPTER 38	367
CHAPTER 39	373
CHAPTER 40	385
CHAPTER 41	399

CHAPTER 1

Time flew by and before we knew it we were landing at Heathrow, where a school minibus driver met us, holding up our name-cards: Sasha Emelianova and Ala Gromova. Then we were on our way, racing down the M4 towards Marlborough. The rather dull suburban landscape originally glimpsed through the car windows metamorphosed into Wiltshire's pastoral idyll: green meadows studded with bluebells, herds of fluffy sheep, and pretty stone cottages set in flowering gardens. It was all reminiscent of water-colours from the children's books we'd read when we were small: we were both in high spirits.

'Well, Sashka, it seems that the sun is shining on us,' Ala jabbed her elbow into my side. 'I feel we will be very welcome here.'

Even at dusk, Marlborough made quite an impression: a characterful town with cobblestone pavements and tile-roofed Victorian houses, decorated at every turn with colourful flowers and bright signs, as if for some festive holiday. We were driven through the main – indeed the only – High Street, then we swept right at a small roundabout, took another turn and drove straight through the impressive college gates, flanked by old-fashioned gate piers and railings. The bus driver soon departed, leaving us and our luggage in the middle of a rectangular courtyard, the centre of which was laid to lawn with a perimeter drive, the size of a football pitch, which was studded with elegant, ivy-covered old English school buildings. We recognised the view from the cover of the Marlborough College prospectus, which had been sent to us the previous summer. My heart was pounding with excitement – though I felt a little nervous too. A female passer-by stopped when she saw us.

'Hello, girls, you look a little lost. . . Which house are you in?'

I turned round to see a pleasant-looking woman, her hair in a neat bob. Ala responded, 'We're in New Court,' upon which the teacher smiled and shook our hands.

'So pleased to meet you. I'm Miss Foxton, your housemistress.'

We introduced ourselves, and Miss Foxton said, 'Perfect, welcome to college! You're just in time for our house meeting. Please, follow me.'

New Court, a recently-built girls' house, was just a moment's walk away, and soon we were breathing in its smell of new wood and fresh cleanliness. Inside, around fifteen newcomers – our new colleagues, I thought – had taken over the hall, which seemed full of lively chatter and laughter. With no free seats left, we slipped to the floor by the back wall, attracting curious glances and friendly smiles from our future housemates. Before we had a chance to speak to anyone, Miss Foxton started the meeting. It turned out that most of the girls there had only just arrived from other schools – including some from all-girls schools, which Ala whispered that she couldn't seem the point of. . .

Miss Foxton told us: 'Our official first meeting happens tomorrow at 7:30 in the Common Room, instead of this evening, as I'm sure that many of you are tired from your journeys. Please put tomorrow's meeting in your diaries: you should all have one in your welcome pack.

'From this point on, I want you to treat New Court as your home; I hope and trust that you'll all be very happy here. However, if you should have any problem – large or small, anything that worries you – you're most welcome to come and speak to me about it. My office is upstairs at the end of the corridor – just ring the bell at the side of the door.

'Now, I hope you've all had time to study the prospectus we sent you, and have found the diaries with picture of the College on their covers. We request that you use these in order to write down your schedule in two blocks: morning and afternoon. In terms of uniforms, the rules for Lower and Upper Sixth are less strict than for Hundreds and Removes, but you must still wear a dark skirt, one falling *below* the knee,' said Miss Foxton, with subtle emphasis, 'along with

CHAPTER 1

a neat blouse, and a sweater, of course, if it's cold. For Sunday morning chapel you'll also need a smart jacket or a dress, and formal shoes. I trust that you all have these in your wardrobes.'

Ala and I exchanged complacent glances. We had read the 'fine print' in the school rules, and had not come unprepared.

Miss Foxton continued: 'Also, you're not allowed to go to town after five o'clock, and "lights out" is always at ten. Either myself or Anna – our prefect, whom you'll soon meet – make the rounds each evening to ensure that no one is reading under her blanket with a torch.'

These are some rules, I thought, feeling a little worried.

'Breakfast is always between six and eight-thirty in Norwood Hall. I'm pleased to see that some of you seem to have already made friends,' she smiled at two girls whispering in the far corner. 'There are two TVs in the house, in the Common Room and in the TV room next to Anna's, though I should warn you that every seat is usually taken when *Neighbours* is on! . . . In addition, there's a small kitchen upstairs. If you feel hungry, you can always go up and make a snack or some toast – there's bread, butter, milk, coffee and tea available – but meals are served in Norwood Hall. Now, will those of you who haven't yet been shown where your rooms are, please follow me.'

Here Ala and I both jumped to our feet, along with several others. And that was when we learned that there had been a mix-up.

We were both in the Upper Sixth, but had accidentally joined the house meeting for the Lower Sixth. This didn't bother us much, until it turned out that there was only one room still available in the Upper Sixth at New Court, so one of us would have to move to a different house. And I already liked it so much, right here! – but I could tell from Ala's face that she felt just the same.

Miss Foxton said, 'It's up to you,' and I glanced at Ala. Ala offered to flip a coin, and – as usual – she was the lucky one, and would be staying in New Court.

'You'll probably get one of the houses with guys,' she told me as we parted, trying to cheer me up. 'It's a petticoat government here.'

I was put up for the night in the room of Anna Price, the New Court House prefect, still on holiday in Antibes. Miss Foxton had apologised twice about the mix-up, but assured me that she could guarantee me a place in a house just as nice – and had even promised that I could visit New Court anytime I liked, including house events, so I began to feel much better. Although I couldn't help thinking: *I just hope I'm as lucky with the housemistress in my new house.*

I loved Anna's room. It was very spacious, and its windows overlooked a courtyard containing a small, well-tended garden, hidden from the rest of the College. However, the room's interior was quite spartan: a single bed, a wooden desk with several shelves above it, a plain wardrobe and a sink with a small mirror.

Miss Foxton wished me good night and then left. About to shut the door behind her, I noticed, to my surprise, that it swung open both ways and had neither lock nor handle. . . *I hope people knock before entering here,* I thought, as I started to unpack. However, in about five minutes my door swung open and Ala raced inside, overflowing with excitement and news.

'The girl in the room next to mine thought I must be either Spanish or Italian. Italian: can you believe it? Must be my hair. She was shell-shocked when I told her that I was Russian. I'm guessing they haven't met many of us before.'

Meanwhile Ala was immediately resolving to become a 'perfect,' as apparently Anna's room was both better and bigger than hers.

'A *prefect*,' I corrected her, 'I think it means a leader of some kind.' I had just been invited to Ala's room, in order to compare it with Anna's, when Miss Foxton's authoritative tones announced that it was time to turn off the lights.

Ala rushed back to her room while I slipped into my borrowed bed, falling asleep almost immediately. I dreamed of Moscow, of my home, of my old school and – for some reason –of a fire-engine with blue flashing lights driving at a full speed towards me. The powerful roar of its siren seemed to get closer and closer and louder and louder each second. . . I woke up with a thudding

CHAPTER 1

heart just before it drove into me. The clock showed 6:00 a.m., but the fiery ringing in my ears persisted.

'Fire alarm! Everybody outside, now, at once!' Surprised, I opened the door. Sleepy girls were hurrying down the corridor in pyjamas and nightgowns of all sorts, multi-coloured robes and even hoods shaped like cuddly animal heads. Some were slipping on their dressing-gowns as they scampered along; others, seemingly without a care in the world, were walking barefoot at a leisurely pace. I grabbed my own dressing-gown and headed for the exit together with the rest.

'Hurry, girls, hurry!' urged a formidable-looking woman, her hair in incongruously pink hair rollers. Ala caught up with me, whispering, 'That's Miss Pope, our dame,' though I didn't know what a 'dame' was.

Soon a crowd of around fifty girls was gathered in the New Court garden, where a roll-call confirmed that no one was missing... *Just like at the summer camp where my parents used to send Ala and me*, I thought, gazing around.

It turned out that someone had felt hungry in the early hours and had carelessly burned some toast, causing the fire alarm go off. As the culprit didn't confess, and as it was almost breakfast time, I grabbed a towel from my room and followed everyone else towards the showers on the ground floor, where a long queue had already formed. I found myself just behind a stocky girl with a thick mane of chestnut hair. She turned around and gave me a rather sulky look from beneath her brows.

'Hi, there. Usually there's enough time for everyone, but what with the bloody fire alarm… Hey, you, you in there! Hurry up, or we'll all be left without breakfast!' she shouted towards the girls in the shower cubicles. A few others backed her up, and the queue began to move a little faster.

'Not that I'm such a great fan of Norwood Hall's 'fine cuisine', she confided, with heavy sarcasm. 'Which floor are you on, by the way?'

'I'm borrowing the prefect's room for now, but unfortunately I have to move to another house. It is too busy here.'

'Anna's room? Fantastic! I've had my eye on that room since forever, but it's always the prefects that get it. Where's your accent from?'

'I'm from Moscow. My name's Sasha Emelianova.'

'Moscow? Wow! I'm Catherine McLockey. From Scotland,' she added proudly.

I said, a little nervously: 'So, you are not new here. How long have you been in College?'

'More than I like to admit: it's my fifth year. Before I was in a mixed house, but when they built New Court, I decided to move in here. I don't want to worry you, but some of the houses are just …' she winced and showed a 'thumbs-down' gesture. 'Especially compared to this one. Such a shame you're moving.'

Then it was her turn for the shower. She moved towards the cubicle saying over her shoulder, 'Join us for breakfast, why don't you? I'll meet you in the hall in fifteen minutes,' then she disappeared in the shower cubicle without waiting for my answer.

After the shower, I changed into my new uniform – a dark jumper and a long skirt – and ran upstairs to locate Ala. I couldn't find her anywhere, so I went to meet Catherine in the hall. She was accompanied by two girls, Christie and Jackie.

Christie, a blonde girl with a plain face, short hair and pale eyelashes, had come to Wiltshire from Sweden in order to improve her English, just as Ala and I had. Jackie, with her doll-like prettiness and porcelain complexion was Catherine's friend from her previous school.

'I'm really from A House in Central Court, but since I seem to spend half of my time here, I feel like a New Court resident,' she told me.

'Yes, they should give you a room here too,' teased Catherine. 'But wait, you already have one – the TV room!' Here she slapped herself theatrically on the forehead. 'But now you'll have competition,' she added, nodding towards me. 'You'll have to share it. . . They want to move Sasha to another house, and she doesn't want to go.'

CHAPTER 1

'I'd much prefer to be in an all-girls house like this one,' said Jackie to Catherine, rather enviously. 'You don't have to dress up or wear makeup to impress the boys. And on Sundays, you can sit in the Common Room and watch TV in your pyjamas.'

'Yes, there are a few advantages,' her friend agreed, 'but we need men! That's why we should merge New Court with B1.' (I later found out that B1 was the closest all-male house.) Catherine continued, 'Let's vote! Everyone in favour of amalgamating New Court with B1, put their hands up!' at the same time comically shooting both arms skywards, though none of her friends followed her example.

'Oh, all right then, let's just go and get breakfast,' she grumbled.

Then I noticed that a girl of Asian appearance, pretending to be reading a newspaper, was watching us rather longingly. 'Would you like to join us?' I asked her.

'Great!' she jumped to her feet, smiling delightfully. 'I'm Nicole, from Tokyo.'

'You're very tall for a Japanese,' I noted when she stood up.

'Thanks! My height is due to my father,' she replied. It turned out that her father was an Englishman who had married a Japanese, and that Nicole and her brother had been sent to the college in order to 'form their characters' before university. We were just moving out of the door when Ala at last materialised, announcing that she was absolutely starved after being stuck in the queue for showers.

'Let's go!' said Catherine and we all followed. Spotting Ala and me dawdling behind, she ordered, 'Hey, Russkies! Stop gossiping in Russian between yourselves! You're in England now!' And as Ala and I hurried after her, trying to keep up, she joked, 'Don't lag either, or there'll be another queue. Although, you USSR types should be used to long queues, right?'

With the clock of the College Chapel striking eight, the Central Court was already filling up with students from every house hurrying towards breakfast in Norwood Hall, whether empty-handed or else weighed down with books.

Two tall male students – obviously sixth formers – cleverly cut a corner across the grass lawn in the middle of the court, just in order to be first in line. I was wondering whether we should do the same where there were heard sharp, triumphant cries and a short, middle-aged man wearing glasses and a long black gown jumped out, seemingly from nowhere, in order to upbraid them.

'Stop! Stop! You two, right there! Can't you read? What does that say?' And here he pointed dramatically towards a sign. 'No walking on the grass! Your names and houses, please.'

'He doesn't seem to take many prisoners,' I said to Ala rather apprehensively, but Catherine was unimpressed.

'That's only Grumpy. Such a bore! You'll be lucky if you miss all his classes. And if you should ever happen to step out of line, you'll get a green or a blue sheet as well,' she added, casting a glance over her shoulder at the teacher and the two young men.

'What kind of sheet do you mean?' Nicole asked, in all innocence, the 'sheet' sounding rather like another word.

'Ha, ha! New kids! So much to learn,' smirked Catherine. 'Aren't I right, Jackie?'

Jackie nodded her pretty head seriously, and added, 'If you break College rules, but not badly enough to be expelled, you'll be punished, with the level of punishment depending upon what you've done. For example, last summer, one of the beaks caught Catherine and me smoking in the bushes.'

'*Who* caught you?' asked Ala, surprised.

'A 'beak' – that's Marlburian slang for a teacher,' Catherine explained patiently. 'For that we had to go for a run across the fields at six every morning for two whole weeks. It was horrible! – I'd rather chop wood or dig up roads than jog. But we were still lucky that our house prefect was on duty occasionally so we could basically stroll half the way.'

'This is one of the prefect's duties, which is why they're not always mega-popular,' added Jackie.

Upon hearing this, Ala whispered to me: 'Right, forget what I said about wanting to be a prefect! I have no desire to wake up early, just to ensure that others are punished!'

However, by then we'd entered the glass doors of Norwood Hall: a huge dining hall with high ceilings decorated with massive chandeliers and old portraits of ancient English lords wearing 17th- and 18th-century wigs.

I should ask Catherine about them, I thought, glancing round. Rows of long wooden tables were thronged with students, but the left corner of the dining hall was separated from the rest. Catherine followed my gaze. 'That bit's for the beaks,' she explained.

A bountiful hot and cold buffet glittered before us, served by smiling cooks wearing white chef outfits. I took a tray and stood in the queue with the others, but Ala went ahead of the rest of us in order to explore, and returned looking quite excited.

'Wow, they've got all sorts of things here! Sausages, omelettes, cheeses and at least ten different kinds of cereals… It's a feast!'

I couldn't disagree, as, having filled our trays with food, we all followed Catherine to a table beside one of the beautiful windows overlooking the Central Court.

'You Russians do eat!' she remarked tolerantly. 'I'd never have guessed it, just by looking at you – especially Sasha.' By contrast, her tray boasted only coffee and cereal, while Nicole's held still less.

'I already miss home cooking,' Nicole admitted, picking at her omelette without much enthusiasm.

'Norwood Hall's chefs haven't learned how to make sushi yet,' quipped Jackie.

Meanwhile, Ala was busy looking around, checking out all the most attractive senior guys as they passed, and occasionally elbowing me, to make sure I'd noticed one. Catherine, always alert, observed this too.

'Yes, there's plenty of talent here and twice as many men as women as well. The best-looking ones are unluckily pretty arrogant, on the whole; but you'll soon find that out for yourselves.' Then she added, in a tone that was meant to be kind, 'Don't worry, Nicole, we'll soon find you someone too. I know there's a Chinese guy in C1 who's supposed to be absolutely brilliant.'

'I am from Japan,' Nicole timidly reminded her, but Catherine didn't seem hugely interested in the differences between the two cultures.

'Do you have a boyfriend?' Ala dared to ask Catherine, who frowned at the recollection.

'Long story!' Then she seemed unusually keen to change the subject. 'Tell us about Moscow! My friend's older brother went there on a school exchange. He sold a pair of jeans for 200 roubles, which allowed him into some of the best restaurants, fabulous caviar included! He loved it!'

'Why don't *we* organize school exchanges to Moscow? I wouldn't say no to caviar,' interrupted Jackie wistfully.

'Even if they did offer them, you'd need to be studying Russian in order to have a chance!' laughed her friend.

'That must have been in the late eighties,' said Ala, impatiently: 'You can't impress anyone in Moscow with British jeans now. . . I'd love to shop in London, though.'

I added, 'It's been our dream forever to see London! So far, we haven't seen anything, except between Heathrow and here.'

'*Moi, j'adore London,*' exclaimed Jackie. 'That big city buzz, eating out, clubs, shopping. . .'

'Well, I can't stand it,' Catherine interrupted flatly. 'For a start, just in order to get anywhere, you have to take that filthy Tube and probably sit next to smelly people . . . and there's way too much traffic.'

'Nowhere's good enough for you, outside of your precious Scotland,' arrowed Jackie, getting her own back.

We were beginning to discuss Stockholm, when Catherine suddenly spotted a group of very pretty girls approaching Norwood Hall.

'Oh look, Serena De Clare with her new entourage!' she crowed. 'She's

CHAPTER 1

certainly found some fresh blood. And who'd have thought it – they're all blondes!'

'So what's wrong with being blonde?' her blonde friend Christie wished to know.

'Nothing, as long as they've at least a little charisma to add to the mix,' replied Catherine, unruffled.

It was impossible not to notice Serene De Clare as she entered the room and haughtily glanced around, her entourage behind her. The food queue had dispersed, but most of the tables were already taken. At last she spotted some girls that she knew, while she and her blonde brigade strode up towards them. I caught Ala staring intently at Serena. I knew that stare: Ala was checking out the competition – and if I were Serena De Clare, I would be concerned, very concerned. . .

Meanwhile Jackie said: 'I feel as if I'm back at my old all-girls school all over again. I don't know why the guys here hardly talk to us. It's as if they'd feel ashamed even to share a table with us,' and here she nodded towards a group of young men engaged in a heated discussion.

'It's a generational issue,' Catherine observed. 'Their fathers got a massive culture shock back in the sixties, when women first arrived – and their sons have been trying to recover ever since!'

I knew from my researches that Marlborough College had been founded in the 19th century, to facilitate the education of the sons of the Church of England's clergy. Who could have then imagined, only a century later, that the college would be the first major British independent school to welcome girls into the sixth form? – though, admittedly, most of the others soon followed its example.

'Check this out.' And with this Catherine hooked a small piece of my sausage with her fork and threw it expertly towards Serena.

I watched, utterly mortified, as the sausage landed, bang on target, in the centre of Serena's plate. She cried out in shock, indignantly glaring around, but Catherine, wearing a perfect poker face, continued with her breakfast as if nothing had happened... To my intense relief our table escaped censure while Serena instead targeted some young man unlucky enough to have laughed at the wrong moment.

'She's the biggest snob in college,' said Catherine to me as we left, 'and probably in all of England, but she's still very pretty – and doesn't she know it!' Then Catherine glanced at her watch. 'Time to go, school assembly's about to start. Hurry up!'

We pushed our trays swiftly onto the kitchen conveyor belt and moved towards the door. At that moment Christy noticed that Catherine had a hand-drawn picture of a fat cow pinned to her back – possibly a 'gift' from Serena – certainly a gift from someone who had passed in the crush behind her.

How childish! Ala and I exchanged grimaces. Not exactly the kind of behaviour we'd been led to expect from well-born young English ladies – but perhaps female rivalry was a universal phenomenon. Christy unpinned the caricature and we all followed Catherine, who was quietly raging against Serena, and utterly convinced that she was the culprit.

Having passed by the Art School, we moved around the corner and down the alley, along a long wall of St Michael and Angels, the College Chapel. It was impossible not to admire its beautiful stained-glass windows. Gravel cracked under our feet, while the boxwood shrubs hid some delightfully flowering gems... Approaching the Chapel entrance, we found ourselves at the top of a long flight of stone steps flanked by clipped yew trees and hedges. There we all paused for a moment, mesmerised by the view of the Memorial Hall – a monumental white building built in the Greek style boasting eight massive stone columns rising from a brick-paved forecourt.

'This is the college's memorial to those Marlburians who lost their lives in WWI,' Catherine told us, momentarily forgetting her annoyance. 'Their names are carved on the walls inside.'

With the clock just striking 8:30, we blended into a crowd of students rushing towards the Memorial Hall, where a group of teachers in black gowns were queuing up outside the entrance to welcome us. With the assembly about to start, the hall was buzzing like a bee-hive. We managed to squeeze inside and found a vacant row in the stepped seats of the semi-circular auditorium, its shape resembling an ancient amphitheatre. I glanced around in some curiosity: the navy and green uniforms of the juniors covering the first rows darkened into more varied colours of us seniors, sitting above. The uppermost row was taken by teachers, wearing academic square-top hats complete with tassels. Then a tall and distinguished-looking professor wearing spectacles, a black gown and a don's hat unhurriedly took to the stage. It was our headmaster, or simply 'Master': Dr. Stone.

He touched the microphone, and the teachers hushed the youngest students, while the rest of the hall fell into a respectful silence.

'Marlburians! I congratulate you on the beginning of a new school year!' he greeted us. 'We all know the motto of Marlborough College – *Deus Dat Incrementum* – God gives the increase. All of you, as true Marlburians, should follow this motto throughout your lives, by giving back what you have gained, with a calm pride in what it has meant to you, to be a Marlburian.'

I'll never forget that moment: I felt so privileged, simply to be included! Holding my breath, I took in his words, hardly believing that he was speaking to me, that I was one of them . . .

Classes didn't start until the next day, so after registration in C House, formerly known as Marlborough House – the brick-red building on the cover of the Marlborough prospectus – Ala and I ventured out to explore our new home, first heading towards some modern school buildings in the distance, each practically covered in summer foliage. We walked past the Mill Mead and C3 houses and soon came to a miniature wooden bridge stretching over a bubbling stream in the shadow of beautiful willow trees.

There we rested, enjoying the fresh breezes, mesmerised by the view of the seemingly boundless green fields and distant Wiltshire hills. Upon crossing the bridge we soon found ourselves in the countryside, in a field in which there were several elegantly-bred horses: I plucked some fresh grass and fed it to one of them. While I was stroking her marvellously curved neck, like something in ancient Greek marble, Ala was trying to figure out where we were from our map. I called her to join me in order to meet the mare, but – strangely – as she approached, the horses all recoiled, neighing wildly and sprinting off in different directions.

'We should have brought a camera,' I said, rather disappointed.

As there were no fences to serve as boundaries, we weren't entirely sure whether we were still on college territory or not. Then I spotted some tennis courts in the distance and suggested we walk towards them: according to the map, we were somewhere in the south-west part of the college, not far from Preshute house.

We soon came to a Victorian mansion, covered with overgrown bushes and rampant ivy, with ornate stone windows protruding from its façade.

'Someone must be pretty lucky in order to live here,' Alka observed enviously, noting the balcony, stone balusters and view over an ancient cemetery.

'That's where we'll wind up if we fail our exams,' I giggled.

We tried, without much success, to read the faded inscriptions on the mossy tombstones. The August sun blazed down as we sank into the grass in order to contemplate our next move. Judging from the map, we still hadn't walked over even a fifth of the entire grounds. . .

'Look,' Ala jabbed her finger at the map, 'More tennis courts, rugby pitches, playing fields, a gym, a theatre, even an observatory . . . And we haven't even gotten as far as Littlefield or Summerfield yet. There's still so much to see!'

However as we were getting hungry, we decided to continue our wanderings some other time and headed back to Norwood Hall, navigating with the aid of the map. As we passed the horses' field I hoped that they would come to greet me, but, for whatever reason, they chose to keep a rather wary distance.

I couldn't help wondering if this was because Ala was with me.

CHAPTER 2

I still think it was because of Alka and because she was my best friend that our dreams had come true and we ended up in England - the fairytale world of English education.

Alka and I had become friends at kindergarten. I remember how I had cried on that first day, longing to be home when a serious little girl with a thatch of fierce black curls came up to me and, taking me by the hand, insisted upon showing me the hedgehog in the pets' corner. Alka continued to take me under her wing throughout our schooldays. For ten years we not only shared a desk, but also our secrets and dreams. Nevertheless we were quite different. Ala, a natural leader, was always the centre of attention. With her sharp tongue she was never at a loss for words: no one wanted to pick a fight with her. I often felt that I was merely painted on the backdrop for Alka's performances although – perhaps surprisingly – I enjoyed it, watching spellbound, feeling proud to have such a friend.

Ala herself did not come from a privileged background, living alone with her mother in reduced circumstances. Their monotonous diet was hardly adequate for a growing girl, so she had a permanent invitation to eat with us. My mother not only tried to feed Alka with delicious food but whenever she bought me a new toy she would often buy one for Alka as well. When Papa was making plans for our summer holiday on the Black Sea Coast, Mama always reminded him to book for Alka as well as for me – and such breaks were not cheap. We went to the best Pioneer camps, including even Artek and Orlyonok, thanks to Papa's good connections. Mama was completely under Alka's spell, often holding her up as an example to me, especially citing her diligence and her determination to achieve her goals. Evidently she thought that this good example should always be with me. At first Papa resisted this wholesale intrusion into our family life but he eventually gave in. Recently Mama had gained a major victory: Papa had agreed to pay for a year's education at a prestigious college in England - for both of us.

We were both just sixteen when we left our schooldays and our Moscow friends behind us. It was the beginning of the 90s and everything about life in our country was changing. Nobodies became somebodies – and vice versa. Whoever you were, your previous life seemed suddenly gone forever. For example, my father had been an academic, someone who, after graduating with a first from Moscow State University, had followed his father into a career in science. In the 80s he had worked first as an engineer in the Soviet Nuclear Centre, before leading a scientific research institute while simultaneously progressing within the Party. During this time Papa managed to gain some enviable contacts in the government and by the time of Perestroika he was already earning very good money – for those times – for his scientific work.

The USSR's collapse presented another opportunity: when state enterprises began transferring to private ownership, Papa bought shares in a factory which did very well, and, by the beginning of the 90s, Papa's business had really started to prosper. His investments increased in value and he expanded into profitable projects connected with natural resources. . . My parents had met at university and married while still only students. I had been born soon afterwards. Mama taught mathematics in a school for gifted children. Together they overcame their every difficulty involved in combining their studies with looking after me: living in student hostels, money shortages, sleepless nights, hunger and exhaustion.

Mama always supported Papa in all his undertakings. She helped him with his postgraduate dissertation and then with his Ph.D, later she advanced up her own professional ladder while running the house and looking after me. When Papa's business became successful he insisted that she gave up the work she loved to devote herself full-time to the family, at the same time giving her every credit and continually emphasizing that everything he had achieved was due to her. At family dinners Papa never failed to propose a toast to Mama, praising her unswerving devotion in the face of difficulties.

Mama herself never seemed to change: a gentle blonde of slender build, she always wore an expression of honest goodness, as if she was always ready to help anyone who needed it, always prepared to take them under her wing. Our acquaintance was unanimous in observing that I looked very like her, you could almost say a younger copy. Although Papa was undoubtedly the head of the family, it was obvious to everyone that he loved Mama and was tenderly protective of her, and that he thought the world of me too. In short, I grew up surrounded by love and attention.

Alka wasn't so fortunate or – to be precise – she wasn't fortunate at all. She grew up without a father: even when he was around, he was scarcely there. According to her mother, when they first got married he had constantly dreamed of having a little daughter with bows in her hair. Then the dream came true and Alka made her appearance. The screaming bundle soon turned into a pretty little two-year-old with big green eyes and apple cheeks. Everything appeared perfect on the surface, but, as often happens, the daily grind cast a long shadow over family happiness. Alka's mother rushed about: between her job and looking after Alka she was often tired and irritable, and the only time she got any rest was when her husband took Alka out to the children's playground in the evening. Alka's father was a sports master at a school, and was correspondingly fit, energetic and good-looking – he was very well aware of this. He had a proud bearing, a lithe gait and a commanding voice. One evening, on the usual outing with Alka to the playground, he met his true love, in the form of a cheerful, sporty woman with two boys a little older than Alka. Meanwhile Alka romped in the sandpit with the neighbour's little boy, little suspecting the heights of feeling to which her father was subject. Tired of the wife who was always exhausted caring for her family, he decided to abandon both her and Alka in order to start a new life. In fact, he only resurfaced in Alka's life when she was sixteen, and required his official permission to go abroad. . . At the time he was openly surprised to see how his little daughter had turned out, however, as is well known, other people's children grow very fast . . .

Alka's mother had constantly wept with mortification, and was never able to understand how he could swap his longed-for daughter with ribbons for two sons – someone else's children, and almost teenagers. Yet her father was happy with his second wife, who was also his best friend. They went on outings with friends, made bonfires and sang songs to her guitar, barbecued *shashlik* at the father-in-law's dacha, and enjoyed lively discussions about films and politics in the kitchen and the meal table. His in-laws were delighted with their wonderful new son-in-law and their daughter's new-found happiness: they did their best to look after their two noisy grandsons so that the young couple would be left in peace. Alka's mother never forgave her husband, or – especially – his new wife. Instead of crying in her empty bed she had simply, without a single pang of conscience, taken someone else's husband from the children's playground. Victory always comes to the strong.

In addition, Alka's mother, having suddenly become an abandoned mother, discussed her personal business with everybody. At first her friends listened eagerly to details of her perfect husband's infidelity, and were curious about details, asking 'When did you start to notice?' and 'Was he different in bed?' and 'How did he dare to tell you?' Against the background of such a situation their own self-respect grew, and they forgot their family quarrels, while their own husbands seemed almost ideal. Gradually, however, everyone got fed up with this sad, long-running saga and Alka's mother found herself quite alone.

Alka was of course the prime witness of her mother's sufferings. From childhood she had learned that all men were merely there to be exploited, as 'that woman' had done with her own father. Alka early on made up her mind that she would never spend her nights crying like her mother, that she would take her revenge on the entire male sex. She would squeeze them for everything she could get and make them whine and suffer. From childhood she disliked staying at home with her grieving mother; instead she was often sent to her grandmother for the summer holidays in the Altai, where they wandered in the forests. Berries, mushrooms and especially herbs – these were her grandmother's elements, and chimed too with something deep inside Alka herself.

Her grandmother was quite different in character from her mother – strong and confident, with an answer for every question, although Alka could not understand everything that she told her immediately. She also had a constant stream of visitors. In the neighbourhood she was thought to be both a witch and a healer: visitors came for both purposes. People were a little afraid of her, the women especially tried to avoid falling out with her. There were rumours that she had lured one early rival into the forest and left her there and for some reason the rival didn't even try to find her way home, although the locals knew every bush, every path. She was found in the forest, stiff with cold and sitting quietly on a tree stump as if someone had put a spell on her, depriving her even of will. This story had inspired lurid fear in more than one generation and had been handed down to both children and grandchildren. Thus, even as a teenager, Alka realised the fearful power of being confronted with some unexplained strength: people tend to fear attributes that they lack themselves. This something can grow, capturing the imagination, until it turns into a huge shaggy beast, like one of the bears which prowl the *taiga*. If you allow this shaggy bear-bogey into your imagination, into yourself, then you can perish. And on the other hand, if you can direct it towards your enemy, he will perish. This was one of the lessons Alka learned from her grandmother: there were many others.

CHAPTER 3

The second of September was officially the first day of school and, straight after breakfast, Ala and I hurried to Leaf Block building for our first geography lesson. Since I'd never been any good at maths – unlike Ala, who excels in everything –I'd decided that it was a safer bet to opt for the humanities, including English and geography. And, upon learning about the possibilities of exotic expeditions to places all over the world, Ala had, for once, unhesitatingly followed my example.

As it turned out, we were the only girls in our geography class, which to my embarrassment seemed dominated by male eyes, all gazing at us with real – or possibly – feigned indifference.

'I'm starting to like it here even more than I did already, if this is possible,' Ala whispered to me. Then she spread her files and textbooks across her desk, making herself quite at home, and boldly looked round, eager to make new acquaintances. How I longed for the same kind of confidence! Instead, before the lesson even started, I discovered to my annoyance that I'd forgotten my pen.

'Hi, do you happen to have a spare pen, by any chance?' I asked a friendly-looking blonde guy sitting next to me.

'What? A pan? Why would you need a pan? Do you plan on cooking?' he inquired, turned to his neighbour and shrugging his shoulders in an exaggerated fashion. I blushed to the roots of my scalp.

'She's talking about a *pen,* idiot!' His neighbour, darker but just as good-looking, held one out to me. 'A pen. A writing utensil. Look it up, why don't you?'

'My God, where's she from?' I heard the first guy whisper, which made me blush even more intensely.

My first – and very awkward – interaction with male Marlburians was then interrupted by the entrance of a distinguished-looking man with an aquiline profile.

'Hello, I'm Mr. Green, your geography teacher. Let's introduce ourselves, shall we?' He cast a piercing glance from under his glasses towards the young men in the middle.

Once all the others had introduced themselves – Ala as confident as any – I thought with despair that I would never remember all the English names (and especially surnames). Edward Gibson de Saint Anthony – how can anyone recall a name like this, all at once?

'We'll call him Eric,' whispered Ala to me in Russian, always thinking on her feet. My only comfort was that the confusion appeared to be mutual.

'E-me-la-no-va,' Mr Green attempted, rather doubtfully, 'Gromov.'

'Gromov-a,' Ala calmly corrected him. 'We are Russians, from Moscow.'

Mr. Green seemed thrilled: 'To be honest, I was hoping that this might be the case! What did you study in this subject in Moscow?'

Here – very luckily for me – Ala immediately took the initiative, launching into a detailed explanation of our former curriculum, quite pleased to take centre stage. I heard some of the guys next to me laughing at her accent, but our teacher warmly encouraged her.

'What is so funny?' Ala whispered to me crossly. Then it was my turn to get the giggles.

'It's our accent, I believe. Maybe the pronunciation we were taught at home wasn't quite as good as we believed it was.'

'Well, they'll have to just get used to it. *I'm* not going anywhere.' Thus my Ala continued to shine, just like the star that she had always been, so nothing unusual there! Gradually the guys became genuinely interested. Suddenly questions were shafting towards us from every corner:

'Ala, what did you think of Gorbachov? . . . Ala, what was happening during the putsch in Moscow? . . . Ala – or Sasha, is that right? – what do

CHAPTER 3

Russians *really* think about Western European culture?'

Meanwhile Ala was in her element: smiling coyly and batting her long eyelashes, basking in the male attention like a film star deigning to give an interview . . . in fact, as I reflected later, our first geography lesson was a triumph for us both.

At lunchtime in Norwood Hall Miss Foxton arrived to give me the good news: they were already expecting me in Littlefield House, and Mr Graham, spouse of my future housemistress, hoped to be able to pick me up at 3:00 from New Court . . . First thing after lunch I headed to New Court to find Catherine, and to hear –rather fearfully, I must admit – her verdict on my new house. I went upstairs to search for her room, carefully checking the nameplates on the doors, and at last finding hers next to the kitchen, where three girls in Hundred's school uniforms were busy making tea. I knocked on her door and heard a snappy, 'Come in!'

The windowsill was occupied by Freddie Fitzroy, whom I had already met, dangling her legs in black Dr Martens from under the navy-green chequered skirt of the Remove girls. Catherine herself was lying on her bed, her arms beneath her neck and her feet relaxed, and – at least judging from the look she shot me – I appeared to have interrupted some juicy gossip. Still, she patiently listened to my news, resolving it all in a very business-like manner: 'Well, there are cons, of course: you'll be living with Serena de Clare, so you'll have to learn to stand up for yourself. But there are pros as well as cons. Mrs. Graham, their housemistress, is really nice, and more importantly, it's a mixed house – so I must admit that I feel a little jealous of you!'

'Yes and besides, there are some really cute guys in there,' added Freddie and they immediately started discussing whom among these they might want to snog.

'Of course, James Brown, the rugby team captain, is the best, but Serena's already got her hooks into him – at least for this term, or until she gets fed-up with him, whichever happens first. Then she'll find herself some other prey. . .

. By the way, I got off with Ian, that rugby back, at the Summerfield House party. He's a very good kisser. Or at least he was, before Serena got hold of him . . . I don't know what he's like now,' finished Catherine.

'What happened after your encounter? Did you get in trouble?' I asked, rather fearfully.

'Nothing happened, really. The next day in Norwood Hall we both pretended we'd never met, which is normal. In fact, that's what always happens! . . . Well, good luck with settling in, keep your eye on the ball and don't forget us here in New Court; we can always go out for supper together. And if Serena starts messing with you, you only have to tell me,' she said, rather belligerently – and I believed her.

Then I returned to Anna's room and started packing up my things. At 3:00 p.m. sharp I was in the hall, where an energetic man in his forties was already waiting for me. He put my suitcase in the boot of his car and immediately drove me off to my new place of residence.

'It's only a five-minute walk from the Central Court,' explained Mr Graham, as he exited the College gates and turned onto Bath Road, 'Much closer than it seems when you're driving around. Our house is very friendly. You'll be only the fourth girl, the other 40 – no, hang on – 44 students are boys, from thirteen-year-olds Shells right up to young men in the Upper Sixth. . . That's the main reason why we were so pleased when the College Registrar told us they needed to find a place for a girl: we've got enough boys already, and I'm sure you'll be a civilising influence! . . . My wife has already found you a nice room; I hope you like it. Anyway, we swap rooms each term in order to keep everybody happy, that's only fair.'

'That sounds very good,' I said, as some answer seemed expected of me, but he continued cheerfully, 'We have breakfast in-house in our own dining room and we also supply dinners three times a week. We often have guests from other houses over for dinner: of course, you may invite whomever you like! You'll find that we're really like one big family – I hope you'll soon feel right at home.'

CHAPTER 3

By then Mr. Graham was parking next to a lovely three-storied Victorian house with a steeply pitched roof and redbrick chimneys, attached rather incongruously to a building clearly in the architectural style of the sixties.

A smiling woman wearing a stylish haircut and a smart trouser-suit greeted me at the front door. 'Hello, Sasha! Welcome to Littlefield! I'm Mrs. Graham.'

I was delighted and relieved at such a kind welcome, although the entry hall of my new home mostly impressed me with the masculine smells of sweat, socks, and grass. Mr. Graham grabbed my suitcase and headed up the creaky staircase with me following behind, still engaged in polite conversation with his wife. Suddenly, galloping down the stairs in rugby boots with metal studs, came a bunch of Littlefieldians, all attired in their trademark black-and-red striped tops.

'Hello, Mr. Graham…Oh, sorry, Mrs. Graham!'

Darting curious glances in my direction, they stepped aside for a moment to allow us to pass.

Mrs Graham explained to me, rather unnecessarily, 'They have a practice match,' before continuing with what she had been saying before. Upstairs, we found ourselves in a small, squared-off corridor, which – judging by a small fridge, microwave and cooker – also served as a kitchen. Various doors led to student bedrooms, while the girls' bathroom was down a small flight of steps.

'Here's your room,' Mrs Graham announced, opening the door to a spacious, south-facing room overlooking a well-manicured lawn. 'Please make yourself comfortable. You'll meet everyone else at the house meeting after supper tonight. Meanwhile, I'll ask Natalie Cox, our prefect, to show you around.'

The Grahams soon left me, but I wasn't alone for long, as someone briskly knocked on my door.

Without waiting for an invitation, two heads inserted themselves inside the door, with broad smiles on their curious faces. One belonged to a redheaded young fellow with dimples, the other to a sassy, good-looking brunette wearing a gorgeous red top over her jeans.

'Hi, I'm Natalie Cox, and this is Tom Perry. Are you really from Moscow?' asked the brunette, inviting herself in.

'Yes, I am Sasha Emelyanova. I'm here with a friend of mine, also from Moscow. She is in New Court.'

'Lucky thing! New Court's brand-new, no comparison to this wreck. And it's right on the doorstep of Central Court, although it's still much more fun over here, right, Tom?' (And here Tom winked at her, rather mischievously.) 'Still, guys are basically trouble, if you ask me . . . they're always doing first and thinking afterwards!'

Tom laughed. 'I'd love to move to an all-girls house, like New Court. Half the Upper Sixth there come straight from all-girls' schools, meaning that they haven't so much as *seen* a guy for years! It's time they were educated, at least in that respect!'

Natalie looked at him reproachfully, shaking her pretty head. 'You see what we have to put up with in here, Sasha? There's only one thing on their tiny minds.'

'What's wrong with that?' Tom asked, unruffled. 'I'm sure your heads are filled with stuff like that, too. Anyway, great to meet you Sasha, I'll catch you later. I've got to get to a rugby match, James is waiting for me downstairs.'

And Natalie added, 'Anyway, I'll pick you up for supper at seven-thirty. Since its Wednesday, we'll all be eating here in Littlefield. Good thing, too. It's no fun plodding to Norwood Hall when it's dark and muddy outside.'

'She's nice,' I heard Tom approve me behind the closed door, 'and very slim too, not the *matreshka* you'd expected.'

I couldn't hear Natalie's response.

Well-pleased with my reception, I started unpacking my suitcase, first rescuing Winnie, the teddy bear who had been with me as long as I could remember, then setting my framed family pictures, books and school files on the shelves above the bed, and finally neatly hanging my few clothes in the wardrobe. . . Then I heard another knock on the door.

CHAPTER 3

'Come in!' I called, vaguely expecting Natalie.

Instead, it was Serena herself, making a grand entrance, escorted by a rosy blonde girl who barely reached her shoulder.

'Hi, I'm Serena de Clare.' Her charming smile made me instantly warm to her. 'Tom told me that you're just arrived from Moscow. Is that true?'

I nodded. 'My name's Sasha.'

Serena and her companion exchanged a surprised glance. 'Sorry, thought Tom was kidding us,' Serena explained, 'Sasha who?'

'Emelianova,' I said, adding rather apologetically, 'I know it's hard to pronounce.'

'Eme..la…Sorry, I'll just call you Sasha E., shall I? I had this room last term. Now I'm in the room opposite, which is slightly bigger and has an even nicer view. . . And this is Penny Preston,' she nodded at her friend, who smiled shyly. 'Her room's a floor below, but she does get her own bathroom.'

She was casually glancing over my modest belongings when one of the photographs caught her eye. 'Your parents?'

I nodded, pleased.

'How old's your mother then?'

'She's 39. And yours?'

'What kind of question is that?' she demanded, quite indignantly. (I couldn't understand this, for had she not asked me the same question?) However, Serena breezed on, as if she had never said it: 'By the way, has Natalie visited you yet? She's borrowed my favourite red cashmere jumper without even asking me, so now I have to chase her all over College to get it back!. . . By the way, do you have a boyfriend in Moscow?'

I was shocked by such openness but couldn't imagine lying. 'No,' I answered.

'I see. Well, have to dash, see you later!' and, with that, they both disappeared.

'*I guess Catherine was right about Serena,*' I concluded disappointedly, rather stunned by the entire encounter.

Of course, I didn't know what was to come. . .

CHAPTER 4

During a short break between English and geography I dropped into New Court hoping to find Ala and Catherine there... I couldn't wait to tell them about my new house. To my disappointment they weren't around, so I made myself a cup of instant coffee and settled in a cushy armchair in the communal hall to glance discontentedly over the press headlines, until I heard Ala's familiar voice through the doors.

'Hi, there! What's happening?' Whereupon she dumped her files on the floor and flopped into the armchair opposite mine.

Eager to share my news, I started telling her about my new house and its residents. 'You know, I think Serena isn't really as scary as Catherine makes her out to be,' I concluded.

'Really? Why does she hate her so much then?'

'Well,' I said, 'All this is all off the record, as they say here, but they had a catfight over some guy, but it all happened years ago, when they were both in Remove.'

'Which guy?' asked Ala.

'Someone called James Brown, maybe the rugby team captain? He's very popular and also lives in my new house. He's going out with Serena now, not Catherine.'

Ala didn't seem very intrigued. However, later on she mused, 'I really must visit you sometime in Littlefield, just to see how you've settled in. When will you finally invite me?'

'Invite you! You can come any time you like. How about later this afternoon, after classes? I'll show you my room.' I brightened at the thought of showing my childhood friend my new quarters.

'I'd rather come for supper; it'd make a nice change from Norwood Hall. When can you next invite guests?'

'I'll find out and let you know,' I promised her blithely.

Then she said, as if an afterthought, 'By the way, New Court is throwing a joint house party with B1 tomorrow night and, of course, as your best friend I'm inviting you. . . You have to dress up as a cartoon character though, with the main problem being, of course, that we watched different cartoons from the British.'

Besides Disney's *Tom and Jerry*, which lucky VCR owners showed to their USSR offspring in the late 80s, nothing foreign and original came to our minds. Mickey Mouse and Donald Duck were equally uninspiring. Suddenly, I had an idea. 'Hey, do you remember that funny rabbit cartoon? With Danny DeVito?'

'Brilliant! I'll go as Jessica!' vowed Ala. 'All I need is to find a red wig. With these babies,' and here, to my amusement, she embraced her full breasts, 'I'll be the best possible Jessica Rabbit! Maybe you could be Thumbelina?' and here she examined me critically, from head to toe. 'We should maybe find out if they know this character, but we'd need to do it discreetly, so that no one steals the idea. I'd ask Catherine, she could never be Thumbelina, anyway!'

I glanced at my watch. It was 10:45 already and Mr. Green detested anyone running in late, even by a few minutes. We grabbed our books and sprinted to Leaf Block.

As far as the B1 party was concerned, I'd decided to go as Malvina, so after lunch we headed straight to town to find a fancy dress shop with colourful wigs: a red one for Ala and a blue one for me. Although there were no such shops in Marlborough, we were still lucky enough to find what we were looking for. In one of the tiny little alleyways we stumbled across a vintage clothes shop, reeking of mothballs and old shoes. We swiped Ala's wig from a display mannequin – it seemed surprisingly new – while its long reddish locks and stylish fringe suited her perfectly.

CHAPTER 4

As I had no luck finding a blue wig anywhere, I bought a white one instead, its demure curls reaching the middle of my neck. Once we returned to College, I borrowed watercolours from my arty friend, Nicole, and dyed it a pale blue. Then, once the paint had dried, I carefully put it on, examined myself critically in the mirror and concluded that my hard work had paid off.

We agreed that I would bring along a few dresses from my wardrobe for us to try on with the wigs in front of the mirror in Ala's room before the party. My choice was easy – a summer dress in pale-blue silk suited Malvina perfectly. Ala's outfit, however, proved a rather bigger problem. Neither of our wardrobes held anything even remotely resembling Jessica Rabbit's, so Ala went round New Court asking the girls for help, until Mary Jones, her next door neighbour, generously lent her a very tight black skirt with a split up the back. Ala straightaway put it on as a strapless dress – every curve showing, cleavage really more obvious than entirely appropriate, red lipstick on. Pleased, she looked herself over in the mirror, eyes sparkling. 'I think it's super sexy. Am I not a real Jessica?'

'Alka, you look stunning,' I said admiringly.

'Thanks. Your outfit suits you, too. It's a shame there's no Buratino to match.'

Suddenly, the door swung open.

'Ladies.' Catherine was standing in the doorway, wearing jeans, a black T-short and a tweed jacket.

'But who is your cartoon character?' asked Ala in bewilderment.

'I'm going as Catherine,' she announced. 'I'm tired of this annual carnival. Look at you, all dressed up! I won't be walking anywhere near you, that's for sure…Such a shame Jackie has tonsillitis – we'll probably never find out who she was going to be, and she was really looking forward to the party. By the way, where're Christie and Nicole? I've got a bottle of Malibu that I bought in duty free when coming back from Barbados last Christmas,' Catherine patted the inside pocket of her jacket. 'Hurry to the kitchen and fetch some cups – we need to warm up before the party, while Miss Foxton's away,' she said, putting her bottle on the desk.

When we rushed back with the cups, Nicole was sitting on Ala's bed, wearing black leggings and cat ears on her head, fumbling with a furry end of her tail. 'I'm Catwoman,' she explained, unnecessarily. Christie was sitting next to her, wearing blue jeans and a white shirt. ('Don't know any of their cartoons. We have different ones in Sweden,' she complained.)

After a few gulps of Malibu everyone felt better.

'Next time we'll meet in my room,' said Catherine. 'Ala doesn't even have any music.'

'Actually, I do. Is Vysotskiy fine with you?' Ala turned on the tape recorder.

'He has almost iconic status in Russia, a talented actor, a bard and a rebel against the Soviet regime,' I explained to our uncomprehending colleagues. . . For a moment, everyone listened to the hoarse male voice pouring from the speakers.

'Very sexy voice,' approved Catherine. But it's all in Russian, and the melody could be better. What are they like – Russian men?'

'Mostly machos, drunkards and troublemakers,' said Ala.

'Alka, what are you talking about? Don't listen to her,' I protested.

'Isn't it time we left?' suggested Ala, obviously trying to change the topic.

We could already hear loud music thumping from B1 next door; the party was on and there was no time to waste. Jumping to our feet we hurried downstairs.

'Is anyone from Littlefield coming?' Christie asked me.

'Serena and her friends have been preparing for days, but all in secret. Also, James Brown – of course, he and Serena go everywhere together,' I said.

We walked out of New Court, and after only a few steps found ourselves on the doorstep of B1, the all-boys house opposite, where the Housemaster and various colleagues were standing in the doorway, trying desperately to control the flow of cartoon characters, as more and more students were arriving.

'Wow,' whistled some guys in X-men T-shirts, looking at Ala. 'Who's she?'

CHAPTER 4

'All I need from a man is a sense of humour,' she quoted Jessica Rabbit and looked at them intriguingly.

We squeezed inside.

'Follow me!' Catherine obviously already knew her way around B1, the house designed by a Victorian prison architect whose expertise in security and iron bars apparently made him the best possible choice to build a house for teenage boys. . .

Eager to join the disco, we weaved down the narrow stairs into the dark basement, lightened with powerful UV lighting, which made my dress and Christy's white shirt fluoresce in the dark, much to our delight. With multiple lasers and blinking lights the disco was already in full swing: hundreds of student feet trampled on a floor soaked with spilled beer, which instantly stuck to one's shoes. The DJ was pumping the latest chart tracks, and soon we couldn't hear a word of what anyone was saying, and were reduced to yelling and gesturing. Catherine went to a bar in the corner to get us some free beer, while I glanced around trying to spot someone I knew. Two guys in streaming capes and weird masks nodded at me passing by, but I didn't recognize them.

'Batman and Robin,' they introduced themselves. They turned out to be James Brown and Ginger Tom and were immediately joined by Serena, wearing a black cat outfit complete with whip.

'Serena! Who are you?' I asked.

She instantly grasped James's hand.

'I am Batwoman!' she shouted, cracking her whip before dragging him to the dance floor, leaving me with Tom.

'Who are you, Sasha? Marge Simpson?' asked Tom, looking at my wig.

'Who's that? No, I am Malvina,' I explained.

'Marge has blue hair too, but yours is much cuter!'

'What? I can't hear you!'

'Doesn't matter, let's dance,' gestured Tom, waving me towards the dance floor.

We joined my friends from New Court, dancing next to Serena and James in the special effect smoke. I thought: *How cool is this?* I had never even been to a disco before and this was well beyond my wildest expectations. I longed to share my joy with Ala, but she was nowhere to be seen. I looked around, but it was impossible to spot her in the multi-coloured student crowd.

Suddenly, the music has stopped and the lightening went out, leaving us all in complete darkness. Angry voices rang all around me, 'Hey, what is going on? . . . It's a power cut! . . . Someone in B1 didn't pay his bills! . . . DJ, where are you? Turn on the music! . . . Fuck! Watch where you're going, it's my feet you're jumping on!'

After a few minutes the lights went back on with the dance remixes thudding powerfully from the speakers, exactly as if nothing had happened. Everyone was in exactly the same place, with one exception: James was no longer around. I wasn't the only one to notice his absence. Serena was glancing round in every direction, trying desperately to locate him in the crowd. 'Where's James gone?' she begged Tom.

'How should I know?' he shrugged.

It was getting very stuffy inside, plus they'd run out of beer, and I yearned for some fresh air.

'Let's go back to New Court. There's my half-bottle of Malibu hidden in Ala's room,' suggested Catherine and moving through the crowd we headed towards the exit. Miss Foxton and the B1 housemaster were already standing in the doorway, taking note of those who weren't steady on their feet. 'Going to bed, girls? Well done,' she praised us.

'You go ahead, I'll visit the ladies and follow you,' hissed Catherine, and disappeared.

Back in New Court, I went upstairs, opened the door of Ala's room and absolutely froze in surprise. It was almost dark, with all the lights turned off, and James seemed to be asleep on Alka's bed in his Batman costume – though without his mask. Alka was standing above him holding a mirror with a

CHAPTER 4

burning candle and muttering something unintelligible under her breath.

'What's going on here? What's wrong with him?' I asked, alarmed.

Ala calmly turned around and blew out the burning candle.

'He followed me to New Court, but I guess he'd had too much to drink, so he just fell asleep. I made him some herbal tea and was trying to revive him with traditional methods, but it just isn't working.' She turned on the light. 'Hey, wake up!' she whispered, shaking him lightly by the shoulder.

James opened his eyes, but still looked very confused, as if he didn't understand where he was or what was going on.

'Sashka, why are you standing uselessly there? Make this guy a cup of strong coffee!'

I rushed to the kitchen as ordered, but when I came back with the coffee, James had already gone. Instead Catherine and Ala were sitting on the bed, and Catherine was trying to find out if they had kissed.

'He tried, of course, but I want him to chase me first,' said Ala calmly.

'You wish! Why, everyone's chasing him, even Serena,' scoffed Catherine. Ala narrowed her cat eyes and said nothing. A light smile touched her lips.

'Hey, look what he's left behind!' called Catherine, picking up the Batman mask from the floor. But Ala snatched it from her hands. 'I'll give it back to him personally, when I'm over for supper in Littlefield,' she said, addressing me.

I couldn't help feeling rather uneasy. What had she been whispering over him? How had he left so quickly? And what on earth would Serena say?

CHAPTER 5

On Thursday, I invited Ala for supper in Littlefield. 'See you there at 7:30. Don't be late.'

'I will be on time,' she promised.

'And please, don't touch James. Serena will never forgive such a thing, and remember, I still have to live with her for the whole school year.'

'Don't worry! Why would I want him, anyway? I've heard he's not the brightest spark around. Besides, I have my eye on a few more promising guys,' she assured me, and I almost believed her.

At 7:25 p.m., I went downstairs to the communal hall, nearly tripping over Penny and Natalie, who had been sitting on the stairs gossiping with some guys in comfortable armchairs next to the front door.

'Hi, Sasha,' Ginger Tom greeted me, while Natalie gave me a friendly smile and made some space on the stairs for me to sit next to her. *It's a nice house after all,* I thought to myself, though still preferring to stand.

With dinnertime approaching everyone was getting impatient, randomly checking their watches and throwing occasional glances towards the entrance in anticipation of the arrival of guests from other houses. Soon the hall had filled up with rowdy and hungry Upper Sixth males, by far outnumbering us girls – for a moment I wondered what it would be like for a few of them to live in New Court if it suddenly decided to go mixed. Recalling Tom's musings about the girls' need for an 'education,' I concluded that they wouldn't mind in the least. . .

'So, who's coming over tonight?' asked Charlie Phillips, a guy in my Geography class.

'Frederic Wood from Barton Hill, from my Chemistry class. Chris invited him,' said Penny.

'Chris Parker?' Charlie asked her

'Yes.'

'He's our House Captain,' Natalie reminded me, good-naturedly trying to include me in the conversation.

'I know Frederic. Tall, geeky guy in glasses. He dated Fifi Lewis-Harbour from Summerfield last year, until she dumped him for Billy Milton,' commented Penny. 'Apparently he snogs like a hoover. Who else?'

'Azaan somebody . . . I don't remember his last name – and anyway no one can pronounce it correctly,' said Natalie.

'Ma-ha-ra-shtrian. His father is an aluminium king in India,' added Charlie knowingly. 'I invited him.'

'And your friend from New Court. Ala, right? What is her surname?' Penny asked me.

'Gromova.'

As soon as I said it, the clock of the College Chapel ominously struck half past seven, which made us all involuntarily look through the window. Talk of the devil! Ala Gromova wearing a confident smile was approaching Littlefield. She had kept her promise to be on time.

'Hello, everyone, I am Ala – Sasha's friend,' she said, granting a gracious look to the Littlefieldians, as if they were her guests instead of the other way around.

'Would you like a seat?' Chris Parker jumped to his feet, making his friends shuffle uncomfortably, secretly wishing that they'd had the wit to offer theirs first. Natalie and Penny exchanged surprised glances, but before Ala had a chance to take up the offer, Mrs Graham swung open the door of the dining room and we all hurried inside to take places at a large wooden table in the centre.

Ala sat next to me, opposite James. They casually greeted each other, and if I hadn't known better, I'd have thought that James was meeting Ala for the first time, which as we knew wasn't the case.

Maybe he's just pretending, in case Serena suspects something, I thought, looking around the table for his girlfriend, but she appeared to be running late.

CHAPTER 5

Ala and I had just filled our plates to the brim with spaghetti and grated Parmigiano from the buffet and were about to tuck into a salad, when Serena strolled in, tossing her blonde hair and accompanied by a tanned Indian guy, whom I guessed was Azaan.

She gawked in our direction, but since there were no free seats left next to James, she had to sit at the opposite end of the table with Azaan, which didn't appear to make her very happy.

In the meantime, Alka was telling me the latest news from New Court, snapping her eyes at James and Chris Parker, who soon joined in and made us all giggle at his impersonation of Grumpy, hiding in the bushes on the look-out for wicked students daring enough to walk on the grass lawn. Ala trilled with ringing laughter, tossed her beautiful hair, and asked Chris to do Grumpy again.

Meanwhile, James and Tom had already started competing with Chris for her attention, outdoing each other with amusing anecdotes and stories. Nervously I peeked at Serena, who – though pretending to be fully engaged in a conversation with Azaan – was clearly all ears, while Azaan, unsurprisingly, seemed most taken with her. Chris emptied his plate first and stood up from the table.

'I promised to pay Vicky Saunders a visit before prep.' He winked at James. 'See you all later.'

Instantly leaving poor Azaan behind, Serena rose and took the recently vacated place next to James. There she wrapped her arms around his neck, planted a kiss on his lips and gave Ala a winning look.

'I'm having a birthday party in a few months in my house in Gloucestershire. All of Littlefield and all my closest friends will be there. I'm having a marquee and a super cool band, oh and the fireworks, of course!' she boasted.

'I'm Ala Gromova, so nice to meet you,' Ala was quick to introduce herself with the loveliest smile she could muster – that smile which she usually saved for the opposite sex.

'Sasha's told us about you,' said Serena sweetly, 'Is it true that her parents are paying your tuition fees?'

I couldn't imagine who had told her that – it certainly hadn't been me! But Ala was equal to it.

'Yes, it is. They're like a second family to me,' said Ala, and looked at me for affirmation.

'Yes, we have been close friends since forever,' I quickly added, hoping that Ala didn't think that it was me who had told Serena about her fees.

'Are you an orphan then?' asked Serena, refusing to release the subject. I thought of her mother – and of mine, suddenly missing her quite a lot. Not deigning to answer her, Ala turned to James instead.

'I have something for you.'

She pulled his Batman mask from her bag.

'I found it on the floor in B1, when the disco was over,' she lied, ignoring Serena's piercing gaze.

'Great! I was wondering where it had got to,' said James, well-pleased. Either James really didn't remember anything that had happened after the B1 party or else he was a first-class actor – which seemed unlikely, judging from his genuine appearance.

'Well, thank you for supper, it was great meeting you all,' Ala stood up from the table. 'Let's go, Sasha, you can show me how you have settled in here. I'll have to be back at New Court in time for prep. Although I think I'd rather do my prep in the library,' and with this she gave James a speaking glance.

'How could I have forgotten!' exclaimed James suddenly, without even looking at Serena. 'I have a paper on Disraeli for Monday's history class. I'd better shoot by the library, too. Shall we go together?' he offered.

'Sure! Let's meet in fifteen minutes in your hall,' she said, paying no attention to Serena, who sent her a stare so deadly that I felt shivers down my spine.

We left the dining room and went upstairs to my room.

CHAPTER 5

'Not bad. And the view is nice,' Ala approved, idly looking around my room. But I had another topic on my mind.

'Listen, you promised me you wouldn't touch James.'

'It's not my fault that he fancies me!' she said indignantly, staring at me with rounded eyes. 'Don't you see? He's even following me to the library, as if I'd invited him there. . . Anyway, I must run. Let's meet tomorrow at New Court during the break and catch up.'

She kissed me lightly on the cheek and rushed downstairs. My door hadn't even closed before someone gave it a light knock and then burst in without an invitation. It was Serena – she must have practically collided with Ala on the stairs. She was coiling her white-blonde locks in her fingertips, nostrils flaring, a threat hiding in her steel-grey eyes.

Something's going to happen, I thought with sinking heart. Upon seeing my face, though, and to my intense relief, Serena came back to her senses and put a token smile on her lovely face.

'Sasha, I need to talk to you,' she went straight to the point. 'You know, we treat you well here. And we all like you,' she forced herself to say. I guessed by 'we' she meant herself and her slavish entourage. 'I've even thought about inviting you to my birthday party – and, believe me, the entire college wants to be there! But your friend, Ala simply spoils your image. She's an absolute man-eater! Didn't you see how she almost swallowed James for supper today, and not just James either . . . While you seem to be pushing him into her arms! Why did you invite her here at all? If you had asked me before, I'd have told you that we only invite the most popular students for supper. You're still new, and you want to improve your status, rather than ruin it! Anyway,' Serena changed her tone abruptly, 'I didn't mean to lecture you, and I'm ready to forget this evening, if you do me a small favour,' she paused waiting for my reaction, but I remained silent and fearful. 'I have to know what is going on between James and Ala. She'll surely tell you everything tomorrow.'

'Why don't you just ask James yourself?' I asked.

'Sweet naivety! If something *is* going on, he'll hardly tell me, will he? And I'm not going to have the entire College laughing at me behind my back. Do you understand?'

'Perfectly,' I answered. 'But I'm not going to spy on my best friend either.'

'No one's asking you to spy! Just keep me posted about any of her intrigues that concern James. I don't care about the rest. She can have the lot.'

'If you are so uncertain about his loyalty, maybe you should just leave him?' I dared to say.

'You don't understand!' Serena hastily gathered her hair up in a ponytail, looking annoyed by my stupidity. 'James is madly in love with me. Every girl in College is after him, and I'm not going to lose him to some Russ… I mean, some floozy, who's only been here less than a term and thinks that she can easily steal the most popular guy in College from me. Look, will you help me or not?'

'I told you I wouldn't spy on anyone. I don't care about other people's relationships. And besides, I have to do my prep now,' I announced, somehow finding the nerve to open my door in front of Serena's nose.

'I see . . . And I'd thought that you and I might be friends! Well, you'll regret this,' she vowed, striding out of my room.

I could have done without that, I thought, sinking in exhaustion into my armchair. It was time to do prep, but I couldn't concentrate. I pulled a geography book from the shelf, sat at my desk and opened the page with homework for tomorrow, but the letters went blurry.

I don't really care, there's always New Court, I have some real friends there, I think. I wonder who will join Serena, though I thought to myself. Then my thoughts went back to Ala: such an attention-seeker, always looking for an audience, always convinced that she was the centre of the universe. However, Ala had always been like that, nothing new there, but she was still my best, first and most loyal friend and I love her for just being – herself.

For that reason I was glad I had stood up to Serena.

CHAPTER 6

The next day, Ala and I were the first to arrive at our geography class, with the exception of Mr. Green himself, who hurriedly greeted us and just as swiftly continued writing something in his teacher's journal. Before the lesson got started, I had plenty of time to give Ala the highlights of yesterday's talk with Serena.

'I'll show her! Who does she think she is?' she fumed. 'She doesn't rule here!'

'Ala, I'm not trying to cross swords, not with you or with anybody. . . By the way, have you done your geography prep?'

'No . . . Can you believe it, I didn't even get to the library last evening! Instead, James suggested going for a walk past the playing fields before prep, and we enjoyed the walk so much, that we, um, lost our way. It was time to study, though, so we decided to be diligent students and have private lessons – outside.'

'Alka! Did you do it?!'

'If you mean sex, then no, of course not; but we were kissing under a full moon for the entire prep and finished our evening in a local pub. He's so romantic, I would never have guessed it.' Here Ala sighed dreamily, as if recalling pleasant memories. 'He wanted to come to New Court as soon as today, but I told him that first he would have to break up with Serena and then propose. . . No, I am joking, naturally! . . . I mean, he has to break up with Serena and then he has to ask me officially whether I would like to go out with him. I've heard from the girls in New Court that this is how it should be done.'

'You went to a *pub*?' I cried.

Fortunately, Mr. Green didn't speak Russian, and this is why it is so fortunate: going to a pub on weekdays was a serious crime for Marlburians, the crime aggravated by the fact that it was during prep and the Marlburian in question happened to be underage. However, as usual, Ala had managed to violate all the rules and still to avoid punishment.

I breathed: 'You were so lucky that a beak didn't catch you! You could have been expelled! As you well know, there are no mitigating circumstances in such cases.'

'He who takes no risks never gets to drink champagne!' she said lightly.

'You drank *champagne?*'

'No, they don't drink such stuff in pubs here,' she told me. 'James ordered us snakebites, a crazy mix of beer and cider. Luckily he definitely looks at least eighteen, so no one asked him for an ID. If we hadn't had to leave in order to hide from a maths beak, who by some coincidence came into the same pub, James would've had to carry me back to College.'

'Alka, truly you have to behave here; you can't afford to be so careless. . . Think what my parents would say, if you were expelled!'

After a few more arguments, which seemed to do nothing either towards ruffling Ala's calm or else towards calming myself, I recalled something else: 'By the way, Freddy Fitzroy and Catherine invited me to watch a rugby match. Our team is playing with a college called Radley. You could come with me, and cheer for James!'

Ala frowned. 'You know how much I dislike being in a herd. It's more Serena's thing: this role would suit her well. Anyway, don't worry about her; she'll freak out for a bit, but she'll soon calm down . . . As for her silly party, I didn't want to go anyway.'

Soon afterwards the rest of our classmates had arrived, and Mr. Green started the lesson.

After lunch, I returned to Littlefield to prepare for my afternoon classes. I was heading towards my room, when I heard loud sobbing coming from Serena's, directly opposite. Her door was slightly ajar, and, unable to resist, I peeked inside. Serena was lying face down on her bed, weeping into the pillow. Penny and Natalie were beside her, vainly attempting to calm her down, but she didn't seem

CHAPTER 6

to be listening. Remembering our frosty previous encounter, I longed to pass by, but then decided I shouldn't be unforgiving and knocked very softly on the door – so softly that only Penny heard me, and came to see me.

'What's happened here?' I asked. 'Can I help at all?'

Penny looked at me, wide-eyed, as if to prepare me for some unbelievable news, and whispered voicelessly, 'James has broken up with her.'

I didn't know what to say – as it was not completely astonishing to me, at least – and remained standing there, until I noticed Penny's obvious disappointment at my lack of reaction. Then I did my best.

'No! It cannot be!' I said, whereupon Serena lifted her swollen face, spotted me standing in the doorway and cried, 'Penny, shut the door!' before burying her face deeply back into her pillow.

'So sorry,' whispered Penny, shutting the door gently in my face.

So, Alka did steal James after all, I concluded, going to my room. And in that moment I felt really sorry for Serena, grieving inconsolably for her former boyfriend. Though I couldn't help thinking also *should you really mourn someone who doesn't love you back?* To be honest, I felt unsure on this point, being unable to picture myself in her shoes.

I sat on my bed and paused to think. Unlike Ala, I had zero experience in love affairs, but I did feel fairly confident that true love shouldn't make you cry – and who would wish for a relationship that was fake? At first I decided to share my thoughts with Serena, when I got the chance, but then remembered her threatening tone towards me and changed my mind. Perhaps, after all, it was none of my business.

That day I'd arranged to meet my friends for supper in Norwood Hall. Catherine had arrived early, in order to ensure that we got hold of our favourite table near the window: the perfect vantage point from which to watch the Marlburian crowd go by. I spotted her there chatting to Chris and Jackie but decided to go first to the buffet before joining them. By the time I arrived at Catherine's table, Jackie, who was captain of the 'A' house hockey team, was in the middle of heatedly describing an unfair penalty card she received during a match against New Court earlier that day. I absent-mindedly listened to Jackie's grievances while wondering whether I was justified in telling my friends about Serena and James. *This can wait. Probably I should talk to Alka first,* I concluded, at the same time noting that my best friend was running late.

The canteen was buzzing as usual at such an hour, with students and beaks forming a long queue for the buffet, where some boy had slopped his dinner all over the floor, causing a minor traffic jam. Suddenly, Catherine rolled her eyes at the window and cried, 'Look!'

Ala and James were strolling across Central Court hand in hand, giggling for no apparent reason, apparently oblivious to the fact that they were being watched by hundreds of pairs of curious eyes. They made quite an entrance: James' arm encircling Alka, who was also wearing his jacket on top of her school dress. Together they headed straight to the buffet to join the queue of other latecomers, followed by stares from every table and a hushed silence.

'There's going to be a show,' Jackie warned me knowingly, while Chris and I exchanged confused glances.

It all started with a few whistles here and there, which served as a signal for a storm to explode in Norwood Hall: the males began tapping their cutlery on the table, stamping their feet and whistling, while the girls stopped eating to enjoy the occasion, though only improving the deafening soundtrack with the occasional girly giggle. I couldn't believe it.

'Whe-hey, James!' yelled some guy.

'Hey, man, congrats!'

'This is how they greet new couples here – whether they want it or not,' explained Catherine to me, rather loftily.

I shivered with sympathy, imagining myself in Alka's shoes. But she wasn't me, so she just smiled triumphantly, without a hint of embarrassment, glanced around and then kissed James, who flushed with pleasure at this attention.

Then, after filling their trays with food, they casually strolled over towards the table usually taken by his rugby teammates.

'Move over, boys,' Ala smiled, while they gawked at her, open-mouthed.

'I don't believe it! When did this happen?' breathed Catherine at last, looking towards me, as if shell-shocked. 'And what about Serena?'

I had no answer, except that I suddenly recalled one of Alka's favourite sayings: all is fair in love and war.

But: which one was it, I wondered. Was it love, or war?

CHAPTER 7

Alka's 18th birthday was approaching and, wishing to rub Serena's nose in her loss, she decided to celebrate it in Littlefield.

Without wasting any time we started our secret preparations for a party, first running into town to order a rich birthday cake and some alcohol. The cake itself was easy, as the town possessed a posh bakery much patronised both by locals and by College students during parental visits. My mouth would sometimes water just eyeing its window display, and I often longed to try everything – chocolate éclairs, appetizing fruit tarts, layered cream cakes. . .

Our choice on this occasion fell on a delectable strawberry and cream gateau, leaving us with only the main task yet undone. However, although the town abounded both in wine shops and supermarkets, as minors we stood no chance of buying any alcohol – unless there happened to be a secret Russian black market somewhere of which we had never heard . . . And even in this case, we would still have to somehow smuggle our contraband into College . . . The rules were very strict on this matter and one could easily get expelled. Still, what kind of birthday party could it be, without champagne? Puzzled and bemused, we stood outside a wine shop, staring at a large bottle of Bollinger displayed in the window. Then we suddenly heard a voice behind us.

'What's the occasion, girls?'

I turned around and found myself staring straight into the eyes of a tall, dark young man. To say that he was handsome was to say nothing at all – he was astonishingly handsome. Beside him, James seemed very ordinary indeed and James was probably the handsomest young man in College, with his clean-cut looks, wonderful complexion and wavy brown hair. In fact, I'd never seen anyone remotely as good-looking as this stranger before, not even in films, where both men and women often have an improbable sheen of near-perfection.

Two other guys were standing next to him, but I didn't even notice them. Tall, lean, broad-shouldered yet elegantly built, his thick black hair was brushed back in order to display an intelligent brow and perfectly sculpted features. He was wearing a black leather jacket, denim jeans and cowboy boots.

'I'm Quentin, by the way, and these are my friends Chris and Will,' he nodded towards his companions. 'You're from College, right?' His slightly crooked smile was bewitching. In fact, everything about him – even the crooked smile – was so attractive that I for a second doubted that so gorgeous a specimen of manhood actually existed, and that I hadn't dreamed him up out of thin air.

While I was standing, frozen and dumbstruck, Ala – always equal to anything – took the initiative and offered her hand.

'Nice to meet you! I am Ala and this is Sasha. We are Russians, studying over here.'

'Really?' Quentin looked rather amused. 'I would never have imagined that there might be Russians at a posh school like this! – No offence meant, of course.'

'None taken, so get over it! However, there *is* something you can do to benefit international relations,' and here Ala nodded towards the window display.

Our dilemma was solved almost immediately and soon, loaded down with heavy bags, we headed back to College, accompanied by our delightful new acquaintances, merrily chatting along the way. . . . We soon found out that Chris's dad owned the popular local pub favoured by the Sixth Formers, and that Will had been expelled from College a few years before for doing drugs. As for Quentin, having graduated from a local grammar school with honours, he had won a place at Oxford and was intent upon enjoying his gap year. Judging from what I heard, he seemed incredibly smart – and also modest about it.

On the way back Ala grew more and more excited, supplying most of the conversation while making eyes at the gorgeous Quentin. Occasionally she'd nod in my direction and say 'we' – but once, apparently to her surprise, Quentin elected to speak to me instead.

'So, Sasha, how do you like it here? Do you get teased about your accent?'

'My accent is not that strong!' If I sounded defensive, then it echoed my true feelings, for why had he not said this to Ala?! – I had always secretly thought my English accent at least equal to hers. 'Anyway, to answer the question, we really enjoy Marlborough, but I still miss home – and Moscow, as well.'

'Speak for yourself!' snapped my Alka. 'I'd rather stay here forever than go back home!'

'And are you really from Moscow? I was there three years ago, on a school trip. I'll tell you all about it someday.' Quentin told me, rather to Ala's annoyance.

Just as we reached the College gates it suddenly dawned on us that it was far too risky to attempt to smuggle our purchases inside, and yet we were extremely unwilling to part with such good stuff.

'Listen, guys, why don't you come to my birthday party tomorrow evening?' coaxed Ala. 'It starts at eight, in Littlefield House. Bring our bottles too. We're counting on you!'

'Deal!' said Quentin, looking me right in the eyes, which made me feel a little dizzy. 'See you Saturday then.'

His look left me gasping for air, and observing that I had, for the moment, forgotten how to breathe, Alka immediately grabbed my hand and dragged me home to New Court, gloating *en route* about how even the most popular girls in College would expire from envy upon seeing someone like Quentin at her party, and then adding, more prosaically, 'I only hope they won't drink our stuff on the way.'

'Maybe Will would prefer something to sniff,' I suggested, rather rudely, which made her laugh.

On Saturday evening I was on pins and needles, I was so looking forward to Quentin's reappearance. For Ala's party Mrs. Graham had kindly given us permission to use the Littlefield dining room, which we had diligently decorated with colored ribbons stating, 'Happy Birthday, Ala!' along with paper garlands.

Our cake, decorated by me with eighteen candles, loomed on the table, surrounded by various Waitrose delicacies. Alka herself looked truly stunning in a red silk dress with a deep cleavage which she'd borrowed from someone in New Court – especially by contrast to the rest of us girls, who were attired in casual T-shirts and jeans. She had even put her hair up, revealing a robust neck adorned with a silver heart-shaped pendant – a generous birthday present from James.

'Birthdays should happen at least twice a year,' Ala sighed dreamingly, stroking the pendant and perhaps thinking about something only she knew about. . .

By 8:00 p.m. Littlefield was packed. Ala had not only managed to invite every single person she knew, but she had also used the occasion in order to invite everyone whom she wished to know – in particular a group of extremely popular and well-connected students, which she wanted to find her way into, in order to run the show. . . Unsurprisingly, Serena and her clan didn't show despite being invited, which was a relief – to me at least.

With the music thundering from the speakers practically shaking the floor and everyone in eager anticipation of promised booze, which we had schemed to put in large lemonade bottles in case our housemistress suddenly appeared, Ala was the centre of attention. Surrounded by males she was telling some racy Russian anecdotes from her endless supply, her distinctive Russian accent ringing loudly across the room. James, of course, was particularly smitten, hardly ever releasing her hand and fondling her possessively whenever he got the chance.

Meanwhile Tom was buzzing some gossip in my ear, but, unable to concentrate, I could not respond properly, my attention being glued to the entrance door.

'Hi, Sasha!' Quentin suddenly emerged next to me, with that just-so-slightly crooked smile across his stunning face. 'So sorry we're a little late. Will had to fix something . . . but it looks as if your party's in full swing without us!'

CHAPTER 7

As before, I was secretly astounded – those angular features with the razor-sharp cheekbones and those warm yet still dancing dark eyes: I absorbed every detail in just a few seconds. You could imagine the most handsome aristocrat, sports star or Hollywood leading man looking similar but, as I later learned, Quentin came quite from a modest background, and had no desire to be famous.

The gift of such looks didn't go unnoticed, of course, and although his two friends had come along too, the spotlight was firmly on Quentin. The girls were whispering in excitement, unashamedly ogling him and nudging each other while the Marlburian males gazed at him with – to my eyes, at least – unmasked hostility. . . However, Quentin didn't seem to notice the reaction he'd stirred up.

'Doesn't he even realise the effect he has on people? How modest he is!' I thought, marveling with the rest.

'So glad you could come and thanks so much for bringing our stuff,' I muttered, feeling annoyed to be so tongue-tied in his presence.

He said easily: 'You're very welcome, anytime. So, this is where you live… Your house seems so old, even the floors are creaky! Which floor are you on? I bet the view's good from the top.'

'It is! My room is at the top, along with all the other girls in this house. I was told that the building was reconstructed after a fire in the sixties, but it's still one of the more historic ones – in comparison New Court, where Ala lives, is completely up-to-date.'

While I was talking, I tried not to glance at him too much, so as to not to lose the thread of what I was saying, which – given his distracting appearance and my still pretty lame English – was easy for me to do. I was thinking hard of something else to say, when Chris Parker's slightly irked voice interrupted: 'Who are all these people, Sasha, and what are they doing in Littlefield?'

Quentin's presence seemed to be causing trouble already.

'I invited them – they're all friends of mine. These heroes saved the day,' stated Ala in a voice that brooked no argument. 'Open the champagne, boys, and let's get a real Russian party started!'

Soon enough the bar was emptied, but the party flowed on. Some guests spilled outside into the courtyard, while others broke off into couples and disappeared into various regions of the house, obviously eager to make the best possible use of Mrs. Graham's temporary absence.

'Shall we wander?' suggested Quentin.

We went outside together. There was a new moon, the contours of its crescent barely visible, but the stars, with that electric-blue tinge, were glinting brightly in the charcoal sky and the crisp autumn air chilled my lungs.

Quentin said: 'Did you know that there's an old chapel nearby? I stumbled across it when I was on my way to see you. I'll show you if you like,' and with this he took my hand. . . The warmth of his touch stung as if an electric current had shot through my veins.

When I was on my way to see you I dreamily repeated to myself, smiling in near-disbelief and squeezing his hand back. Had he really come to see me? We walked about ten minutes before he found it, a mysterious little chapel, half-hidden in thorny briars, and half buried in a copse. It felt as if no one had been there for ages. We groped for the door in the dusk, but, even once we'd found it we struggled to open it, as it had become throttled by ivy and half-locked in muddy ground. . . Quentin had to use all his strength to shift it, shoving hard with his shoulder until the door, to his immense satisfaction, scudded sulkily open.

Timidly, I peeked inside and felt a rush of freezing cellar damp, which made me shiver and almost recoil: however, Quentin then put one warm hand on my shoulders and flicked his Zippo lighter with the other, illuminating deep-set stone walls and a low, damp ceiling. The place was so tiny, that it was impossible to move without brushing against each other. Glancing round, we found some half-gutted old candles littering the ground next to a small bench opposite an altar, which Quentin managed to light, turning the space in an instant from forbidding to cosy.

He had spread his jacket on a narrow stone bench, and we sat there in silence very close to each other. My heart was pounding so loudly that I was certain that he could hear it, so I was relieved when he was first to interrupt what seemed to me to be a protracted silence.

'What an atmospheric place! It can't be later than the 12th or 13th century. Just imagine how much time has passed away, Sasha – and how many generations have visited it! Though I don't think there can have been many Russians here before.'

'In which case, let's call dibs on this place,' I offered bravely.

'I don't mind at all.'

His perfect face was only inches from mine, his dark eyes gleaming in the light of the candle: I could just trace his breath on my cheek. How I longed to touch his face, slowly tracing each flawless line with my finger, just to convince myself that this wasn't a dream, that he was indeed real, and truly beside me! As if reading my mind, he firmly but gently turned me towards him, pulling me close and sending a flood of powerful feeling through the whole of my body. My heart was hammering so wildly that I felt my head spin and my legs tremble: I was so glad that I wasn't standing!

That was the moment when I first diagnosed my illness: that illness for which there is so often no antidote. . .

The moments we spent there were lost in time, our passions so fervent that we were no longer able to register the cold. It was the College's Chapel bell persistently striking ten which finally pulled me back to reality. My head was still dizzied from his kisses and my tongue to his taste and, while the sensation was overwhelming, I knew that it was time for me to return. We left the chapel and headed back to Littlefield, although the last thing I wanted to do was to let him go.

By the time we reached the house, the party was over: most of the guests had returned to their houses and Quentin's particular friends, we were told, had moved on to a local pub. Alka was also nowhere to be seen: she must have returned to New Court without waiting for my return.

Quentin kissed me goodbye right in front of the house, paying no attention to passing Littlefieldians openly gawking at us across the way.

'If you are free, I will come tomorrow night,' said Quentin burning into me with those deep velvety eyes, until I felt that I was in danger of melting away.

If! It was all I could do not to sing with joy! But I composed myself and said, 'See you at 9:15 then, right after prep.'

It was as I turned away that I suddenly had the strangest feeling that I was being observed.

A pair of almond-shaped green eyes were glittering like tiny headlights from the nearby bushes. These belonged to a large black cat, who had paused, paw lifted, as if deliberately eavesdropping on our conversation, but the moment I spotted it, it disappeared into the darkness of the approaching night.

CHAPTER 8

It is hard to recall where the next day went, the whole of which I spent impatiently looking forward to the evening. During classes, all my thoughts were consumed by the upcoming date. In what I was pleased to call my brain I was extraordinarily busy, trying on outfits and adjusting my hairstyle in my imagination. I was about to select my lipstick colour, when Mr. Green interrupted with some tricky question about a global warming.

'There is no warming. It's -20° every winter in Russia,' I blurted out, not knowing what else to say.

'I can tell at once, Alexandra, that you haven't prepared for today's lesson,' he shamed me.

'It's a good thing that they don't rush to give bad marks here, like in our old school,' Alka whispered to me, in the meantime raising her hand confidently.

The rest of the day didn't pass without incident. After lunch in Norwood Hall, I was due at a tennis court near Preshute for a coaching with Mr Reed, our PT beak. I felt light but strong, hitting from every corner of the court, and he was extremely pleased.

'Really, you play splendidly, and that backhand down the line is damn good. Keep it up, young Sasha, and I'll include you in the regional competition next term,' he promised me.

I had been playing tennis ever since the age of six in Moscow and felt delighted that my efforts hadn't gone unnoticed. To my utter surprise, Alka, who had never played sports in her life (and who used to regularly skip PT lessons back in Moscow) also had a sporting achievement to report: she had been included in the College grass hockey team. Her first match was later on that same afternoon – and I would have prepared to give everything up in order to see such a show! – but unfortunately, Mr Green had given me some extra homework, presumably so that I would never feel relaxed in his lessons, ever again. Which is why, once released by Mr Reed, and still wearing my tennis gear, I rushed straight to the library, although admittedly thinking of Quentin along the way.

However, all my good intentions to become a straight-A student failed that day: geography was the last thing on my mind. I cudgelled my brain over the book, feeling hopelessly unable to focus. In addition to everything else, I met Catherine in the library, who suggested that we share a short break in order to get some 'fresh air' – which, in Catherine's terminology, meant to go out for a smoke.

Together we left the library, crossed Central Court and headed towards the new school buildings, discussing the latest college news on the way. Then, having ensured that we weren't being observed, we sneakily turned off the path and slipped behind the two nearest trees. Catherine then pulled out a creased pack of cigarettes from her jeans' pocket and offered me one, although – staying true to my hopes of future tennis stardom – I declined. She drew deeply on her cigarette and then asked me in her usual business-like manner, 'So, who was that ridiculously handsome guy everyone was talking about at Alka's party? And won't you introduce us?'

But while I was eagerly telling her all about Quentin, we didn't even notice that Grumpy had spotted us.

'Your names and houses, ladies!'

We gave them sulkily, especially on my part, for I had not been smoking but only chatting . . . however, there was no arguing with Grumpy! 'You'll each run five kilometres each tomorrow, starting at six in the morning,' he ordered, skilfully extracting a pair of blue sheets from somewhere from under the folders of his gown, like some annoying magician.

Catherine immediately dropped her cigarette on the ground, stomping it furiously with the heel of her shoe.

CHAPTER 8

'I've had it with this! Anything but running, please!'

'And I wasn't even smoking!' I protested.

'Too late, I'm not taking any objections,' he snapped, filling in the blue sheets with our details before giving us copies for our prefects.

'Some fresh air,' grumbled Catherine, as we dragged ourselves back to the library at a snail's pace.

I didn't feel like studying anymore, so I simply fetched my tennis racket from the library, waved good-bye to Catherine and hurried back to Littlefield.

Despite everything, I was in high spirits: not even tomorrow's early morning run and extra geography homework could bring me down to earth. With my head up in the clouds, I couldn't wait for 9:15 to come.

Immediately after supper in Littlefield I quickly disappeared into my room, intending to cope with my geography, no matter what. After some struggles, I somehow I managed to finish the homework, as well as to hurriedly brush my hair, change into a black evening top and apply some lipstick, which on second thoughts I nervously removed, choosing some lip-gloss instead. At 9:15 sharp the College Chapel bell signalled the end of prep, and with it the house roared to life: loud voices accompanied by slamming of doors heralded the usual banging of feet on the stairs and general sense of jubilant chaos.

With just over an hour left before bedtime, each Littlefieldian was keen to seize the moment in order to do something he or she had probably been looking forward to for most of the day. This was the time for night walks, secret dates, and clandestine visits to neighbouring houses, for not everything in our student life was as innocent as our teachers wishfully believed to be the case.

Just as I glanced out of the window, I spotted Quentin's tall, broad-shouldered figure being rewarded by curious stares from the students rushing outdoors. Involuntarily I stood still for a brief moment by the window, admiring him: he had unhurriedly lit a cigarette and drew on it calmly, with none of Catherine's gulping desperation . . . That same moment, I saw Mr Reed, presumably on beak's night patrol, approach him with torch in hand, delighted to catch such a bold student red-handed. I tore myself away from the window and hurried downstairs. Yet when I arrived outside, Quentin seemed to be in the middle of having an amicable conversation with the beak. Seeing me, he put out his cigarette. I greeted him awkwardly, secretly wishing that Mr Reed would disappear into thin air.

'Mr Reed was just telling me how brilliant you are at tennis, Sasha. What a fantastic thing to be good at – I wish I was! So, how much time are you allowed? Until midnight, like Cinderella?'

'The doors are locked at 10:30, so you must be sure Sasha's back by then, unless you want her to get into trouble,' said Mr Reed in a firm but friendly tone.

I shot Quentin an apologetic look, secretly thinking that I'd never be able to get used to his extraordinary looks. 'In that case we better leave now,' he said, claiming my unresisting hand, and sending enough invisible sparks between us to ignite a forest fire.

Quentin said a polite farewell to Mr. Reed and strode confidently into the dusk, taking me with him. The old stone steps were dimly lit and broken in places. I squeezed Quentin's hand tight, afraid to trip over while attempting to keep up with him.

The feeling of feverish excitement which had hovered just under the level of my consciousness all day grew even stronger in his presence, holding me in a steely grip. Upon reaching the bottom of the stairs Quentin turned and pulled me to him, making me recall his height – even in heels I hardly reached his shoulder. His proximity was making me feel weak as if slightly intoxicated (not that it was difficult for me to feel intoxicated, as I had never been much used to alcohol. . . .)

'I wanted to show you a bit of the neighbourhood, but we're too short of time. Anyway, I've thought of a better plan.' And with this he nodded towards the opposite side of Bath Road.

Holding hands we ran across the busy road and continued on the footpath along the College's western boundary. The outlines of the Chapel's gothic spire pierced the dying sky.

CHAPTER 8

'Where are we going?' I asked breathlessly.

'We're going to Merlin's Mound. I've always wanted to go there, but you're not allowed unless you're from College... or going out with a Marlburian girl,' and here he winked at me, making my heart skip a beat.

Does he mean – could he mean that I was actually now going out with him? I wondered, half-dizzy, half-doubtful. It seemed altogether more likely that there had been some mix-up, and that it was Alka he was after.

'Which mountain?' I asked uncertain as to what he meant.

'Merlin's Mound. Haven't you heard of it?' he asked in astonishment. 'Merlin was supposedly the most famous wizard during King Arthur's reign. . . Of course, you haven't been over here very long.'

I vaguely remembered Merlin being mentioned on a general tour that we had had soon after arriving, but the abundance of the new information that had been processed since must have pushed it clean out of my head. Quentin instructed me. 'The motto of Marlborough is written in Latin on the town coat of arms: "*Ubi nunc sapiens assa Merline.*" This means, "Where now are the bones of wise Merlin?" Legend has it that the Mound is his burial place, making it the town's most famous legend – in fact, one of the sights of the whole area. I read somewhere that in Old English it was called Merleberge and that Merlin's real name in Welsh was Myrddin . . . Have they heard of King Arthur in Russia?'

Quentin's amazing knowledge of history captured my imagination, taking me straight back to the world of medieval kings with their castles, the Knights of the Round Table and the crusades in search of the Holy Grail. Listening to him, walking hand-in-hand, I felt somewhere far away. Glancing at his noble profile, its contours glowing in the moonlight, I secretly decided that he would have been the most handsome knight at the Round Table, Lancelot included. . .

The mysterious mound, which, as Quentin had told me, had served as the foundation for a Norman king's castle, was right in the middle of the College and, as I now vaguely recalled, strictly out-of-bounds to College students. (It's a measure of my confusion that this recollection made almost no impression upon me.)

It turned out to be about twenty metres high, shaped like a large pudding, and peppered on its summit with bushes and random conifer trees, like candles on a huge birthday cake, while its foot was adorned by a small shell grotto. While admiring it, we spotted a spiral ramp shielded by a thick hawthorn hedge and without wasting any time, went up the stairs two at a time.

To my surprise, Merlin's Mound turned out to be much wider at the summit than I'd suspected, offering amazing views of the famous White Horse on Granham Hill, carved into chalk, as well as various College buildings, which seemed comparatively rather unimpressive from above. We sat on the ground next to an unused water-tank, admiring the view, our arms wrapped around each other. The stars hung so low from the sky that it seemed I could just stretch my hand and pick whichever one I liked.

'The White Horse is very fine but you should also see its big sister – Silsbury Hill in Somerset. It's not far from here, just along the A4 on Bath Road. I'll show it to you next time. By the way, what are your plans for the weekend?'

'I am available!' I replied, singing in my thoughts.

Inspired, Quentin launched into telling me about Silsbury Hill, while I was listening to him, star-struck, admiring my inexplicably beautiful new friend and basking in the feeling that something very precious and real was happening to me. . . Eventually though, just as before, the sound of the Chapel bell interrupted our date and it was time to get back. This time he escorted me right up to the stone steps of Littlefield, where – utterly unable to part – we continued kissing in the darkness until I heard Mrs Graham's light step approaching with the keys and hurried upstairs.

There all the excitement took its toll on me and sleep took over. I vaguely remembered soaring over a medieval castle, watching a knight in silver armour depart for another crusade before, in the early morning hours, the very vividness of my dreams escaped my recollections.

CHAPTER 9

I was really looking forward to the weekend. Apparently, Quentin's mum had mentioned that she wanted to meet me – and had invited me over for Sunday lunch.

I wondered, more fervently than ever: *what might his parents be like?*

I imagined them – or at least one of them – to have been absolutely stunning when they'd been young. I secretly thought the person concerned most likely to have been his mother – a graceful beauty, perhaps resembling the young Vivian Leigh. Or perhaps Quentin took more after his father? Most of all, though, I worried: *will they like me?*

Finally, Sunday came.

At 12:00 sharp Quentin was already waiting outside the Littlefield front door, looking devastatingly handsome in jacket and tie. Hand in hand we headed towards his house, which turned out to be only a ten-minute walk from College. It was a lovely old cottage surrounded by well-tended rose bushes; one immediately sensed the caring hands of its current owners.

When I met Quentin's parents I was astonished to find that he didn't look anything like them. Their faces were friendly and pleasant but quite ordinary; one could not imagine either of them having been particularly good-looking, even when young. They introduced themselves as Debbie and Peter and we followed them inside.

Their living room was in classic Laura Ashley style: fabric sofas covered with attractive tapestry cushions; while pretty china figurines, jewelry boxes, miniature houses and framed family photos adorned various wooden chest of drawers and faux antique cabinets. Through the chintz-patterned curtains I could see a small, well-kept back garden: trimmed grass and immaculate pots of flowers all round. In fact, everything seemed so picture perfect – outside as well as in – that it seemed almost impossible that anyone could be actually living there.

After some small talk and delicate cut-glass helpings of sherry, Debbie summoned everyone to the dining room. The dinner table was dressed with a starched white tablecloth and matching table-napkins in gold napkin-holders, all arranged around an elegant vase with fresh-cut flowers; it was obvious that my hostess was a perfectionist. Which made me a little nervous.

'So, how are you enjoying the College, Sasha?'

'Very much, thank you.'

'What do they feed you there for lunch?' asked Debbie, after serving us generously. Peter solemnly opened a beautiful bottle of wine, carved the roast and asked me a few questions about Russia, but spent most of his time echoing his wife, who seemed to lead the conversation. I told her about our cafeteria selections, and then she said, 'Sasha is a lovely name. Do you know, even before Quentin was born I somehow knew that we'd have a son and I'd already chosen his name. You may not be aware of this, but Quentin is a rather popular name in the upper-class circles. I feel sure that he'll meet my high expectations!' she said, smiling proudly at him.

Quentin and I exchanged understanding glances. Quentin, like myself, was an only child, and he had already described to me his close relationship with his parents, especially his mother, who – as must be obvious – entertained great hopes for his future.

She continued: 'Peter and I are so proud that Quentin got a place at Oxford. Actually, he'll be the first in either of our families to receive a university education. Still, no one could have imagined his going to Oxford . . . What about you, Sasha? Have you thought about what you might do after College?'

'To be honest, university seems too far off to contemplate. I have my hands full at College,' I admitted.

'How lovely it would be if you both went to Oxford!' said Debbie.

CHAPTER 9

'It would! You should certainly try your best, Sasha,' laughed Quentin.

The atmosphere at the table was friendly and seemed relaxed, but I fleetingly believed that I caught Debbie looking attentively at me, which made me worry that my posture wasn't quite correct, or that I needed to work on my table manners – or possibly my English. I could have been wrong, but I somehow felt that, in Debbie's eyes at least, I fell a little short of her ideal of what a young miss from Marlborough College ought to be.

Our conversation was interrupted by a phone call: Debbie apologized and left the table to take it in the living room. 'We have a guest for lunch – Quentin's girlfriend from Marlborough College,' she told the caller, which cheered me somewhat.

After dessert, Quentin seemed to have had enough of his parents and suggested that he show me his room. Leaving them to put on the TV (and possibly to discuss me) we went upstairs, where I discovered that his room, far from fitting in with the rest of the house, seemed to enjoy a life all its own.

The walls were plastered with posters of famous rock bands and colorful prints; a wild variety of books and music overfilled the shelves; while a broad desk by the window hosted a brand new PC and a huge tape-recorder, complete with loudspeakers.

'Do you like Van Halen?' asked Quentin, putting some music on.

I nodded, without having a clue what he was talking about. To be honest, I really didn't care what music he chose, as long as I was next to the beautiful Quentin. 'Let's talk about love . . .' High energy screams of hard rock broke into our silence.

'Hang on, here's a better one,' said Quentin, interrupting the song despite its promising lyrics. While enjoying the music, I continued to study his room. I couldn't help being both surprised and impressed by such a volume and a variety of books: history, astronomy, politics and geography were mixed with adventure novels and classics. . . Clever boy! I gave him a secret 'thumbs-up' in my mind, feeling proud to have such an exceptional boyfriend. Suddenly a watercolour painting above his bed, depicting some medieval theme, caught my attention.

'Do you like it?' asked Quentin, noting my interest.

'Who is the artist?' I queried in return.

'No, no, you have to guess . . .'

I came nearer to take a closer look. The focal points were clearly King Arthur and his knights, all gathered at the Round Table. In the background however I saw some odd, fantastical creatures who seemed to have borrowed something from Merlin, something from dwarves and something even from interbred humans and animals. 'And what are those?' I inquired, indicating the strange creatures, who seemed to be conjuring up mischief behind the backs of the knights.

'I'll tell you another time,' said Quentin, leaving me mystified.

Suddenly, I noticed an unfinished sketch on his desk.

Quentin caught my eye and immediately turned the painting over before I had a chance to see it: 'Ah that! That's a surprise!' he said, putting his arms around my waist and instantly sending a powerful electric charge through my body.

I immediately forgot about the painting and about everything else in the world, feeling the hot brush of his lips on my neck and the magnetic touch of his hands on my body . . . lips locked together we sank down onto his bed.

We were brought back to reality some time later by a knock on the door, barely audible over the rock music thundering from his speaker system. Quentin immediately jumped off the bed and turned the volume down.

'Quentin, Chris is here,' we heard Debbie's tactful voice from behind the door.

Hurriedly we got dressed and rushed down to the living room, where Chris had made himself very comfortable in an armchair and was chatting agreeably to Quentin's father, Peter.

'Would you like some tea, perhaps?' Debbie proposed, but Quentin refused, on all of our accounts. Then I thanked Debbie and Peter for the lovely

CHAPTER 9

lunch. Before we parted, Debbie gave me a warm hug and promised to invite me for tea at the rather posh local bakery, the one where I'd gotten Alka her birthday cake.

As for Chris, he couldn't wait to leave the house and have a smoke. 'So, have you had enough of the old folks?' he asked, impatiently drawing on his cigarette. (Quentin also reached out for a smoke, but far more gracefully.) 'I'm not so good with family dinners, as they always end badly between my dad and me. I just can't stand his after-dinner lectures,' said Chris, rather mournfully.

Unlike Quentin, Chris had no university prospects. Nor did he appear to be in any great hurry to find a job, instead spending most of his time in pubs and bars with friends and girlfriends, enjoying life as much as he could. But he was always full of funny stories – some about himself – which he related brilliantly, with a poker face, while everybody around him was bursting with laughter. His black curly hair was tangled into greasy braids, which he was continually tucking behind his ears, a sight which made me long to give him a brush, or even to escort him to a decent local barber. Even in my own experience, he often told fibs, but he still had such stunning, crystal-blue eyes – and I couldn't help liking him, especially as he and Quentin had been best friends since childhood.

It was getting dark when we finally arrived at a local pub, squeezing inside through the rowdy crowd. Once there, we landed at one of the tables covered with pints of beer where a noisy company of local lads and girls, who all seemed to know Chris, were at different stages of getting merrily drunk.

Quentin got us some beer from the bar and was, while still holding my hand, quite engaged in a conversation with his friend Ben, at the other side of the table. I was glancing around in an attempt to spot some Marlburians without paying much attention to their chat. Above the noise I heard shreds of Ben's phrases. ('Everything's ready. The weather also looks great. So, as agreed...')

'OK, yes, fine,' nodded Quentin rather absently, stroking my knee. Suddenly as if struck by a notion, he slipped off to the jukebox. He soon returned to the table singing along with Guns N' Roses' 'Paradise City.' Then he wrapped his arms around me and kissed me on the lips, before carrying on chatting to his friends. In that moment I felt, as the English say, 'over the moon' I was going out with Quentin – and I'd met his parents, and his friends as well. I loved College; the UK had answered my every hope. Everything was wonderful!

Just then I caught sight of Natalie and Tom waving to me on their way out and recalled that it was time to return to College. I kissed Quentin goodbye and, leaving my beer unfinished, followed them through the door.

CHAPTER 10

Through heavy sleep I heard a sound, as if something had pinged against my window. Grudgingly, I opened my eyes, but then decided that I dreamed it, flopped over, and was about to drift back to sleep, when the sound occurred again.

My alarm was glowing one zero five, but somebody obviously couldn't sleep. Jumping out of bed I ran barefoot to the window, flung open the curtains and glanced out into the yard. Quentin was standing in the darkness, shifting his feet on the grass because of the cold and preparing to toss another pebble at my window. Having spotted me, he waved. I opened the window wide and leaned out, filling my lungs with air pierced with deliciously crisp night freshness.

'Come down, let's go for a walk,' he called softly.

'I'll be right down,' I whispered back.

Then I began rushing about the room, trying to figure out what to wear for such an unexpected night date, so as not to wind up looking like a complete scarecrow. . . But apart from my wardrobe, I began to fret about a more difficult problem: how could I slip out of the house unnoticed and then slip back in? The front door was out of question, as it was connected to an alarm system, which Mr. Graham activated every night. Maybe the window? I immediately rejected this idea: the height from the second floor was formidable. In the end I decided to make a reconnaissance on the ground floor and check out more sensible options.

Having slipped on a heavy coat over my pyjamas, I tiptoed out of the room carrying my sneakers in my arms and scuttled down the stairs like a guilty scullery-maid, trying not to creak the old floorboards and tensely listening out for any unusual sound . . . however, the whole of Littlefield seemed to be slumbering peacefully. Downstairs, in the moonlit hall, I could see Quentin gesticulating towards the closed windows. I unlocked and released the nearest of these, half-frozen in fearful anticipation of Mr. Graham's sudden appearance or the sudden screech of an alarm, but the house remained quiet.

'Hurry up!' I heard Quentin's muffled laughter as he gallantly held the window open while helping me through.

Once outside, I immediately heard the window slam tightly behind me, cutting off my escape route. Quentin noticed my concern.

'It's impossible to open from outside, but it's not so long till morning,' he whispered cheerfully. Then he pulled me to him for a lingering kiss, which made my knees go weak. Once released, I hurriedly slipped my feet into the sneakers, while Quentin added, 'Well, if you do feel cold, we can go straight to my place: I can warm you up quickly. What cute pajamas you have – next time I'll wear mine too!'

I immediately forgot, not only about the window but also about everything else in the world. It's just impossible for any person to be quite so beautiful, I thought, admiring him in the moonlight and feeling as if I was melting beneath his gaze. Quentin was rather more practical. 'Right, let's get out of here before your housemistress wakes up.'

This jolted me back to reality. The last thing I wished for was to be caught red-handed at the crime scene! Breaking off our embrace, we rushed down the steps leading to Bath Road and once there, headed in the direction of the town.

'I can't go to the pub in pyjamas,' I said, becoming suddenly obstinate.

'What makes you think that we're going to the pub? They've all been closed for hours already. We're going for a drive instead. You're perfectly dressed for it, except that your big coat prevents me from hugging you properly!' And here Quentin squeezed my hand tight.

'Drive?' I asked, taken aback.

'Why not? I think that car would suit us perfectly,' and here he nodded casually at a battered red Ford with dented sides parked by the side of the road,

CHAPTER 10

probably a friend's. However, having tried the door, Quentin laughed and said, 'I knew it! We'll have to break in!'

'What! We might be arrested for that!'

'Don't worry, I was only joking,' he grinned, pulling car keys out of his jacket pocket. 'Though I wouldn't mind claiming some insurance all the same!' He opened the door for me and I made myself comfortable, wondering where on earth we might be heading to in the middle of the night.

Quentin started the engine, turned on some music, and we got under way. Shortly after leaving Marlborough, we took a very bendy road through some picturesque villages, until we found ourselves on a major road, rushing along the inky contours of hills along Wiltshire's fields and meadows.

'I always said that I'd show you Stonehenge,' Quentin told me, squeezing my hand again. Greatly touched, I recalled that, even before coming to England, I had read about the world-famous archaeological Wiltshire monument, and longed to see it. Another dream was about to come true for me! A few minutes later he nodded towards the window. 'Look!'

Huge boulders of vaguely rectangular shape were seen on the clouded horizon, enigmatic as sphinxes, stretching towards the sky. Having approached, Quentin stopped the car. 'Come take a closer look,' he told me, and I followed him out of the Ford, speechlessly. 'They're supposed to date from about 3,000 B.C.'

'I wonder who made such a thing?' I breathed.

'Merlin,' Quentin said quietly, wrapping his arms around my shoulders. As if to confirm his words, a hoarse croak pierced the night silence, sending shivers down my spine. A black raven seemed to have become frozen, silhouetted atop one of the stones, eyes locked on us. Hand in hand, we were walking towards the rocks, when suddenly the winds whipped up, rain clouds appeared from nowhere, startling a shy young moon, and a strong gale rose, as if determined to haul us off our feet. Backs to the wind, we tried to continue, however the wind was lashing more and more furiously, threatening to turn into a real storm.

'Let's go back,' I suggested nervously. Quentin willingly supported this idea, and we hurried back to a warm safety of his car, cuddling up on its backseat. A powerful surge of hard rock music whooshed from the car audio, almost loud enough to drown out the winds raging outside. Having removed my coat, Quentin turned his attention to the buttons of my pajamas, marking each area of capitulated territory with the lightest possible touch of his lips until my unbuttoned top had disappeared under the seat, and I, like the wings of a butterfly, was trembling from his kisses.

No! Such kisses should be prohibited by law, I thought, rising from my seat to pull his shirt off. The mere sight of his torso took my breath away. Quentin quickly helped me to cope with his shirt, breathing hard. Observing my temporary confusion, he reached out for the drawstrings of my pajamas bottoms, burning me with a questioning look.

I caught his arm, having no intention of going that far. Quentin continued kissing me until we'd both run out of air. We didn't even notice as the storm calmed down and the whirling winds died into a stiller dawn.

Quentin wiped the misted window and began collecting our clothes scattered around the car. Despite the hour, I felt wide awake, but it was time to return to Littlefield before my disappearance was discovered.

Having parked in the same spot, Quentin escorted me back, along the way concocting a strategy for plan A of my entry back into the house, along with a back-up plan B and a fallback plan C in case of an emergency. If I was caught, I would be expelled on the spot, which I wanted less than anything in the world.

Tom's room was on the ground floor, right next to the housemaster's house, but it still seemed the best option, as I softly knocked on his half-open window. Tom didn't even stir and, after waiting a couple of minutes, we tried again. 'Tom! Tom!' I called, trying to keep my voice down. Then Quentin managed to pull the window a fraction wider and peered in.

'Looks like he's sacked out, he's even snoring! If he wakes up, tell him that you were in his dreams!' he grinned, lifting me onto the windowsill. 'See you after prep.'

CHAPTER 10

The gap was – just – wide enough. Quentin kissed me goodbye before helping me through the window, sneakers under my arm. Tom, his arms wildly outstretched across his bed, was loudly wheezing in his sleep and didn't even budge while I, awakening every floorboard, tiptoed to his door. Upon opening the door into the corridor I immediately met the astonished gaze of a sleepy Chris Parker in his pajamas, which were horizontally-striped, like a Russian *telnyashka*.

'Wow, you and Tom?' he asked, scratching his head.

I blushed furiously. 'Don't you dare to say such a foolish thing! I was just on a morning jog and sneaked in through his open window.' And I waved my dirty sneakers as proof.

'Hey, I don't care!' he retorted, heading on to the bathroom, while I rushed to the female section before anybody else could see me and spread more gossip around the college. . . A few minutes later I had thrown my coat off and was safely wrapped inside my cosy duvet. It was almost six, and I had only two hours to nap before my classes.

That evening, Quentin visited me in Littlefield after prep. He'd never been in my room before, and I noticed him glancing curiously around my humble setting. 'I thought everything would be much newer and better here, considering how much you pay a year,' he commented disappointedly, taking a seat in the armchair pureed with holes. Then he drew me close, pulling me on to his lap. I wrapped my arms around his neck, admiring the strong yet delicate lines of his gorgeous face, which I had only been able to daydream about during school hours.

'Well, I can't complain, I don't think it's bad here at all!' I said loyally.

'I like it when you wear short skirts,' Quentin told me. His hands were traveling along my bare legs, which I enjoyed very much. He threw an eloquent look at my bed, which I caught.

'Ha, ha, I would definitely be expelled for that! They're very strict here,' I warned him. 'Could I get you some tea?' Suddenly, there was the briefest of knocks and, without waiting for an invitation to enter, Mr. Graham flung the door open. I saw a giggling Serena and a wide-eyed Natalie behind him, and realised in an instant who had reported the guest in my room. . . I hurriedly slipped off his knees, discreetly straightened my skirt, and tried to appear more confident than I felt, not knowing in the least what to expect from this visit.

'Sasha, I think it's time for me to meet your friend here,' said Mr Graham glancing towards Quentin rather frostily. The introduction however, was most successful: it was obvious that Quentin's manners made a most favorable impression on Mr. Graham – especially when he learned that Quentin was heading off to Oxford in the autumn. At this point Mr Graham started reminiscing about the glorious years he had spent there as a young student. We hung on to his words, nodding encouragingly in hopes of prolonging his trip down memory lane and distracting him from the equivocal nature of our immediate situation. . . As he left I thought how strange it was how nostalgic one could become after, say, thirty-five years or so. Left alone again, we didn't even notice how the time flew until the church bells were heard.

'Oh! I almost forgot!' said Quentin, at the door. 'I've got a little gift for you.' From his bag he pulled out a rolled canvas, which he carefully spread on my desk. It was an oil painting, beautifully done, of a knight in silver armor – which I was stunned to recognize from my recent dream.

'It's perfect!' I breathed.

'Do you really like it? He asked, 'I had to wait quite a while for the paint to dry. I also signed it.' He turned over the picture and handed it to me.

'To dear Sasha, with love from Quentin,' I read. What immaculate handwriting he had!

'But if we should ever separate, I'll want it back,' he warned me.

'Separate?' I repeated in confusion.

Quentin hastily put his arms around me. 'I certainly hope that will never happen – forget I said it! It's just that I like this particular painting quite a lot myself,' he finished, rather sheepishly.

CHAPTER 10

I couldn't blame him for liking it, as I loved it! 'Well, that's a deal,' I generously agreed, but in my heart I hoped against hope that the Knight and I would be together forever. . .

CHAPTER 11

On Thursday, Dad called unexpectedly with some great news– apparently he was London! – and his company had approved his opening a branch office in Mayfair, meaning that we should be able to see each other much more often. We were happily chatting away, when he suggested my coming to London for the weekend.

'I'm staying at Lanesborough, in Knightsbridge. Let's spend some time together, especially since Christmas is just around the corner. I'd love to spoil you a little! By the way, your mother sends her love; she really misses you.'

'That would be lovely – The only thing more perfect would be if Mum was over as well!'

'Yes, yes, of course. My driver will pick you up on Saturday morning. Perhaps ten?'

'Ten is fine. I can't wait to see you again!'

Bouncing off the walls, the first thing I did was to run to New Court in order to share my news with Alka. I bumped into her in the hall and instantly blurted out about the phone call and the trip to London. Alka, without blinking, stared at me with rounded eyes, smiling with closed lips, as if deep in thought about something. After a short pause she firmly declared: 'Cool! Let's go together!'

I found myself at a loss for words. Dad and I hadn't seen each other for so long, and we had so much to talk about - and besides, I longed tell him about Quentin. But how could I tell Alka to her face that she wasn't wanted, without hurting her feelings? She was my best friend, after all!

I suddenly felt ashamed at wishing to leave her behind, especially since we'd been jointly dreaming of being in London together for years and years. I thought: *Well, why not?*

'He's sending his car at ten on Saturday morning, I told her.

Alka clapped her hands in wild delight, then threw herself on my neck. 'Hooray! Just imagine how much fun we'll have!' Then she was bombarding me with questions, chattering non-stop, as if the trip had been planned to involve both of us all along. It only then occurred to me that – just as so often happened - Ala had got her wish and everything was turning out just as she'd wanted . . .

On Saturday morning, having secured the requisite permission to leave College for the weekend, we settled comfortably into the Mercedes' soft leather seats and were soon rushing up the M4 towards London. In less than two hours our driver was approaching Knightsbridge, eventually pulling in before a magnificent, four-storied, sand-coloured building adorned with massive columns. A dazzling Christmas tree lit up the second floor balcony, and it seemed to me that Santa Claus, with a bag full of gifts, was just about to appear. The doors were flung wide, as if welcoming us inside what I imagined a royal country residence of the last century might have looked like, and only the appearance of the hotel manager – a suave American with impeccable manners - reminded me of where we really were. I introduced myself, and was told that, of course, I was expected. At reception I was given a message from my father, explaining that he'd been held up in a meeting and was running a little late.

Our luggage having already been taken care of, we were taken to our room, which impressed with its size and splendor. It represented an elegant combination of Regency style with modern amenities and boasted a stunning view of Hyde Park, just across the road. The room also featured a king-size canopied bed, and without thinking twice we switched on the radio at full blast before bouncing on the mattress in a fit of joyful giggles, like children on a bouncy castle.

'I love it!' Alka screamed. 'Here we are in a palace in London, commanding a butler, just like the Queen. . . And the manager said that Buckingham Palace is only a five-minute walk away. London, here we come!'

(In fact, as we learned later, every hotel room commanded a private butler, who looked after its residents, night and day.)

We soon got hold of a map and, mostly talking over each other, started making plans for various 'must-see' places. Two days had originally seemed like two weeks, but there was so much that we wanted to do!

'We've got to see late-night London. I know, let's go to Soho! I've heard that this is really something!' Alka pronounced.

Because of our thudding music we failed to really register that someone had been knocking on our door for some time. A charming elderly gentleman in a gold-cuffed red uniform was standing in the doorway with a friendly, if mildly reproachful, expression on his face. He introduced himself as our personal butler.

I awkwardly jumped off the bed and swiftly turned down the music, feeling like a schoolgirl caught out by a teacher in some mischief-making.

From our butler we learned that the hotel, which had only been recently opened, was named after Viscount Lanesborough, who in the 18th century had held 'suburban' entertainments for English nobility on the premises. Now of course its position counted as immensely central, in the prestigious neighbourhood of Apsley House – home to the Duke of Wellington – as well as enjoying views over Hyde Park and Wellington Arch. The building had been designed by the same architect who had designed the National Gallery in Trafalgar Square. . .

Our butler was interrupted by a phone call – Dad was waiting for me in the Conservatory Restaurant on the ground floor. Having thanked our attendant and hastily fixed ourselves up, we rushed downstairs. Papa was sitting at a table by the window and, as we entered, was just glancing at his watch. His face lengthened perceptibly at the sight of Alka, or so I imagined. . . I thought that I read discontent in his eyes, but he hugged me warmly, saying, 'My dear Sasha! So you arrived here all right? Nice to see you again as well, Ala. You've both grown up since I last saw you. All that English fresh air is obviously doing you both good!'

The atmosphere quickly eased and Papa asked the waiter to re-set the table for three. While Alka studied the menu, my dad and I bombarded each other with questions. After all we hadn't seen each other for such a long time! *If only Mum was here too, how she would have liked it!* I thought, glancing around. The interior design was wonderful: luxurious cherry-toned wood gradually flowed into tawny brown and then gleamed into golden-beige under the soft rays of the winter sun through the high, glassed roof. Large palm trees shielded hotel guests from prying eyes.

'British colonial style,' Dad commented, following my gaze. 'An exceptional hotel, my business partner recommended it. Well, let's go ahead and order, shall we?'

The cuisine was really fine, even by comparison to our favourite Norwood Hall. Alka ordered monkfish with mustard vinaigrette, and both Dad and I chose roast beef in Burgundy sauce. After dessert Dad settled himself comfortably with a glass of Hennessy to hear our rather sketchy account of College life. . . We did our best, but basically our story boiled down to the fact that we had been studying diligently, making friends easily and had managed not to upset any teachers so far.

Dad also had news to share. He started quite bluntly, 'The truth is, Sasha, the current economic and political situation in Russia worries me . . . Foreign investment at the moment seems largely discouraged, and, as a result, many of us are trying to access Western markets before the door slams shut altogether, as well as to secure a solid base abroad for own families. Your mother and I are particularly pleased – partly for this reason – that we've been able to give you an English education.'

'I'm very grateful, Papa.'

'I know you are. And I know you hope to remain in the UK after graduation in order to complete the experience. With a good UK university degree you should be able to pick and choose what you wish to do in the future . . . I've also taken some modest steps in the British direction, having recently persuaded my partners to open an office here, in Mayfair, in fact. . . Here are my new London contact details, by the way,' and with this he handed me a thick, embossed business card. Then he continued, 'After graduation, perhaps you might think about working in the business yourself, Sasha – though it's entirely up to you, of course. . . I'm also considering purchasing some property here, so that you and your mother have the option of spending time in the UK, wherever you might choose to work, America, the Far East. . . wherever.'

I was happily listening, though to be honest not particularly interested in the current Russian economic situation, when, fleetingly glancing at Alka, I caught her admiring gaze firmly fixed on my dad. When he paused to sip his coffee she sighed and then added 'Oh, Sasha, you're so lucky! You have such a wonderful, warm and loving father – I only wish I had the same! I love your family so much, although I can't help sometimes envying you a little . . . '

My father was rather pleased, saying, 'Well, you're almost a member of the family; we seem to have known you since Sasha's days in the nursery! And if everything works out, we might be able to find a good job for you too - unless you marry young and decide to become a housewife,' he added jokingly. 'Which reminds me, Sasha, what are your plans for the New Year? Are you planning to come home?'

'I haven't decided yet. I'll let you know after the Christmas Ball in mid-December,' I replied, though well aware that Alka was certainly not planning to spend Christmas with her own mother in Russia.

'Very well, girls. What would you like to do next? I've rather unluckily got landed with an important business meeting, for which I need to prepare, but you could join me for dinner later this evening.'

'Thanks so much Dad, but, if you don't mind, we thought we'd go out. Our concierge guy knows a bunch of cool places around here – and we thought we might do a little shopping before dinner.'

'Fine, as long as you're back in your room by eleven,' he agreed. 'I'm responsible for you, don't forget!' Before returning upstairs, he gave me a small parcel and a letter from my mother and an envelope from himself, adding, 'Do buy yourself a Christmas gift and something for your friend too. Have fun!'

Once back in our room I opened up the parcel. Inside was a stunning garnet necklace with matching bracelet which I instantly recognized - my mother only wore it on very special occasions. There was an exquisite flower in the centre of the necklace, inlaid with delicate garnets and pearls. Alka exclaimed over it and tried it on – it looked wonderful with her dark colouring - preening before the long mirror while I opened my mother's letter.

Mum had written that the house felt very empty without me and that she was missing me so much. My father was busy with work and was anyway often away from home on business trips, coming back tired. She greatly feared he was working too hard. As for herself, she had, along with some several other business men's wives, recently set up a charity to fund orphan homes and affordable schools for kids with special needs . . . It was clear that my mother was still devoting herself to her favorite pursuit: taking care of other people . . .Finally I opened the envelope from my father, which to my astonishment contained five hundred pounds – a whole fortune!

Alka immediately said that first thing we should do was to go shopping for outfits for the upcoming ball. No sooner said than done! Half an hour later, we were leaving a taxi and entering Selfridges, where, as far as we could gather, every fashionable girl from College went shopping when in London. We rushed from floor to floor of the huge halls, flying up and down escalators, racking up kilometres, until the abundance of clothes, designer names and fellow shoppers began to make me feel almost dizzy . . .I soon felt completely lost: sometimes I would pause to consider some dress I rather liked, but Alka immediately grabbed my hand, criticized my poor taste and dragged me on. Suddenly, however, she herself seemed utterly rooted to the spot near a stand featuring stunning evening dresses by Vivienne Westwood.

'It's the dream of my whole life! I'm simply going to die if I don't get that dress!' And here Alka pointed at an extravagant strapless dress on a mannequin, featuring a black velvet corset and a silk black and red, very full, skirt. I glanced dubiously at the price, which came to more than a half of my father's cash gift. Also, in addition to the dresses, we needed shoes for the ball – and, above all, I wanted to get a Christmas gift for Quentin. . . But Alka was already heading towards a fitting room, accompanied by a smiling sales assistant. I hadn't been particularly taken with the Vivienne Westwood dress on the mannequin but when the door of the fitting room opened, I couldn't help gasping: the dress had been *made* for Alka. The corset perfectly fitted her ample shape, while the combination of black and red patterns on silk fired her complexion, giving her the look of a femme fatale – or an opera Carmen. Alka's cheeks were crimson with emotion; her eyes, shining with happiness, were looking at me pleadingly. I couldn't refuse her, and asked the saleswoman to wrap up the dress. . . As always, Alka's gratitude was stormy and short. She threw her arms around me and hugged me, and then, with rather a guilty look added, 'But we should dress you up as well!'

I had neither the strength nor the desire to circle round Selfridges again, but on the floor below I saw what I needed, and easily imagined myself in it. A small black velvet dress from Episode fitted me perfectly. On the same floor, we quickly found two pairs of shoes with impossibly high heels and, just before the store closed, despite Alka's protests that it was time to leave, I still had time to rush through the men's department and to choose a green cashmere scarf for Quentin.

Our plans for the evening were to drop off our purchases at the hotel and then, without loss of time, to head out to Soho. We had no intention of letting my dad know where we were going: why should we worry him for nothing? The main thing was to be back in our room by eleven. So we set off, though we had no idea of where exactly in Soho we should be going.

'We'll see once we get there,' suggested Alka and, having jumped into a taxi, we were soon speeding towards the West End, with Alka telling the cabbie, 'Just drop us off in the heart of Soho,'

The taxi raced through twisting back streets, its meter climbing higher and higher, and soon the bright neon signs of cabaret shows, strip clubs and sex shops were flashing across windows in the darkness. Some untraditional-looking gentlemen were clustered outside a crowded pub with full pints of beer, whilst a group of Japanese tourists was busy photographing the local attractions.

'Great Windmill Street OK?' our taxi driver asked us and, upon seeing our confusion, pulled over. 'Look, it's no distance from anywhere, just look out for the Mill,' and here he pointed to an old building across the street.

'Is that a theatre?' I asked politely, paying for the trip.

'Nah, not anymore, now it's a table-dancing club. Good luck!'

Having got rid of us, the cabbie spurted onwards, leaving us standing on the pavement, gazing around in bewilderment. There certainly was plenty to see: night butterflies - local working girls - were carelessly passing by, neon signs suggesting 'Go-Go-Girls' brazenly winked on the corner. Giggling, we looked at the windows of a sex shop, not daring to enter, but lingering until we began to attract suspicious looks from passersby. Having wandered enough around the streets of Soho, we returned to the Mill and decided to experience a local pub. Our choice fell on the Red Lion. In the hubbub inside, in air saturated with cigarette fumes, we ordered two glasses of wine and, after making ourselves at home in a corner of the bar, were soon engaged in animated discussion.

'Moscow? Leningrad?'

Our Russian language had attracted the attention of the barman, who wrongly imagined us as a grateful audience for his fable about some secret congresses held here by Marx and Engels in the previous century . . . Eventually he left us alone, and soon after finishing our wine, we headed for the exit. It was time to return to the hotel, but, as every taxi seemed to have been taken, we decided to walk a little. Chattering on the way, we failed to notice how we somehow took a wrong turn into a back street, which seemed suspiciously quiet, although I spotted a young girl in an unbuttoned long coat over a leopard print bikini, her tragicomic baby face looking out sadly from under cheap makeup. She was smoking in a doorway under the sign 'Model Girls' - and partly obscuring a steep narrow staircase, probably leading to somewhere dodgy.

Suddenly we heard obscene Russian slang, with a heavy accent which I instantly recognized as being from the Caucasus region of the former USSR: it was emerging from an open window in the floor above. Suddenly two burly guys appeared and, grabbing the collar of the young girl's coat, started demanding information from her in poor English, simultaneously shaking her and slapping her hard.

'We should call the police!' I whispered to Alka, who returned coolly, 'I think we should clear out first!' However, it was too late to fade into the woodwork: we had already been spotted.

'Hey, look at these tender goats!' This was spoken in Russian with a heavy Georgian accent. A skinhead swaggered towards us, while I broke out in a cold sweat.

'Yes, our girls, from Russia, I can tell . . . All alone, beauties, at the hour? You look for the job, right?'

'No, we're visiting with our parents. And we're students,' I stammered feebly.

'Why your parents look after you so bad?' the skinhead scoffed, seemingly surprised. He was clearly the leader, as his sullen companion was merely staring at us in silence – at Alka especially. Then he seemed to make up his mind.

'Belles, we find you a good job! You do nothing, only smile to the guy for the champagne in the bar, and then we take care of it. You get the big bucks, believe me. . . We look after you great! Let's go and share the bubbly, right? OK? OK!' And with this the skinhead put his arms around both our shoulders and the situation began to take a serious turn – the two clearly did not intend to lose their prey.

Now all along, Alka had been keeping gravely silent, with downcast eyes, but now, staring straight at the skinhead, she cooed cutely: 'What a bit of luck for us to meet you two gentlemen! It must be so dangerous around here for a couple of Russian girls! And I'm sure you'll have the knack of hailing a cab, too, right?'

The Caucasian Russians were at first taken aback by her audacity, while she kept smiling at them – a strange, somehow significant, smile I'd never seen before, letting her green eyes rove speculatively over them. Then, leaning over, she started whispering in the skinhead's ear. I only heard snatches of this: 'The eyes on the back cannot see . . . treachery . . . re-hide the money . . . the dock' and either seven or else seventeen years – I couldn't be sure. I was too shocked at the sudden alteration in the previously swaggering skinhead, who had blanched and was staring at her with eyes full of horror.

'Put them in a taxi,' he snapped hoarsely to his sidekick. Then he swerved 160 degrees and moved away, walking swiftly, without looking back.

His colleague, although clearly baffled by the command, made haste to carry it out, and soon we were in a safety of a taxi speeding back towards Knightsbridge.

'Alka, what were you whispering to him back there? Whose eyes on whose back? . . . It was as if you'd bewitched him!'

'Oh, it was nothing: I was talking rubbish, but fortunately he believed me. Well, you know about those hidden talents from my grandmother!' and here Alka winked at me. 'As for the eyes - it's was nothing, just a tattoo, though it was pretty clear to me that those boys have serious issues with the law. We were lucky to get rid of them so easily!'

I still couldn't imagine how Alka had guessed about some tattoo on the skinhead's back or even whether he had a tattoo at all. . . But I was also very tired. In fact, I couldn't wait to get into a warm bed and fall asleep.

In the room everything had been meticulously prepared: our pajamas and bathrobes had been laid out on the silk bedding, our bags unpacked, and our clothes ironed and neatly hung up. After all the excitement, we felt terribly hungry, so we asked the butler to bring us some hot chips and mini-burgers. While we were dining, I noted a beautiful writing set on the desk – personalised paper with our names engraved above the heading, along with the address and logo of the Lanesborough. Alka had already scribbled several notes to friends at College, although they would reach it much later than we would. *Tomorrow before breakfast I'll write to mum and Quentin,* I vowed sleepily, before calling Dad to tell him that we were back safely, and with that I soon fell into a deep sleep.

At dawn I was awakened by the sound of a burr or even a drawl, which turned into a loud, throaty snore. Alka was wheezing into my ear with a full force of her lungs! I lightly touched her shoulder, whispering, 'Alka! Alka, you're snoring!'

'What do you want? She grumbled irritably, turning over, but soon the snoring had resumed, and grown perhaps even louder. This time I pushed my friend gently, in hopes that she might stop. I was stunned when she jumped up furiously on the bed and started shouting at me, pouring out a stream of accusations. I'd never seen Alka behaving like this before!

'I can't even get a decent night's sleep because of you!' she screamed at me. 'You're such a spoiled, ungrateful egoist! I only came to London for you, so you wouldn't get too bored, and now you can't even let me get any sleep! You're just so used to having everyone tiptoeing around you, as if you're some kind of frigging princess: you probably just decided to wake me up, pretending that I snore as some kind of a lame excuse. I never snore! Never! And if I did wheeze a little, perhaps this is because I've caught a cold. Why are you looking at me, like a calf at the new gate? Call the butler, why don't you, and ask him to bring me some tea with honey and lemon. I can't sleep any longer anyway, and that's all your fault!'

She had never talked to me in such a tone before, and I felt both shocked and offended. I silently went off to take a shower, leaving Alka to fume by herself. Whilst washing my hair in lukewarm water, I felt a deep resentment building up inside me, as I replayed her harsh words in my mind. (*'An ungrateful egoist!'* Well, I thought, *look who's talking . . .*)

When I returned to the room, however, I was startled by Alka's change of mood - she had completely mellowed and was peacefully drinking tea in front of the TV, even offering me some. She then admitted that she had overreacted, an apology which I accepted, and then we started discussing our programme of the day. Despite our previous, very unpleasant, exchange, I decided to forget about it and got busy writing my letters, in order to be on time for breakfast with Dad.

Over breakfast Dad naturally asked what we had gotten up to the previous evening, and we made up some story about having dinner at a local Pizza on the Park. In fact, Alka excelled herself, being very witty and amusing about all the people we'd supposedly met and making my father roar with laughter. I felt guilty about our lies, as well as about our frivolous trip to Soho, but I also felt I shouldn't worry my father - right after breakfast he had to catch his flight to Moscow. I gave him the letter I'd scribbled for Mum, and we hugged each other goodbye.

I felt a bit wistful that we hadn't in fact spent much time together, and that I hadn't had a chance to tell him about Quentin, but he promised to visit me soon - next time with my mother – which made me feel happy again.

Meanwhile Alka and I had the whole day free until five o'clock, when we were due to be picked up by a College driver. We left our bags, beautifully packed by our butler, at the hotel, and jumped into a red double-decker bus at Hyde Park Corner, comfortably settling ourselves on the upper deck, full of excitement about our day. The bus turned into Park Lane, passed Marble Arch, and was soon opposite the now-familiar Selfridges before heading towards Piccadilly Circus. On a sunny December day it all seemed magical.

We watched the 'changing of the guard' at Buckingham Palace, explored the Houses of Parliament, enthusiastically climbed to the top of Big Ben, and wandered among the cold marble tombs of Westminster Abbey. *So much excitement for one day!* I thought, feeling myself falling in love with this amazing city. . .We ended our trip in the austere and haunted Tower of London, where a cold wind raised up clouds of ravens and an early darkness - then it was time to reluctantly return to College.

CHAPTER 11

We reached Marlborough just in time for supper, and I decided not to join Alka in Norwood Hall. Since we'd perhaps seen a little too much of each other over the weekend, I preferred supper in Littlefield, where the girls bombarded me with questions about my London trip. I was describing our adventures, though missing out some parts, when Mr. Graham entered with the information that Quentin had called. After supper, I ran eagerly to the phone to call my boyfriend, but Debbie told that he'd gone off to the pub with his friend Chris. We chatted briefly, and I went back to my room to unpack.

There, to my surprise and disappointment, I couldn't find Quentin's scarf anywhere. I hunted through all my belongings twice to no avail, so again I ran downstairs to the phone, this time to call Alka - perhaps the scarf had mistakenly ended up in her suitcase? Alka seemed surprised at my question, and told me that she definitely didn't have it: most likely it had been stolen in the hotel, presumably by the same butler who had packed our things. 'Though he seemed such a gentleman! Who would have thought a cashmere scarf would tempt him?' she marveled.

I was so upset that I couldn't sleep for a long time, turning over and over in my bed, and only around dawn fell into a disturbing dream.

CHAPTER 12

Ala's grandmother, known as a babushka, lived in the southern-most part of Altai, in a settlement forsaken by God and men. Her home was hidden in a cedar taiga, or snow-forest, in the valley of Ak-Alah near the Chinese border, surrounded by high mountain ridges, beyond which stretched the sacred Ukok plateau. Less than a hundred people lived in her village, their timber houses well scattered – which didn't prevent everyone being almost perfectly aware of everyone else's business.

The villagers both feared and respected the grandmother, but behind her back called her different names: a Kam, a witch, a sorceress or a shaman. Still, people came to see her, not only from the Altai and Siberia, but from all over the country. She could predict the future, treat sicknesses, cure the evil eye and cast spells. Some even claimed that she could prevent a natural disaster – even conjure up a storm or an earthquake. A few even suggested that she was a black shaman, and served the evil spirits of Erlik, ruler of the underworld.

Ala's babushka had not chosen to become a shaman. Long years before, as long before as on the eve of her own eighteenth birthday, a young woman not much older than herself appeared to her in a dream. She had long golden hair under a tall headdress decorated with carved feline figures, wore silk tussah clothes and beautiful ancient jewelry. This was Princess Ukok herself, a great shaman of ancient times, who according to local legend was buried in a barrow of the Ukok Plateau.

In her dream the Princess told the young girl that she had been chosen as her successor and that she would soon be sent her own spirit-protector, who would serve her as he had previously served the Princess. The grandmother did not at first believe in the dream – partly because she had no desire to become a shaman, partly because she was about to be married to a young shepherd from a neighbouring village in the valley. In fact her daydreams centred upon nothing more dramatic than a large family and a comfortable home.

Thus she was both dismayed and terrified when a mythical animal showed up in another of her dreams, one who resembled a deer, but with a griffin's beak and with horns like a goat. The spirit told her that he was now her faithful servant, come to accompany her to the underworld kingdom of spirits, where she was called to accepts the claims of her ancestors, but the girl was frightened, and chased the creature away.

Soon she married her shepherd, and had almost forgotten her unsettling dreams, when, about half a year after the wedding, Princess Ukok again visited her in the night, her luminous eyes filled with disappointment, shaking her golden head with disfavor before disappearing into a mist . . . In the morning the new bride tried to get the dream out of her head, but the next night the Princess visited her again. This time she was furious, her beautiful eyes fiery, her voice no longer silent:

'You should not oppose the things I have foretold for you. You are the chosen one, selected by the spirits of your ancestors the shamans, as you have a great gift. If you want the daughter you bear under your heart to be born, you must accept your fate.'

The young bride had no notion that she was already expecting, and terrified for her unborn child, she instantly promised the Princess that she would carry out the will of the spirits.

A week later, she fell suddenly deathly ill with an unknown disorder, and lay unconscious, unmoving and very nearly not breathing for almost a month. During all this period, during which she neither ate not drank, she only briefly flickered into awareness on one occasion, only to instantly lose consciousness again. Her husband and relatives despaired of her life, but one day she returned to her body, singing an unknown song in a voice that no longer resembled her own. In her hands she was holding a taut, moose-skin tambourine, which had appeared from nowhere, while some black and white mythical animals had appeared to have been drawn upon its skin. She was alive – just – though dry as a stick, and in desperate need of food and vitamins. Yet ever since that day, her eyes had begun to see, her ears to hear, what others could neither see nor hear.

In time a healthy baby girl was born to her, who was to become Ala's mother, while the grandmother continued to practice her craft. Her daughter grew up tall and beautiful and went to study at Novosibirsk Pedagogical Institute, where she met her future husband. After the marriage, the newlyweds moved to Moscow and only a year later Ala was born. Meanwhile Ala's grandmother stayed in Taiga village, at the end of the Altai, where her granddaughter often came to visit her throughout her childhood.

To conduct her shamanistic ritual, Ala's grandma had a special outfit: a heavy deerskin coat decorated with colored ribbons, kerchiefs, serpentine borders and hemp rope, lined with cotton and iron pendants complete with snakeheads and copper bells, in order to frighten away any evil spirits. Her collar was adorned with owl feathers and on its back and sides iron clacks rattled. On her head she wore a hat made of owl hides of pyramidal shape with owl feathers decorating its top and cowrie shells, constructing a thick fringe, at the front. In the summer, she simply bandaged a colored kerchief around her head, to stop her hair from falling into her eyes and to prevent her from seeing the spirits.

Ala's grandmother's tambourine, which had reputedly belonged to Princess Ukok herself, was her pride and treasure. She cared for it as if it was the apple of her eye, and prohibited anyone else even to touch it. During her lifetime, she had used many tambourines, but each was an exact replica of her first one, which had crumbled into dust a long time ago. The same patterns of black and white animals were reproduced with paint made from rubbing special stones from the upper reaches of Ak-Alakh River; while the rusted iron pendants were shaped like sharpened arrows in order to scare away evil spirits. There was an ear and an earring on each rim, signifying with its bells the spirits' will, which, belonging to her first tambourine, was effortlessly transferred to her every new one.

It was rumored that once upon a time – no one remembered exactly when – the police authorities of the Altai region (called Militsiya in the Soviet days) sent for 'the shaman who conjured throughout the village.' A warrant was issued, and the threat of deportation and imprisonment hung over the babushka's head.

In those days the Soviet authorities strictly persecuted shamanism: suspected shamans were either thrown into prison or else sent to forced labour camps, from whence almost none had been known to return.

And yet, strangely enough, none of the police officers could reach Ala's grandmother, as something terrible always seemed to happen to them just as they were about to set off: one contracted a serious illness just before his departure, another – in strange circumstances – lost all his family and relatives, while two promising young policemen drove to their deaths in the Altai mountains on the way to her village. After this the police were too afraid to go after her, and she was left in peace – in fact, after a while she was forgotten altogether, and continued to quietly perform her shamanic rituals despite all official prohibitions.

Once the young Alka decided to snoop on her grandmother, and when the latter, as she normally did at sunset, took a walk in the forest, she followed her at a safe distance, hiding behind the trees, and trying to walk without treading on any dead branches. Her grandmother meanwhile was diligently gathering brushwood, muttering something under her breath, and, once she had gathered up a bundle in her hands, she chose a place in the forest, threw the brushwood to the ground, hunched down upon her haunches and kindled a fire. As dusk started to descend on the forest, Alka, though not easily frightened, hid in some dense juniper bushes, her heart thumping fast. Having built up her fire, her grandmother rose and calmly headed directly towards the area where Alka was hiding. Alka, terrified, believed that she had been discovered, but instead her grandmother merely plucked a few juniper berries for her fire from her bush. Then, from an inside pocket of her coat, she pulled out a can of kumiss, sprinkled a little in the air while downing the rest, and retrieved her precious tambourine. Then she got to her feet and raised the tambourine horizontally above her head, beating it with her mallet, first slowly but gradually faster and faster, singing in some strange language all the while . . . Gradually the tambourine got wilder, the singing more powerful, until Ala's grandmother was dancing on the spot, her whole body vibrant, first bending, then straightening, tiny beads of perspiration appearing on her forehead, while the iron pendants of her coat fluttered wildly in the air, and the sound of rattles and bells clashed with the tambourine. Her singing was interrupted by the hiss of a snake, the snarl of a bear, and sometimes by what sounded like a cuckoo's cry or other unsettling sounds. In places, it seemed that she was talking an invisible creature in an incomprehensible language, and even laughing at someone's jokes. . . Finally, however, the tambourine beats intensified, almost ecstatically, as if possessed: she began spinning like a top on one foot, while still beating the tambourine and singing.

The entranced Ala had had no idea that the grandmother could dance so stunningly. After some time however the music grew softer and the dancing wound down while the tambourine began to beat a rhythm like horses' hooves, as if in preparation for a long journey. Finally, exhausted, her babushka fell motionless to the ground.

After a moment Ala grew so concerned that she was about to rush to the village for help, when, suddenly, her grandmother opened her eyes and rose to her feet. She then pulled out a pipe from her coat and sat smoking it in quiet contentment near her dying fire.

Suddenly she called, 'Come out, granddaughter!' without turning her head, and there was nothing for Ala to do but to slip out from her ambush, feeling shamefaced and guilty.

However, her grandmother didn't scold her, but instead strictly ordered her never to follow her again and never – even with the nail of a single finger

– to ever touch her tambourine. ('Otherwise, you will anger the spirits,' she warned.)

Then she beat down the fire, carefully wrapped the tambourine into her coat, and led Alka back to the village, in order to get back home before blackness fell. To her eager questions about what significance to her actions she retorted that Alka was still too young to know about such things, but then added rather more kindly that, once she was older, she would tell her everything.

Alka immediately longed to grow up, if only to learn all of her grandmother's secrets.

'When I am grown, perhaps I'll also dance with a tambourine around the fire,' she said wistfully, but her grandmother shook her head.

'Yours is a different destiny, my granddaughter: you will be rich and happy, your life ruled by another force. But a shaman's fate remains unenviable. . . ' and here she sighed. 'Let's go home and make dinner.'

Then she was silent the rest of the walk back home.

CHAPTER 13

A few days later, a small parcel on The Lanesborough's own stationary arrived for me at College. Expecting to find the missing scarf I couldn't believe my eyes when perhaps a thousand soft green scraps of cashmere fell out instead. Also enclosed was a letter from the hotel manager. It turned out that when a maid cleaned the room after our departure, she had discovered, behind the wardrobe, these remnants of a scarf resembling the one I had described as lost. The letter concluded:

> *'Thanks so much for choosing to stay at The Lanesborough. We look forward to welcoming you back in the very near future.'*

Meanwhile I looked in confusion at what had once been a hugely expensive cashmere scarf, slit mercilessly by some sharp object. *Perhaps a pair of scissors or even a knife,* I thought uncertainly, examining the edges. I instantly knew that Alka must have been the culprit. There were no other suspects. In fact, remembering that day, I thought: *no wonder she had so suddenly cheered up, while I was taking my shower!* The truth came to me in a flash, as our morning quarrel at the hotel floated, in retrospect, before my eyes.

And yet, deep inside, I continued to entertain doubts. It just seemed so hard to believe. Could Alka have really done such a thing to her best, her oldest, and her most loyal friend?

I couldn't decide.

I didn't mention the parcel to Alka, but instead started acting icily cold towards her, and keeping my distance wherever this was possible. I reasoned: Alka wasn't stupid, she would figure out the reason for this, if she was guilty.

And indeed, having observed and absorbed this sudden change in my attitude, Alka became like silk, fawning upon me and buddying up into a pretense at our previously close friendship.

'Sashenka, you know that you are my only true soulmate. We've been best friends since forever!' She cast other such lines, but I still chose not to take her bait.

Christmas was by this point close at hand, and in fact the very next night would see the long-awaited Christmas Ball, an event at Norwood Hall for which every Sixth Former – especially the girls – had been preparing in excitement for the last few months.

'I won't eat anything tomorrow – well, maybe just a small salad,' announced Serena on the way to morning class.

'Me neither,' echoed Penny, throwing a questioning look in my direction.

'I will pass on this idea, as I get dizzy without food,' I replied honestly.

'Well, we don't want your ball gown falling off you, do we?' giggled Serena before turning towards the Leaf Block, where our ways parted. Ignoring her usual smuttiness I headed to the museum block for an English lesson.

After lunch Alka surprised me by turning up in my room while I was doing my English prep for the next day's lesson. Having shut the door behind her, she solemnly declared that she had something special for me, and with a disarming smile handed me a yellow Selfridges bag, which turned out to contain a green cashmere scarf identical in every respect to the one that had been shredded, beautifully presented in glitzy gift paper. I stared at her, speechless.

'Well, I know how much you wanted to give the same one to Quentin, if only it hadn't been for that old thief!' (It was in this fashion that she accused the butler.) 'And as your best friend I decided to make you happy again. I hope Quentin will enjoy wearing it!'

Touched, I warmly embraced her and our quarrel was patched up on the spot.

Later, I marveled. How had she managed that? Had she really returned to London just for me? Only Alka could have so effortlessly achieved the near-impossible! In spite of everything, I still possessed a truly great friend there! And, after all, in a fit of anger, who is truly responsible? I thought, recalling the ruined scarf. This could happen to anyone! Or perhaps it wasn't even Alka who had done it? Anyway, it didn't matter – not in the least – not now that I had a gift for Quentin!

The next day after morning classes, I dropped into New Court, seeking some company for lunch at Norwood Hall. Alka was in her room, where I found her spinning exultantly in front of a mirror in her Vivienne Westwood creation. She seemed thrilled to see me.

'Sashka!' she exclaimed breaking into a delightful smile, 'Well, how do you like me in this jaw-droppingly divine dress? Beautiful, isn't it?'

I told her, 'Yes, it looks stunning! You will be a complete knock-out tonight! Shall we go for lunch? Or are you also on a diet for the day, like all the rest of the girls here?' And here I must admit that I couldn't help thinking to myself that it wouldn't hurt Alka to lose a few centimeters around her waist.

'Me? A diet? Alka laughed. 'Help me out of this dress and let's go get something to eat!' she ordered, turning her back for me to unzip the dress and lifting up her long hair, shiny as raven's wings.

We bumped into Catherine on the stairs. 'Ah, here you are!' she said, strongly resembling a shepherd who had lost his flock. 'Where are the others?'

Alka shrugged: I could tell that she was getting a little bored with Catherine's patronage.

'I saw Nicole in the art studio earlier. Probably she will go straight to lunch,' I reported. We also picked up Chris in the hall, leafing through magazines with her feet on a chair, and headed together to Norwood Hall, discussing what each of us was planning to wear that evening.

Norwood Hall was already glittering with festive Christmas lights, and in the corner, next to the beaks' table, a noble Christmas tree was glowing on a pedestal, featuring dizzyingly flashing lights of every hue. At the opposite end of the hall was a small stage erected for the College rock band where some students, having set up a pair of massive speakers, were testing the DJ's equipment in a very businesslike manner. A lively line had already formed at the buffet, and, glancing at the happy faces all around, it was obvious that the Marlburians were all in joyful anticipation of their Christmas Ball, followed of course by their long-awaited holiday! My friends and I filled our trays with food and hurried to occupy our usual table by the window, occasionally glancing at the neighboring tables and commenting on the contents of the girls' trays.

'Where does the dance take place? On the stage, or where?' asked Alka, looking around with interest.

'The tables are always moved, so there'll be more than enough space!' explained Catherine, and then added, in a tone which brooked no dispute: 'Before the ball we all meet up at my place for an aperitif. As usual, I've stocked up some ammunition – more than usual, for such a special occasion. Let's rush for the mood! I've got Jackie, Nicole and Laura Jones from Summerfield to join us.'

Chris gleefully promised to replenish her alcohol reserves with some Swedish liquors.

'I will be with James in Littlefield, so I cannot promise to come,' Alka reminded her.

'Sounds perfect, but I have to run at the moment, as I'm meeting Quentin. See you tonight!' I said hastily, upon hearing the clock strike 2:00.

First I ran to my room to get the immaculately wrapped scarf: then I rushed to my date with Quentin, whom I was meeting at the usual place, by Littlefield's stone steps.

Quentin was there, as always patiently waiting, and as ever never evincing even the slightest concern at my delay. When he saw me, his face broadened into a beatific smile. He moved to meet me on the stairs, and then wrapped his arms around me, firmly kissing me on the lips.

'What, is this for me?' he asked, receiving the bag. Seeing his surprise and gratification at his gift, I immediately slipped the scarf around his neck,

CHAPTER 13

enjoying the sight of such an impossibly handsome and stylish young man. Green can be a hard colour to wear – but it suited Quentin divinely.

'I will even wear it to bed, thinking of you!' he promised, rapturously hugging me to him. I was thrilled at his reaction. As for his promise to think of me, I didn't mind that at all. In fact, I thought: *Let him think about me as often as possible, especially once I go home for Christmas. . .*

On the walk to his house I told him about my plans for the Christmas holiday. He seemed disappointed. 'What a shame! I was just chatting to Mum about you – and she was hoping to invite you over for Christmas. You couldn't delay your flight, could you? It'd be so amazing to spend Christmas together!'

I was very touched. His offer was truly tempting, but I'd already promised my parents to come home, my tickets had already been purchased and many old friends were also awaiting me in Moscow. Moreover, despite the closeness of our relationship and my overwhelming infatuation with Quentin, we still were not intimate in the fullest sense of the word, and I had decided to postpone that stage of our relationship until my return. I'd also thought, more than once, that an absence would also give me a chance to test his feelings for me – although, of course, I had no real doubts, either about him or his constancy.

After our afternoon date in his room, Quentin, with his usual thoughtfulness, walked me back to Littlefield. The day had passed so fast! Whenever I was with Quentin I never noticed where the time went, but I intentionally dragged him up to my room, in order to seize the opportunity to show myself off in my tasteful new cocktail dress.

'Let him see what an attractive girlfriend he has!' I thought gleefully, hoping that I wouldn't come across as vain and self-centred at the same time . . . We met Alka and James in the Littlefield doorway, both gorgeously attired for the ball. The rest of the girls seemed to have already gone.

'See you there!' she caroled to me, tossing just a glance of her emerald eyes towards Quentin.

'It's so unfair! I'd love to accompany you as well,' Quentin sighed, watching James rather enviously. I immediately felt guilty, though of course it wasn't my fault that I hadn't been allowed to invite him, as only Marlburians were permitted. I thought: *How selfish and self-centred I am! Here I am boasting about a stupid ball to my boyfriend, knowing that he can't come himself, and that instead I'll be dancing with other men!*

Recklessly, I told him, 'Well, if you want, I won't go anywhere tonight and we can spend the evening together.'

I made the offer, but I admit that I made it hoping that Quentin wouldn't agree. I so longed to experience my first Christmas ball!

'Don't be ridiculous!' he protested. 'Go, and have fun – but don't forget about me,' and he pulled me close by the waist, and we indulged in a last lingering kiss.

'How lucky I am to have met such a wonderful guy!' I thought, kissing him back with unadulterated adoration.

Then, having donned my new dress from Selfridges, I spun round the room fishing for compliments, which Quentin paid with his usual generosity. Flattered and pleased, I hung possessively on his arm all the way to the school gates, where we – again unwillingly – parted company.

Then I remembered that I had promised to stop by Catherine's, in order to join the other girls and 'warm up' before the ball. I crossed Central Court, already bustling with suddenly grown-up Sixth Formers in their dinner jackets and ball gowns, and headed towards New Court. On the first floor, where Catherine's room was, an eclectic music mix flooded out from the girls' closed doors into the hallway. In Catherine's room the party was already in full swing.

'Oh, I hardly recognized you, you're all so beautiful and with such stylish hair!' Thus I complimented my friends, noting with some amusement that we were all wearing slinky black dresses cut just below the knee.

'Sasha, you're so late! We've already polished off the liqueur, but I think there's still some vodka with orange juice left,' Catherine told me, producing a bottle of Russian vodka – Alka's contribution, meant to compensate for her absence.

CHAPTER 13

'I think it's time to go. The ball's already started,' said Chris, impatiently glancing at her watch.

'Really? And what's going on in the Court?' Jackie asked me.

'Not much,' I told her.

'Anyway, we don't want to arrive at Norwood Hall first, and still sober!' Catherine interrupted, and without waiting for any response, filled all the tea mugs with more vodka and orange juice.

'Cheers!' Nicole sang out, preparing to take a photo of us. 'No, wait! Take the vodka bottle out of the picture, my mum will see these shots.'

'So, which of the guys would each of you like to score with at the ball?' Catherine wanted to know, back on her favorite topic. 'D'you know Harry Edwards from B3, the one with the big eyes and gorgeous floppy hair? He's so horny! And John Masters from Preshute, wow, he's got to be the fittest guy around!' Noting my lack of interest she added sardonically, 'Of course, Sasha's not interested, since she's got herself a man! Quentin doesn't have a twin brother, by any chance, does he?'

I laughed, shaking my head, and soon we'd all warmed up so much that, without feeling the December chill in the least, we scuttled outside in our party dresses and hurried towards Norwood Hall, from where the music could be heard all the way across Central Court.

So this is what the balls are like here, I thought, looking around with unmixed curiosity.

Lit like a gilded palace garlanded with gold, Norwood Hall was hard to recognize in the dark. The college rock band was pounding hard from the DYI stage to the utmost enjoyment of the rowdy Marlburian crowd swinging on the slippery dance floor in black-tie and evening dress.

Disco with ball gowns! Great! Without hesitation I followed my friends, bravely diving into the crowd. But after three plastic cups of white wine I suddenly felt sick and lost. Unfamiliar faces appeared to be flashing around me, and some tall guy in glasses seemed to be chatting me up, but it wasn't a good game anymore.

I still know so few people at College! I thought, half-panicked, turning my head from side to side and feeling horribly affected from mixing various spirits with white wine. Then, a dense ring of boys, buzzing like a swarm of bees, caught my eye. 'Do you know what's happening?' I asked one guy. He shrugged his slim shoulders. 'Hey, let's go and take a look!' he suggested, summoning up a few friends with a glance.

I joined them, and having squeezed between the crowd, curiously peered inside the circle.

Right in the center, like a fireball, Alka, roaring with joyous laughter, was spinning in James's arms, her silky black hair spraying round her like a whip. It seemed that she was always about to fall out of her scarlet dress, which – by some miracle – still clung to her. She looked wild and eerie, and scarily beautiful.

'Who *is* that?' asked one of the guys, his eyes locked onto Ala.

'Don't you know? That's Ala Gromov from New Court, James' hot new Russian girlfriend!' came the instantaneous response. Alka's popularity in college was clearly rising!

The spectacle was indeed hypnotizing, especially for the normal type of British guy: her teasingly strapless dress, opposing every law of physics, remained in place as if glued to her form, despite Alka's reckless pirouettes, and demonstrated just enough of her assets to make every male in the vicinity long for it to fall down. . . I stood with the others for a moment, loyally admiring my friend, before heading out to look for the girls. It was then that Will from Barton Hill asked me for a dance.

'With pleasure, a little later, but to be honest I feel slightly sick right now,' I told him. Will was about to prudently disappear when an enormous, sleek black cat leapt out from right from beneath my feet and immediately disappeared among the dancing crowd.

I grabbed Will's shoulders. 'Did you see that?' I breathed.

'See what?' Sympathetically, he embraced me by the waist, at the same time squeezing my free hand in his warm, sweaty palm.

'That enormous black cat, of course! It jumped straight inside!' and here I nodded towards the stage.

'Ha, ha! Will it sing for us too? I think you've had a bit too much to drink, Sasha. Never mind, let's dance!'

Indeed, I must be enduring alcohol-induced hallucinations, I thought, freeing myself from Will's embrace. Then someone suddenly smacked me on the back.

'Where have you been? We're all here!' Catherine barked in my ear, and having grasped my hand, dragged me away, half-deafened and entirely defeated.

After the ball we all gathered in Catherine's room to discuss the successes and failures of that tumultuous night until Mrs Foxton chased all the others to their rooms – while I had to sprint to Littlefield in order to get there before Mrs Graham locked the doors.

The next day was the last day of class before College broke up for Christmas. Straight after school I met up with Quentin, to spend the rest of the afternoon with him before my departure to Moscow. When it was time for me to return to Littlefield Quentin walked me, as usual, right to the door.

'I miss you already. I'll write to you!' he promised, kissing me goodbye. Then he added, rather shamefacedly, 'Also, well, you know that painting that I gave you, the one you really liked? I just wanted to say, well, can keep it forever.... whatever happens!'

I believed that I understood what he was trying to say: that his feelings for me were growing stronger, just as mine were for him. We parted reluctantly and I hurried up to my room in order to pack. I also wanted to drop to New Court to see my friends before leaving for the airport. For Christmas, much to Alka's amusement, Quentin had presented me with a colorfully hand-embroidered cushion from an Indian shop in town.

'I want you to always think of me when you cuddle this,' Quentin had explained, hugging me hard.

'Ha! James would have found himself very unlucky had he chosen to give me such a Christmas gift!' Alka had told me, roaring with laughter. 'Catherine!

Come see what Sasha's boyfriend gave her for Christmas!' she yelled into the corridor, and I once again regretted sharing something important with her, especially as my feelings towards the cushion were very tender.

'Well, at least she'll have something to sleep on, unlike every other passenger on Aeroflot,' said Catherine rather tartly, throwing a disapproving glance towards Alka, which seemed to bother her not at all.

Meanwhile, Alka had managed to share with everyone that she would be spending Christmas with James, at his parents' elegant home in west London. As she had told me, 'Here's the number there, so be sure to call me before the New Year. Say hi from me to everyone and for God's sake don't forget to visit my mother. In fact, she'll be counting the hours until she sees you.'

As we hugged each other goodbye, I thought regretfully that it just wouldn't be the same, flying back to Moscow without my dear friend. . .

CHAPTER 14

I was playing with a narrow white envelope thickly stuffed with paper. It had been sent Royal Mail first class a week after the beginning of school holidays, with my name and my parents' Moscow address carefully written in dark ink. I could just imagine Quentin, head bowed over the envelope, eyebrows almost meeting in a frown as was usual when he was concentrating, scrupulously tackling the Russian letters. Having savored the image, I rushed up to my room, shut the door and bounced onto my bed, simultaneously tearing open the envelope. The letter turned out to be ten pages long, written on both sides in a small, elegant hand that I immediately recognized. *What a long letter! Whatever could it be about?* I thought, starting to read the first few lines.

'Dear Sasha, I hope you are enjoying your holiday in Moscow and are not freezing there too much. It's such a pity that we're not together for Christmas; I already miss you so much and often think of you, especially whenever I pass by 'our' steps! For Christmas we had our relatives over: my grandmother from Bath and Uncle Roger and Aunt Sarah from Manchester. Imagine, Gran is entering her ninth decade, and still chain-smokes at least ten packets a day – which naturally upsets my mum. But she still seems sound as a bell and actually really cool; I'm sure you'll like each other a lot when you meet.

'Unluckily however my uncle and his wife were constantly at each other's throats. The walls in our house are thin and all we could hear was her nagging: poor Uncle Roger without doubt is hen-pecked. I couldn't help wondering what he saw in Aunt Sarah – mousy hair, scrawny build and always-pursed mouth – in the first place, but perhaps this is unkind!'

I skimmed through the description of a family dinner, a trip to a local pub and the Christmas Carol service. Then I read with more intentness.

'Four days before Christmas, Chris, Sean and I decided to get together at Will's place, to listen to the music, play snooker, and most importantly to get high on magic mushrooms.'

What are magic mushrooms? I marveled.

'Will's parents had gone to visit relatives in Somerset, and around seven I drove them to Will's place. His family lives in this marvelous old cottage, build around 1690, tucked away in a tiny village between Avebury and Marlborough. I don't know if you've yet been shown cottages with thatched roofs – if not, I'll show you one sometime. I wouldn't mind living in one someday.

'Will was waiting for us, having prepared the mushrooms: parts he'd wrapped into spliffs for us to smoke, and he'd brewed up some tea from the rest. To start off we had some tea, while listening to the music, then Chris and I battled in snooker. We played worse and worse as the mushrooms started to work and we all had a good laugh at Chris, who kept repeating the same words over and over, as if unable to change his channel. It's hard to describe but basically everything seemed quite funny and we all seemed to bond as we'd never done before. But after a while we got bored with snooker and then Will had a better idea, to get high in the Valley of the Rocks (or the Devil's Den, as the locals call it), an ancient burial chamber believed to date back to the Neolithic period.

'He'd heard some scary rumours about it, and decided that it would be really cool to test our nerves on the mushrooms there in the middle of the night. Having filled up our backpacks with a flask of mushroom tea, spliffs, torches and sleeping bags, we immediately set off on our night picnic.

'Soon we were all walking single file on a well-trodden path through spacious green fields, the whole surrounded by ploughed expanses studded with Wiltshire forests. The December air was mildly damp, and a full moon lit up the way, which Will knew quite well: it seemed almost unreal that Christmas could be so close at hand. It was a couple of miles trek until we got to the place, where ominous outlines of rocks, like giant tombstones, appeared on the horizon. The mushrooms were making me feel a little dizzy but quite excited as we arrived at the rocky monoliths, most with a height of over six metres, really impressive! A capstone, which accordingly to Will weighed around twenty tons, lay horizontally across two of these perpendicular giants, and between two fallen stones was what had once been the entrance to an enormous tomb.'

Here Quentin had drawn a little sketch to help me better imagine what it looked like. (I was entranced by the idea of the ruins – rather less so by the notion of the 'magic' mushrooms.) At any rate, I read on.

'We tossed the sleeping bags near the rocks, and gathering in a circle, finished off our remaining tea. Under its influence, the stars seemed to be dancing across the sky, playfully chasing each other, while the moon appeared to me to be growing by leaps and bounds, rapidly increasing in diameter until it suddenly imploded, transforming into a giant yellow ring with an inner black hole. The voices of distant owls sounded like a symphony played on magical instruments, the plants around were growing with startling speed and, looking closely, every blade of grass seemed separately visible in the moonlight, wavering in the wind as if dancing to its own secret music. In every living thing there was everything, the entire universe!

'Then Will remembered the spliffs and we smoked these at once. Our sensations intensified as we walked around the entrance to the ancient tomb. I felt unsteady on my feet while Chris felt a little nauseous: in order to steady ourselves, we held on to the cold stones. Then I suddenly noticed that the rocks seemed to be breathing, in and out, pulsing under my hands like some predatory creature, lying in wait to ensnare its prey. Suddenly my hands began to go inside these soft-as-butter stones, with every atom of the stone structure exposed to the inner eye. In blind panic I recoiled from them before they swallowed me!'

The next few pages appeared to be more delusional descriptions of weird hallucinations. I understood very little: there were many unfamiliar English words and eventually I gave up. Having skimmed through the bit where 'the tomb opened up and a young Tutankhamun in a golden headdress carrying a live cobra loomed before us,' Quentin concluded, 'It seems that my imagination ran riot following a recent BBC program about Howard Carter. Wouldn't it have been amazing had I really found the treasures of Egypt! But while I was chatting to Tutankhamun, Chris was running around looking terrified to death and shouting wildly, much to Sean and Will's amusement. He was furiously waving his hands in the air, as if fending off some invisible enemy, while alternately yelling and muttering something under his breath . . . Suddenly, he turned around and charged into the darkness, away from the stones and the rest of us. He only managed to run a short way before he tripped and fell to the ground, but then almost immediately jumped to his feet and looking completely paranoid, rushed off again.

'"Just look at him! What the fuck is he doing?" Sean was guffawing with laughter. "Hey Chris, come back!"

'I ran after him, shouting. "Wait, Chris! It's me – Quentin!" but he didn't even turn around. I was still tripping hard myself; everything seemed in a bizarre blur. Of course, it would have been smarter to stay with Sean and Will in the valley, but no way could I leave my best friend alone. What if he fell off of a ledge or something? Finally, I caught up with him.

'"Quentin, man, it's you!" he said, seemingly very happy to recognize me. 'And I thought I was being chased by that creature!'

'However, his joy almost immediately turned into panic: "We have to get out of this damned place. Let's run to your car! How far are we from Will's house, anyway?" Seemed he was having a pretty bad trip.

'"Calm down mate, nobody's after you."

'I felt for the pack of Marlboro Lights in my jacket pocket and lit a cigarette, inhaling deeply before handing it to Chris: "Fag'll make you feel better."

'Chris drew heavily on my cigarette, which seemed to calm him down, and we staggered on. On the way, I talked in colours about Tutankhamun, but Chris paid no attention, mumbling some nonsense to himself. I didn't even notice how or when we lost our way. Instead I noticed that the surrounding trees were swaying and creaking, their thick roots crawling, like snakes, wriggling deliberately under our feet as if hoping to upend us. Strange rustling sounds too, despite the lack of wind: I felt my heart sinking into my boots. Something was glistening in the bushes; I thought these were crickets, but looking closer, I realized that these were hungry eyes of some animals, following us (maybe the ones Chris had seen?) It seemed that we'd never get out of there, and a crazy, almost primeval fear gripped us. We broke into a senseless run in the darkness. Branches stretched out to whiplash my face, but, overcome with fear, I didn't feel any pain and continued sprinting, until one – unless I imagined this – actually reached out and grasped me, twisting my foot painfully. In the process, I lost my balance and flew head first into a steep ditch, almost a ravine. When I came round my head was spinning, and everything felt misted over. Somewhere close by owls hooted and a vague outline of a glade seemed to beckon through the trees: a yellow moon disc lit the dark sky. My back and legs were aching, but I was very happy to be alive.

"'Oh fuck!' I heard Chris groan, from somewhere nearby. I managed to turn my neck towards the sound and made out his silhouette: he was cradling his head in his hands.

"'Are you alive, man?' he wanted to know.

"'Yeah. But what was all that?' With an effort I lifted myself off the ground and sat up; my hands and knees were skinned and half-burning in pain, I was aching and bleeding from about ten places. Chris had gotten off comparatively lightly in terms of scratches but had a large lump on the head. While contemplating what to do next – I doubted we could find our way back in the dark and without Will – I found myself staring at the outlines of a glade through the thinning forest. I suddenly had the strangest feeling, as if something was urging me towards it.

"'Let's head towards that glade and find somewhere to sleep till dawn,' I suggested, and Chris agreed. Limping, we began to wade through the bushes and branches towards the glade, until we were standing on its edge. It was a green circle of almost perfect shape, as if someone gently shaved a round bald patch on a thick crown of the forest. Its bareness seemed almost to gleam, reflecting the brightening moonlight. We picked a spot under a huge centuries-old oak tree at the edge of the glade. Almost immediately, whether because of fatigue, mushrooms or the shock of our falls, we both felt extraordinarily tired, as if our eyes were intent upon closing. Chris rolled himself into a ball and fell asleep almost immediately. Despite the rock-hard ground I had also drifted off when I was awoken up by voices. I opened my eyes resentfully and unwillingly – then they widened in disbelief.

'On the glade, lined up in a large circle, stood a number of figures dressed in long black robes with hoods, mumbling something in what sounded like a foreign tongue. In the middle of the group stood an elevated circular altar which had certainly not been there before, facing north, adorned with jet-black candles burning incense. And – and this was probably the weirdest part – someone in a creepy mask with goat's horns and a similarly shapeless robe was standing on it, a long knife in one hand. I shook Chris awake, after first pressing my hand all over his mouth, so that he wouldn't shriek out. Once I had his attention, I pointed towards the group. Hardly breathing, we continued to watch. Then we saw a huge cat, almost blue-black in the light and very nearly panther-sized, preceding a candlelight procession consisting of three male figures – I think they were men – in hooded robes emerging from the forest, leading a girl with her hands tied. She had her back to us, so all I could see then was that she had jet-black, waist-length hair and was wrapped in a green sheet instead of wearing a robe like the others. The accompanying group led the girl inside the circle, which parted to let her through and instantly closed up behind her. The light of the full moon shone softly on her, just illuminating the steps of the candlelit altar, which she unhurriedly ascended. There, the horned figure awaited. He made a step towards her and pressed the tip of his black-handled knife right up to her heart. Chris and I froze with fear, expecting bloodshed, but something kept our eyes fixated on the altar, and the horned figure didn't

CHAPTER 14

press in the knife: instead he said something I couldn't catch. Then a breath of wind carried this towards us: a hoarse male voice: "Are you prepared for death and rebirth?" and a clear woman's voice saying, "I am."

'"And what name will you be called in our Sacred Circle of Georgina?"

'"I will be called Lilith," she replied.

'The horned man – to our intense relief – then freed her hands by cutting the rope with his dagger: "We welcome you, Lilith, with perfect love and perfect trust."

'"Welcome, Lilith!" was repeated in unison by all the hooded figures in the circle, and then this Lilith turned around to face them with a haughty look on her face, as if well-pleased with the outcome.

'She was wearing a black, Venetian-style mask, but her eyes were of that rare piercingly green color, which I've only seen once before and – I swear – were looking straight at me, which made the skin on the back of my neck absolutely crawl. In astonishment I realized that she was an absolute double of your friend Alka – in fact, if I hadn't known that Alka was in London, I'd have sworn that it was she. I remember almost nothing afterwards, as I fell into a deep sleep, but in my dream I saw screaming witches flying across a burning fire, all dancing in a circle around Alka's lookalike.

'I woke at dawn to find the grass lightly covered with crystal beads of ice, and Chris's breath steam, like smoke from a cigarette, leaving traces in the moist air. It was so chilly that my teeth were chattering, while of course my whole body was aching and throbbing after the previous day's adventures. The glade seemed innocent and empty: with no trace left of all that had happened.

'I then woke up Chris – who can sleep forever – and immediately asked him what he had remembered about the previous night, but he had a rotten headache and, apart from our trip to the Devil's Den and getting lost in the forest, could recall nothing else.

'I now doubt whether all I've scribbled here really happened or whether it was only my imagination, inflamed by a mushroom trip. However, at the time I was still curious enough to explore the glade – and went through it with a fine-tooth comb – but I must admit without finding any trace of an altar, or even a single footprint. However, I was just about to return to Chris when I found the stub of a jet-black incense candle. I squatted down to pick it up. There was no doubt about what it was.

'Lost in thought I rubbed it between my finger and thumb, remembering what I believed I recalled of the events of the previous night. I kept thinking: *had* it really happened?

'I immediately decided not to say anything to Chris. I'd normally have mentioned it, but some instinct was telling me to remain silent about it all. And in any case – as you well know – Chris can be a bit of a loose cannon! What if he teases Alka by calling her Lilith when by chance we meet in town? I was shivering at the very idea, recalling that wicked blaze of the green eyes I'd seen above the altar, when Chris interrupted my thoughts.

'"Hey, Quentin, c'mon! Let's hit the road before I freeze to death!"

'I headed back to the oak. On our way back we kept our eyes out for the great dip we'd both tumbled into, but we never found it: instead, we almost at once located the path. We couldn't help wondering how we'd managed to get so desperately lost the previous night. The sky was brightening, morning birds were welcoming the sun, and we soon left the forest behind, treading through the damp fields towards the Devil's Den.

'"Hey, let's scare Sean and Will," suggested Chris. "Why don't we jump out from behind and yell?"

'"I think they'll get enough of a fright just by looking at us," I told him, and Chris roared with rueful laughter. The spectacle was truly not one for the fainthearted: Chris's clotted hair stood on end, one of his eyes was blackening, the swelling on his head was turning purple and he was still trembling from cold. (I looked no better: scratched and blood-stained, my new jacket, grainy with soil, looking second-hand.) I thought, I couldn't turn up at home looking like this! How lucky that my relatives were only arriving that evening: there should be enough time to take a bath and rest a little.

'We approached the rocks, where Sean and Will were still snuffling peacefully in their sleeping bags, all unaware.

'"Look at them – two ideal victims, should any robbers be passing, snoring away!" whispered Chris, tiptoeing towards them.

'"Yeah, but what would be worth robbing?" I observed. Chris leaned over them gleefully. "Hey, sleeping beauties!" he yelled just above their ears, making them practically leap inside their sleeping bags.

'"Fucking idiot! I nearly had a heart attack!" Sean was indignant, while Chris was growling with laughter, holding his stomach.

'"Ha, ha! That's so funny! If you could only have seen your faces!"

'Having wriggled free of his bag, Will cunningly kicked Chris's feet out from under him, which stopped his giggles. "Hey, what the hell happened to you?" They were looking us over from head to foot. "Did you get into some kind of fight or something?"

'"Tell you later," I promised, and we all headed back towards Will's house, both two of us extremely aching and sore.

'On the way Chris was – at least as far as I was concerned – very creatively describing our night's adventures in the forest, fibbing wildly about us being chased by wild boars. I didn't mind, in fact it was something of a relief not to be questioned about what had really happened. In fact, I have yet to breathe a word to anyone, except you, about what really happened last night.

'Once back at home, Will loaned me a pair of his jeans, though the length, of course, was some inches too short for me. I bundled Chris with Sean into my car and rushed home, dropping them off in town. Having parked in a side street, I sneaked into my parents' house and indulged in a long hot bath. As you can imagine, the recollection of the previous night never once left my head.

'At breakfast my mother, worried, wanted to know what had happened to my face. I gave her a song and dance about how I fell, very awkwardly, after leaving a country pub, and she believed me. Then, the relatives arrived and we all got wrapped up in the usual festive preparations.

'See how badly I get along without you! You should definitely rush back soon, before I get into trouble again!

'Love, Quentin

'P.S.: My mum has broadcast to the relations that I have a Russian girlfriend from College, so all my relations really look forward to meeting you, although I doubt you'll like Manchester much.'

I finished the letter with a sense of disappointment: Quentin had written so little about his feelings for me. Why had he bothered to write all the nonsense about his drug trip? I didn't understand even half of all I've read, as the letter was full of English slang.

Why do we still have such wacky dictionaries from the old Soviet times, which can hardly be applied to the modern youth language? I thought acidly. *As for the rest of it, well, of course, my boyfriend has a terrific imagination and a rich inner world, so it's not surprising he's got into Oxford,* I reasoned to myself. *Medieval kings, and Egyptian Pharaohs …He knows so much that he seems to view the world somewhat differently from the rest of us. I wonder how he sees me? And what about Alka? Why did she appear to him that night at all? I didn't really believe in her ability, allegedly passed to her by her grandma, but it would be best if Quentin didn't know about it at all, as he's already labeled her a witch. Perhaps it was a dream. . . And yet, what a strange one… I should call Alka and find out how she's spending her time with James in London. She left me his phone number somewhere.*

And yet part of me was simply jealous that Ala seemed to have invaded Quentin's dreams, pushing me aside. I went over the parts of the letter that had pleased me over and over. ('It's such a pity that we're not together for Christmas; I already miss you so much and often think of you, especially whenever I pass by 'our' steps! . . .') However, there were too few of them, and I went downstairs again in a state of vague discomfort and discontent.

CHAPTER 15

While Lilith was being inducted into witchcraft in the pinewoods Ala Gromova was sleeping serenely in the guest room at the Browns' house in Chelsea. At 8.30 a.m. the maid Annette knocked softly on the door, wishing to know if she might like a cup of tea or coffee in bed before breakfast. Alka accepted the offer, stretching herself languorously. 'Wow, what a night that was,' she thought, drowsily propping herself up in order to enjoy the tantalizing aroma of coffee, gently steaming in a bone china cup.

Still half-asleep, still wondering why the English keep their houses so cold, she sipped a mouthful of rich coffee before curling back under her duvet. . . There was something special about today, now: what was it? Then she remembered.

'Oh yes! A happy birthday to you, dear Lilith! What a celebration we had yesterday!' Alka couldn't help smiling, remembering the nocturnal flight into the woods, the dancing that followed her initiation and the welcoming kisses, scented with mead. . . 'She is special among us,' she remembered, the words echoing in her head.

Alka had known, ever since childhood, that she was special. She clearly remembered the first night that something astonishing had happened. She had been just thirteen when her mother had sent her to spend the summer with her grandmother in the Altai, mainly in order to be able to continue her love-life unhindered by Alka's presence.

That particular night Alka had dreamed a dream. In it she had been a great cat: she had hunted birds and mice in the woods, lain in wait for them to emerge from the bushes, climbed trees like a panther, destroyed birds' nests with nestlings in them, and dug out mouse holes. She found that she could distinguish everything as clearly as if in broad daylight. The intoxicating woodland smells had led her ever deeper into the woods. She had returned home in the early morning with her black cat's face and paws stained with blood. . .

In the morning she had scampered to tell her grandmother about her dream. Her grandmother's first reaction had been strange: she had looked searchingly and intently at her, and sighed deeply, as if distressed. Then she had silently boiled up some kind of beverage, which itself smelled of the wild woods.

'What's this?' Alka had asked, puzzled.

'It is for you, said her grandmother. After a moment, she had continued, "Granddaughter, you and I are cut from the same cloth. Your mother is not, and never will be, but I will teach all that I know – at least, as long as I'm alive – and even after I've gone I'll still help you."

'I don't understand.'

'Not yet. The main thing is that you remain fearless. Believe me, you will get answers to all your questions when the time is right.'

From that night Alka didn't fear anything, wherever her dreams took her. But however much she enjoyed rushing about as a nocturnal predator in the Altai's hills and grassy meadows, hunting for mountain deer, snow sheep or woodland game, as an Ussuriysk tigress or a savage panther, she still preferred being her true self, Alka, hovering above woods and high snowy outcrops of rock, basking like a mermaid on deserted sea beaches or slipping into grey-green mountain waterfalls.

At first she pestered her grandmother with questions, including, 'When I'm asleep, why does my soul fly off and roam about, or even turn into a wild animal?' Her grandmother frowned. 'Your being is not subject to mind or body, as is the case with ordinary people: instead, it belongs elsewhere, to another power. Everything will come to you, granddaughter: beauty, power, fame and riches. You will be loved and adored. But it's far too early still to be thinking about such things. . . When the time is right you will learn how everything will come to pass.'

'Will I have teachers?' the young Alka had persisted.

CHAPTER 15

'You will, of course, have many teachers but until then I will help you as much as I can. You have a great future ahead of you, granddaughter, but meanwhile, enjoy the simple things in life. Let's go and gather herbs. There are wonderful medicines growing unrecognized here in the Altai hills.'

***

Nearly five years had passed since. Her grandmother was already dead but her predictions were beginning to come true. While she was staying in Wiltshire Alka's favourite nighttime activity was to explore the local surroundings, and she felt especially drawn to those otherworldly places for which the area was well-known. Apart from her grandmother, Alka had yet to meet anyone of her own kind: she was unconsciously waiting for such an encounter with a mixture of curiosity and an almost animalistic fear.

One night, a couple of weeks after she had started college, Alka decided, as usual, to go for a wander in the woods, and at the same time to check out Wooten Bassett, a small town near Marlborough. According to legend, whole tribes of witches had inhabited this little town in centuries gone by – some of whom had been burnt on bonfires, as witchcraft had been considered a heinous crime, exacting extreme legal punishments. Even now, despite the law against witchcraft having been abolished in the 1950s, fears of persecution persisted and young witches imbibed it with their mothers' milk.

On her way Alka came across some sorcerer spirits in the older streets of the town. Gleefully, they tried to brush against her, but she ignored them, being only interested in the human representatives of this breed. The town didn't seem particularly remarkable to Alka and she had already made up her mind to wander into the nearby Savernake Forest when she conceived the idea of instead flying over the place where – at least, according to tradition – a renowned witch had lived during the previous century. Her house was in a secluded spot on a steep hillside, and Alka was able to find her way quite easily. At first glance, the three-story house of dull grey flagstone had an ominous appearance. The windows were narrow and set with dark glass, while the metal-studded black door was thoroughly forbidding, yet something drew her nearer.

Flying round the house she saw a candle burning in one of the back windows. Alka's grandmother had expressly forbidden her to approach people during her nighttime expeditions. 'But if someone chances to see your face at night, I can teach you a few spells so that when the human wakes up they will have forgotten everything. To them it will all vanish like a dream.'

The window blinds were up and moonlight was shimmering silver into the room. Alka saw twelve people gathered around a table covered with a red cloth, apparently listening to a bald man with his back to the window, reading aloud from a thick book by candlelight. Ala clung to the window, forgetting the chill in her bones, because, from the barely audible murmurings that reached her, and from what she could see, she concluded that she was witnessing her first witches' sabbath. . . Frozen with the strongest possible curiosity she continued to observe – and who knows how long she might have remained, rapt and motionless – had not a large black cat suddenly leaped onto the windowsill below her, met Alka's wide-eyed gaze and let out a wild and penetrating cry. Startled, Alka jumped back from the window and hung like a bat to the ivy clinging to the greystone walls. Then, to her dismay, the window above her flew open.

'Who's there?' said a man with a high voice, leaning out of the window. 'I can sense that someone is there. . . In addition, Mavr too sensed someone, and he is never mistaken in such a case.'

'What do you think, Mia?' asked another male voice, and – with sinking heart – Alka heard a soft Scottish woman's voice respond, 'I think – I think that it is she, at last!'

A moment later the front door opened. On the threshold stood a rather wizened elderly lady with a black and white scarf round her neck. There was nothing particularly unusual about her appearance, yet Alka felt irresistibly drawn to her. . . She moved forwards, rather hesitantly, as

CHAPTER 15

if caught out in some crime. The woman's eyes met hers. No word was spoken, or had to be . . . Alka felt both an instant kinship and a silent summons. As if mesmerized, she followed Mia into the building and up the stairs, and into room that she had spied upon. Twelve pairs of eyes scrutinised their guest, not counting the alert eyes of the cat Mavr, who was indignantly watching her every move from his place on the window sill.

'It is she,' repeated Mia, addressing the bald man – or so it seemed to Alka – in particular. A thirteenth chair had somehow materialised, causing a mild sensation, and the bald man gestured Alka towards it.

'It's a sign!. . . The prediction has come true!' Alka heard the whispering and glanced around, alert and nervous yet still challenging. The bald man coughed meaningfully and the whispering immediately ceased.

He said, 'Welcome. We've been awaiting your arrival for a long time. You've had to make a very long journey in order that we might meet at last. It has long been said that a Special One from the land of Grigori Rasputin, where our name, Georgina, means a beautiful flower, would join our clan, but we didn't know exactly when this would happen.'

'Georgina is Dahlia in Russian …I'm sorry, but I don't understand,' interrupted Alka. 'How did you know that I existed?'

The old man smiled at her. 'Witchcraft is not like most gifts. If you aren't born with it, no training, no diploma can possibly assist . . . In short, not only can your spirit freely travel during sleep – a feat beyond even many advanced witches nowadays – but when you wish you can retain the form of your own body while simultaneously a sleeping copy slumbers in a warm bed. Am I correct, Ala?'

Ala, too shocked to speak, only nodded. He turned to the others.

'Unlike the rest of us, she doesn't have to seek out animals, people or other beings. Only Gertrude, founder of our clan, and her two sisters, possessed such powers. Just imagine, what potential is invested before us!' he exclaimed delightedly. 'With our help she will master displacement to temporary spaces, time travel, reaching the Otherworld and will be able to utilise secrets of both present and future for the good of our clan. . . Gertrude herself foresaw such developments but unfortunately before she and her sisters could achieve them, the royal inquisitors had them burnt alive. But their spirits still assist us in our undertakings.'

'Just one moment, I pray,' came, rather querulously, from an aged fellow in spectacles. 'In my opinion, Higgis, you might be rushing things a bit. First of all we need to tell our night visitor about our clan. Yes, yes, I know,' he replied to the witches round the table who were exchanging glances: 'our oath forbids talk of this with outsiders, but I sense – do not we all? – that she is the one of which we were told.'

'I can be trusted,' said Alka eagerly.

The old man continued, 'Even if she decides not to join us, everyone will soon know about her manifestation here, upon which all the other clans will try to curry her favour. So I very much hope, young one, that we might be able to impress you. Mia, this is your time.'

'Greetings, novice,' said the old woman. 'We are one of the seven oldest and most powerful clans of hereditary witches in England, and we are called the Sacred Circle of Georgina, so named by the great Gertrude in honour of her grandmother, Lady Georgina. All members of the Inner Circle are hereditary witches to the third, fourth and even – in one case – the fifth generation,' and here she awarded Higgis a small smile.

'We have been practising our art for centuries, transmitting its secrets from one generation to the next. The Outer Circle consists of our pupils: we choose only a select few, and only the elect ever reach us. They must be hereditary witches, brilliant, talented, promising and – most importantly – witches guided by the spiritual values of our clan. It is common knowledge that witches can both cure illnesses and also put the evil eye on people, but as the ancient proverb puts it, "He who knows not how to kill knows not how to cure." In both cases the same magic energy is used, the difference being in how it is directed – and with what intent. When the members of our clan use magic powers they must follow strong ethical principles –coincidentally, the first thing that we teach.'

Alka listened with bated breath, still disbelieving that here – at last – she had met her kindred spirits.

Mia continued: 'Unlike some other clans, the Circle of Georgina has a definite hierarchy, with one's position within the circle being defined by one's qualifications and level of expertise in witchcraft. We are a clan with a strong academic bias: knowledge is food for the starving soul. So our study programme has five diploma levels, the fifth - and highest - allowing the candidate to assume the role of High Priest in our circle. It requires a near-flawless mastery of our arts, and a minimum of seven years' training. Higgis is our High Priest, and I am the High Priestess but Wise Raven – she nodded towards the old man in glasses – remains our sage, with as much experience of magic as Higgis and I put together: thus, all attend to his advice.

'In terms of tutelage, every pupil has a teacher from the Inner Circle – an extreme privilege, as in other clans there might be one teacher for ten pupils. Should you choose to join us, your teacher will be your mentor as long as you are studying in the Circle of Georgina but you will have to obey him or her in everything. . . You would also have to choose a magic name by which you will be known. Some take the names of spirits who are the patrons of their arts, or of demons, birds or even wild animals. Traditionally one has to study for exactly a year and a day before their initiation.'

At this point Higgis intervened. 'I think, taking into account her special gifts, that we might exempt her from the period of waiting.'

Mia turned to and look inquiringly at Wise Raven.

'May I ask how old you are, Ala?' he asked gently.

'I am seventeen.'

Everyone around the table exchanged glances. 'We do not initiate minors,' explained Mia.

'But my birthday isn't far off – on the 21st of September.'

Higgis rubbed his hands. 'In that case I propose to postpone your initiation for three months from the day you reach your majority, permitting your rebirth to coincide with Yule, the rebirth of our great Angel of Light – that is, if the Circle approves.'

'Shall we vote?' suggested Mia, and the vote was agreed and taken, to offer a place to Alka. Everyone except Mavr was 'for' – he looked rather grumpy and waved his tail in a rather marked manner – but the day of Alka's initiation was still set for Solstice Night of the 21st of December.

'In the meantime, you will learn much and get to know us better,' said Higgis. 'The decision is entirely yours: whether to join us – or to join others – or to continue as you have done so far, living as a witch in a human world.'

'We shouldn't detain our night visitor any longer, it will soon be light,' warned Mia in her warm Scottish accent. 'Ala, this is not goodbye, it is only farewell. Take yourself safely home now: we will find you again soon, as you have found us.'

'The thirteenth witch in our circle, that's another sign,' muttered Wise Raven to Mia, as she departed. . . Alka took her leave, inspired by the revelation of her future, and positively skimmed through the air back to college.

A week after her meeting with the Georgina Clan she set off for town, first dropping into Crosby and Lawrence, the school outfitters shop, directly opposite the college, for a new hockey stick and a new pair of gloves. In truth, hockey was Alka's latest passion. As soon as she had learnt the rules of the game she had excelled, swiftly becoming the best attacking player in the College team.

Of course none of the other students knew that Ala had only been playing for three days: in fact they knew very little about her in general: she seemed rather reserved, even withdrawn, to her new colleagues. . . Yet this was purely a defense mechanism against being misunderstood: her character was so powerful that at times even she was afraid of it. She had partly chosen to play hockey because of

CHAPTER 15

the stick. 'Not a bad vehicle,' she'd thought, admiring the elegant shape with the delicately hooked end. 'Cooler than flying on a broomstick like some old biddy!' Alka enjoyed wandering round the shop, trying on a dozen pairs of gloves in front of the mirror and even flirting with the red-headed sales assistant, more out of habit than for the 10% discount that the dazzled young man offered her. She had only gone a few paces down the road when a large black cat appeared out of nowhere and, with seeming deliberation, directly crossed her path.

'What luck!' she murmured. Then Alka noticed that the cat had stopped a little way away and was staring fixedly at her with impatient yellow eyes. Mavr! – she thought, and sped up in order to follow him. The cat crossed onto the parallel street at a leisurely pace, and then dived smartly into a lane. Alka tried to keep up with those elegant black haunches. They dodged through various backstreets until Mavr stopped at the entrance of a two-story second-hand bookshop with an old sign, apparently ready to fall off its copper hinges, reading: 'Antiquarian and Rare Books.' Mavr gave her a long, appraising, possibly faintly disgusted glance, prompting Alka to half-open the door and to glance inside. An antique bell clanged loudly to announce the arrival of a customer but the shop itself seemed empty. Daylight scarcely reached the interior, mostly because every window was blocked up with books. . . Row upon row of bookshelves reached almost up to the ceiling but they didn't seem arranged by any particular system, either by subject or author. 'How could you possibly find anything here?' wondered Alka, wandering around. Suddenly she heard the scrape of the storeroom door and a little cough. Alka whirled round. 'Higgis!'

'Greetings, greetings,' Higgis welcomed her, and then, 'Thank you, Mavr, you did precisely as we asked. . . I have great news for you, Ala. Wise Raven himself has agreed to be your mentor, although he has only agreed to act as a consultant these fifteen years – yet for you he has decided to make an exception.'

'I am honoured,' said Alka.

'Had circumstances been different I myself would have been only too delighted to take on this task, but as High Priest I must remain impartial. . .

As for this,' and here he glanced around looked around vaguely, 'this is simply to distract curious eyes. Our real library with the ancient demonic texts lies securely in a safe behind a hidden door. Would you care to have a look?'

Alka said that she would be delighted, whereupon he said, very politely, 'Please follow me.' And they all, including Mavr, followed him up the staircase.

On the second floor, to Ala's surprise they found themselves in a spacious conference room with black-and-white checkerboard flooring, comfortable soft arm-chairs equipped with remote control and an enormous flat-screen TV on the wall. Wise Raven was there, reading a book about fifty centimetres square, with pages that gave off gold-filtered dust. He rose courteously as they entered, and greeted them.

'Here we hold sittings of the Global Committee together other regional groups and colleagues from the headquarters in London, as well as Moscow, Rome, Brussels, New York…' he explained.

'Moscow?' she interrupted, shocked.

'Of course. Who do you think was behind the 1917 revolution under our shiny pentagram? *"All religion and all morality is abolished, and everything is permitted."*

'Was Marx one of you?' Ala was astonished.

Wise Raven smiled. 'Our people are everywhere. The seed was planted long ago, it sprouted green, and the sprouts grow ever stronger. Soon we will only have to reap the fruits of the harvest. We can't be stopped now.'

'Did you really have something to do with the collapse of the USSR?' she asked, almost disbelievingly.

'Made it one day, collapsed it the next,' Higgis told her. 'In politics as in magic, nothing happens by chance... But one can always choose between the good and evil. These powers are as interlinked as are day and night, yin and yang, life and death. In the same way our mission of light is intertwined with darkness. We test humanity with darkness for the sake of its spiritual evolution. In this way we are true servants of this planet... See, I have prepared a few books for you.'

CHAPTER 15

'Oh, thank you!' said Alka, her head spinning. In fact it looked rather a strange-looking parcel, wrapped in old newspaper and bounded with black rope.

'Please, read them before we meet again. Be careful with them, especially the one on top – it was written by a notorious wizard and close councillor of King Charles V. I do not agree with everything he has written but I still recommend it to all our apprentices. The second book, the *Book of Shadows*, will be your daybook on the way to becoming a powerful witch. Don't forget to place protection upon it, so that no one else can see it, wherever it might lie. . . And here in addition is my own work, on demonology.' Proudly, he offered her a large volume with a well-thumbed, almost shabby binding. The dedication simply read: 'For Wise Raven.'

'I don't know how to thank you,' said Alka gratefully. 'The truth is that my grandmother has been my only teacher, and she couldn't read, although she was hugely wise.'

'And there is one other thing of which I must remind you,' Higgis instructed: 'Our classes must not be allowed to interfere with your College education. No successful witch would allow her regular life to be interrupted, especially not a witch from our particular clan. Private education, money, status and social position are very important for our clan members. We remain weak and vulnerable without them, and our enemies and competitors – who are the same thing, in truth – are eager to see us make a wrong step. In such a case we wouldn't be able to fill our ranks with gifted, brilliant and beautiful young people, as others will take them. That's why our apprentices are encouraged to work hard in all arenas. You will meet some of these shortly, from the best universities in the country. And, of course, with your many advantages –' Here Higgis glanced approvingly at Ala, taking her in from head to toe, 'you have every possible chance to make a successful marriage. I mean marrying into money, of course.'

'She will have plenty of time to get married! First, she needs an education,' Wise Raven objected. 'We take our classes in the attic above,' he told her, 'and, as I need more sleep than I once did, I suggest we meet on Fridays, after your college classes are over. Magic energy should be channelled in the right direction, not casually frittered away. . . This is why we will need to work on both theory and practice. It's crucial for us both to understand how your magic powers can be interwoven with the power of the other Inner Circle members. In order to do this, we will ask you to join us for a casting spell in the Magic Circle at the next full moon. Ginger Sparrow, our administrator, organizes these events. Once he has chosen the correct place on the night, Mavr will find you.'

At this Mavr stopped licking his elegant paw, to cast a faintly patronising glance in Alka's direction.

'And if you need to contact us before Friday, put a letter into the mail slot in the door of the shop. The landline is not safe, which is why we cannot recommend it. . . If you ever need to contact us urgently, I will give you the means to call Mavr to you – as long as he is willing to agree.'

He glanced towards the cat apologetically, and Mavr just deigned to briefly lower his head, indicating an almost regal consent.

Alka was surprised when Wise Raven and Higgis then whispered swiftly between themselves. However, Wise Raven then tore off a page from a book apparently chosen at random, folded it neatly into a triangle and gave it to Ala. 'Here. Learn this and then burn it. It is a risk, I admit: we've never trusted any of our apprentices with something quite like this before.'

Surprised but eager, Ala unfolded the tiny paper triangle but saw nothing beyond three tiny lines of what appeared to be minutely-written spells. She neatly folded it back, tucking it into her left shoe for safety.

'Yes, she'll do fine,' Higgis laughed, scratching Mavr behind his ear.

'Until Friday then,' said Wise Raven. 'I'm sure you'll find the way back easily, but beware those who might try to mislead you!'

Alka collected her books and purchases and left the shop to find her way back. She roamed the various alleys for a while, trying to get a feel for the neighbourhood, then found her way back to High Street and into college.

CHAPTER 15

Soon Alka was immersed in learning. On Fridays she practiced with Wise Raven – a demanding mentor but still impressed by her enthusiasm. With a near-photographic memory, she had no difficulty in getting whole textbooks by heart, while – to her secret gratification – everything her grandmother had taught her was only reinforced, gaining higher sense and greater meaning through the confirmation of wizened, century-old works of the ancient greats. She learned so many new things, but the old, herbal spells especially reminded her of her grandmother.

'A good witch first of all is a good practitioner,' Wise Raven told her, rather austerely. 'There are frankly far too many theoretical types about nowadays, particularly in teaching circles.'

Everything was used: fire, salt, special stones, dog hair and even frogs. Alka's magical power was taking off.

'You will rise high, young one!' When Wise Raven repeated her grandmother's words, she felt the glow of knowing that she must be giving of her best. 'Soon you will be ready for us to invite you to our circle. The spells pronounced by those in the circle own a tenfold power. But, of course, you have to learn them first,' Raven added, sensing the girl's impatience.

Only three weeks after their first meeting in the bookshop the full moon reared up again. As usual, at ten o'clock every light in the New Court went out – yet still, Alka couldn't sleep. Instead she was utterly absorbed by the book of magic spells that Wise Raven had given her at their last lesson. She was reading in her bed with a candle – Miss Foxton would no doubt have had a heart attack had she seen it – and didn't even notice when midnight came . . . Suddenly, an imperious meow sliced through the night. Mavr was perched on the windowsill, licking the tip of his right paw and obviously in a bad mood – the full moon having cruelly put paid to his plans for hunting forest mice. Not to mention the fact that this head-tossing princess didn't instantly leap up upon his arrival! . . . Alka felt his annoyance and responded.

'I'm almost ready, Mavr,' she promised, leaping nimbly out of bed.

Sticking her head into some random jumper, Alka wandered about her room seeking a clean pair of jeans somewhere in the heap of clothes on the floor. . . Mavr, gentlemen that he was, turned his gaze away, staring gloomily out of the window. Once completely dressed, Alka put out her candle and headed towards the door, when a cross hiss surprised her from behind. Swivelling round, she saw that Mavr had grown to the size of a huge panther, lithe, blue-black and glowing, his yellow eyes scorching the darkness of the room like two headlights. Alka climbed on his back, firmly grabbed the fur surrounding his muscular neck and shut her eyes tightly. The cat made three counter-clockwise turns and sprang out of the window. They jumped over the New Court in one leap, rushed through the school gates and raced on. Alka was enjoying the ride so much that she didn't even notice how soon they reached the ancient witch's house where she had met Georgina's clan for the first time. Mavr stopped at the doorstep, permitted her to dismount and swiftly melted into the neighbouring forest. Suddenly it occurred to her that her had forgotten to put on her shoes and had indeed elected to attend her first Sabbath in her favourite scarlet slippers. *Well, who cares now*, she thought as she entered.

Guests were already taking their seats around the table, but a few vacant chairs remained. Having greeted everyone, Alka sat next to Mia, who was intent upon pouring a fragrant herbal potion from a cast-iron pot into various glasses. Suddenly the windows started trembling, eventually being flung open with a protesting creak. . . A cold gust of wind blinked out every candle burning on the table, while Higgis, together with Ginger Sparrow, the former clutching a black leather briefcase under his arm, swooshed inside astride their broomsticks.

'So sorry for the delay! We were just checking out some new places for the next European Witch Conference,' said Sparrow, rather loftily.

'How many times must I ask you to simply use the door like everybody else!' sighed Mia. 'Just look what you've done' – gesturing towards the table, with glowing teas spilled from over-turned cups.

Higgis apologised. 'But now, ladies and gentlemen! – and here he tapped the candlestick with a teaspoon. 'Listen! I declare our full-moon meeting open. Where's the agenda?' he asked, in an undertone, of Sparrow.

Sparrow obligingly delved into his briefcase, fishing out a bundle of papers. Thick white sheets with the elegant, slightly raised Georgina watermark, stating the following in rainbow ink:

1. General welcome, greeting Alka (Higgis)
2. Introducing twelve members of the Georgina clan (Higgis and Mia)
3. Making a spell in the circle. . .

'Whose turn is it to take the minutes?' inquired Higgis in morose tones. No one volunteered. 'Fine, then, as usual, the Chair will have to do it, himself,' he grumbled. 'Sparrow, where's the quill?'

Sparrow fussed about for a few moments: then a ginger quill together with matching inkpot emerged on the table before Higgis.

'Fine, well done,' continued Higgis rather grudgingly, 'And so, who is absent today?'

'Mavr.'

Someone had turned the cat in.

'Officially, he has half the night off,' explained Higgis hurriedly.

'Very well,' said Mia disapprovingly. 'In addition, Harvest and Willow are on a family holiday, while Jade and Tara are addressing the witch conference in California.'

'It's all right for some,' noted Sparrow, rather enviously.

'Yet everyone else is here, well done,' Higgis coughed. 'On behalf of the attendees, I would like to greet Ala formally, especially as it's her first full moon meeting. Wise Raven has told us you are making progress even swifter than he had hoped.'

Wise Raven roused himself sufficiently to add, 'In just ten days this young lady has already mastered the curriculum of the first degree and started practicing. We have even attempted some third-level spells.'

At this, an approving muttering swept around the table.

Higgis adjusted his glasses and consulted the agenda sheet.

'Number two – introductions,' he muttered to himself. 'Ah yes. Well, as Ala does not yet know us all, I would be grateful if you would introduce yourselves. Let's start with Mia, moving counter-clockwise.'

'The candidate and I have already met, of course,' Mia smiled at Alka. 'My name is Lady Mia, but everyone calls me Mia. I was awarded the title after reaching the sixth level. Sir Perushen himself initiated me, almost ten years ago. Unfortunately, he is no longer with us. Five years after my initiation I first became High Priestess. I do many things, especially Kabbalah, spiritualism, prophecies and creating rituals. Not long ago I gave up private practice in order to pursue my academic work.'

'I am called Spider,' continued Mia's gaunt neighbor. He had piercingly sharp, multi-layered eyes and long thin fingers that appeared to be constantly twitching. 'I am involved in general practice and, of course, Kabbalah. I also specialize in working with animals, mind-reading and energy work. I have a level three diploma and have spent eight years with the clan.'

Next came the Gothic twins, Pixie and Kiki, both entirely in inky black, with heavy kohl-lined eyes and pallid, mask-like faces. To Alka they didn't look any older than she was herself: she was secretly astonished to learn that they both had third-level diplomas.

While absorbed in watching them – for they had a weird synergy – she missed the part about their specialities. Something related to astral prophecies and some 'isms' - druidism, Sufism, pantheism, who knew what else. . .

On the other side of them was a shy, blue-eyed, dark-haired man called Silverwolf. He was a quiet thirty-year-old accountant who – oddly enough – turned into a wolf at the full moon. Alka, a little disappointed, asked why in that case, as it was full moon, he still looked like a man. 'I am not a werewolf,' he explained, 'I transform only in the dream-state. I'm taking exams for my second-level diploma. It's my first year in the clan.'

CHAPTER 15

At this Higgis took over the meeting, with effortless authority. 'Now you know almost everyone in the Inner Circle. Soon you'll meet our apprentices and also Harvest, Willow and Jade. But you would be surprised how many of us are infiltrated our chosen society: higher-ups, financiers, and celebrities, not to mention film idols and other role models. . . The reason? People long to be like them, these darlings of the global media. To rule people, one has – of course – to be prepared to become the main piece on the chessboard – the rook, at least, if not the Queen herself. . . Pawns are there merely in order to clear your path, while a person who wants nothing is far worse than a pawn – such people can be pushed from the board! You, our latest candidate, are gifted, ambitious and beautiful. With assistance from the demons we will teach you to read minds, to find out your enemy's intentions and to keep ahead of any action against your own interests.'

Everyone muttered approvingly while Alka secretly thought how lucky she was to be there.

'Forgive me, I am too chatty today,' said Higgis, recollecting himself. 'It is now time to get down to business. As I've already said, we need to know how your magic energy blends in with ours. That's why you were invited, Alka. We pursue no specific agenda tonight: we will just do the usual: raise the Cone of Power, ask it for prosperity of our clan and then release it to Cosmic World. It is only after initiation that you will truly become one of us – should you choose to, of course – only then will you take part in spells, or elect to fulfill certain tasks for our mutual benefit. . . If there are no questions, let's commence.'

Suddenly, the table and the chairs disappeared, as if they had never been there. The roof peeled back to reveal the beautiful night sky. Members of the circle themselves were thrown together, reaching out and grabbing each other's hands, weaving and dancing in the wind of the spell. With her entire being Alka felt the circle drawing her power towards itself, like a magnet. The power mingled with the circle's intrinsic energy, picking up speed until it turned into a coil of power, deeper at its base, widening at its rim, like a great silver cone of energy. It seemed to spin on its axis faster and faster each moment, before finally soaring through what had been the roof and into the wild open sky, until it passed from their sight. . . Almost as suddenly as they'd been spun together the grip of their hands was released, and everything in the room returned to normal.

'Good work,' said Higgis to Alka, well-pleased. 'You can perfectly direct and, most importantly, control your magic power in the Circle, which is usually a difficult knack to master for a novice. We have great hopes for you, well done!'

Everyone looked at Alka approvingly, as Higgis adjourned the meeting. Mavr was already awaiting her, flicking his great tail from side to side, He was in high good humour, signifying a successful forest hunt, and soon Alka was fast asleep in her New Court bed.

All too soon – it was actually almost nine – someone knocked politely on her door. Alka pulled herself unwillingly from dreaming to consciousness and said, 'Come in.'

It was Annette again, wearing a starched white apron over a black dress which vaguely reminded Alka of her school uniform back in Moscow.

'You have a phone call, miss. Someone called Sasha.'

Despite the hour, Alka was happy to chat in Russian and hear Moscow news. She slipped into a soft white dressing-gown and followed Annette into Mr. Brown's study.

Closing the door behind her, Alka grabbed the receiver.

'Sasha, hi! Merry Christmas! What's the news?'

'All our former classmates say "hi" to you. We're getting together at my place for the New Year. Such a shame you won't be here! And how's it going with James?'

'Great . . . we're getting ready to celebrate Christmas. There will be lots of people; it should be fun. And James's mother is absolutely charming. She's more like an older girlfriend and guess what – she's even trying to teach me how to be a proper lady!'

CHAPTER 15

'Good luck to her!' teased her friend.

They chattered for a while and Sasha promised to visit Alka's mother before the New Year Eve to deliver her presents.

Alka hung up and paused to think. Despite the light tone, it was obvious to her that Sashka was hiding something. It was as if she desperately longed to ask her a question, but couldn't summon up sufficient courage. Could it be about Quentin? How did he and Chris even get to the place of initiation that night?

According to all she'd learned, only the most thoroughly checked and vetted places could be selected for such events: hidden forest openings, mysterious glades and other sights forgotten by people – places known only to the Inner Circle and protected by spells from unwanted guests. Ginger Sparrow was an experienced coordinator of Sabbaths, initiations, witches conferences and conventions, who had never failed. . . But even this didn't bother Alka as much as what happened next.

After her initiation everyone flew to celebrate Yule at Stonehenge, where witch clans from all over the country would converge by dawn. Alka, however, decided to check up on the two drug addicts in the woods before joining them.

'I know them, after all, and they depend upon me,' she told herself. 'It would be horrible if demons or werewolves might find them there at night, and that risk was surely increased with it being the longest night of the year.' She felt an unusual sting of responsibility. She flew in, only to find that nothing seemed to be happening in the glade – the two friends were peacefully slumbering, the spells of the circle were still working and it was clear that no unwanted guests had paid a visit in the night . . . The dawn was growing close and she must get to Stonehenge in time: there was therefore nothing else to do but to awaken Quentin. Alka pushed a few stones under his side and hid in the branches of a nearby oak, watching intently. Luckily, she didn't have to wait long. Quentin twisted round, met the pain in the back, awoke and started shaking his friend.

Listening to their conversation she realized that her grandmother's spells, which had always worked before without a hitch, had – for whatever reason – failed to work upon Quentin. He remembered everything: he had even found traces of fire. His friend, however, as she'd expected, had suffered a total memory lapse – which was one lucky thing, at any rate.

Alka flew down upwards from her branch, heading as swiftly as she could to Stonehenge, reflecting on the way. She recollected her first meeting with Quentin in town, when those charms in which she had always trusted had unexpectedly failed her.

'And now it turns out that even my spells don't work on him!' she hissed, freewheeling above a motorway. 'At this rate I'll get an inferiority complex. Something's all wrong about this.

He's a tough nut, but I swear I'll crack him in the end!'

Mulling things over, she forgot all about breakfast, until James slipped into the study, interrupting her thoughts.

'Here you are! I was looking for you everywhere until Annette told me you are here. I thought we might go out last night,' he complained looking at her with those love-struck puppy-dog eyes. 'Where were you? I knocked on your door, but it was locked. You were in your room right?'

'Where else could I have been?' she teased, thinking: *you wouldn't believe me where I was, even if I could tell you. . .*

'I wanted you.'

'Sounds good to me, said Alka, tossing him a smile that made him feel weak with longing. 'Why don't we do it right now?' And the next moment his lips were on her breasts, her arms around his strong shoulders.

CHAPTER 16

For the first time in my entire school life, I was looking forward to the end of a holiday. I couldn't wait to return to College, and - still more - to see Quentin, whom I'd missed so badly. While at home, I'd buzzed so often in everyone's ears about my wonderful boyfriend that my parents were anxious to meet him upon their next visit to England – a visit that Dad, at least, was planning in the very near future.

Finally, the long-awaited day of my departure arrived. I said a guilty goodbye to Mum, who was already missing me, and left for Sheremetievo airport with my Dad and Nikolai, his new driver.

'Well, my dear, you should expect an early return visit from us. We can get acquainted with your groom then,' said my dad, warmly embracing me, while Nikolai was unloading my luggage out of the trunk.

The groom! Thank goodness my 19-year-old boyfriend isn't around to hear this! I thought gratefully, though all I said was, 'Of course, Dad. You'll see, you'll love him!' I turned round and waved good-bye once again; yet as I rushed towards the departure gates in my heart I was already back at Marlborough.

I reached College in the early evening. To my chagrin, Littlefield was still locked up and, as I learned from a passing College gardener, the Grahams weren't expected back from their holiday until the next morning. . . In fact, I'd managed to arrive at College a whole day too early! Utterly at a loss I sat on my suitcase outside the door, watching the sky growing darker and feeling my teeth beginning to chatter from cold. Then, a bright idea blessed me: *I should call Quentin!*

Leaving my suitcase behind I headed to Bath Road, where opposite the school gates was a traditional red phone box, in which Azaan had once boasted of having had sex with an exchange student, a girl who had long since returned to Italy. This unconvincing tale had nevertheless aroused real jealousy among his friends, who had all longed to have been in his place. . .

I immediately dialed the number, which I knew by heart. Quentin picked up the phone.

'Hi! It's me, Sasha!'

'Hi there! No need to introduce yourself. As if I could ever confuse your voice with anyone else's!' he rejoiced.

'Guess where I am?' Gladly I disclosed my current location.

'You're back at last! Great! Stay right where you are, and I'll pick you up straightaway.'

Ten minutes later, having picked up my case as if it weighed nothing, Quentin was driving us to his house, while relaying the breaking news in Marlborough. On the way, I couldn't take my eyes off his beloved face, in exultant anticipation of the moment when we would finally be alone in his room. . . . *How could I have such a stunning, handsome and generous boyfriend?* I marveled, admiring his athletic figure while he was unloading my suitcase.

'Mum, we're here!' announced Quentin, entering the house with my hand locked in his.

Debbie greeted me warmly and offered me a bite to eat, but, filled with excitement of seeing Quentin, I didn't feel hungry. We couldn't wait to be left alone and, hand-in-hand, quickly disappeared upstairs.

'I prepared the guest-room for Sasha. . . ' Debbie's voice trailed off: nobody was listening. Soon, the familiar thundering rock music filled the room and I was back in Quentin's world, which I never wanted to leave again.

'I missed you so much!' Quentin told me, undressing me on the bed and covering my face with hot kisses. 'I hope you were thinking of me in Moscow.'

'Every second!' I promised, dissolving in the pleasure of kissing him back.

Our enthusiastic reunion lasted all evening, the rest of which we spent lounging together in his bedroom until we finally got hungry. Having gone

CHAPTER 16

downstairs to raid the kitchen, Quentin eventually returned with two cups of tea plus ham and cheese sandwiches.

'Did you receive my letter?' he asked eagerly, biting into his sandwich. Clearly, he couldn't wait to discuss it. Having answered in the affirmative I listened as he continued: 'So, what do you think about it, now that you know everything?'

I was ashamed to admit that I hadn't completely understood some parts of his letter, between his handwriting and colloquialisms and my own poor English.

'Well, it was great! I mean awesome,' I said, not knowing what to say, or even what kind of reaction was expected. Quentin stared at me with sudden suspicion.

'Did you read it carefully?' he asked.

'Of course! And more than once!' I lied.

'And?'

'Well, I have to tell you, it's complete nonsense about Alka, for a start! I called her from Moscow, and she spent the whole of the Christmas holidays in London with her boyfriend James.'

'You could have called me as well, not only your girlfriend! I didn't even know whether the letter had arrived safely,' Quentin objected. 'Though I thought the postage would be hugely expensive, but it was only pennies!' he added, rather more cheerfully.

'Well, OK, but please don't get cross! Honestly, I *was* going to write you back, but, knowing only too well how the Moscow post office functions, I knew that I'd get back myself much sooner!' And I gently kissed his earlobe, as a peace offering.

'Hmm. Well, I'd still advise you to be really careful with that friend of yours. I know what I saw,' he told me, although afterwards he suddenly seemed far less confident, saying, 'Sasha, now that you know all about me, do you still like me and want to be with me?'

Do I like you?! Don't you know that I'm completely crazy about you? I thought, astonished.

'What are you talking about? If it's about those silly mushrooms, I really don't care! By the way, Alka and I also tried something like this once,' I lied, for no particular reason.

'Really!' Quentin's curiosity was piqued. 'You never told me. How was it?'

'Oh, um, actually great! Yes, definitely!' and then I hurriedly changed the subject. Carried away, we failed to notice the time until it was already 2:30 a.m. Then we cuddled up tightly on his cramped single bed, and I fell asleep listening to his breathing. . . In fact, I never managed to spend even two seconds in the bedroom that Debbie had so beautifully prepared for me!

The next morning I thought: *I slept with Quentin without sleeping with him* and smiled to myself at such a paradox. *Soon it will happen! He's so amazing. . .* I recalled my sleep, drifting into dreams inside his strong arms.

Immediately after breakfast Quentin drove me to Littlefield, which was already a hive of activity: some boys in the Hundreds were making up for the lost time with friends, perched right on their trunks in the lobby; and parents were unloading luggage from family cars, while their offspring rushed off to their rooms to resurrect their school lives. Classes weren't due to start until the following day, so we had plenty of time to catch up.

'Sasha, hello! How was Moscow?' Penny called on the stairs. 'Or perhaps you didn't even get there?' And with this she threw an eloquent glance at Quentin, escorting me with my suitcase in his grasp.

'It was great, minus twenty degrees, though! While you have such a lovely tan!'

Penny drew level with us. 'Yes, well, we had ten days in the Canaries, right after Christmas! Come on up to Serena's room, we're all there.'

Quentin delivered my suitcase into my new room, as I'd exchanged with Penny for the term.

CHAPTER 16

'You'll want to catch up with your friends, so I'd better be off . . . but I'll see you this evening,' said Quentin, hugging me tight. Then he kissed me and left me to unpack the few things that I needed immediately.

The door of Serena's room was flung wide and the room itself full of Littlefield girls, all vying with each other in their efforts to brag about all that they'd done while on holiday and what presents they'd got for Christmas. Serena, of course, had the longest and most impressive list of gifts and, pretending not to see me, continued with her solo performance. ('And then my grandmother excelled herself! Beside my plate on Christmas Day was a one of the family's double string of pearls and a Selfridges' gift card. . . ')

She must be still sulking about James and Alka, but really, what do I got to do with that? I fumed but tried to be gracious all the same.

'Hi, everyone! It's great to be back!' I cheerfully greeted them.

Natalie and Penny gave me warm smiles, but didn't dare to interrupt Serena. For a while I hung round in the doorway, not saying much, but after a while wearied of the recitation and returned to my new room. There I hurriedly dumped my things on the bed and headed off to New Court – I couldn't wait to see Alka and to hear about her vacation with James.

New Court was also in high gear: every five seconds the house doors swung open with more and more girls arriving, some from other houses, all gleefully screaming and hanging on each other's necks.

I found Alka in the lobby, chattering and laughing with Catherine and Nicole. Nicole had clearly gained a little weight during Christmas holidays with her lovely cheekbones slightly plumper than before; her mother's sushi had clearly been missed! Alka instantly jumped from her chair to embrace me: 'Sashka! How glad I am to see you!'

Utterly relieved, I thought: *what a lot of nonsense Quentin's dream was!*

'I was just telling the girls about my Christmas holiday with James in London,' Alka continued.

I hugged the others and joyfully joined the conversation, responding to questions about my vacation in Moscow and my solo arrival at College the previous night.

'Wow, so you were with Quentin!' Alka screamed.

'Tell us everything, in full detail!' commanded Catherine.

Then I had to disappoint everyone, explaining that Quentin and I hadn't done *it* – not yet, anyway.

'Alka's vacation was much more interesting than yours!' said Catherine reproachfully. 'And, as for mine, I met two gorgeous guys at the New Year's Eve party at my sister's house in South Kensington. They don't know about each other, of course, but Matthew promised to visit me here at College, and Chris has already invited me to spend a weekend in London. . . Older guys are so much more entertaining than our contemporaries here, who seem stuck in late childhood!'

Soon Catherine and Nicole returned to their rooms to unpack while Alka invited me to hers, promising that she had 'things' to show me. As I'd anticipated, she couldn't wait to show off the gifts with which the Browns had showered her for Christmas. For starters, she pulled out a huge Christmas stocking, full of covetable feminine paraphernalia, from brand-name cosmetics, perfumed candles and chocolates to fashionable tights, soft leather gloves and cashmere socks. Obviously, James' mother had taste! . . . Then she impatiently swung open the closet door to demonstrate her main gifts: a gold-sequined evening gown and a designer long cashmere coat.

'This is unbelievable, Alka! They're so generous!' I cried, in astonishment.

'Yes, I know! And it's all so wonderful!' Ala lovingly stroke her soft-as-velvet cashmere coat. 'But here's the main thing that I wanted to show you!' And saying this she lifted her lustrous hair up with one hand and smiling mysteriously, stared at me, without blinking, rather like a puma, or other large cat.

'The pearls are lovely!' I praised the pretty studs in her ears.

'Oh, those – James' gift,' she said, dismissively. 'But you're looking the wrong way!' And here she threw a meaningful glance downwards. Only then did I spot the stunning owl tattoo on her right shoulder.

'Do you like it? James was thrilled. I had it done secretly, in Notting Hill, just before Christmas. I could hardly dissuade him from following my example; but I preferred not to ruin my friendship with his mother, as I didn't want my first holiday in Chelsea to be my last! So, what do you think?'

'I really don't know . . . doesn't a tattoo last forever?' I asked hesitantly. 'And what if Mrs. Foxton or one of the other teachers notices it?'

Alka released her lustrous black hair over her shoulder. 'How could anyone know, if you, of course, do not tell?'

'Of course I wouldn't tell! How could you suggest such a thing! But why an owl, Alka?'

'I like birds, and an owl is wise, unlike a parrot, for example!'

Catherine and Jackie then pounced inside the room without knocking, in order to chivvy us towards Norwood Hall. Alka enjoyed the opportunity of displaying her gifts once again, and I had to listen to another round of her boasting before we reached Norwood Hall, where she instantly spotted some of James' male friends, with whom she'd celebrated New Year's Eve. She brought us along to join their table, which seemed to cheer Catherine somewhat. As she whispered to me, 'Life at Marlborough is getting *so* much better!'

However, classes started the next morning and soon life at College was back to normal.

CHAPTER 17

A month of College had gone by, half-term was near at hand and all the students were busy making plans for going places, home and away, all over the world as well as all over Britain.

In Littlefield everyone was vying with each other in consideration of the best holiday destinations, their own current plans and their preferred future arrangements. Skiing in Courchevel or sunbathing in sunny Marbella had featured at the top of the lists, until Serena, much to all the other girls' envy, announced that she would be attending a masked ball during the Venetian Carnival in a made-to-measure designer ball gown.

To my own disappointment, my parents had been obliged to postpone their visit, but promised to come in the spring, for sure. Unlike many others, neither Alka nor I much fancied going home for half-term – and not just because of the fiercely cold weather typical of February in Moscow. I really didn't want to be parted from Quentin, not even for a short while: besides, having been home for Christmas, and busy with my new independent life at College since, I had not yet had time to grow homesick.

As for Alka, I don't believe that the thought of going home had even occurred to her: the idea of spending time with her depressed mother was really uninspiring. In addition, James had announced that he had some surprise in store, so Alka told Mrs Foxton that she would be spending her holidays with the Browns, which Mrs Brown duly telephoned Alka's Housemistress to confirm.

I still couldn't decide what to do for half-term, although Catherine had most kindly invited me to stay with her in Scotland, so when Quentin asked me to spend the entire period with him, I jumped at the opportunity. Moreover, this half-term coincided with Valentine's Day and I was really looking forward to our first celebration together. I kept thinking: *I wonder what Valentine's Day is like and how the English celebrate it?*

From talking to other girls Alka and I understood that it was something like a combination of the International Women's Day of March 8th and the Red Army Day of February 23rd – both hugely popular public holidays dating from the Soviet era. In other words, chocolates, perfume and cuddly teddy bears. . . Well, what could be better?

Judging by Quentin's paintings of knights and castles – and by everything else I knew about him – he was a true romantic. *So: what can he be planning for our very first Valentine's Day?* I wondered, in high spirits, looking forward to our first holiday together.

Apart from the celebration, I was most concerned about losing my virginity. Both Quentin and I had managed to tactfully avoid this sensitive topic so far. . . In fact, knowing, or at least suspecting, that I wasn't prepared for such a big step so soon, he hadn't even mentioned it, perhaps believing that, once I'd made the decision, he would be the first to know. . . As for me, I couldn't even begin to imagine this happening with anyone else, but – whether from nerves or for some other reason – I continued to postpone this serious moment.

Quentin was so patient with me, he wanted to make it utterly beautiful and exactly the way I wanted it to be. Every time our hot love-making got closer and closer to ending every boundary between us, I always pulled away, shunning the happy ending in favour of still being able to call myself a virgin. As to how or why I managed to such a thing, I couldn't give an answer, not even to myself: just looking at the gorgeous Quentin, I felt completely ready, and could imagine melting in sensual pleasure from his lightest touch. . . As a result, my virginity had persevered until we were both more than willing for it to fall: there could be no more appropriate or symbolic date for such an event than St. Valentine's Day.

'That will be your present,' replied Alka matter-of-factly, to my question as to what I should get Quentin as a present. 'What could be sweeter than losing your cherry to him?' And she laughed at the silly English slang for this event adding rather smugly, 'Look at me, I don't miss mine at all!'

I knew – although her own mother did not – that Alka had lost her virginity in the eighth grade with her first 'grey' love, as Alka later jokingly called her whirlwind romance with a popular football player in his senior year, Sergey, or Seriy (meaning 'grey' in Russian), as he was known to everyone in our former school.

I thought: *How lucky I am that my love is nothing cynical like that: instead a bright rainbow of warm feelings overwhelms me each time I think about Quentin. Because this is not just some silly first love – some grasped-at chance to attempt to become a woman far too soon – but instead a deeply serious, all-consuming feeling, which will last for eternity. . . Every ripened cherry in my own cherry orchard was destined only for him.*

But despite these powerful feelings, I had never once heard Quentin tell me that he loved me and, following Alka's advice, I ought not to be the first to say it, no matter how much I longed to.

'A man should be the one to say it first,' she had warned me. 'Imagine, what if you say that you love him and hear only silence in response? You must never even think of giving anyone that kind of power over you – at least, not without receiving something in return.'

At the same time I couldn't even begin to imagine such a scenario. I knew in my soul that Quentin had strong and deep feelings for me. Everything he did told me that. And what about that beautiful painting that he had given me: didn't that speak for itself? Moreover, he had signed it, 'Love, Quentin,' as I recalled, perhaps trying to reassure myself. (Although signatures don't really count, I decided, after further thought. . . For example, soon after our arrival in England, Ala and I had discovered that many well-mannered English people signed everything in this way, which did not mean that they were all in love. . .)

And yet, was Quentin's and mine a real love? I couldn't find the answer to this question within my own experience, as I had nothing to compare it with, so in the end I decided to leave it to fate.

There were five days separating the beginning of the school holidays from St. Valentine's Day: five days and nights under the same roof as Quentin! The mere thought made me giddy with excitement. I couldn't help wondering: *Would we have enough patience to wait?*

On the last day of College, straight after classes, my irresistible one and only was already waiting for me outside Littlefield. As usual, I was seized with excitement at the mere sight of him; my heart pounding loudly in my chest, my breathing getting faster and faster. Quentin walked towards me, and cheerfully wrapped his arms around me, saying teasingly, 'Well, and are you ready for our first vacation together? It'll be great, you'll see!'

We rushed to collect my things, on the way up encountering Tom Perry and Chris Parker, both loaded with the heavy bags full of dirty clothes that many students, especially boys for some reason, seemed to accumulate before every holiday. We even heard a discontented female voice from a Range Rover parked in the backyard: 'Tommy! How *can* you manage to collect such piles of washing? Tell me, why do we pay the equivalent of a new BMW for you to attend here every year if they don't even give you access to a washing machine?'

Quentin and I fruitlessly attempted to squelch our laughter as we moved aside to let the boys pass. Quentin murmured to me, 'Yes, this school of yours is certainly great, but frankly I'd prefer the new BMW! You can get into Oxford *without* going to Marlborough College, after all!'

But Tom was as good-natured as ever, saying in passing, 'Hey, I wish you two a hot vacation!'

Having said goodbye to the girls, I gave my bag to Quentin and, hand in hand, we headed towards his parents' house.

He was in high spirits, saying, 'Sasha, this is so great! We'll be able to spend so many days together! I've hardly been able to wait for your holidays to start. Finally, you won't have to run to Littlefield upon hearing the church bells!' And with this he pulled me to him and planted a kiss on my cheek. 'Mum's prepared the spare room for you, but in the morning, I have to warn you, you'll be bound to have two visitors: our cats! They've become used to sleeping on that bed when the room was empty. . . As for me, I probably won't be able to fall asleep at all, knowing that you're just next door. I wish Valentine's Day would come sooner!'

'And do we have any special plans for the day?' I asked, pretending innocence.

Quentin stared at me in surprise: 'What, have you forgotten?'

'Yes, I remember, of course. I was only joking,' I assured him hastily, upon noting the distress on his face.

'Phew! I was afraid that you'd changed your mind,' sighed Quentin. 'Are you sure?'

'If you ask me one more time, I really will change my mind,' I teased him.

'Then I'll just shut up!' Absorbed, we had almost walked past his house. Quentin took the key from under the clay flowerpot at the threshold and opened the front door.

As was apparently usual on weekdays the house was empty, and even the cats were tactful enough to disappear. Seizing my hand, Quentin led me to my bedroom on the first floor, right next to his. White cotton bed linen and Turkish towels on the bed possessed the fresh scent of washing powder; a bouquet of wild flowers adorned the dressing table and the window opened onto a lovely view of rich green fields stretching behind a wooden fence.

'Here's where you'll officially sleep,' he told me, tossing my bag on the bed and pulling me close. Utterly conscious of every molecule in his body, I felt as if thousands of butterflies were fluttering inside of me, ready to fly up.

'What about unofficially?' I lowered my hand, stroking the hard bulge visible through his jeans.

'Sasha!' Quentin groaned and grabbed my hand, freewheeling me into his room. Soon his favourite brand of hard rock was sounding through the house, our clothes were scattered about, and we were completely lost in a hot embrace on his narrow bed.

'No, it's impossible! Five days is too long to wait!' I thought, half-opening my eyes in order to admire the face that had, from the first time I'd seen it, driven me half-crazy with its beauty.

Feeling my gaze upon him, Quentin opened his eyes, which burned into mine:

'Why wait until Valentine's Day? Let's do it right now!' he whispered, caressing me irresistibly, as though reading my mind.

'Not a chance! We've waited for so long, we can bear a few more days!' I whispered, showing my will-power, while feeling my body quivering with pleasure under his fingers, and almost instantly regretting my decision.

The next few days we continued to drive each other crazy, barely being able to contain ourselves. And then, the day before the long-awaited St Valentine's Day, Quentin announced that he had a surprise for me. 'Pack your things! We're not celebrating our big day at home.'

'But where?' I stared at him in astonishment, but Quentin remained mysteriously silent.

After lunch, we loaded our luggage into the boot of his old Ford and waved goodbye to his parents, who, like me, claimed to be unaware of our destination, but also seemed pleased at having their house to themselves again.

Soon the landscapes of Wiltshire's spacious fields and downy meadows were floating past us, to the sounds of The Who blasting from the car radio. Though winter, the weather in England seemed almost spring-like, a fact that never ceased to amaze me: I certainly didn't miss Moscow's drifting snows and biting February frosts.

'So, where are we going?' I asked impatiently, turning down the music.

'We're heading towards Salisbury, but that's not quite our destination, at least not today. But tomorrow, I'll certainly show it to you. We'll visit the famous Salisbury Cathedral – it's stunning – but as for the rest you'll just have to contain your curiosity for now. You'll find out soon enough!'

CHAPTER 17

Wow, I can't even crack him! I thought. This surprised me, as usually Quentin gave away to me in everything: as far as I was concerned, there were no secrets between us.

'And what's your friend doing for Valentine's Day?' Quentin asked, in what I hoped was an effort to distract me.

'She must be really busy organising another witch orgy in the woods,' I joked, recalling the letter he'd sent me in Moscow.

'It wouldn't surprise me,' he muttered, continuing along the A-road. About an hour later we arrived at a picturesque Wiltshire village, complete with delightful stone-built cottages and an ancient limestone church close to a riverbank. Slowing down, we passed an attractive old pub, probably the only one in the area, and turned left on to a narrow path meandering through various fields, where cows were phlegmatically finishing up last year's grass.

'It's somewhere along here.' Quentin murmured, slowing down to accommodate a tractor. As it passed he rolled down his window and called, 'Hi! Do you happen to know where Rose Cottage is?'

The ruddy-faced tractor driver beamed. 'You've already passed it, mate! Turn right at the store, and it's the third house along.'

'Great, thanks!'

'Rose Cottage? What a romantic name!' I breathed.

'Well, it wasn't me who named it, but apparently in the summer it's literally drowning in roses. . . Okay, since you already know where we're going, I can tell you that I convinced John to loan us his home for a few days while his whole family are in Austria, skiing. His only condition was that we don't do it in his parents' bedroom!'

I burst out laughing: 'Well, I hope they won't turn up in the inopportune moment. . . '

'This wouldn't be funny! But they have another ten days of skiing in front of them. And given that the house has four bedrooms, my promise shouldn't be too difficult to keep! There's also a snooker table, a dining table, a washing machine. . . .' Quentin gave me a meaning look and I pretended to be unimpressed, merely saying, 'You had better watch the road or we'll take that hedge with us!'

'Here's the store. I'll recognize it from here' Quentin indicated a small grocery store, which we had nearly overshot. Then he took a sharp turning to the right and pulled in by a low wooden fence behind which could be seen the reddish tiled roof of Rose Cottage.

I jumped out to open the gate and Quentin drove the car up the gravel drive.

'Apparently John's neighbours only pop up from London on weekends, so we don't have to worry about being taken for intruders.'

'Well, that's reassuring,' I mused, looking around me in delight. The freshly whitewashed cottage was set in a huge front garden and covered in climbing rose bushes, each one pruned for the winter by caring hands. 'It must look amazing, all in bloom. What a shame it's not summer now!'

Meanwhile Quentin grabbed our bags from the car boot, and headed towards the house, telling me, 'It used to be a farmhouse before the upper floor was built, turning it into a proper cottage. Apparently the core of the house dates back to the 17th century, but it's been extended, although you can tell that the interior is really old.' Quentin unlocked the door. 'Hope you're not afraid of ghosts!'

'Not while you're here,' I told him as we entered. While Quentin was unloading our food supplies in the kitchen, I peeped into the living room opposite. *So this is what a 17th-century English cottage is like* I thought, examining the setting as meticulously as if I was in a museum. . . The low whitewashed ceiling was lined with coarse wooden beams, the oak floorboards before the fireplace were covered by a Persian rug, and all the furniture appeared antique except for a comfy two-seater sofa and plushy chairs in cherry fabric. Bright summer landscapes dotted the white walls and the cross-casement windows opened out onto a back garden featuring a glorious maple tree.

CHAPTER 17

Overwhelmed with emotion, I recalled that it was here that Quentin and I were to spend our first night together, and – although I hadn't cared where it happened before – I couldn't dream of a better place than this.

'Sasha, where are you? Come here.' I heard Quentin calling from the kitchen. When he saw me he added, 'I suggest that we start celebrating right now.' Then he opened the fridge, removing a bottle covered with ice. Having expertly coped with the cork, he filled two long-stemmed glasses with effervescent white foam.

'A sparkling cava from Waitrose, supposedly just like champagne – except for the price of course! To us! Cheers!' And here Quentin raised his glass and took a gulp before asking uncertainly: 'Well, what do you think? I don't know… I never tasted cava before, but I think it's OK, although beer, of course, is miles better!'

'Not bad,' I told him, approving his choice. To be honest, the ice-cold cava could have been lemonade as far as I was concerned. Looking at him, I couldn't help thinking how strikingly handsome he was: in short, I was feeling rather weak in the knees.

Having caught my gaze, Quentin put his glass down and moved towards me. 'Let's go choose the bedroom,' he said in a low voice, pulling me close for a lingering kiss with his hands slipping down to my bum, which he enthusiastically squeezed, saying, 'Mmm, lovely!' I was thrilled to feel his excitement. We disposed of my jeans, then Quentin pulled off my sweater, alternately caressing my breasts. Then he scooped me up into his arms, putting the cold cava on my lap.

All the bedrooms were on the first floor, and he carried me up, passionately kissing and stumbling up the steep staircase. Halfway up Quentin got tired, as he stopped to gently put me down.

'You weigh a lot more than you look,' he told me, taking a gulp from the chilled bottle to catch his breath before handing it back to me.

'I'd be even heavier if I still had my jeans and sweater on,' I giggled, and following his example sipped a little more sparkling wine. The cava started to work its magic, making me feel delightfully lightheaded, as if somewhere inside me butterflies were fluttering their wings, struggling to break free.

Upstairs, we found ourselves in a long corridor with doors on all sides. Quentin opened the first to disclose a total mess: the single bed covered in clothes, posters of rock bands plastered all over the walls, and the carpet covered in boots and shoes.

'This has got to be John's room, and definitely not what we are looking for,' Quentin commented with a grin. I opened the second door to what was obviously John's parents' room, featuring a king-size bed and silver-framed family photos on the dressing table. Keeping our promise, we left it in peace.

The third room gave off a distinct whiff of damp: used primarily for storage, there were lots of cardboard boxes and in the corner beside the bed stood an old bicycle with deflated tires.

'Probably the former bedroom of John's brother Alistair, now at university in the States,' explained Quentin, slipping his hot hand into mine. He had the exquisite long fingers of a pianist, which I loved as much as I loved everything else about him. 'Well, we still have one last hope.' He nodded towards the door at the end of the corridor and we moved towards it, holding hands.

When Quentin flung the door open I gasped, not quite daring to believe my eyes: a fiery crimson velvet bedcover was almost hidden under wild petals of red roses. To my dazzled eyes it seemed to be about to burst into flame. *And I'm like a flying moth darting into the fire* I thought, throwing my arms around Quentin in a burst of love.

'Well, I couldn't possibly deprive you of roses on Valentine's day!' he told me. Then he lifted me by the waist and lightly threw me on top of the bed. Watching my manipulations with my lingerie with burning gaze, he hurriedly took off his clothes and joined me. We fell into each other's arms on an unimaginably soft blanket of fragrant roses, rolling, kissing and caressing each other with the full heat of passion on a fiery bed.

CHAPTER 17

'It's good that my friends can't see this,' Quentin murmured, covering me with rose petals from head to toe. 'Now let me kiss you properly,' he whispered, going down on me and gently playing in turns with the petals and the hot tip of his tongue between my legs. *Quentin is a genius at love!* I thought, in ecstatic anticipation of the main event. Later he joked, 'Lie back and think of England!' as he lightly lifted himself up over me.

Taking a deep breath, I leaned back on the silk-down pillows and wrapped my arms around him, my whole body thrilling to his heaviness inside me. But before I could follow his advice, it was over.

'Is that it?!' I lifted my head from the pillow in genuine surprise.

'What do you mean?' Quentin seemed quite offended. 'What did you expect?'

'I don't know… I thought it was still ahead,' I said, not even trying to hide my disappointment. I thought *Sex is so overestimated! Was it really worth waiting for it for so long? All that preceded it was so much more stunning!*

'Well, wait, let's rest a bit and we will do it again. This is only the first time. We have everything ahead of us. As my friend Will always says, the first pancake is always lumpy. For example, when Liz and I did it for the first time. . .'

Great! Now he'll start telling me about sex with Liz, I thought resentfully, sitting up and gathering my underwear, which was strewn over the floor. I glanced at Quentin, not knowing what to say.

'Sasha, I love you!' He said perplexed, peering anxiously into my eyes.

You could have said it before I thought, subconsciously feeling that what had happened between us required these or similar words.

'I love you too,' I replied, feeling numb.

'And, believe me, I'm sorry you weren't the one I lost my virginity to. It should have been you!'

This moved me deeply. Overcome by unexpected tenderness, I wrapped my arms around him and lovingly kissed him on his soft lips, while the underwear slipped from my hands back on the floor…

That evening we went to a local pub, which, according to Quentin, served the best ale in Wiltshire.

'Now we're a real couple, Sasha!' He sounded extremely pleased with our new status. 'Let's go to Salisbury tomorrow and spend the whole day there – though you may be a little tired because tonight I'll probably end up holding you all night long . . . You know, I'm almost glad I had to wait for you for so long, I'm just so lucky to have you. You're so special and wonderful – beautiful, of course, but nice at the same time. Really nice! You're the truest and realest and best. Oh Sasha, I've really fallen for you!'

Tell me more! I thought greedily, contentedly smiling while, as usual, admiring my amazing boyfriend. We quickly finished off our ale and in high spirits rushed back to the cottage. *All these months it took before I heard those longed-for words!* I thought, glancing at Quentin along the way. It all seemed worth it.

We drove to Salisbury the morning after our first grown-up breakfast together, with heated chocolate croissants, coffee and orange juice which Quentin had bought in previously.

Salisbury, known as 'the city in the countryside' turned out to be a charming old town, surrounded by a quintessentially English landscape of luscious green meadows, boundless fields, rivers and lakes. Its biggest tourist attraction was the famous Salisbury Cathedral, where we headed on Quentin's initiative, as he always enjoyed being my guide.

'This is the most stunning example of English Gothic architecture; you won't find another place like this in the whole world! Just look at the spire, the highest in England! Let's go in: I want to show you the Magna Carta.'

'The Kama Sutra?' I teased him.

'No, that's for another time,' he smiled. 'The Magna Carta is the charter of the medieval law of England, the Great Charter, and one of the only four copies remaining in the world is kept right here in Salisbury.'

Quentin slipped his arm around my waist and led me to the Chapter House, recounting its history along on the way. *I'm so in love with Quentin!* I

CHAPTER 17

was singing in my thoughts, listening to his impassioned history lesson with only half an ear.

After the Charter House we easily covered the 300 or so stairs to the very top of the Cathedral in order to admire the splendor of the view. *Life is just so wonderful! With him every day is like Valentine's Day!* I thought, fervently kissing Quentin in the teeth of the surprisingly powerful wind.

The following five days and nights we spent in the Rose Cottage, until we had exhausted our Waitrose food supplies. Occasionally, we went to Salisbury or visited the local village pub: with Quentin every place was incomparable, but most of our time was spent in bed. *Sex is just so bloody marvelous!* I had concluded by the time it was time for us to return to Marlborough. . .

On the last day of our holiday we carefully removed every trace remaining of our presence and bade farewell to our love-nest. I had to return to College while Quentin was looking forwards to seeing his Marlborough friends. I couldn't help wondering how all my own friends had spent their Valentine's Day, while I was looking forward to telling them about mine – though not all about it, of course! With classes starting the next day, that evening I reluctantly returned to College, already missing Quentin.

As it turned out, on Valentine's Day, Ala had gone to Paris with James (and with his parents, which didn't seem to please her quite as much) where they had all stayed at the Ritz Paris.

'A magnificent city! You must see Paris before you die, as they famously say back in Russia. I am just so in love with Paris!' she marveled.

'With Paris? What about with James?' I asked.

'Let men fall in love with you, but never fall in love yourself!' she advised me in rather a patronising tone. However, I couldn't have agreed less with this philosophy.

My other friends from New Court had also had Valentines: it turned out that Catherine had enjoyed two, while Nicole, returning from Tokyo, had met a young countryman on the plane who was planning to study in the UK, and they had already made plans for the upcoming weekend. For her part, Chris was still wondering about a secret Valentine who had sent her a card (written in a hand suspiciously similar to Catherine's, in my private opinion) and Jackie declared that she didn't need a man at College, but naturally none of us believed her.

CHAPTER 18

Quentin was blissfully happy with Sasha – happier than he could have even imagined only ten months ago, when Liz had dumped him for a cricketer. The last thing he had expected was to fall in love again – but from the moment he had seen Sasha's sweet face he had felt as if he'd come home.

It no longer hurt to remember how inconsolable he had been over Liz – how he had gone so far, hot-eyed and worn out with weeping in the blackness of his room, as to briefly consider overdosing and even to imagine his funeral: Liz remorseful, his parents wishing that they had offered more generous sympathy, his aunt and uncle – for once – not arguing but instead united in sorrow for such a promising life cut short. . . He had imagined Swindon Grammar School subdued and stricken, including the words the Headmaster had used ('Popular and gifted, even brilliant . . . thoughtful and caring . . . a stunning career ahead of him.')

Sentimental, affectionate and deeply attached to his first love, Quentin had certainly suffered more than most when the relationship had ended, but the natural resilience of youth, the excitement of getting his exam results and the beckoning pleasures of Oxford University had all served to console him – along with his favorite music, which during that period featured mostly hard rock and heavy metal.

In Quentin's mind the beauty of rock – so hard, powerful and incredibly intense, but also mellow and at times fragile – was almost spiritual: it would always answer his soul's silent prayer in its 'hour of need' with some perfect song.

The gut-wrenching pain of betrayal felt like his darkest hour, something which Megadeth, one of his favorite bands at the time, really understood. They sympathetically looked down at him from the posters on his walls as if telling him: 'Hold on, friend! We stand by you!' whilst their sorrowful anthem bled from his speakers.

In my hour of need
Ha, you're not there
And though I reach out for you
Wouldn't lend a hand
Through the darkest hour
Grace did not shine on me
It feels so cold, very cold
No one cares for me

Too right, Quentin had thought, and *Wow, even the toughest, most talented, world-famous rockers feel really sad when betrayed and abandoned.* He listened to this song over and over, identifying passionately with Mustaine, the king of metal, who also must have been once left by someone with no mercy, someone who '*in his hour of need just laughed, ha, ha, bitch!*' Quentin also felt obscurely validated by his suffering, altered overnight into an adult, someone with a tragic past from which he had emerged strong, as strong as Megadeth . . .

Their bond must be perpetuated for posterity! decided Quentin one day without realizing that art, at which he was gifted, was another part of his recovery.

He turned his sound system to its wildest level, until his ears were almost ringing with it, and begun enthusiastically mixing the paint for his masterpiece. He was soon completely swallowed up in the process of designing and decorating the back of his secondhand black leather jacket. Completely intent, he didn't even notice that it had grown dark, that his parents were about to return from work, and that he was both hungry and deeply thirsty.

Finally, he tossed the brush aside and gave his work a long, critical examination. With a surge of pleasure he could not find no faults: a steel plate was covering the eyes, the mouth, eternally silent, was ruthlessly clamped shut, and the ears deafened with metal caps, while the skull was macabre and the juxtaposition of timbres perfect! An inscription «Megadeth» in yellow acrylic was added, but still the bare vulnerability of the skull looked so sad and lonely. . . He thought with an uprush of sorrow: *What if I never fall in love again?* Suddenly Quentin took up a new brush and plunged the skull into blood-red roses with prickly thorns, which he could almost feel piercing his heart. '*Love is not all a bed of roses, it has thorns which could make you bleed. . .*' Finally, he carefully lifted up the jacket, admiring his own artwork: Megadeth with roses, but without weapons, so no sensible person could accuse him of plagiarizing Guns 'N Roses. Only then did he realise that the entire room was stinking with pungent paint chemicals and, except for his direct lamp, almost entirely in darkness. Flinging the window open, he carried his precious cargo to the empty garage to dry, anticipating how the next day everyone at school would gasp in admiration when he turned up wearing it . . .

From his earliest years, Quentin had been unusually forward. Having learned to read at three, by the age of five he was studying everything he came across – comic strips, the children's encyclopedia, fantasy books, and even bits out of the newspaper, while his vocabulary, confidence and articulateness impressed everybody who met him.

Nobody knew that the youthful Quentin occasionally saw things that the rest of the family had never seen: he had secret friends who played with him and kept him company: when he couldn't sleep, they visited him.

When he was staying with his grandmother in Bath, he had made friends with little Becky. She seemed to him such a sweet, fragile girl, who also spoke in a fascinating way – no one he'd ever met used such old-fashioned turns of phrase. She wore unusual clothes too: a frilly cap and a long white lace dress, clothes that reminded him of a porcelain-faced Victorian doll that he had once seen in an antique shop. Quentin saw nothing odd in the fact that Becky lived in his grandmother's attic, and he solemnly promised her not to tell anyone about her. When he had asked how old she was, Becky evasively replied that she had passed her eighth birthday. Quentin was quite satisfied with this: he had always liked older playmates. She knew his grandmother's house from top to bottom and at night, when his grandma was safely asleep, they ventured into the cluttered closets, the dusty attic, and even played hide-and-seek in the huge cellar, which, according to Becky, had been used as a place of punishment when the house had been part of an orphanage.

Quentin was never bored by Becky, and eventually Becky introduced him to Jack, a mischievous lad, also sporting very old-fashioned clothes, who lived next door with an elderly couple. He often played tricks upon them: creaking old floorboards, moving things at night, hiding jars of jam, and switching round the hands of the clock, but the old couple had poor eyesight and sometimes failed to notice. Offended that he had been ignored, he would sometimes ran over to play with Becky and Quentin, swearing he'd never return home, but always forgave the oldies at the end of whatever game they were playing.

In addition to his secret playmates Quentin also loved his aunt Esther, his mother's elder sister, who lived with her husband in Oxford but often visited. This childless lady took great pleasure in showering her precocious young nephew with presents, but she also talked to him like to an adult, asking for his opinions and sincerely admiring his answers. 'You're so lucky!' she told Debbie enviously one day, unaware that Quentin was hidden close by. 'How I wish I had a son like yours!'

Later Quentin, who was four at the time, confided to her that he would be happy to be her son and to have two mothers. Greatly touched, Aunt Esther shed a tear, which made Quentin worry that he had upset her. On his seventh birthday Aunt Esther gave him a beautiful electric train set that Quentin set up in the garage. The train made a long hoot and rushed around the tiny village before disappearing in a tunnel through the plastic mountains. Quentin was utterly entranced. However, his Mom warned him that it was a very expensive gift, and that he had to be truly careful with it, so he was only allowed to play with it on weekends (at which point he did indeed regret that Aunt Esther was not his second mother. . .) As it turned out, his aunt was enduring treatment for a terminal cancer, and when a few months later Quentin's mother told him

CHAPTER 18

that she had gone to heaven, he was extremely hurt that she had left without saying goodbye. So he was not in the least astonished when one night, just before he drifted off to sleep, she came and sat composedly on the edge of his bed. As usual, they talked and laughed; at the end of the chat she kissed him on the forehead exactly as she'd used to and left through the door. The next morning the eight-year-old came downstairs for breakfast and told his mother blithely, 'You're a fibber. Aunt Esther can't be in heaven yet, because she came to visit me last night!'

'Poor little love, he misses his aunt so much that he's been imagining God knows what,' thought Debbie. She was a materialist, and didn't believe in other worlds.

One of Quentin's favorite pastimes as a young lad was to explore the local woods. He was forbidden to go there, but it was his favorite place, so he tagged along with some older boys whenever he could. There they climbed trees and scuttled around the woods with toy guns or pretend swords, fighting numerous invisible enemies. One day they were playing Romans and barbarians. Quentin, the sole barbarian, was sitting in a small, overgrown ravine expecting an assault from the Romans – Andy and Gavin – at any moment. It was difficult to say for how long he had been waiting, but his legs were numb and his hands had grown very tired from holding up the heavy sword, so he put the sword down. Perhaps Andy and Gavin hadn't been able to find him and had either given up or run home for lunch . . . *I wonder what we'll have for lunch,* he thought. Quentin remained in ambush for a short while longer, until his stomach started to growl. He had just fetched his sword and emerged from the ravine when he saw a beautiful dappled doe, poised as if frozen, only few steps away. The pink lobes of her ears were slightly twitching, her high forehead featured black and beige oval markings resembling eyebrows while her fine nostrils were delicately distending. Suddenly turning his head, the creature stared at Quentin with a worried look in her huge velvet eyes. For a moment both stood absolutely still, as if hypnotized.

'Should I run or not?' the idea flashed across Quentin's mind. 'He doesn't seem dangerous – he's small and there's no rifle. If he moves I'll leap into those bushes, and he'll never be able to catch me up.'

Stunned, Quentin realised that he was listening to the thoughts of the doe. He took a hesitant step towards her; the doe startled as if awakened from a trance, and instantly disappeared in the bushes.

Elated, Quentin thought, over and over, about what had happened: had he really 'heard' the mind of the deer? Longing to make sure, every time he ran into the woods, he rushed to the place where he'd seen the doe, hoping to see her again. He never did however, and eventually the powerful impression was almost erased from his memory and he decided that he must have made it up.

When Quentin turned ten, his mother brought home a couple of tiny twin kittens with white spots on the chest and white cuffs on the paws. They were touchingly squinting their hardly-open eyes – they had only just left their mother, and drank milk through a pipette. Quentin couldn't bear to leave them for a moment, fussing over them and playing with them. At first Debbie worried that he had abandoned his fascination with learning in favour of the tiny creatures but eventually Quentin returned to his books and the kittens grew up, though they remained attached to him, following him around the house and bringing him gifts of dead birds and mice after a night's hunting. Quentin could occasionally 'hear' what the cats were thinking too – which made him immediately revise his opinion of what had happened in the woods with the little doe.

Both cats, once grown, became remarkable predators and local troublemakers: hunting, enjoying fights with neighboring male cats and, of course, pursuing any female cats in the area. The neighborhood abounded in other cats and, fearing complaints from the neighbors, Debbie decided to sterilize them both, making an appointment at the vets for the following Tuesday.

Upon returning from school, Quentin was surprised that the cats failed to greet him. Instead, they were huddled in different corners of the sofa, looking crushed, while the bowl of dry food on the kitchen floor was untouched.

'What's wrong with you, guys?' asked Quentin, thinking out loud. 'Maybe you need to see the vet.'

Suddenly he heard Tom's thoughts: 'No, no, no! I don't know what Harry's going to do, but I will definitely run away before Tuesday, in order to remain a real man.' Meanwhile his brother Harry was silent, apparently deeply depressed.

When his mother returned from work, Quentin started fervently begging her not to take the cats to the vet on Tuesday.

'But how did you know?' Debbie marveled. 'Did your father spill the beans?' But Quentin didn't say, for fear of sounding silly.

However, the boy loved the cats so much, his beautiful eyes were filled with tears, and in spite of all her commonsense objections, his mother allowed him to talk her out of it. 'All right, but only until I hear a single complaint from the neighbors,' she warned him and the threat of the operation was lifted.

The cats cheered up immediately and ran to devour their food, but Quentin warned them, 'Behave yourselves, guys, if you want to stay out of harm's way and keep your jewels!' However, they either didn't listen or didn't understand for soon they were back to their old habits and, after a number of complaints from the neighbours, they were both sterilized. The cats didn't hold this against Quentin however: they knew he had tried his best.

From his birth Quentin didn't resemble anyone on either side of the family. By his thirteenth birthday he was a tall, somewhat lanky, but strikingly handsome teenager who looked like a fostered child. The boy's academic prowess was as extraordinary as his appearance, a fact that didn't go unnoticed amongst his parents' friends and acquaintances. Two main hypotheses were secretly conjectured: an adoption or a questionable paternity. Those who had known the family for a long time rejected the adoption theory: Debbie had certainly been pregnant and had just as certainly given birth to a baby boy at Swindon maternity hospital. In any case, the version of the mysterious paternity was far more exciting to the imagination.

Debbie, a pleasant but quite ordinary and undistinguished woman was thus invested with an aura of mystery. Some recollected that a handsome, raven-headed Italian nobleman had stayed in the vicinity the year before Quentin was born. Others recalled a famous if elderly Hollywood actor who had briefly hid from paparazzi in a Wiltshire manor house around the same time. Yet nobody quite believed these stories either, as no one could quite conceive what interest Debbie could have aroused in noblemen or celebrities. . .

As a very young child, Quentin had thrilled to the idea of starting school; however, he was almost immediately disappointed. The curriculum was too simple for him and he quickly lost interest, as the lion's share of every teacher's time was focused on very basic school material for the benefit of the rest of the class. Quentin could answer almost any question offered, something he had at first demonstrated with such unconscious superiority that it made some of his contemporaries term him a 'smart-ass'. Later, he decided not to stand out too much, sometimes even purposely giving wrong answers in class. (Some of his cleverer teachers guessed the reason why.)

At heart Quentin yearned to break free from school into a world where his talents would be noticed and appreciated. From a very young age he longed to go to university, but just at the moment – whichever moment it happened to be – his immediate objective was to assert his position at school, and to become one of the more popular boys. This was harder than it ought to have been but Quentin was always a little shy, a little sensitive, and perhaps a little sophisticated for his age, while at the same time very susceptible to criticism. He had left school joyfully, though keeping in touch with a few close friends, and had just been looking forward to Oxford when he had first met Sasha in town outside the wine shop. . .

Which, of course, had changed everything.

CHAPTER 19

Warm April sunshine streamed through the window as the Lent term came to an end. My romance with Quentin was in full bloom and we were really looking forward to spending Easter together in Marlborough. I had already asked Mrs. Graham's permission to remain in Littlefield, and – having taken a short time to consider – she had agreed, on condition that I continued to abide by College rules and to diligently prepare for my final examinations. Overjoyed, I had promised to be on my best behavior, especially as I was planning upon spending most of the time at Quentin's anyway . . . In addition, my parents were coming to London for Easter and I longed to introduce my boyfriend to them.

Alka didn't choose to go home either: apparently she had a new boyfriend who had invited her to spend the vacation with him in London. For the first time since I'd known her Alka had turned secretive – so secretive that, no matter how hard I tried to find out about her boyfriend, she would tell me nothing.

In fact she slammed the door on my curiosity, saying only, 'He's quite a well-known person in certain circles and I can't just drop his name here and there. He wouldn't like anyone finding out that he's dating a schoolgirl, even one from Marlborough College. Besides, when the time comes, you'll be the first to know everything!'

I only hope he's not married I thought, but said nothing. I still felt truly sorry for James: he'd been looking like a ghost ever since Ala had dumped him a few weeks ago. I couldn't understand how she could have behaved so cruelly to someone as good-natured and pleasant as James.

At last the final day of Lent term arrived. By lunchtime a massive queue of parental Volvos and Range Rovers was already lined up around Central

Court, together with two white mini-buses collecting students for the airport; while the sluggish driver of a stretch Rolls Royce – to overall resentment – had succeeding in blocking the drive to the College gates. In Central Court everyone was rushing around, loaded with trunks, golf clubs, tennis racquets and rugby balls, their arms full of boxes of books, files, clothes and God knows what . . . Some students I knew waved me goodbye, or wished me a happy Easter before I heard the revving of their departing cars and they swept away.

The College soon emptied, and I returned to Littlefield with the keys Mrs Graham had entrusted to me in order to look for something to eat in the kitchen pantry. . . 'Not bad,' I thought, upon triumphantly spotting a jacket potato and some baked beans to microwave.

Afterwards I couldn't decide how to occupy myself until my date with Quentin, so I wandered around the deserted house thinking over my further plans. How I missed Alka's lively chatter! To kill time I decided to sort out my wardrobe but, as I didn't own a lot of stuff, this took only ten minutes.

'I need to make a study plan for my A-levels,' I told myself, but the idea of doing this on the very first day of holidays didn't appeal at all. . . Finally I decided to walk into town. I had just reached that High Street and was heading in the direction of Waitrose when suddenly somebody called my name from Café Rene. It was Chris, having a coffee and a smoke with some friends at one of the outside tables.

'Sasha! Where have you left Quentin?'

'Hi, Chris! He's got some family commitment in Bath but I'll be meeting him in about an hour's time.'

'Tell him I was looking for him,' Chris suggested. 'How come you're not surrounded by all your College friends?'

'It's the holidays,' I replied, rather sadly.

'Of course. By the way, we all like you – especially since Quentin told us that you were cool about his hobby.' And here Chris chuckled, tucking one of his hair braids behind his ear.

CHAPTER 19

'What hobby do you mean?'

'Ha ha, very funny! Just tell him from me, that tomorrow evening there's going to be a massive party – Sean's parents are out of town. We're all meeting at the Royal Oak at seven before heading over.'

Chris must have noticed the look of bewilderment on my face, because he added, 'Tell you what, just tell him to find me in town; I should be playing snooker in the Green Dragon later on.'

I agreed, then waved goodbye and headed on down the road. Upon returning to Littlefield, I found Quentin waiting for me on a bench outside the house.

'Hi, I've missed you!' He folded me in his arms, adding ecstatically, 'Finally, we can be alone!' We rushed up to my room, passionately embracing on the stairs. An empty Littlefield felt strange, but rather thrilling too.

'It's time we baptized that bed of yours! Who knows when we'll have another chance like this one?' teased Quentin, preparing to lingeringly undress me.

I didn't mind – not in the least – but suddenly, we heard a firm step ascending the stairs, and, just as we sprang away from each other, the door of my room swung open.

Mr. Graham was standing in the doorway. I'd had no idea that he was even still in town. 'Hi, guys,' he greeted us, peaceably enough. 'Just checking who it was. Thought I heard voices in here.'

Mr Graham had always been well-disposed towards Quentin, especially since he had discovered that my boyfriend had been accepted by Oxford University.

'Hope you two haven't been up to anything naughty,' he joked, probably noticing our crimson faces. 'It's too nice a day to hang around indoors!' (Indeed the weather was great: I was wearing a tank-top and jeans.) 'Hey, here's a thought. Quentin, why don't you help Sasha to prepare for her A-levels? Although her grade forecasts are encouraging, it's not going to be a pushover, what with English not being her mother tongue.'

'I'd be delighted to – though I'm sure that with her determination she'll pass with flying colors,' Quentin assured him.

Mr Graham looked pleased. 'Well, Sasha, you've got the keys to the house, so please make sure you don't lose them! As you know, we'll be spending Easter in Somerset with my relatives. I know that my wife has shared our phone numbers with you already. Should there be an emergency or if you simply need something, don't hesitate to call.'

'Thank you,' I told him, very gratefully.

'Also, most of the housemasters will be staying in college for the Easter break. They're aware you'll be here, so they might pop in to see you – and Quentin, if he's here, of course.'

'To be honest, Mr. Graham, I'm not entirely happy about Sasha being here entirely on her own,' said Quentin suddenly. 'I think it'd really be better if she came and stayed with my family. We're only just around the corner.'

'But what about your parents?' I questioned. 'Did you ask them about this?' But I was only asking out of courtesy: inside I was already triumphing in eager anticipation of our being together throughout the holidays.

'It's fine. My mum will be only too glad.'

'Excellent!' approved Mr. Graham, clearly much relieved that he wouldn't – even at a distance – be directly responsible for me. 'Have a lovely Easter, both of you!' With this he hugged me, in his usual paternal fashion, and left us alone.

I quickly tossed some clothes and make-up together. Then Quentin threw my back-pack over his shoulder and we headed towards his house in high spirits, looking forward to our freedom.

Except for the cats, the house was deserted and we had plenty of time to ourselves before his parents returned from work. We went up to his room, and soon all our clothes was scattered around, while we were lost to everything except each other, and the howling of Jimmy Hendrix in the background of course.

CHAPTER 19

'Foxy lady,' repeated Quentin, kissing me tenderly afterwards. 'Let's listen to his "Angel" now – such a cool song, it's also about you – oh Sasha, I was so lucky to meet you in town that day!'

'No, it was me who was lucky!' I protested, kissing him back.

'Well, you were lucky too,' agreed Quentin, swapping Hendrix for Led Zeppelin. Then I suddenly remembered my earlier meeting with Chris. Quentin frowned when I gave him the message, adding: 'I don't want to take you to that party – and, of course, I won't go anywhere without you. Let`s just spend the evening together instead. Perhaps we could rent a video and watch a movie?'

'But why? I don`t mind going to a party,' I said obstinately, digging in my heels.

'It wouldn't be the kind of party you probably have in mind,' he told me. Then he grew thoughtful. 'But you have tried drugs before, right? You told me you had after reading that letter of mine last Christmas.'

I vaguely remembered telling him about experimenting with drugs while back in Russia . . . a slight exaggeration on my part. I wasn't sure what might be the correct English word for the scruffy rollup Alka had assembled using some weed or other that she brought back from her grandmother's home in Altai. I think I inhaled it – at most – only once, before breaking into a nasty cough. I'd hastily returned it, having no desire to have another go. . .

How Quentin or Alka or anyone else could possibly enjoy getting high on something like that, I could not grasp. In fact, my entire knowledge about drugs beyond this single experience had been culled from lessons and warnings about 'Class A' drugs: heroin, cocaine and some amphetamines: all of which struck me at least as scary, dirty and prohibited.

The very word 'drugs' conjured up images in my imagination of a hopeless drug-addict, arms pock-marked with injections, or a prostitute, giving themselves for the cost of a single dose, or possibly runaway teens from vaguely delinquent families. All the kinds of things which couldn't possibly have anything to do with Quentin or me.

Everything in my life was so perfect: I was head over heels in love with Quentin and I had no desire to leave my reality for any other world – after all, I had everything that I could possibly wish for right in front of me! At the same time, though, I so longed to be 'cool' – and I also longed not to disappoint Quentin.

'It's such an incredible feeling!' He'd suddenly become inspired. 'You can't even imagine it until you've tried it. And if we did it together, we'd grow even closer. . .'

The feeling hadn't sounded all that incredible in his endless Christmas letter, but I was too polite to remind him of this. Especially when he pulled my hand to his lips, tenderly caressing my palm and saying, 'I want to share everything with you, Sasha. I'm tired of hiding anything from you!'

Seeing that I wasn't protesting, Quentin continued: 'Just imagine what a high you could experience having sex while on drugs. Not that I've ever tried it,' he added hastily, 'but Will once said. . . Of course, it isn't for novices, or to be tried in the forest either – it's practically impossible not to freak out in there! . . . Well, anyway, if you're sure, we could go to Sean's party tomorrow. However, it's not too late to change your mind. Just tell me if you feel doubtful,' he added, observing my hesitation. 'I just want you to be happy. But it might be the most exciting evening of your life!'

'I'm happy,' I told him. 'Let's go to the party together.'

'Fantastic! Let's go find Chris, just to confirm.'

Without wasting any more time, we wandered around town, where we finally discovered Chris, playing snooker with Sean in one of the pubs. We all got some beer while Quentin joined his friends in a game. I spent most of the time serenely admiring my devastatingly handsome boyfriend, and not giving a second thought to the party.

After 'last orders' we left the pub to get a couple of hamburger from a local fast-food place before hurrying to his parents' house, taking Debbie and Peter rather by surprise.

'Sasha will be staying with us for the holidays,' declared Quentin. Luckily, they had no opposition to make and, refusing dinner, we slipped upstairs together.

CHAPTER 19

The next evening, as planned, Quentin and I headed towards the Royal Oak. Just inside the door we bumped into Chris, Sean and two other guys whose names I didn't catch, all heading off to Sean's house.

'See you at Sean's,' Chris told us, 'but you'd better hurry up before he leaves,' and here he nodded towards an older-looking, rather scruffy guy, sitting on his own in a corner with his hat half-covering his eyes. 'He can't hang around for long. The police have caught him before and the local barmen know his face.'

'Great, see you later,' Quentin nodded and moved towards the bar, still holding my hand. Having ordered us both half-pints, he discreetly wandered over to the older guy, asking him for a light. The deal clearly came off, as Quentin returned looking pleased and whispered in my ear that he'd got me 'a strawberry'. He opened his hand to reveal a tiny scrap of paper with a bright red berry drawn on it, as if by a child.

'Put it just under your tongue and don't drink anything, except for maybe a few sips of beer,' he advised.

For himself Quentin had chosen a cute Mickey Mouse, which immediately disappeared inside his mouth.

'OK, we can go now,' he said, glancing at his wristwatch. 'The others are waiting for us at Sean's.'

Still holding hands, we sauntered along the High Street towards St. Peter's Church. 'His house is quite nearby, so we don't have much time before it kicks in,' advised Quentin.

I didn't feel any effect at all. *But what could you expect from a scrap of paper?* I thought incredulously.

'Do you feel anything?'

'Not a thing.'

'You will,' Quentin promised me.

We soon reached Sean's house, where his friends had already occupied most of the lounge, slumping on couches and armchairs in front of a TV watching *The Doors* with Van Kilmer as Jim Morrison. We brought in some chairs from the kitchen and joined them.

'Hi, guys! The party's started!' exclaimed Chris in great excitement, appearing from the kitchen and then running gleefully back again.

'He dropped some acid well before us,' Sean told us.

Meanwhile, Chris's exultant screams could be heard from the kitchen: 'Look at the knife! It's doubled in size and is still growing!'

'Put the knife back, kid,' his friend advised. 'You'd do better to come here and join us.'

Chris's behavior when he did was pretty strange. 'Oh, Jim, the Lizard King!' he cried, pointing at the TV, 'How fucking brilliant you are, Morrison! How many times I have heard that song but this is the best ever, do you hear that, Jimmy? – I love you, man!'

He was about to kiss the screen, but then flopped back into an armchair, still staring intently. 'What! He's getting out. . . . Look! Just look! Wow, what's the matter with his head? Turn it off, turn it fucking *off!*' he suddenly protested, almost violently. 'I hate watching TV on acid, let's just put the Stones on.' Nobody made any objection as he switched off the TV and turned on the music: we just continued sitting around, occasionally glancing tensely at the clock on the wall.

'Over half an hour,' murmured Quentin, turning to me. 'How are you, Sasha? Do you feel any different?'

'Not yet,' I replied, not having the vaguest idea what to expect anyway.

'What about your leg then?'

I looked at him puzzled and suddenly noticed that all of us except Chris were sitting with crossed legs, and in each case the upper leg was reflexively jumping up and down, faster and faster, gaining speed. 'Like synchronized swimming,' I thought, giggling along with the rest.

'That's it, it's started,' said Sean.

'The ceiling's moving!' exclaimed Quentin, 'Don't you see it?' he asked me.

CHAPTER 19

Something was happening to the ceiling: it was crawling and quivering under my stare, my leg was shaking, my heart was thumping and the weirdness of it all didn't appeal to me in the least.

'Check out that vase, the vase with the flowers!' howled Chris, 'I've seen gorgons there!'

The vase was a real work of art: brazenly colourful, it was textured like something out of Van Gogh: how had I never noticed that before? And the music! The Stones were so mind-blowing! I could hear each note as keenly as if I'd been playing it. 'From now on I'll listen only to the Rolling Stones,' I thought, and shared this vow with Quentin.

'I told you it'd be great,' my boyfriend rejoiced. 'Believe me, this is just the beginning, it'll get even better!' His voice sounded somehow unusual, as if from inside a deep tunnel. Then everyone got rather rowdy, running around the house in excitement, or giggling to themselves while admiring something strange. The objects around the house suddenly seemed to spring into life, moving and gleaming, their colours vivid, wired, unreal. I seemed to be able to hear every sound, even from a distance, while the carpet was crawling like green snakes under my feet, and I could feel my heart speeding faster and faster in my chest.

But where was Quentin? I glanced around, not seeing him anywhere. Suddenly, an idea rushed into my head: 'What am I doing here? Who are these guys? I don't know them! What do they have on their minds?'

I felt my palms sweating, my heart kept skipping beats and the mirror on the wall crept noiselessly out of its frame, casting its metallic eye on me. In sudden panic I cried out, 'Quentin? Quentin! Where are you? I'm scared!'

'Oh shit, that's just what I was afraid of,' murmured Quentin, springing towards me. 'What's wrong? Have you seen something bad? It's all not real, nothing's real, just relax and enjoy the show!'

But I grabbed at his arm.

'Is it her first trip?' Sean asked.

'Yeah, I think so.'

'Go upstairs into one of the bedrooms and let her get some sleep.'

We fell on an upstairs bed fully clothed, and simultaneously the panic I'd already experienced gripped me in its steely embrace: some huge shadows were reaching up to smother me, even though Quentin hadn't switched the light off. I snuggled into the pillow face down, shuddering, while Quentin attempted to console me: 'Everything'll be fine, Sasha, I'm right here. Remember, I love you so much and by tomorrow absolutely everything will be back to normal. If only I'd known you'd never tried it before, I'd never have given it to you. Why did you pretend?'

'I don't know, I can't remember!'

'Well, just try and relax. What can you see?'

But I was hardly listening to him because at that point my consciousness, as if detached from my body, was going hell for leather somewhere up into the vast darkness. It felt amazing! I was gaining more and more speed, flying straight up into the blackness of the star-studded night. Soon I was glancing down from a bird's height, then from a skyscraper height, spotting College buildings and roads I recognised and Quentin's house itself. . . Then, I circled around some castle on the hill and flew above a huge haystack before rushing off again, gaining height at tremendous speed.

Perhaps, I'm somewhere in space I thought, admiring some stunningly ice-blue stars along my way. But just as suddenly, I panicked: *But how will I get back, having flown so far? I don't want to stay out here! I have to get back!* – And I cried out but nobody was listening, and I was spiraling higher and higher into the empty darkness…

My heart was beating fast enough to leap out of my chest, when I heard a voice from somewhere over my head: 'A heart attack. Just wait until the hospital. . . ' and then I was back but still not inside my body. Instead I was being rushed along endless hospital corridors, watching myself from somewhere just above. Heavy doors swung open before me, but I was being taken, I was helpless. It felt almost as if I'd been locked in some different dimension, a parallel universe, or as if I had been kidnapped into appearing in some terrible film, in which I was playing myself.

Maybe I don't even exist anymore? – but wait, I probably do or I wouldn't be hovering like this, thought the person inhabiting my head, and *I might not know it, but everyone else knows that I've been put in some mental hospital. . .*

All night I was either writhing around in terrified anguish, storming somewhere in the darkness, or else crying in Quentin's arms. I felt I'd lost myself and couldn't find my way back – I felt utterly devastated. Eventually I fell into some crazy dream . . . but if the night had been a nightmare, the next morning turned out even worse.

I woke at dawn, alone. 'Thank you, God! I came back!' I thought, looking around the bedroom joyfully. Then I heard voices from the kitchen below. Soon after, Chris appeared in the bedroom doorway. . . Yes, I thought, it was Chris, but he looked terrible, as if he'd aged overnight, and both puffy-faced and strangely gaunt.

'How are you feeling, Sasha? Quentin's downstairs. He was so worried about you that he didn't sleep a wink.'

'I think I'm better.'

'I'm still coming round after mine: it was wicked! But you must have had a bad trip. . . '

While he blundered on I was intently gazing around. Everything seemed pretty normal, but strangely in motion and eerily quiet. The white ceiling was still crawling and the bedside lamp seemed to be shimmying. I felt upset and disappointed not to feel completely normal, recalling bitterly that Quentin had promised that I'd be fine in the morning. . .

Then Chris left and Quentin appeared. His face was troubled; he crossed to the bed and hugged me tight: 'Sasha, my love, I told you that it would be over in the morning! Listen, we need to leave as soon as we can, because Sean`s parents are due back any second. He's busy cleaning up the mess Chris made last night. . . '

He continued, but I had stopped listening. My attention had been drawn to my inner monologue: *So, everyone else is OK now, but I seem to have gone mad and stayed in a world where everything, even inanimate objects, seems able to move and wriggle and behave as if they were alive! What will happen when everyone finds out that I've gone mad? I'll probably be put in hospital, but who knows whether I can be treated? And what if they take me to a hospital in Moscow? – what would happen? What about College and my A-level exams? How could I possibly have been so stupid? Everything was so great but I had to go and wreck it!*

I was consumed with despair, and objects still seemed to be rearing and roaring at me from every corner of the room.

'Sasha, are you listening?' Quentin's voice sounded from miles away, though he was close by my side. 'I didn't get any sleep,' he told me, gently stroking my hair. 'Let's go home and get some rest. Please, get ready! I'll be waiting downstairs. . . ' As he left I thought I heard him say, 'Love you,' as from an enormous distance.

I slowly got out of bed and moved towards the wardrobe, which featured full-length mirrored doors. Some crumpled stranger looked back at me, strangely at a loss. She was dressed the same way I was, I thought doubtfully, in a Miss Selfridges sailor top and fashionably faded Levis, but she was a dwarf, as if in a fairground mirror, with ugly stumpy legs. . . Oh God, it *couldn't* be me! I had long, elegant slender legs – my tennis coach in Moscow had told me that I had the build of a professional player! . . . As for this person's face, I couldn't bear it! No, it was definitely not me! I was on the verge of actual hysterics as my most tormenting fear seemed confirmed: I had really lost my mind: I couldn't even recognize myself in the mirror.

The window, which had been left slightly ajar, then caught my eye and some strange, almost magnetic force seemed to pull me towards it.

'Yes! I simply must jump! I'd be able to fly, just as I did last night,' I thought, with a huge wave of relief. The idea represented itself to me as the

CHAPTER 19

perfect method of escape from my predicament: the notion possessed me, I could think of nothing else.

I opened the window. From above, it looked sufficiently high for a nice take-off, and I was just taking a breath when suddenly someone caught my arm from behind. 'Hey, what do you think you're doing?'

I turned around to see one of the guys from the party, who had luckily left his jacket in the same bedroom. He yelled, 'Quentin! for chrissake come and get your crazy girlfriend! She was about to jump out of the window!' He was still grasping my arm so hard it hurt.

Crazy! I repeated to myself. *That's exactly who I am now! He knows!*

Suddenly I remembered the local schizophrenic, an older guy who meandered around Marlborough with his headphones on jabbering incessantly about time warps and outer space.

Oh, my God! I thought, horrified, *I'll be like him. Quentin will be ashamed of me and dump me and everyone will feel sorry for me and pretend not to see me. . . I've got to try to still seem normal!* By this point Quentin had reappeared, looking extremely concerned.

'It's not what he thinks! I just wanted a little fresh air!' I reassured him hastily, and, making a real effort to collect myself, followed him down the stairs.

On the way to his house I felt chilled to the bone so Quentin thoughtfully covered my shoulders with his leather jacket – the one with the Megadeth skull skillfully drawn on its back. I tried not to look around too much: the High Street itself seemed to loom towards me. Covertly, I attempted to dry my tears which, probably together with smeared mascara, were quietly streaming down my cheeks.

Quentin tried to cheer me. 'We're lucky it's only half-six and nobody's about. Don't get so upset! I'm also still tripping a little: the acid was really strong this time. Give it until lunchtime, and everything'll be all right. . . I've done it dozens of times, and everything's always worked out perfectly. All we both need is to get a little sleep.'

Quentin's parents were still asleep as we tiptoed upstairs, fell limply onto the bed, limbs intertwined, and soon slipped into sleep.

When I woke up, I immediately looked at the ceiling: it was still crawling, but much less than it had at Sean's house. I happily tickled the still-drowsy Quentin.

'What time is it?' he yawned. It was almost noon, so Debbie and Peter must both have been long gone to work. He added, 'I'm absolutely washed-out, so even if you insist on making love, I just can't. . . '

I wasn't going to insist at all – in fact, it was the last thing on my mind! How much everything had changed in just one day! At that moment I only wanted one thing: everything back to exactly as it had been before.

The living room was filled with bright spring sunlight. Quentin settled me comfortably on the sofa and went to the kitchen to make some coffee. He soon came back with steaming hot mugs, seemingly absolutely fine, while I was distressed by – seemingly out of spite – objects either glazing over or else moving weirdly under my gaze . . . The unnerving fear about madness hadn't left me either.

I felt that I had been irreversibly changed, possibly damaged forever, and that it was no longer possible to get back to the self I had been before taking the drug. A deep wave of sadness coursed over me as I looked over at Quentin; he looked so heartbreakingly handsome holding his cigarette while glancing thoughtfully over the sunlit garden.

As for me. . . Not only was my strong sense of self seemingly dissolved, but I was still too afraid to examine myself in a mirror… I thought, hot with panic: Quentin doesn't even want to look at me anymore! Soon he'll leave me and find himself a normal girlfriend. He doesn't want to make love to me either. . . These thoughts seemed to press themselves deeply in my mind, as if they were making imprints in my skull.

'Why are you so sad, Sasha? Everything's good now, right?' he asked, looking searchingly into my face.

'No, I haven't come back and I don't think I ever will,' I responded, very sadly. 'The old Sasha doesn't exist anymore. It's as if part of myself has stayed behind, in that other world.'

'Stop talking stupidly! You're absolutely fine!' he raged.

'No, I'm not, I know that I'm not!' I argued, my knees pulled up to my chest, and swinging myself back and forth like a wild thing. 'And you'll leave me – I know that too,' I added, with conviction.

Quentin calmly drew on his cigarette but I thought I caught a glimpse of anxiety in his eyes, which suddenly turned to sadness. He slipped his dark Ray-Bans on, hiding sudden tears in his velvety eyes. 'Just because of the sun,' he told me quickly, but I knew better.

Yes, he's finally understood! I thought.

'Listen, I know all this is partly my fault,' he confessed, 'but how was I to know that something so bad would happen? You told me yourself that you'd tried it before, but maybe we misunderstood each other. . . As it is, if they ever find out about it in College, I'll be in trouble, massive trouble. I could even lose my place at Oxford, do you understand? I could lose everything!'

'But what about me?'

'I don't know, you should have thought about that before, shouldn't you?' And with this he crossly threw the cigarette stump into the ashtray and disappeared into the kitchen.

I thought *he only cares about his own future. He doesn't really give a damn about me. He doesn't love me anymore.* Then I thought: *this is the saddest day in my whole life, which has been so happy up until now. . .*

However, by late afternoon, to my unutterable relief, I seemed to be back to my old self, haunted neither by unutterable strangeness nor by terrifying fears and doubts.

Quentin was jubilant, 'You see, I told you! And you got so scared. . . Oh you silly girl, I do love you!'

'I love you too,' I echoed, but still a shade of disappointment cast a tiny shadow over my happiness. At the same time I blamed myself for my foolishness and also felt hugely grateful to Quentin for looking after me through that horrible night. God knows what could have happened, had Quentin not been there – perhaps I might really have thrown myself out of the window!

When his parents returned from work, we were curled up in the living room watching TV. Debbie and Peter greeted us warmly and Debbie went into the kitchen to make some dinner. Life seemed perfectly normal again.

'Will you ever tell what you saw on that trip?' Quentin whispered to me, later that evening.

'No, I don't want to talk about it to anyone,' I told him, although I did certainly intend to have a serious conversation with Quentin about his 'hobby' – if not perhaps on that particular evening. I was too happy to have found myself again.

CHAPTER 20

The next morning I was awoken by a persistent scratching outside my door from the cats, who were counting upon being invited to share the guest bedroom. I happily recalled that it was Saturday and felt a sudden wave of gratitude wash over me for being back to my usual self – so great a rush of gratitude that I rashly got up to let the cats in.

Ignoring me, they burrowed joyfully inside the warm goose-down duvet, demonstrating who was really in charge, while I tiptoed into Quentin's room next-door. He half-opened his sleepy eyes, and having spotted me in the doorway, grinned widely and, raising the edge of his duvet, silently invited me in. I dived under the covers and we merged in a tender embrace. Quentin's parents' muffled voices could be heard downstairs, so we didn't have to worry about waking them up.

Everything is just as before! I rejoiced. Quentin was in love with me again, so tender, thoughtful and passionate. We dissolved into each other as effortlessly as if the previous day had never happened – '*Today, all my troubles seemed so far away*'. . . In my head I was happily paraphrasing the famous Beatles lyrics, my body responding like a finely-tuned instrument to Quentin's expert touch. . .

Later we decided to go for breakfast at Café Rene in town.

'Let me treat you to a full English breakfast: free-range eggs and crispy bacon, sausages and fresh orange juice, just the way you like it. Anything you wish for,' Quentin offered generously. 'And afterwards perhaps we could go somewhere? We could even drive into Bath, spend the day there and come back in the evening. You'd love it, the architecture, the history, the elegance. . . '

'Great! I'd love to!' I agreed.

It was obvious that after my recent misfortune Quentin truly wanted to please me, and (knowing him as well as I did) I suspected that he was probably feeling slightly guilty about it as well. In the café we selected an outside table and ordered pancakes with strawberry sauce for me and a full English breakfast for Quentin. We were still enjoying our strong filter coffees, when Chris, Sean and one of the other guys from Sean's party approached. We exchanged greetings and they joined us.

'So Sasha, how are you?' Sean asked, drawing everyone's attention to me.

'Thanks, I'm fine,' I responded, in some embarrassment. The last thing I wanted was to be reminded of the previous night's experiences.

'Are you still recovering from that "bad trip" you had? You still look a little pale to me. Anyway, what'd you see out there?' persisted Chris, always slow to take a hint. 'Maybe zombies or a monster? I once had such an awful trip, in fact two, as I'd taken a double portion of acid at once, like a fathead. Anyway, these monstrous bugs were eating me alive while I was running around screaming and trying to shake them off . . . Ask Sean, if you don't believe – '

'Listen, why don't you guys just leave her alone?' Quentin asked sharply. 'Can't you see she doesn't want to talk about it?'

'OK, OK, sorry, Sasha, I'll shut up. By the way, has anyone here ever had any "flashbacks?"'

'A "flashback"? What's that?' I asked Quentin, a bit worriedly.

He frowned. 'It's nothing to worry about, as it only happens incredibly rarely. Basically it's when you haven't taken any drugs – none at all – but for some reason your brain still retrieves and scrolls down some images from a previous trip . . . But you don't need to worry; only junkies get them. I've never had one myself and I've been really into acid, off and on.'

About five minutes later it seemed to me as if every person there but me was engaged in a lively description of his personal 'trip' at Sean's house, describing his most memorable thrill, enthusiastically interrupting each other – when all I wanted was to forget it all! Suddenly resolute, I finished my coffee and stood up. 'I need to get back to Littlefield,' I told Quentin.

'What for? Have you forgotten something? Why don't we go together?'

'I just need to be alone for a while,' I told him, rather sternly.

'Sure you're all right? You shouldn't be on your own. Why don't I walk you over?'

'Please don't. I'll find you later.'

I hastily said goodbye to the others and, avoiding eye contact with Quentin, headed swiftly towards College – though I sensed Quentin's anxious gaze upon me until I'd disappeared from sight.

I felt overwhelmed with contrasting thoughts, emotions and imaginings – so much so that I desperately needed to be alone, to at least attempt to sort them out. . . Fortunately, I had my Littlefield key with me and ran straight up the empty staircase to my room where I lay down on my bed, deep in thought.

Now that I'd had learned the truth about Quentin's 'lifestyle,' did I really wish to continue our relationship? I pulled up the image of him in Sean's house, putting on his shades to hide his tears, basically only terrified about losing his place at Oxford… Of course, I could understand his panic: he'd worked so hard for so many years to achieve it, yet still a feeling of being hurt, even betrayed, clouded my feelings – though I also thought that I was probably being slightly unfair, and even expecting too much from his love.

I spotted the mirror opposite my bed and nearly kissed my reflection in my delight that it was the usual Sasha, and not that horrible dwarfish Sasha, inquisitively staring back at me. I thought *No, the girl in the mirror there can never make friends with drugs, but Quentin seems pretty hooked… he gets such a high from each 'trip' that it might prove to be an endless journey on the road to nowhere! Perhaps, without drugs, his life would seem a blank and futile existence, even with me in it? Perhaps . . . perhaps he loves drugs even more than he loves me. . .*

The realisation of my powerlessness to make Quentin completely happy felt so disappointing. . . And yet, of course, it wasn't him alone. Almost all of Quentin's friends seemed to live in eager anticipation of the next, still more thrilling, 'high,' united by the enjoyment and recollection of previous such experiences. For a moment I wondered whether I myself might have been desperate to repeat the experiment if I'd had a great time the previous night – but I couldn't bear to think about it. Acid had proved to be the first stumbling block in our relationship and I was determined not to share Quentin with anyone or anything, especially not such an unpredictable beast! It seemed that my decision had been made, almost without conscious thought.

We have to break up! I told myself and, in the white heat of determination, immediately settled behind my desk in order to write him a letter. It was difficult, almost impossible, to put my feelings into words, but basically I told him that I was clearly not enough to make him happy, but that I would always cherish the joyful times that we had shared. I then indulged myself in a little storm of tears – but still my actual decision never wavered. This gave me at least a little hope, that I could bear it.

I had just put the letter in an envelope and was preparing to go out to post it, when I heard Quentin calling me. From the balcony I saw him, just outside the Littlefield back door.

'Sasha, there you are! What are you doing? Come on down!'

Apparently, explanation was unavoidable. I took a deep breath to steady my nerves and walked downstairs, feeling utterly miserable. Then I opened the door and silently handed him my letter.

'What's this?' he asked me lightly, but noticing the look on my face, he guessed immediately: 'You're leaving me, aren't you?'

His velvety eyes were looking anxiously and sadly into mine and I felt a sharp pain stab me – I still loved him so! And he entreated me in his warmest tones, 'Oh Sasha, you can't! Is it because of what happened at Sean's? If it is, then I'm really and truly sorry. But you have to know that it'll never happen again! In fact, if you want, I'll give up drugs altogether, and will never touch them again. . . Oh, Sasha, I love you so much; I'd do anything for you! You know that, don't you?'

CHAPTER 20

I said unsteadily: 'Can you really promise me that you'll give acid up for good?'

'Of course! I was actually going to anyway,' said Quentin, relief flooding his face.

I hugged him hard. 'I love you too, but I was so worried – and you have Oxford waiting as well! What were you thinking of?'

'I know, I know. And I really hope that we'll be at Oxford together as well. . . By the way, when are you actually going to start revising for your A-levels? We need to work out a revision plan.'

I didn't mention that I would have been doing this, had I not been distracted by being obliged to write the letter to him, and Quentin continued eagerly, 'Look, why don't we get your books and files from your room and head home to study together? And as for this,' and here Quentin waved the envelope with my letter inside it, 'let's just tear it up and forget all about it!'

I threw my arms around him, feeling 'over the moon' about his resolution. I even thought: *perhaps this could even make our love stronger?* Then, firmly grasping Quentin's hand I followed him up the stairs and into my room, where we stormily 'baptized' my bed.

Later, completely loaded down with files and books, we headed joyfully to Quentin's house, where we appropriated the dining-room table in order organize my A-level revisions. . . After a very short time I caught myself thinking what a genius Quentin was: I couldn't stop admiring his brilliance. For example, upon just leafing through my geography textbook, he picked a topic at random and launched into its detailed discussion, going far beyond the curriculum – and eventually getting so involved with the subject that he leaped up to fetch some book he had read a couple of years before. . . I could listen to him for hours, admiring his turn of phrase and trying to absorb his passion for knowledge. *If only I could be as erudite as my stunning boyfriend!* I marveled, and: *How could I even contemplate breaking up with you?*

Eventually Debbie and Peter returned home, loaded down with groceries, and rewarded us with approving looks upon seeing our heads so diligently bowed over my textbooks.

'Surely it's time you two bookworms took a break for lunch,' Debbie suggested, lightly kissing Quentin's forehead.

I was helping her unpack their shopping bags, merrily chatting about our plans for the Easter holidays, when Debbie suddenly recollected something. 'Hang on,' she said, extracting the Saturday *Times* from her bag, 'there's an article about some Russian with the same name as yours. Perhaps you might know him?'

I grabbed the paper eagerly. The third page was taken up with a black-and-white photo of my dad at some business conference or other. Most of the article involved an interview with him about the future of telecommunications in Russia and his forecasts for the economic situation there.

'That's my father!' I exclaimed.

'No, really! I thought there was a resemblance! Peter, it is Sasha's father, just as I thought!' Debbie called triumphantly, though Peter was by then preoccupied with some football match.

'So when you going to introduce me to your famous dad?' Quentin teased.

Then I guiltily recalled that I hadn't talked to my parents for several weeks and that it was about time that I learned about their Easter plans.

'I hope you'll meet him next week,' I told him and begged Debbie's permission to call home, which she kindly gave me immediately.

My mum was overjoyed. 'Sashenka! How lovely to hear your voice! How are you? Are you calling from College?'

'No, we broke up for the holidays and I'm just staying with Quentin and his family. They all say "hi," by the way! We've just seen the interview with Dad in the *Times* so I just had to call and congratulate him. When are you coming to London?'

'Dear one, I'll tell your father the moment he gets back. He's away on some trip concerning the Union of Russian Industrialists, which he recently helped to establish, and I'm not entirely sure when he'll be back – that's why we've unfortunately had to postpone our trip yet again.'

CHAPTER 20

I was disappointed, but tried to be cheerful, and my mother consoled me, 'Never mind! I can't wait to see you during the summer holidays – if not earlier. . . It depends on your father, really. Do give our regrets to Quentin and his parents for us, will you?'

Despite the too-cheerful tone of my mother's voice I could sense her own disappointment, even though she was doing her best to hide it. I put the phone down and shared the news with Quentin.

After lunch Debbie and Peter went to their neighbors' to play Bridge. We made ourselves at home in front of the TV, immersed in the mystical world of *Excalibur,* our favorite film about King Arthur. My head was on Quentin's lap as he gently stroked my hair, accompanied by 'O Fortuna' and armored knights charging across the screen.

'It's you, Sasha! You're "the one,"' and here Quentin paraphrased Merlin's words from the film script, which we both knew by heart, 'You know, I will always love you,' Quentin whispered in my ear.

'Always!' I replied, without hesitation.

My life seemed so wonderful once again: Quentin and I were back together, I loved and was loved, which – like the blade of Excalibur – seemed to me to make the two of us invincible. It seemed that nothing bad could ever happen to us ever again . . .

CHAPTER 21

With the A-level exams fast approaching the whole of the Upper Sixth had turned into reclusive hermits unwilling to leave their lonely habitats except to eat at Norwood Hall or to cram in the library. Littlefield was no exception and like the rest of the houses at College was possessed by exam fever.

After lunch everyone peeled away to their rooms to swot for these exams, upon which depended not only admission to university but even (as it then seemed) our whole future.

Having settled myself comfortably at my desk, I surrounded myself with books and files and was just beginning to get down to some serious work when suddenly I heard raised voices and pop music coming from Natalie's room. It sounded as if there was an all-girls' party to which I hadn't been invited. *Never mind! I wasn't about to waste my time on idle gossip anyway,* I thought. I was just opening the file filled with English mock exam questions when I suddenly heard Natalie's thrilled voice: 'I ran into Quentin in town earlier. He's just so incredibly horny! Even the handsomest guys here don't come anywhere near him in my opinion.'

She clearly had the hots for my boyfriend – while the others were only too happy to consider a favorite subject, comparing the male 'talent' at College. I could distinguish Serena's voice laying down the law, echoed by muffled tones of agreement, probably from Penny.

'No way! They can't even hold a candle to him,' I heard Natalie disagree about some contender for the role of Mr. Hot Marlburian. It was obvious that none of the girls was in much of a hurry to study for finals. I was losing interest in my accidental eavesdropping when the conversation returned to Quentin, reigniting my curiosity.

'Most likely he's thick and his parents live in a council house,' Serena decided, making way off the mark assumptions about my boyfriend.

'*Are* there any council houses in Marlborough?' asked Natalie doubtfully.

'Certainly, but not close to College,' Penny informed her.

'But I've heard he's very smart,' Natalie persisted. 'Sasha told everyone that he got a place at Oxford with five A grades at A-levels, apparently!'

Serena was incredulous. 'And you believed her? It's not like he showed her his A-level certificates! – Anyway, with her English, Sasha doesn't always understand what's going on around her. He probably simply bullshitted her (and Mr Graham too!) and she believed him, of course.'

'I don't know,' Penny hesitated.

'I don't like him at all,' Serena concluded. 'Just a townie with too much time on his hands having fun with a girl from College. And what does he see in her anyway?'

'I don't know!' Penny echoed. 'She's quite boring.'

'Well, some guys in the Upper Sixth were asking me about Sasha and when I told her about it, she didn't even believe me. But personally I think she's stunning.' Natalie had very kindly stuck up for me, making me instantly forgive her for fancying my boyfriend.

At the same time I couldn't help but carry on eavesdropping, as my curiosity had been piqued. The idea that I might be considered stunning had never really crossed my mind before. Then I heard a cross: 'Fucking not!' from Serena, of course. 'She's too skinny and flat-chested!'

'Maybe she's good in bed then,' Penny-the-virgin chuckled.

Well, what gets in your way to try it yourself? I answered her back in my mind, but then I suddenly heard Penny's muffled voice add, 'But you wouldn't believe what her friend Alka told me about her!' Penny for once had seized the limelight, but didn't seem to be in a hurry to put all her cards on the table. The others all tried to get her to tell them, but she was too coy.

CHAPTER 21

Which of my secrets did Alka so shamelessly betray? I thought. In a sudden fury I first dropped a heavy geography file right on the floor, causing a loud enough crash to provoke a sudden, guarded silence next door. Then I flung the door of my room wide open and marched straight into Natalie's room without knocking.

'Wow, you're all here! What have I been missing?' I inquired. The girls exchanged quick, shamefaced glances. Then Serena smirked, 'Oh, we were just talking about one of the beaks who used to teach here… you wouldn't know him, anyway. Right, girls, the break's over! I'm going back to my room to revise.'

Everyone scampered back to their rooms and I returned to mine, determined to focus on my studies and not to think about Alka's betrayal. This wasn't easy, though. The trust which had been the cornerstone of our long-standing friendship, suddenly seemed shattered. It was true that we no longer had our usual heart-to-hearts and seemed to be drifting apart, especially since last half-term when Alka had so secretively disappeared in London with her new boyfriend. (However, I thought, *isn't this normal, when boyfriends first surface? Don't those relationships always take priority?*)

Yet I had to confess that I'd also kept a few secrets to myself – for example, I'd never told anyone, not even Alka, about my drug 'trip' – and just as well too! The last thing I needed was her telling on me at College. Still, it suddenly felt rather miserable, no longer having my best friend by my side.

The day before my first exam Quentin unexpectedly turned up in Littlefield and grandly presented me with a scintillating card depicting a medieval knight with raised spear on a black horse rearing up against a white background. In pencil, it was masterfully drawn in intricate detail, which made it look almost like an antique piece.

'I hope, Sasha, that it will bring you good luck at exams.' He lovingly wrapped his arms around me. 'Do you like it?'

'Of course! I love it!'

With bated breath I ardently opened the hand-made card to read what he had written for me, as more than anything else I enjoyed his declarations of love – I still couldn't quite believe that such a truly amazing guy had fallen for me. My possessive feeling was wonderfully strong: this incredible guy belonged to me! I also felt blissfully happy, because in his eyes I could read the same message as in the card: 'I will always love you, your Quentin.'

Overjoyed, I repeated it aloud.

'You haven't even looked at the knight, and it took me almost five hours to draw,' said Quentin sulkily, taking it from my fingers. 'Just look at the detail: the knight's helmet, the sun on the cutlass. . . But the horse took by far the longest. I was visualizing something, as I was still coming down from a trip I had taken earlier, and I got so lost in the process that when I glanced at the clock, it turned out that I had spent almost three hours on the horse alone!' He laughed, but then broke off, having caught the expression on my face.

'You haven't been taking drugs again have you? After everything that happened? And you promised! You promised that you'd give it up for good!' I was indignant.

'I know I did, but it was only once – it just so happened that Chris had some mates over. . . I wasn't going to, but everyone else did, so I then had to as well. What else was I supposed to do? But it was the last time, I absolutely swear!' Quentin was trying his best to justify himself, probably ardently wishing that he hadn't put his foot in it.

Then, seeing a stern look on my face, he resorted to emotional blackmail, raising the eyebrows over his big puppy eyes to give a 'hurt little boy' look to his perfect face.

'But I can tell that I wasted my time on this – you don't like my knight at all!'

'I like it very much,' I grumbled, 'but I have to study.' Sulkily I saw him out, trying my best to ignore those puppy eyes.

'See you tonight then,' he said, as if it went without saying, and disappeared behind the door.

Some knight on psychedelic drugs I thought to myself, though I did look at the 'tripping' horse with renewed interest.

However, it made me recall the night of the bad trip again and I hastily put the card away, trying to focus on my revision instead. Less than half an hour had passed when I heard a knock on the door – it was Catherine and Nicole.

'Let's go out and buy lots of sweets and vitamins – a working brain needs sugar!' suggested Catherine, while Nicole added: 'Also Pro Plus caffeine tablets for me, as I'm planning to revise all night.'

'What's to revise for in an arts exam?' snorted Catherine. 'Some of us have maths tomorrow!'

'Are you sure Pro Plus is a good idea?' I asked Nicole uncertainly, but she had spotted the picture.

'Wow! What an amazing sketch!' Nicole exclaimed. I proudly handed it to her, keeping quiet about the circumstances of its creation.

'You'll need to open a gallery soon – I seem to remember that brooding man on the wall since first term!' observed Catherine tolerantly.

'You're so lucky to have such a great boyfriend who loves you so much,' Nicole told me, having read Quentin's message.

I couldn't disagree with her: in fact, my resentment with him was utterly extinguished and I happily joined my friends for a brisk walk into town.

Right after prep Quentin picked me up and without wasting any time we rushed to his house. We didn't revisit the subject of his 'hobby' and as soon as his parents left we disappeared into his room, where for quite some time we enjoyed our own life . . . Afterwards, Quentin, as usual, walked me back to Littlefield.

'Sasha, I wish you best of luck with your first exam – not that you need it! Remember, I love you whatever happens,' He told me, kissing me by the steps. I fervently kissed him back and happily rushed up the stairs, imagining us together at Oxford.

CHAPTER 22

The next morning I skipped breakfast, as I felt too anxious to eat. Unfortunately, exactly an hour into the first exam I felt an insistent murmuring in my stomach, breaking the deathly silence in the gym, where the exams were taking place. To me it sounded absolutely thunderous, but, glancing around, nobody else seemed to have noticed: someone was biting a pen, straining to gather his thoughts, whilst others, in fear of losing theirs, were scribbling at what seemed to be lightning speed.

I glanced over at Alka, who was sitting quite close to me. She was unhurriedly tracing the letters with the pen in her left hand – on the ring finger of which sparkled a huge diamond, which I had never seen before. With this I completely lost the thread of my thoughts. I frantically tried to recollect what I was about to write about, while becoming every moment more horribly conscious of the clock on the wall, which seemed to be ticking restlessly, faster and faster. . . At last I managed to focus on the exam paper instead of on Alka's glittering ring and finished writing precisely on the blast of the ear-piercing bell, signifying the end of the exam. Sighing with relief, I handed in my paper to Mr Green. Although geography could have gone better, at least one exam was behind me!

Afterwards all the students heatedly discussed the shared examination experience, jealously comparing their answers and feeling either happier or rather more upset, depending on what they heard. On the way back to Littlefield I caught up with Alka who was walking with Eric (the one who won the prize for the longest surname): they were chatting about the exam but she was no longer wearing the ring. Perhaps she had hidden it in her pocket? We soon lost Eric, who turned towards C3, and continued our walk alone, but the conversation soon flagged, as I lacked enough nerve to bring up the subject of the ring.

'Well, see you around,' said Alka outside the main gates, where we parted.

On the way to Littlefield I thought sadly about how Alka and I had drifted apart, and resolved to do my best to bring us close again once all the exams were over...

A week later light summer rain was drumming on the gym roof all through my last exam and I couldn't wait to meet up with Quentin afterwards to go to London, where we planned to shop for my Leavers' Ball dress. Having finished my English essay a few minutes before the bell, I was one of the first to head for the door and then in the direction of Bath Road. I spotted Quentin from afar, sitting lonely on a wet bench like a sparrow in the rain.

'Why are you getting drenched? You'll catch a cold!' I called out and he looked up with that dazzling smile of his and moved to enfold me in his arms.

'Well, I knew you were coming out any time soon, and I didn't want to miss you. How did it go?'

'Freedom at last!' I cried blissfully, waving my notebook in the air.

'Finally! Let's celebrate first and then head on to London,' Quentin suggested, and in high spirits we set off for his house, making wild plans for our summer holidays on the way.

His parents, as usual, were at work, so the whole house belonged to the cats and us. We hurriedly got rid of our wet clothes and rushed together under a hot shower, after which we passionately celebrated my freedom in his single bed. By lunchtime however my prediction seemed to have come true: poor Quentin was coughing and sneezing non-stop. I made him some hot tea and stayed with him until his parents returned. Of course, our London trip was postponed, and in the end I decided to go to the ball wearing the same dress I'd worn at the last Christmas Ball. The only thing that worried me was its long sleeves, but I comforted myself with the recollection that, if it rained like today on the evening of the ball, the sleeves could come in handy...

CHAPTER 22

Over the next few days Quentin helped me move my things from Littlefield to his house and I bade farewell to everyone till the Leavers' Ball. With all exams completed, there was nothing else to do beyond enjoying the remaining few days at College before the summer holidays. It was a lovely, carefree time of lazy summer days, strawberries and champagne in the Wiltshire countryside, evening trips to local pubs and hot sleepless nights. At the same time this summer idyll conjured up for me a beautiful sadness of the inevitable parting which was rapidly overtaking Quentin and me.

My melancholy seemed to have seeped into Quentin's own mood. I noticed that he looked more and more gloomy, but assumed that this was due to my impending departure to Moscow. At the thought of parting we both became unbearably sad, but I consoled myself with Quentin's possible Moscow visit during the late summer – and even to my secret hope of getting into Oxford myself.

The day before the Leavers' Ball Quentin suddenly announced: 'If you don't return from your ball before midnight, I'll throw your stuff out of the door!'

I stared, not quite believing my ears. His jaw was clenched, and his face, which so often drove me half-crazy with its beauty, was black as thunder. I had never seen him like that before, but I had no doubt that he would carry out his threat.

My files and books were stored in boxes in his parents' garage, while part of my wardrobe was hanging up in the guest bedroom. For a moment I imagined my stuff randomly scattered along Marlborough High Street and wondered bleakly which things I would miss the most. A bright fire seemed to be blazing before my eyes, swallowing my teddy Winnie up in its flames together with my favorite silk dress.

'Of course I'll be back before midnight,' I promised.

Quentin's face was instantly transformed: he clearly hadn't counted on such an easy victory. He hugged me joyfully, saying, 'I'll be waiting for you just outside the school gates, but don't be late, as it'll be very dark.' He seemed utterly content, while I felt at a complete loss.

I couldn't understand either the condition or the feelings behind it. I had never given Quentin the slightest reason to be jealous: he was absolutely sure of my strong feelings towards him. Was there something I had missed?

In the end I decided to ask Alka's opinion, despite promising myself hundreds of times not to share anything personal with her anymore. With these resolution I walked over to New Court, where I found Alka packing up her things. Next to her there was a large black bin bag, and I was stunned to see about half her things, including the Vivienne Westwood dress which I had given her the previous year, shoved in the bin bag. Having caught my glance, she silently tied the bag tightly. *I'll never give her anything else ever again,* I thought, feeling quite hurt, but decided to say nothing about it.

It seemed at first as if my trip had been wasted, as Alka was going shopping in London with her new boyfriend. It was also evident by her annoyance at my arrival that she had no intention of sharing any further details about him. ('Sashka, what's up? If you need something just tell me. Can't you see I'm rather busy? – I have so many things to do before I leave!')

When I finished telling my story, Alka laughed heartily: 'I can't believe it! Well, you're like a first former, I swear! The boy is just learning how to manipulate, and you take it just like a lamb. . . Anyway, that Quentin will go far!' She glared at me with her vivid green eyes, boastfully declaring: 'If he'd dared to say that to me, I'd have put him in his place straightaway!' I didn't care for her verdict and regretted sharing my feelings with her. *She's just jealous of our love,* I decided, upon leaving New Court.

On the day of the Leavers' Ball I told Quentin that there was no need to accompany me to the gates: I still felt a little sulky about such an unfair restriction of my freedoms, especially on my very last day in College. At 7:30 p.m. sharp, all dressed up, I hurried to Central Court, where on the lawn outside Norwood Hall was gathered a beautiful crowd of Marlburians, parents, and teachers, all merrily chatting away. I spotted a bunch of Littlefieldians and hurried to join them. Serena in a stunning pink ball gown was hanging on

CHAPTER 22

James's arm, accompanied by Natalie, Penny and Tom – all gorgeously attired in black-tie and ball gowns.

'Hi, Sasha! You look lovely,' Natalie welcomed me.

'Who'd wear a long-sleeved dress in the summer? Only the Russians!' Serena smirked, glancing over at James. It was obvious that she couldn't forget his love affair with Alka. *Just as well that I'm leaving at midnight,* I thought, immediately forgiving Quentin.

Having idled a little with Littlefieldians, I was moving on in search of Alka and my friends when Jacqui grabbed my hand. 'Hi, Sasha, great to see you! Why don't you join our table for dinner?'

I told her that I would love to, whereupon she hurried to introduce me to her parents, who were engaged in conversation with Miss Foxton and Nicole.

'Straight after dinner and speeches I'll be sending my parents back to the hotel. Only the true Marlburians will be having fun until morning!' she whispered. . . Soon we were joined by Catherine in a red silk dress, accompanied by her parents, Chris and her elderly mother. *Such a shame my parents are not here,* I thought with regret, *but where is Alka?* I glanced around but my best friend was nowhere to be seen.

'Have you seen Alka?' I asked Catherine.

'Don't you know?! Why, she took her things and disappeared, without even saying goodbye to anyone! It turned out that her mother called Miss Foxton and said that Alka had to return to Moscow at once for her grandmother's funeral.'

But Alka's grandmother had been dead for years! *How strange.* I was still wondering when Dr Stone formally invited everybody to take their places for dinner. After dinner, dancing and a few glasses of wine with friends, in the blink of an eye it was midnight and time for me to rush off like Cinderella. . . My eyes unexpectedly filled with tears as it suddenly dawned on me that I was saying goodbye forever. Overwhelmed with emotion I hugged everyone who happened to be nearby and, holding back yet more tears, hurried towards the exit.

At midnight sharp I reached the school gates, where Quentin was waiting, smoking nervously in the darkness. When he saw me he tossed away his unfinished cigarette and decisively headed towards me. 'Oh! You're right on time! Did you enjoy the ball?' and he took me in his arms, with a proprietorial air.

'Why are you upset?' he added, gazing into my eyes in bewilderment.

The College band's music could still be faintly heard, even from such a distance: the Leavers' Ball was still in full swing. I suddenly felt unbearably sad that College and all my friends were being left in the past forever. With tears welling, I turned around and shouted at the top of my lungs into the darkness of Central Court:

'Farewell, Marlborough!'

Some Upper Sixth males in black tie slowed down and cheered me before hurrying back inside Norwood Hall.

I'll always love you, Marlborough, I said under my breath.

Then Quentin gently touched my shoulder: 'Shall we go, Sasha?'

I sighed throwing a farewell glance towards Norwood Hall and thought longingly: *Just one last dance, so that it could be imprinted on my heart forever.* . . However, I nodded silently and hand in hand we started slowly walking towards his parents' house.

'Why are you so upset? You should be happy that school is finally over and university ahead,' he said trying to cheer me. 'In any case, we'll be here often and you can always meet up with your College friends.'

He's not a Marlburian, he doesn't understand, I thought, not even hearing him. Soon Quentin noticed how tiring it was for me to walk in my high heels.

'C'mon baby, I'll piggyback you the rest of the way,' he offered, looking at me with tenderness.

'OK, but don't drop me,' I warned with a smile. I wrapped my arms around his neck and Quentin easily hoisted me on his back and started walking faster towards his house. I was no longer so sad, because I had Quentin. 'Would you really thrown my stuff out if I'd been late?' I whispered in his ear.

CHAPTER 22

'Of course not! I was just afraid you'd forget about me that night with some Marlburian or other.'
'How could a thought like this even cross your mind!' I fondly caressed his hair. *My boyfriend is the best*, I thought, though I forgot to tell him that.

All the rest of the night I kept tossing and turning, waking up and then falling asleep again, seeing fragments of dreams, which the moment I was fully awake I couldn't quite grasp hold of. . . However, just before dawn I fell into a deep slumber, my dreams as vivid and clear as if I was watching a film about myself.

It was again my childhood, and my father and I were somewhere in a mountain forest with a gorge at its edge. I ran up to the gorge to see where it ended, when suddenly the rocks and even the ground beneath my feet began to give way on the steep slope. Terrified that with just a single skid I'd fall down the deep gorge, I cried out, stretching out my hand towards my father to save me, but all I could see was his departing back as he walked away from me. I felt certain that I was about to slip straight into the gorge. There was nothing to hold on to, not even a tree branch, so I grabbed hold of some grass instead – only to have the roots come away in my hand.

I was still crying out, 'Daddy, daddy, help!' when I woke up, sobbing, with Quentin's face bent over me. 'What's wrong? I heard you crying. Did you have a nightmare?' But I already felt so much better! – in fact, I couldn't believe my luck that it had only been a dream.

Oddly enough, after breakfast my dad suddenly called. To my utter astonishment he told me that he was in London and would love to come round to see me, even if only briefly. He suggested that he drive down to Marlborough and meet me there. Thrilled but utterly exhausted after my terrible night I replied: 'Of course, how lovely! Let's meet at the Castle & Ball Hotel in High Street. I can't believe you're in the country!'

Before the appointed time I arrived excitedly at the Castle & Ball and saw my father already awaiting me at a corner table.

I gave him a big hug, perched opposite and said: 'Well, what a wonderful surprise this is!' In response I saw a strange expression on his face – something between a smile and a smirk, which made me feel vaguely uneasy. Swiftly I added, 'Are you well? Has something happened? How's Mum?'

Dad stopped me with a glance. 'Your mother is fine. You'll both be fine, as of course you have everything that others can only dream of. This is because I've devoted my whole life to you and your mother: providing for you, carrying out your whims and caprices… That's why your mother's girlfriends have always envied her and longed to be in her place.'

I was unsure about this, so I said nothing, and he went on, 'Anyway, you're an adult now, and you've started to live your own life. To be honest, I don't really approve of your relationship – I think that you probably need someone older and more serious, but, in the end, it's your choice.'

What does he know about my relationship with Quentin? He's never even met him! I thought fiercely, completely taken aback by such an unexpected start. However, I didn't dispute the point and Dad continued: 'At any rate, about me… I once loved your mother very much – she was my first love, in fact – it was all brightness and romance. Everybody envied us. But this was back in the time of our youth . . . although, you know,' and here my father perked up amazingly, 'unlike your mother, I still feel so young! Yes! I feel full of energy, even more so than I did ten years ago! And why should I be considered worse than some mere greenhorn? I'm in terrific physical shape, and besides, with my life experience and mature mind I have everything to offer. There's no reason at all why I shouldn't start a new life, even have more children, perhaps, no reason at all. Really, why should I refuse myself the chance of having all this?'

All what? I wanted to scream, but really, it was perfectly obvious: *He has fallen in love with someone else.* Why should he 'refuse himself' the chance? Because we are a family, because we love each other, because families belong together! I wanted to say all this, but the words somehow got stuck in my throat.

Instead, I asked distantly: 'So, what is the situation?'

CHAPTER 22

'The situation is that for the past several years I've been living in a dream. I wanted to experience a thrilling flight, as in my youth, to fall head over heels in love again and to long even to move mountains for my beloved! Do you see how romantic I can be?' and with this a sugary, dreamy expression appeared on his face.

I thought resentfully: *Yes, and I also see exactly how you've been betraying us all these years, floating on your rosy love clouds, while only pretending to be a true husband and father. It's a pity that there are no family lie detectors, or maybe actually that is a good thing under these circumstances!*

'Anyway, as I mentioned, I've been dreaming of true love for a long time, but naturally living without it. There were always many beautiful girls around, the kind who would do anything had I only lifted my little finger ... But you know me, I'm a perfectionist, I strive for excellence in everything. Besides, I know human nature all too well: I could see through every woman I came across: the manipulation, the greed, the slyness, and, worst of all, the deceit. In fact, it took years for me to find a woman young and pure, unspoiled by these evils, and truly worthy of me. Women with experience are cunning and treacherous – they disgust me – only the young creature can be unspoiled, truthful and real. I had almost given up on my search when I was most fortunately, blessed – yes, my dear Sasha, I've finally found true love at last! I've finally found her: the kind of girl who doesn't care for money or status, the kind of girl I can't do enough for, just so that she might love me back . . . '

'A girl?' I repeated, blank with astonishment.

'Yes, she is just your age,' Dad said proudly, beaming with pride and happiness. *Oh, God! In front of me was a man with a completely altered consciousness. . . He'd been bewitched!* I wanted to cry out: 'Daddy, wake up! Have you gone mad? What's wrong with you?' It seemed that some middle-aged stranger, having taken the shape of my father, was telling me about his passion for some pouting nymphet. But it was his next sentence that took my breath away.

'Luckily, you know her already,' he added almost casually. 'It's your friend Ala.'

So this *is who her mysterious 'boyfriend' is! No wonder she kept it such a secret! Oh Alka, this is a true betrayal at last – you have betrayed me in little things but this . . . this is beyond anything!* I thought. Unbelievably, my father was still talking.

'So, of course, I hope that nothing will change between you two, which I also think would be in your own best interest.'

Was he subtly threatening me?

'This is never going to happen!' I screamed, all my pent-up rage, frustration, misery and shock exploding.

A prim elderly couple nearby gave us disapproving looks as my father, lowering his voice, said coolly: 'I would advise you to think about it and not to rush into making hasty judgements, I really would.'

Everything was floating before my eyes, there was a strange rumble in my ears, and I felt that I should rise and leave, but I couldn't even move.

It was my father who rose. 'Anyway, so sorry but I have to go now. I have an important business meeting in the City.'

I could say nothing. He was just about to leave, when he added, 'Oh and, by the way, your mother and I have already discussed this and reached an amicable mutual understanding. Perhaps with age you'll understand a bit better . . . Anyway, let's stay in touch. I'll be in London for a while.'

Absolutely dazed, I remained at the table for some minutes after hearing the door click behind him.

CHAPTER 23

Ala Gromova was lounging on the sofa, absently flicking though TV channels with the remote control. British programme choice was really very limited; there was nothing even remotely interesting to watch, not that she was particularly eager to watch anything. . .

It's long since past time to connect to Russian television, she thought irritably, turning the TV off and tossing the remote control onto the glass coffee table.

Topulic, as Ala affectionately called Anatoly Emelianov, had been obliged to go to Russia on most important business. (The nickname had possibly been created by combining 'Tolik,' the name used by friends and family, with 'papulya,' one of the many Russian diminutives for 'daddy.' Or perhaps it was instead related to 'home slippers' – which sounded somewhat similar in Russian – items which could be comfortably put on or kicked off and even, in a tantrum, thrown under the bed . . .)

Ala had been left all alone to patiently await his return, just like his virtuous wife always did back at home. He couldn't tell when he'd be back - everything depended on the situation in Moscow.

Alka sighed and glanced around the room with disdain: a rented three-bedroom apartment, albeit one right in the middle of the 'tiara triangle', wasn't exactly her notion of 'dream come true.' She had been leading a secret life here for some time, as well as keeping safe the expensive clothes and jewels with which Topulik had showered her – as well as those favorite books in black magic loaned to her by Wise Raven.

Reluctantly she left the sofa, stretched languorously and moved towards the balcony for a bird's-eye view. Knightsbridge was a hive of activity: black cabs were constantly dropping off or picking up smartly-attired shoppers, who were then greeted (or else attended to their cabs) by green-clad doormen. . . Meanwhile crowds of Arab women in traditional burqa, eyes twinkling like chips of coal, were swanning out of Harrods flaunting its iconic signature bags, while gay waiters in Café La Concerto opposite swaggered past with their trays, exchanging flirtatious banter in fluent French undertones.

This landscape, which had once so thrilled Ala, now did nothing to lift her spirits. Even recollecting her new best friend - Topulik's Centurion black credit card - from which she hadn't been parted since the moment of his departure, failed to improve her mood. She was bored with opulence and luxury, and required amusement.

Suddenly, for no particular reason, Sashka's image surfaced, as if from nowhere; she even felt that she missed her somehow. And yet: was that really so surprising? There was no one else who would so eagerly listen to Alka's chatter over lunch, like a free nodding-head toy, or else tag along with her shopping, or even just peaceably hang around with her, in comfortable companionship.

Some episodes from their carefree student days passed before her eyes, like promotional clips from a film, and Ala was alarmed to catch herself thinking that there was something pleasantly nostalgic in these pictures. Incensed by such a discovery, all her sentimentality, which had appeared from nowhere, instantly evaporated.

'Sashka has only herself to blame! Did she really think that I'd be one of her charities? I'll take whatever I want from life: I don't need anyone else's permission!' she told herself fiercely.

'Power is taken, not given' – this was the teaching of the circle of Georgina. Ala had known since childhood that the strong get what they want in this life while the weak merely survive – assuming that they're lucky enough not to get trampled on beforehand. . . *I've really tried to make up with her, I've called her over and over, but she couldn't trouble herself even to pick up the phone!* Ala simmered. *What kind of friend is that? Not to mention that it's also extremely silly. Now she'll hardly see her daddy at all, while everything could've been so*

CHAPTER 23

different if only she hadn't been so hypersensitive and touchy! After all, it's not that big of a deal! On the contrary, we should have actually become even closer – more like relatives. At a certain age rich men often trade in the wife for a younger model – really, what sane person would drive an old Volkswagen if he could have a new and glitzy Bugatti? – and Sashka's mother is certainly already over forty. Probably Topulik has long been giving various younger women the eye and I just happened to be there. . . No magic had been particularly necessary – her youth and beauty alone had done the trick. Well, just to be on the safe side, she had cast a love spell during the full moon and then poured her babushka's love-potion into his food, but still – Alka proudly gave herself credit – the seduction of Sasha's father was her own personal achievement. Although she still had to admit secretly that Topulik, like most men of his age, had proved to be easy prey. Without a shadow of suspicion he had eagerly assumed the role to which Ala had assigned him: as Casanova, the experienced seducer of an innocent girl.

'Typical male ego,' Alka chuckled, remembering their first night and her virtuoso performance. 'A-plus!' she crowed, awarding herself her favorite mark.

Yet now, when everything was going so perfectly according to plan, it was crucial to consolidate her position. Ala threw a satisfied glance at the ring finger of her left hand: five carats by Graff were a pretty good warranty. Engagement - what a lovely English tradition! She had told Topulik about it, rather wistfully, immediately after their first intimacy. A true Anglophile, Anatoly was fond of English traditions and did not mind at all: as he had very handsomely said, his love 'deserved only the best'. What was best for Alka's new fiancé to learn, in her opinion, was not that some English engagements dragged on: why put bad ideas into his head? Ala had no intention of remaining a husband-hungry mistress, casually fed with vague promises about some possibly imminent divorce. Quite the opposite! Instead, she wanted a grand, heartstoppingly posh wedding and not 'someday,' but instead as soon as it could reasonably be arranged, something which her own Topulik knew only too well. . . Therefore, it was at least partly his divorce which had taken him back to Moscow.

I hope he won't drag his feet about it. Perhaps, I ought to help Topulik a bit, and with this thought Ala returned to the safe in her bedroom where she kept her book of spells. Lost in thought Alka flicked through its well-thumbed pages. She didn't really want to take any extreme measures against Sasha's mum, as she had known her since childhood and was not ungrateful (especially as it had been Sasha's mother who had insisted upon her being sent to Britain with Sasha, not to mention her many other kindnesses).

'Better to wait until Topulik is back with the news. I shouldn't think that there'll be many problems with this old hen,' Ala decided eventually, slamming shut the book.

Alka had dreamed up the plan of Topulik's seduction over their weekend at The Lanesborough the previous Christmas, when she had so deftly followed Sasha in order to encounter her father again. At first she had hoped that everything would happen that same weekend, and that, whilst Sashka would be busy admiring London, Topulik and Ala would be blissfully getting to know each other in his suite. Then, she had a better idea – she would sneak into his bedroom while Sashka was under her spell, asleep until Ala woke her up the next day - if Sashka was lucky, that is. Although in fact no magical tricks were necessary to lull Sasha's vigilance – she trusted her best friend implicitly and slept quite heavily in any case.

Alka felt gratified as she recalled her expertly-laid groundwork over lunch in the Conservatory restaurant: a white silk blouse primly buttoned to her throat had most innocently hinted at her luscious firm breasts, shimmering curls the color of a crow's wing had flowed over her shoulders, setting off the delicate color of her symmetrical face, bare of makeup except for the soft, pink, full lips of the vamp that she truly was . . . Topulik had not been able to stop undressing her with his eyes – or fantasizing about her in his mind, which Ala could read like a book. Luckily Sashka didn't notice what was going on right under her nose (not that she would anyway, with the head of hers so permanently in the clouds!)

CHAPTER 23

There was no need to be a witch to entice his male interest: the line was cast, the golden sturgeon took the bait. Alka was looking at him in her special way: her endless lashes, like theatre curtains, unfurled eyes promising passionate love-making combined with gentle caresses. Her expression – what an artist she was – was constantly changing, one moment shining with genuine admiration, as if captivated and enthralled by his sure masculinity, then opening wide in almost childlike wonder, then gleaming playfully from under those eyelashes, then sparkling with a delightfully mischievous glint. . .

After lunch Topulik was running late for some business meeting while Ala was eager to buy a provocative dress for the Christmas Ball, consequently she decided to postpone his seduction until the evening. Once everyone had gone to their separate bedrooms, she would put on her stunning new dress and drop in on Topulik for an aperitif –for who knew when another such opportunity might arise?

Following their exchange of meaningful glances over lunch and a love spell expertly cast with her own blood, victory seemed assured . . . However, to her annoyance, Ala ruined everything herself, by falling asleep in exhaustion following her adventures with Sashka in Soho.

'What a stupid idea it was to go there!' she had muttered to herself in exasperation.

Later that night, out of curiosity, she had returned to Soho as a black cat in a dream – something which very nearly killed her, as Soho was one the preferred haunts of guileful evil spirits. Ala was already regretting her impulse when one of them, a toothless old witch wrapped in a coyote skin, told her some wicked gossip: apparently the Caucasian Bucephaluses, the ones who had frightened Sashka so much, slaved for some local Satanists who – along with a young whore – owned the den where they stood. There, exhausted prostitutes were eventually made redundant and sacrificed to the dark forces, while the Bucephaluses gleefully covered up the tracks of the perpetuators. (Alka recollected the words of Wise Raven 'Demons can't be bought with gold and silver: they only need blood.')

Having had her nerves duly shredded, Ala had flown back, no longer in any mood for romance, and had forgotten all about Topulik. In addition, she had been unceremoniously interrupted upon her journey. Alka was enraged if a human – generally some unlucky boyfriend – happened to disrupt her night flights: it was bad for both her health and her nerves to wake up and be obliged to return to her human self in a rush. Unlike the others, Sasha had been lucky to come off lightly: it could have been so much worse than the slitting of Quentin's silly scarf! What good could be expected from a witch without sleep? Yet she had still been obliged to ask Mia, who, fortunately for Ala, loved London shopping, for a favor - to locate and to buy at Selfridges an identical cashmere scarf for her sulking friend...

Had it not been for this ill-fated parcel, Sasha would never have suspected anything, but it can be difficult, even for a witch, to foresee absolutely everything. But now that Ala had put a spell on the scarf, Sasha's relationship with Quentin couldn't last much longer. *All good things must come to an end and better sooner than later!* thought Ala, and besides, Sashka had become impossibly annoying recently, bragging about her beloved. *Let her find out what men are really like! It would do her good to grow up at last and stop living in her tranquil cloudless dream-world!*

Over breakfast at the Lanesborough the next morning, Topulik had matter-of-factly discussed family plans with his daughter, not appearing to give Ala a second glance before hurrying away to Heathrow. Vexed and furious, Ala's eyes had welled with angry tears – how could she have missed such a chance? – but as he hugged her she felt him slip something in her jeans' back pocket. It was a thick, embossed business card with Topulik's London address: *Mount Street, in the heart of Mayfair,* and Ala instantly conjured up a new plan of action. Her mood instantly improved, she happily followed Sasha on a bus tour of London, saving her closest attention to Mayfair and its immediate environs...

When her friend returned to College after the Christmas holidays, Ala casually inquired about her father's future plans. It turned out that he wasn't

CHAPTER 23

planning to be in London often, since his business in Russia demanded near-constant supervision: however, his next business trip was scheduled in only three weeks' time. Ala then called the PA in his Mayfair office, pretending to be a journalist from a fashionable magazine hoping for an interview, as of way of learning his arrival date.

Then Higgis called Miss Foxton and, in precisely the voice (and level of English) of Ala's mother asked permission for her to stay in London overnight, citing the arrival of relatives from Moscow. Permission was granted, on condition that Ala made up her missed classes. Having thus guaranteed that Topulik would be in place, Ala cancelled the meeting arranged by the fake journalist and took a cab to Mayfair.

Anatoly Emelianov had been feeling cranky: he had hardly slept as his PA, only selected because of her long legs, had rashly booked him on the 'red-eye' flight. His anxiety had also kept him wakeful. He had noted recently that his nerves seemed less robust than usual and had promised himself his usual check-up with Larionov, a medical luminary as well as an old school friend.

But his troubles had started before leaving for Moscow airport. First he had been rude to his wife, who had done nothing to deserve it, and his conscience had smitten him. Then, as if in retribution for such meanness, his luggage failed to arrive at Heathrow, while dealing with the airport authorities had cost him well over an hour. (*Time to think about a private jet!* he'd thought.) At long last his luggage had resurfaced, but on the way to London his driver had been stuck in severe congestion and by the time he'd reached the office it was past lunchtime. Then he had learned that, most annoyingly, some arrogant lady journalist had first broken into his hectic schedule and then failed to turn up to interview him. All this and now a sudden burning sensation in his stomach made him regret the double brandy he'd had on the plane. A tempting notion crossed his mind: *Why not reschedule the meeting, go to the hotel and get a good sleep?* The only trouble was, it was an important meeting. . .

He loosened his necktie and leaned back in a leather swivel chair at his oak desk, hands folded behind his head, thinking. However, instead of work considerations other thoughts floated to mind. . . Lately his relationship with his wife, despite her indisputable devotion over the decades, seemed to be waning, day by day. He still appeared to love her – still signed her birthday cards with 'all my love' – but those marital duties, so loyally performed over the past twenty years, now bored him intensely. Lately he had also been conscious of a longing for much younger women, although he had rejected the notion of setting up a permanent mistress and was instead getting by with casual encounters, mostly at hourly rates. After all, he didn't need any emotional complications! – all women were materialistic and grasping, it was in their natures, and it was fortunate for him that he, Emelianov, could see through them all. In particular, he had no very high opinion of young women: arrogant, selfish, careless, disrespectful. . .

However, he then recalled, they were not all like this. Following his last visit to London he found that the image of his daughter's beloved friend Ala kept returning to him. It was strange: he'd known her since her childhood, and had – if anything – rather resented his wife's insistence that he pay her way through life. But she was different from most girls: modest, mannerly, feminine, and really quite extraordinarily intelligent.

At first he saw no reason to worry, believing that, upon his return to Moscow he would forget her. But, strangely, thoughts about her only grew stronger with each passing day. He thought about her in the middle of business meetings, he dreamed of her at night and he mentally made love to her while in bed with his wife. It was turning into an absolute obsession, something he was finally forced to acknowledge after some quite thrilling sex with a hot young prostitute. He simply couldn't get Ala out of his head. . . After the initial shock, he grew scared of such fiercely powerful feelings, but later he became ecstatic - it seemed that he had fallen in love again, just like some teenager. He didn't understand how it could have happened to someone so innately prudent, and

CHAPTER 23

what was most ridiculous about the whole situation (other than the fact that such a modest and demure girl would never dream of obliging him) was that the object of his desires, was not only his daughter's dearest friend but also, and through his own efforts, 2500 miles away. *What a hole I've dug myself into!* Emelianov thought gloomily.

He had only three days in London but still he longed to see her. Perhaps he could simply turn up at College and take her and Sashka somewhere out for lunch. *It would be great if Sasha wasn't around at all,* he thought, rather guiltily – but this of course was impossible.

Still, he had to see her, if only to find out whether he was only imagining this fantastic love or whether he had even a sliver of a real chance. If he had . . . Emelianov recalled how she looked at him at the Lainsborough, burning desire scorching through him. Just recalling the swell of her innocent breast against that silk fabric excited him like a teenager. If only she were his, he'd feel so inspired, so young and full of energy. . .

'After all, I'm still young,' Anatoly Emelianov said to himself as he pushed his hair back with the palm of his hand. It was almost the same shock of hair that he'd had at twenty, except that his temples had greyed, but then, women often preferred men enriched by life experiences. He had no belly, unlike most of his contemporaries – and here he pinched his waistline with satisfaction. In fact, as his last lover had crowed, he was in a better physical shape than some twenty-year-olds! His personal trainer in Moscow, who charged in dollars, made sure of that. After all, forty-five was a great age when you were a handsome, confident, successful and intelligent man with very few bad habits – in fact, once these attributes were added to his high net worth, he was a dream come true for any intelligent woman! . . . They hunted for men like him everywhere, in every nook and cranny, and really his wife and daughter had been extremely lucky that throughout so many years he had chosen to be such an exemplary family man. *Other men, men with weaker willpower than his, would have taken the baited hook a long time ago* reasoned Anatoly Emelianov.

Meanwhile Ala, long black hair swinging, was going through his revolving office door.

'I am Sasha Emelianova, his daughter, no need to announce me. I'll just pop up to Daddy myself,' she cheekily informed the dazed receptionist, heading towards the elevator. *I'll need to fire her later, so she can't inform on me if ever Sasha visits here* Ala thought as she approached the door with 'President Anatoly Emelianov' on it in raised gold lettering.

Ala gave a light knock and, without waiting for an answer, half-opened it. 'Anatoly Petrovich, may I come in?' she sang, peeking from behind the door with a delightful smile that, to her acute disappointment, no one saw – for Anatoly Petrovich was sitting with his back to the door, having turned his office chair towards the window. Ala could see only his thinning crown.

At the sound of her voice he swiveled around to stare at her, quite shocked, for it seemed to him that his thoughts had conjured her up out of thin air. As for her, Ala noticed the dark circles under his eyes, and decided that he looked older than his years, although she had only the vaguest idea as how a forty-five-year-old man ought to look. She closed the door behind her and sailed towards Anatoly, gifting him with another ravishing smile.

'Forgive me this intrusion! I was on a College trip to an art exhibition when I strayed onto another floor and got left behind! Of course I phoned my teacher but she was not happy with my taking the train alone and I haven't enough money for the cab fare – then I thought of you, my dear friend! What a surprise! I can't believe my luck that you're actually over from Moscow!' Ala's soft, pretty tones wove a delicate web, while she further hypnotized Anatoly Emelianov with unerring arrows of those piercing green eyes.

Emelianov at first thought that he was having a more vivid than usual hallucination. Giving no heed at all to her lively chatter he couldn't take his eyes from her – so young, so beautiful and vivacious – he couldn't quite believe that the object of his longings could have materialized so suddenly. He even pinched the back of his hand, under the desk, to make sure it wasn't a dream.

CHAPTER 23

Clumsily he rose from his office chair. *I'll sack that useless receptionist!* he mentally fumed, *Why didn't she warn me about the visit?* He would have preferred time to freshen his breath, put on a dab of cologne and do his tie properly. With quickened heartbeat he approached her: 'But this is wonderful! So glad to see you; It's great that you've dropped by!'

They embraced and almost with trepidation Anatoly Emelianov breathed in the scent of her hair, so soft and silky, and, covertly nuzzled into it. Her black tresses were so lovely!

'Have you eaten?' he asked, reluctantly pulling away from her. 'Surely you don't need to rush back to school, and I'm starving!' Ala readily agreed, trying not to show her triumph.

They went down to the reception and she heard Anatoly ordering his PA to cancel all his remaining meetings for the day and to reschedule everything for tomorrow. To her relief nothing that the PA said gave away the fact that she had just pretended to be his daughter. . .

'You see, I've just stepped off the plane – I've had no time even to go to the hotel yet . . . Tell you what, why don't we go to The Lanesborough now? I'll just drop my luggage off, and then we'll get some lunch. In my opinion, their restaurant is not bad,' said Anatoly Emelianov, although food was the last thing on his mind. He was wondering if Ala remembered the exciting game of provocative glances which they had played there and whether there might even be a follow-up. . . Needless to say, he wanted more.

'How could I forget? It was delicious!' Ala smiled at him coyly.

Soon they were in the back seat of the Mercedes, while his driver sped smoothly in the direction of The Lanesborough. On the way Anatoly Emelianov was feverishly pondering his plan of action. He simply couldn't let the object of his desires and dreams – the woman who seemed to be on his mind 24/7 – to just have lunch and slip away. She had to end up in his room somehow… though he had no clear idea how things could develop once he managed this. All that concerned him at that moment was to be next to her, to dizzily breathe in her scent and to memorise the curve of her lovely long arms and fingers. Later, perhaps, he could explore those ripe lips, and undress her gently and carefully, as if unpackaging a rare and expensive gift. His fatigue had entirely vanished: his heart was pounding as loudly in his chest as a ticking bomb and his palms were sweating – he discreetly wiped them on his trousers after adjusting his tie. Then all of a sudden he found an extraordinary eloquence and couldn't stop talking – about nothing – until his throat felt dry.

I could do with a real drink, Anatoly thought, in exasperation. 'How's Sasha?' he asked, remembering his daughter at last.

Absently, he listened to Ala being amusing about their studies, while his thoughts were running in quite a different direction: *She obviously likes me, but because of her youth and inexperience she may not even be aware of this herself. I must direct her sensitively. Everything between us should happen perfectly in a proper and noble way. . . What an amazing young woman she is, brilliant, stunning, entertaining, modest, exceptional in every regard! I would do anything for her!*

All the while he was still puzzling about how to invite Ala to his room, so that it wouldn't look vulgar and she – God forbid – wouldn't be offended, thinking that he just wanted to get her into bed, like some expensive Mayfair tart. How could he make it clear to her that it was something different, different and utterly meaningful?

They soon arrived at the Lanesborough, where he had his usual suite booked.

Maybe after lunch I could offer her an aperitif in my room? he mused, but then: *Wait, what am I thinking about? She's only eighteen! The last thing I need her to think is that I want to get her drunk! An invitation for coffee or tea would be more appropriate. . .* Yet still he suffered: *What if she refuses or decides that she needs to rush back to College?* His every feeling revolted against this.

To his enormous relief Ala accepted his invitation quite matter-of-factly and followed him and the butler carrying his luggage, as composedly as if she had truly been his daughter. *She's so young and inexperienced*, Anatoly Emelianov

CHAPTER 23

gushed to himself: *She trusts me completely! She doesn't even know yet that all men are only after one thing. How lucky she is that I'm not that type - I have only noble feelings towards her!*

Once they were in his room Anatoly hastily got rid of the doorman with a generous tip.

'Make yourself comfortable!' he told Ala, and she curled up cozily on the sofa and began to study the room service menu.

'Lobster? Hmm. I've never tried it, but they say that it's delicious. . .'

He thought she gave him an expressive glance. Emelyanov took the hint - it was a good sign, to his mind, that Ala wanted the same thing he did.

'Agreed, we'll have the lobster. Why go somewhere when we can be so comfortable here?' he said and went to the phone to order room service. Then, he took a bottle of ice-cold Krug from the bar fridge, popped the cork and filled the glasses. 'To our meeting!' he said as they clinked glasses. Emelianov took a mouthful of the cold, sparkling drink and instantly felt much better, regaining his usual composure at last.

'Don't go anywhere. I'll be right back,' Ala heard the click of the bathroom door.

At last I'm here, where I'm supposed to be - the goal has been achieved! she thought, coming up to the mirror to inspect her long lustrous hair, her glowing complexion, her simple dress (though its simplicity still showed every curve), her sensible shoes (which she hated, but it was part of her act). She could see clearly how Topulik was spinning round like a fly on glass under her softest gaze. Before the mirror she honed her skills: making her eyes open, wide and innocent, and also casting them modestly downwards.

Ala wandered into the bedroom, featuring a king-sized bed, on which she sat down: the mattress felt soft but firm and she was satisfied with her inspection. *What's he doing in there? Maybe I should undress and join him in the shower?* She immediately rejected this naughty idea. *No, I shouldn't frighten him - he might have a heart attack! Then, I won't even get a chance to become a widow . . .*

Meanwhile, Anatoly Emelianov, in a fluffy white bathrobe, was standing in front of the large bathroom mirror, lacking enough confidence to go out. After a hot shower he had put on some expensive cologne and carefully brushed his teeth when suddenly a panic had seized him: *How would it look, if I come out wearing a bathrobe? Would she guess that I want to get intimate with her under a pretext of lunch? What if the bathrobe accidentally became untied? Would she be frightened or – worse – what if she laughed at me? What if I completely misunderstood her and simply mistook my ardent wishes for reality?*

Anatoly Emelianov had never felt so nervous about a date, not even in his earliest youth. With paid girls everything was so easy and straightforward: everyone knew who was calling the shots, but here . . . He was simply afraid, in case he ruined everything.

Suddenly from behind the door he heard a tender voice, 'Tolya!' His name in that lovely voice! Emboldened, he opened the door.

'Come and sit beside me,' she said, using to perfection that wonderfully open look.

'Yes, yes, of course!' her lover agreed. He quickly poured them both a touch more champagne and drank it. Goodness he was slow, thought Alka, rather crossly: how easy it would be if she could just take his hand and entice him to the bedroom . . . but that kind of forward behaviour would not allow him to feel masterful. . . She must play her cards more cleverly than that. She lowered her eyes again and said, 'I don't know what it is but just seeing you makes me feel so much better!'

'What, have you been ill?' he asked, secretly thinking that he'd never seen so exquisite a glow of health on any creature.

'No, only homesick – for Russian voices and friends from my youth,' she said.

'Ah! We should be speaking Russian!' he exclaimed joyously.

'No, the voice is enough, so resonant and rich. It's just that sometimes one feels so – so alone – in a foreign country.'

CHAPTER 23

He grasped her hand, noticing how her firm maidenly bosom quivered, how her full lower lip trembled. She turned her face towards him and almost – was it possible? – seemed to lift that trembling lower lip to his. Could he? Should he? He kissed it. Never had he felt such intoxication. She was – tremulously, of course, she couldn't be very experienced – kissing him back. He undid the topmost button on her blouse and just thumbed the hot soft skin beneath. Oh my God, he thought: I am lost! He pulled her unresisting body towards him: he kissed the top of her breasts: he stroked those blooming cheeks, he caressed those unbearably soft curls. . . They didn't quite make it to the bedroom, in the end, not until all the action was over.

***

After a while they were lying snuggled up in bed, Tolik in complete bliss. The bedroom presented an idyllic picture: the lovers relaxed and relieved after an event so significant for them both.

Due to Tolik's overwhelming agitation it had happened too fast. But the main thing was that it had happened and that his beloved Alachka, her lovely tousled head resting on his powerful shoulders, was clinging to him, gazing into his eyes and saying: 'Oh, Tolik, it felt so amazing! You can't even imagine! I never thought anything could feel like this!' and 'But I feel so terrible . . . we should never have done this thing' . . . and being reassured that sometimes it was impossible not to.

'I'm just so happy . . . so happy and so privileged,' she sighed, while tears brightened her soft green eyes.

'Was it really OK?' he whispered into her ear, as if someone could overhear them. She ardently reassured him on this point, while meanwhile thinking rather contemptuously to herself: *My sugar daddy is hardly a macho man! But that's not the point! What matters is that he's really fallen for me – and that victory is gained!*

Anatoly handled his young mistress's delicate fingers, kissing each reverently in turn.

'These elegant fingers are worthy of the world's finest jewels! My darling Alachka, you must choose anything you want, the price is unimportant. As long as you like it, that's all that matters!'

It is important! Alka thought resentfully, but aloud she whispered 'Thank you, Tolik,' and fluttered her long eyelashes. Then she exclaimed: 'I think it's time for champagne. And what happened to that lobster?' She stretched her limbs like a cat while Tolik, leaping joyfully from the bed, started to fuss.

From that day onward Anatoly Petrovich Emelianov, previously renowned for his shrewd toughness with family, business partners and competitors alike, had only one care in the world: whatever could pleasure or enthrall his beloved Alachka.

CHAPTER 24

My plane landed at Heathrow and, having endured the endless passport control queue for non-EU and otherwise non-privileged nationals, I collected my suitcase and headed for the exit. I spotted Quentin from a distance - his tall, well-built figure was impossible to miss, even in a crowd. Our eyes met and a wonderful smile lit up his face: abandoning my suitcase, I rushed over, ecstatic to see him again after that endless summer, while he picked me up and whirled me around. *How lucky I am to have a boyfriend like him!* I thought.

People glanced at us rather enviously whilst my head began to spin. Finally, Quentin lowered me onto the ground and tenderly wrapped his arms around me. I breathed in his scent, like an addict who, following a period of withdrawal, had finally got hold of another fix. . . Recovering my suitcase, we continuing kissing so passionately that we almost missed the exit!

Finally Quentin glanced down at me and said, 'I must have a really good look at you at last! I've missed you so much – and I was worried about you too.'

I hastened to reassure him. 'There was no need to worry. I'm just so happy to see you again!'

'But are you really OK? You seem to have lost a little weight.'

I had already accepted that the stress of the past few months was mirrored in my appearance: the shadows under my eyes were only partly concealable, whilst my jeans felt a little baggy, as if borrowed from the big sister I'd never had. . . I had made, all the same, a real effort before leaving Moscow: I'd washed my hair and put a fresh white shirt on, as well as a dab of makeup – although, had Quentin not been meeting me, I wouldn't have bothered. The truth is, once a grave misfortune befalls a close family member, everything else pales into utter insignificance, and I'd almost resented having to make any effort at all . . .

At the recollection of my mother in the wheelchair, of her bottomless, empty eyes – suggesting a strange and even frightening detachment – my heart tightened as if it was being squeezed.

The doctors had all assured me that, at her comparatively young age, with proper treatment and care, a full rehabilitation was possible. But Mum seemed utterly lacking in desire, not only to rise to her feet, but even to continue to live. Most of the time she simply lay in bed, her still-pretty face turned blankly towards the wall, accepting if not encouraging the kind attentions of her nurse, an old Soviet-style matron who was caring for her.

I had often stroked my mother's hair, in which had recently appeared silvery strands, while talking to her about England. Mum often pretended to be asleep; though a tear sometimes lingered on her lashes, which I softly wiped away, whispering that everything would be fine. . .

I did my best to chase away these depressing recollections on our way to the parking lot.

We set off on the M4 towards Marlborough with the American band Pearl Jam pouring out from the car stereo: 'Listen, Sasha, it's their latest – what rhythm! And that guitar riff! Superb, isn't it?' He turned the sound up to full blast, but, noting my indifference, then reduced the volume.

'Would you rather I put something else on? Why are you so quiet? Are you still worried about your mother?' He looked at me with sympathy, then stretched out his hand to grasp mine.

'Not too much: she's miles better now,' I lied to him – perhaps even to myself. 'Once she undergoes all the physio everything else should fall into place. The only worrying thing is that the doctors think that there may have been psychological factors behind it – well, you know what happened.'

Suddenly, I blazed with anger inside, picturing Alka. So unbearably, unspeakably ungrateful! Did she never remember all that my mother had done for her – how she'd begged my father to pay for her presents, her education, even for Marlborough itself? But I rushed to change the topic, in order to drown out such livid thoughts about my long-term best friend who – like some werewolf, I sometimes thought – had suddenly turned on me.

'Anyway, how's Chris, and the rest of your friends? And please drive a little slower!'

'Sorry. I've seen quite a lot of the gang, but mostly I've been working towards Oxford and missing you – not in that order! They send us various things to read before our first tutorials, you know. . . And, though I'm certainly excited about Oxford, I just wish it wasn't all happening so soon. I'd hoped to have at least a week with you in Marlborough, just to hang out: to go to the pubs in the evenings and to drive out of town in the afternoons – but I'll definitely see you next weekend.'

As it turned out, my exam results hadn't been good enough for Oxford, but I'd luckily still managed to garner enough points to be admitted to the faculty of law of the London State Institute, or LSI, one of the most prestigious institutions within London University. I'd initially felt sad that Quentin and I wouldn't be studying in the same city, but, as he assured me that we'd meet every weekend and also spend every vacation together, I quickly became more optimistic.

Soon my eye was being refreshed by the familiar Wiltshire landscape of luscious green fields and dark blue hills, set off by a pale blue sky. Soft August sunlight shone through the open car window and I could feel the summer breeze caressing my face. Briefly shutting my eyes, I recalled how, at just around this time a year ago, I'd first arrived in what had seemed like another world.

How much had happened in just a year! While my new world had amazed me with wonderful gifts – here I threw a loving smile at Quentin – my old familiar world had turned from a seemingly iron-clad fortress into a sand castle, shivering away at the assault of the first wave. Everything I'd always believed in – loyalty, family, true friendship – had been proven false, ranking along with my youthful belief in wood fairies and Santa Claus. . .

I thought about Alka and my dad: he had always hungered to fall in love, and she to enslave, so when their well-matched dreams came true in sickening reality, the repercussions had failed to rouse the slightest pangs of conscience – instead, they had willfully set about destroying everything obstructing their way ... As Alka had always used to say: 'It's OK to foul your hands in order to gain your ends.' And I'd been crazy enough to think that she was joking!

As for any other considerations, I could recall no evidence that Alka had ever bothered her pretty head with questions about right or wrong. Instead, this soulless creature had stolen both my father and my mother's happiness: she was despicable!

'Sasha, wake up! We're here! Don't you recognize it?' Quentin's voice brought me back to reality.

As I opened my eyes we were already driving along Marlborough High Street, passing by the familiar pubs, quirky shops and Victorian buildings. Leaving behind the closed College gates, at the sight of which I felt a surge of nostalgia for those carefree days, we continued along the familiar route towards Quentin's home.

The house was empty. Leaving my suitcase by the door, Quentin easily swept me in his arms and carried me upstairs to his bedroom. Overwhelmed with desire I thought *Quentin's all I ever longed for: handsome, loving and altogether mine!* For perhaps the first time I also realised how weak I was: I felt almost breakable in his hands. An overwhelming sense of my own femininity flooded through my body like an ocean wave and I grasped at his strength and solidity, as at a rock that might save me from drowning.

Afterwards, leaving Quentin to enjoy a post-coital cigarette, I was heading downstairs for a glass of water when I suddenly froze on the stairs. I hadn't even realised that his parents had returned until I heard Debbie saying, 'What a horrible situation! I only hope that it's just a rough patch and that he'll soon return to his senses ... Anyway, I can't imagine what an eighteen-year-old friend of Sasha's could see in a man old enough to be her father!'

CHAPTER 24

'Well, he's only 45, five years younger than me, and girls have been known to give me the eye, as well,' Peter teased her.

Debbie half-laughed, adding, 'At any rate, trashy girls like that are only interested in fifty-somethings with money, so I don't have much to worry about, do I?'

And, as I turned round to go back upstairs, I heard them kiss. . .

The next day I awoke early with the thought that soon more than a hundred kilometres would separate Quentin and me. Feeling suddenly utterly bereft, I clung to him, lightly touching his shoulder with my lips. He sluggishly embraced me, but then dropped his arms, lost in sleep again. However, back in Moscow it was already mid-morning and I already felt wide awake.

I wonder how Mum is? I thought guiltily. *I should have stayed with her instead of coming back!* However, when I'd suggested it she'd fiercely protested against any such sacrifice before retreating back into her usual shell of silence. . . I resolved to ask Debbie's permission to call Mum before leaving for London.

The cats were scratching at the door. I let them in, donned Quentin's shirt in order to feel close to him, and then hurried into the kitchen to make some coffee. The house by then was utterly quiet, with everyone else still asleep, though the birds, rejoicing in the summer morning, could be heard. Having opened the kitchen door, I moved out into the garden, treading barefoot on the silky carpet of trim grass. Screwing up my eyes, I lifted my face to the sun's rays and stood still for a moment, letting them gently caress my face before returning to the kitchen.

When I came upstairs with the mugs of scalding coffee, Quentin was awake. He had propped himself up on the pillows and was leisurely stroking the cats: 'Morning! Coffee in bed with you? What could be better?' He waited for me to put the mugs on the bedside table before leaning to pull me onto the bed, noting with delight the absence of underwear under his shirt. . . The dislodged cats lounged by the door, silently protesting their eviction by means of their tails – but soon I forgot all about them.

After breakfast Debbie generously offered me a lift to London, having arranged half a day off of work in advance. Quentin wrapped me in his arms: 'This is only goodbye until next Friday,' he whispered in my ear. 'Call my parents as soon as you settle in and give them your number.'

'Till Friday!' I echoed, as he got into his car. *Only just reunited and already parting...* I thought. I wanted to hold on to him forever as I waved him goodbye.

CHAPTER 25

Ever since my arrival in England I'd always dreamed of London – in fact, even Oxford University seemed only a step on the ladder towards a grown-up and exciting life in the capital. So, despite my disappointment that Oxford and I hadn't found much in common, I consoled myself with the fact that I'd ended up in the city of my dreams three years earlier than originally planned.

In the Halls of Residence I was surprised to stumble upon Jill Nichols from College, but then remembered her telling me that she had applied to the same university, to study philosophy. We had exchanged phone numbers and had even agreed to meet up in London during the summer holidays, although this – thanks to my sudden trip to Moscow – had never happened.

We fell on each other's necks, like best friends reunited at last. Indeed, it felt wonderful to see a familiar face from those happy times, despite the fact that we'd never been particularly close at College. This wasn't because we disliked each other - Jill was a lovely girl. Instead it was much more to do with lack of common ground: we'd been in different houses, taken different classes, and had no particular friends or sports in common. Despite this, she suddenly seemed so close and dear!

Back at College Jill had fitted into the category of a 'very nice' girl: pretty, with rosy cheeks and an exceptional complexion, she was genuinely friendly, lacked any obnoxious ambitions or arrogant delusions about being the centre of the universe, and – most importantly – had failed to attract undue attention from the opposite sex, thus depriving her girlfriends of the opportunity to gossip behind her back. In fact, it had been unanimously agreed that Jill was a 'very nice' girl.

Her room at university was on the floor above mine and she had already succeeded in getting acquainted with several of her neighbours, as well as getting a crush on the guy next door.

'He's Canadian and extremely fit,' she confided. 'I really must find out if he has a girlfriend, in which case I hope she's still in Canada! – I'll point him out to you in the Student Union bar this evening, if he's there. . . Anyway, what about you? Are you still with that local guy you were dating at College?'

'Quentin, yes, I am. He's coming from Oxford for the weekend.'

We immediately started to make plans about our evening trip to the Student Bar to celebrate the start of Fresher's Week.

'Classes haven't even started yet and I'm already missing Marlborough,' Jill mourned. 'It's such a metropolis here and some of the architecture is just awful. . .' I suspected that Jill was referring to a monstrous concrete university building, constructed in the sixties as if to spite all aesthetes. . . I attempted to comfort her.

'Never mind. What really matters is that we're in London - the capital of Europe! There's so much to see in the rest of it, including the architecture!'

'That's true . . . Wait, I know! We should go out dancing in some West End club! When my sister studied art at college here, she met her future husband at some nightclub in Kings Road. He's an Italian banker and admittedly ten years older and also had a child from a former relationship – I mean, Dad wasn't thrilled – but Anne Louise is so happy! By the way, how's your friend Ala? Is it true that she went back to Moscow? There were so many rumours that I didn't know which to believe. . .'

For a moment I hesitated, not knowing what to say, yet imagining only too well how the shameful news about my dad and Alka had probably flown all over College, being chewed over by giggling students and spat out behind the closed doors of the Staff Room. . . Finally I said, 'Oh, we lost touch. Somehow we just grew apart . . . you know how this can happen.'

Jill, though clearly curious to know more, was too polite to press me, and,

CHAPTER 25

having arranged to meet at the Student Bar later, I hurried back to my room to unpack my suitcase.

At seven that evening, I was working hard with my elbows in the crowded bar in search of Jill and her friends. The hubbub of student voices even drowned out the thunderous music: everybody seemed to have descended on the bar at once! Finally, in the busy throng queuing for the bar, I was pleased to spot Jill's turned-up profile and began to work my way towards her.

'This is Sasha – my friend from College. Sasha, this is Claire and Samantha,' said Jill kindly.

'Excellent! Let's drink peach schnapps,' suggested Claire, and, seizing upon the notion, we rushed to order double portions, taking instant advantage of the Fresher's discount.

'A few more rounds and they'll refuse us the discount,' giggled Jill. Before we knew it we were all shouting at the top of our lungs over the thudding music in a collective effort to meet new people rather than have any kind of real conversation. Our first acquaintances were three drunk male 'freshers' (I never caught their names). They were hardly able to stand yet nevertheless persevered in their efforts to work the female student crowd, although soon enough their attention was scattered in search of other exciting UFOs (as in: unidentified female objects).

Meanwhile, we had been spotted by two tall guys at the opposite end of the bar, who had been throwing occasional glances in our direction, and, as soon as the rest departed, they made their move.

'They are definitely not Freshers!' Samantha whispered to me excitedly, watching them swagger towards us.

Stuart and Alex were generous third-years who treated us all to more schnapps and themselves to pints. From them we learned that, following last orders, most students were heading to a Fresher's disco at the University's own nightclub, and hurried to join the crowd as soon as the barman had rung the final bell.

Down in the dark yet spacious basement premises, the 80s pop chart was already at full blast while seemingly recently-formed couples, were hanging in each other's arms.

'In the morning 90% of them won't even be able to remember each other's names,' Alex predicted.

Soon the DJ must have become bored with churning out 80s music, as he switched to the latest, vaguely familiar, boom-boom from *Top of the Pops*, something requiring vigorous bobbing in the air, preferably in close embrace with a neighbour. People without a partner jumped by themselves, clenching their hands over their head to the beat, like passionate football fans watching their team score.

I was about to leave but Jill begged me to stay for one more dance, if what was happening on the dance floor could be described as dancing. 'We can walk to the Halls of Residence together,' she assured me, still hanging on to Stuart's arm and I reluctantly agreed.

Then, suddenly, I felt someone's eyes upon me: a guy who stood out from the rest with his upright posture and athletic physique. Our eyes met: his were light, almost luminous, and displayed a clear interest. Not wishing to encourage him, I hastily glanced down, although I must admit that I was curious to take a closer look. He was wearing a white T-shirt with faded jeans, just like so many of the young men, yet he looked somehow both older and more confident. . . One dance turned into another, and it seemed to me that Jill was never going to leave.

'I love this song!' she screamed, upon hearing one of the latest hits of a Spanish sex symbol, which instantly turned the dance floor into a Latin dance arena. I was just moving to go when someone took me by the elbow. Turning around, I saw that it was the guy in a white T-shirt.

'Will you dance? I'm Robert Lambert,' he smiled – with his eyes, not just his mouth.

I said confusedly, 'I can't dance . . . in fact, I was just about to go.'

CHAPTER 25

'You really can't dance? Looking at you, I'd never have thought it. Never mind, let me teach you. What did you say your name was?' And with that he took me by the hand and led me out.

His easy confidence and friendly manners prevailed and after just a moment's hesitation I followed him to the dance floor, hands linked together, feeling obscurely guilty towards Quentin. I had never even tried the salsa before and at first felt utterly clumsy and self-conscious, and soon began to fret about allowing myself to be talked into looking stupid on my very first night. . . Then, however, everything changed. Robert expertly wrapped one arm around my waist, lifting my hand up in his, so that we were nose-to-nose and thigh-to-thigh, while at the same time hardly touching each other: then he confidently whirled me into a semblance of the dance. Some inexplicable sense of peaceful strength and energy emanated from him and I immediately realized that I was in experienced hands. In fact, he led me so skillfully, spinning around and picking me up on the fly, that all that was left for me to do was follow him, barely moving my feet and trying my best not to step on his toes. . . In fact, I could have been a dummy from a shop window: Robert could have danced with anyone just as expertly as he did with me.

'You must be professional!' I found time to tease him, even with my heart in my mouth, in the middle of a complicated move.

'So to speak,' he winked back.

It turned out that Rob had learned to dance in Toronto, his home city, and that he was indeed a professional – although at hockey rather than dance, having played for the Canadian National Team. He was in London doing a Master's degree, having received his Bachelor's in the States, which (at least in the eye of a Fresher) made him seem almost a mature student. He also admitted to have traveled the world, as his father was a diplomat. All this I learned while dancing the salsa, which I was really starting to like.

'I'd love to speak fluent Russian,' said Robert, after learning about my homeland. 'I'll learn Spanish first and then polish up my Russian. Perhaps you could help me with this? Да?' I shrugged my shoulders, trying not to look too impressed. He added, 'I'll teach you to dance salsa in return. How about it?'

'Sure,' I said casually, not committing myself.

When the Latin music ended, so did our dance. 'Well, it was nice meeting you, but I really must be going,' I told him, although I'd been wondering where Jill was for some time.

'Has your friend gone without you? Never mind, I'll walk you back to the Halls of Residence,' he offered politely.

It did appear that the others had left without me, so I gladly accepted this offer and we headed upstairs together. On the way Robert reached for my hand, but, observing how rapidly I withdrew it, he desisted. . . In the doorway we found Jill and Claire. Jill's pretty eyes widened in disbelief as she spotted me: 'There you are! We've been looking for you everywhere!' – At least, it seemed likeliest that she meant me, but I wasn't completely sure, as she seemed to be glancing at my companion instead.

'This is Robert from Toronto,' I said, and was about to introduce the others, when Jill interrupted, 'Oh, we've already met. Robert's my neighbour.'

'Hi Jill,' he said, flashing her a smile. 'So, girls, how'd your evening go?'

'It was fun! We had a really good bop, although it could've been even better,' said Jill, giving him rather a suggestive look.

Only then did it hit me that Robert must have been the same guy Jill had mentioned earlier . . . Leaving the club, we headed back to the Halls of Residence, chatting on the way.

'Is Quentin coming over for the weekend?' Jill asked me, although she was already aware of our plans.

'Who's that, your boyfriend?' Robert asked immediately.

I nodded. 'He doesn't really like London much.'

'Guess you'll be spending time in your room then!' noted Claire mischievously. 'Personally, I consider myself lucky being at university in London rather than somewhere in the north of England, say in York or Leeds . . . There is so much more to do!'

'What about you, Robert, do you miss Toronto?' Jill asked.

'Definitely: there's no place like home! – but at the same time it's great to travel and absorb different cultures. Once I get my Master's, I'll have to decide where to go next. Maybe Russia, once I've learned Russian,' he said, winking at me as if he'd known me for a hundred years.

Before we knew it, we've reached our Halls of Residence, where I wished everyone good night and headed up to my room, feeling Robert's gaze upon my back.

Alone, I caught myself smiling while recalling how skillfully Robert had twirled me around the dance floor – I suppose I'd enjoyed it more than I wished to admit. It was already almost 3:00 a.m., though and I hurriedly got into bed in hopes of a little sleep. The next day was Friday and after classes Quentin was supposed to arrive.

'I can't wait till tomorrow!' was my last thought before falling asleep.

That night I dreamed a strange dream: some scary men in dark uniforms with epaulettes were chasing me down the street, yelling threats in Russian and English. The action moved to the LSI, where at first I tried to hide, but they were just behind so I ran inside the Halls of Residence and, full of terror, hid in one of the rooms, locking the door behind me. But they followed me into the building and attacked the door. The door shuddered from their merciless blows until it buckled altogether: then they rushed in, pointing their guns at me. There was nowhere left to run; I screamed out loud in utter terror and immediately woke myself up.

'What an action thriller! Lucky it was just a dream,' I sighed with relief.

The clock glowed seven: almost time to get up. For a minute I lay in bed wondering about my dream, but then I got up and started to get ready for breakfast in the canteen - I urgently needed some caffeine remedy following my overdose of schnapps.

After classes, while waiting for Quentin, I called on Jill, who was busy making strategic and long-term plans regarding Robert.

'Wonder what he'll be doing for half-term, Canada's too far away to fly to for a week. I hope we'll be going out by then, so I can invite him to stay with me in Gloucestershire – I'm sure my parents would like him... Oh, look! There's your boyfriend!' exclaimed Jill. She had spotted him even before I had.

Travel bag casually thrown over his shoulder, Quentin was striding towards the Halls of Residence, unhurriedly drawing on a cigarette and looking rather like the Marlboro Man, just stepped down from a billboard. As always, his appearance made my heart feel as if it was about to leap out of my chest.

'Great! Got to run!' I threw over my shoulder, heading for the door.

'See you later,' said Jill, not turning her head, evidently mesmerized. 'He's just so handsome! A cross between Matt Dillon and a young Rupert Everett....' I heard her voice from the corridor.

I dashed downstairs, excitement boiling over, and met Quentin walking up.

'Hi, stranger!' I called, and Quentin looked up, breaking into a wide smile, his eyes flashing. He jumped up the last steps, and lovingly wrapped me in his arms.

'Hope you missed me half as much as I've missed you!'

For a moment we shared a passionate kiss, oblivious to causing a minor traffic jam. When I emerged I saw Robert coming down the stairs with some pretty redhead in a floral dress.

'Hey!' he beamed at me and offered his hand to Quentin: 'You must be Quentin. Robert Lambert.'

They shook hands and Rob continued down to lunch while Quentin and I hurried to my room, impatient to be alone.

'Who was that?' queried Quentin on the way.

'Oh, just one of the students... He's Canadian.'

'He looks older than most,' noted Quentin, upon entering my room. 'And now at last I can say hello to you properly! Let's continue this conversation in bed,' he suggested, pulling me close and, utterly unable to keep our hands off each other, we did just that.

Later, snuggling with Quentin on my cramped single bed I couldn't wait to hear about Fresher's week at Oxford, but, judging from his unusual reticence, I deduced that his first week hadn't quite lived up to expectations: 'I haven't really had a chance to settle in, though it's only been a week. Though I do love Oxford itself – and I can't wait to show you around! What about you? Have you made any new friends?'

I told him about my Fresher's night out – leaving out the salsa dancing, as I thought how much I'd resent it if it had been Quentin dancing with some hot girl . . .

'So, what shall we do tonight?' asked Quentin, getting restless for a cigarette.

'Well, we could always join Jill and the girls in the Student Union Bar. Though it'll probably be crowded.'

'Sounds great!' he said, and with that decided I jumped off the bed to put on some music while he had a fag out of my window.

That evening the Student Union was even busier than usual, including football fans glued to a large television screen. There was a great roar of 'Goal!' just as we entered: we'd turned up right in the middle of a game.

In the rowdy sporty crowd I saw Robert sipping beer out of a bottle within view of the TV. He was exchanging lively banter with other fans, though he spotted us at once and beckoned us to join him.

Anything but football! I thought and, waving politely to Robert, I towed Quentin firmly in the opposite direction, where I had already spotted Jill and her friends at one of the tables.

Jill didn't wait for the introduction. 'Hi, Quentin, I've often seen you at Marlborough. I'm Jill Nichols,' and with that she kissed him on both cheeks – which I rather disliked – before introducing her own friends, who, upon hearing where Quentin was studying, suddenly became interested in life at Oxford University.

'Have you seen Robert, by any chance?' Jill asked me.

'Yes, he was watching the football.' Meanwhile Quentin threw me a loving glance and then, pulling me close, kissed me lightly, saying, 'Next weekend Sasha's coming over to see me at Oxford. Isn't that right, darling?'

We hadn't discussed it but I instantly said, 'You bet!'

At that moment I heard a cheerful voice close by: 'Hello, all!' and, looking up, locked eyes with Robert. He rewarded us with one of his 100-watt smiles, pulled a free chair over and unobtrusively monopolized the conversation, which ranged over subjects such as travelling, food, and local places of interest. Then Quentin said to me, 'That reminds me. Tomorrow I'd like to take you to see the Temple Church. It was built by the Templar Knights in the twelfth century and the most heroic of them are buried inside.'

'Ah, the valiant knights of King Solomon's Temple,' grinned Robert. 'A couple of years ago I was in the north of Israel when I met some British weirdos who had been fruitlessly searching for the lost treasures of the Templars.'

Quentin sat up straighter, saying rather haughtily, 'I've got no doubt that these treasures exist - something confirmed by any number of leading historians. They'll be found someday, and perhaps by the British, too.'

'Neat! I wish you success,' said Robert graciously. 'Anyway, I've got to run. Enjoy your evening!'

He left our table and headed for the exit, leaving Quentin and me to end our evening in the company of Jill and her friends. When, around midnight, we got back to my room, I was in the mood for a romantic finale, but to my annoyance Quentin felt more like talking about Robert.

'Walks like a peacock with his chest thrust out,' he sneered, strutting around the room like King Kong.

'You're pushing your tummy out rather than your chest,' I teased, getting ready for bed. 'Robert's into sports, he used to be a Canadian hockey player.'

'No wonder he's so dumb, then. And all those annoying Canadian buzzwords like, "Neat!" He needs to get an English girlfriend and learn how to speak the language properly. For example, your English is much better since we met – although it's still easily susceptible to bad influences.'

I gave him a questioning look.

'I can always tell by your accent whom you've been chatting to,' explained Quentin, 'so I'd advise you to avoid any foreigners, the Irish – and the Mancunians while you're at it!'

'You missed out the Scots,' I reminded him mockingly, recalling my Scottish friend Catherine and imagining her righteous indignation, had she been present.

'The Scots are fine,' he admitted, sinking onto the bed beside me. 'They have lovely soft accents; for example Gail's from *Good Morning, Britain*. I wouldn't mind waking up to that of a morning. . .'

I felt his hand gliding down my inner thigh.

'Oh, I see! So my accent is no longer good enough for you!' I seized his hand, stopping it, meanwhile snapping my brows together in a frown.

'Your accent's the sexiest of all,' replied Quentin intensely, locking his lips into mine.

The next morning I was unceremoniously awoken by a severe toothache. Unfortunately, as it was Sunday, all the dental clinics were closed and there was nothing to do but to suffer until Monday. Unable to eat, I aimlessly wandered in pain from one corner of the room to the other, Quentin's scarf wrapped around my aching, swollen cheek. Quentin was truly sorry for my misfortune and went out instantly to buy me some Nurofen – though unfortunately it didn't do much to alleviate the throbbing pain. Not being a dentist himself, he could do nothing beyond, although he tried his best to reassure me with sympathetic hugs and an occasional kiss, with which he rewarded my healthy cheek. His train to Oxford wasn't until mid-afternoon, and time seemed to drag on endlessly. . . I couldn't wait until Monday while Quentin was probably secretly wishing he could simply slip back to Oxford. I could hardly blame him – who'd enjoy a weekend in the company of someone unable to endure mere toothache patiently? The clock hand was sluggishly crawling towards three, Quentin was busy packing up his travel bag and I was nursing my ill-fated tooth when my eyes fell on my sour expression in the mirror.

Did I really spend the whole of today with such a long face? I thought in dismay, hastily forcing a feeble smile. However, despite a triple dose of Nurofen, my dental torture persisted, turning into a shooting pain which I self-diagnosed as pulpitis.

'Poor thing!' said Quentin and glanced at me with sympathy.

He zipped up his bag and then came up to put his arm around my shoulders in front of the mirror. Standing next to such a handsome man, with my own swollen face, lack of make-up and pained expression did nothing to lift my spirits. I attempted to move away from the mirror, but Quentin, not taking his eyes off our reflection, pulled me close.

'It must be difficult to be with someone like me,' he remarked, addressing the mirror. 'So perfect in every respect,' he continued, when there was no response to his 'mirror, mirror on the wall…' 'Even my teeth are perfect,' he added, grinning like a Cheshire cat. 'Never been to the dentist in my life. They probably can't stand even hearing about someone like me.'

And they're probably not alone, I thought, freeing myself from his hold and sinking onto the bed to hug Winnie instead. For some reason his presence was beginning to annoy me. I just wanted to be left alone.

'Only joking, darling,' Quentin said, probably realising that he had overstepped the mark. 'You're the most beautiful and wonderful girl I know,' he added, attempting to kiss me, but I still sulked.

'Every joke has a shred of joke to it,' I said, trying to be cute in response, but the English translation somehow didn't sound right and we failed to understand each other.

'Well, really must go now, otherwise I'll miss my train,' he said, rising. 'After you've seen the dentist, please call me. In any case, I'll love you even without your tooth!'

CHAPTER 25

He kissed me goodbye and left me in bed, where I covered my head with a duvet in a vain attempt to go sleep. Despite Quentin's assurances I really didn't want to part with a tooth, but as the pain failed to abate I soon realized that I could forget all about sleep. . . Soon afterwards there was a brief knock on the door.

It must be Quentin! I felt instantly thrilled, certain that he'd decided to stay with me until Monday.

'Come in!' I cried, ducking my head out from under the duvet. The door swung open, but instead of Quentin, it was Robert.

'Get ready, we're going to get you some help,' he said, as if by prior arrangement.

'What are you talking about? It's Sunday and everything is closed!' I protested in disbelief.

'Don't worry! I know just the place.' And with that Robert disappeared behind the door, leaving me staring, dumbfounded. 'I'll be waiting for you downstairs,' he called from the hallway.

As if in response my tooth suddenly seemed determined to kill me, fiercely shooting as if from a built-in micro-mini machine-gun. Without further ado I threw my coat on over my clothes, pulled my hair up in a ponytail and hurried downstairs.

How did he even know about my tooth? I wondered for a moment, although I really didn't care as long as anyone, anywhere, could ease my suffering.

Robert was waiting for me on a shiny silver motorcycle in which I could, as if in a mirror, admire my swollen reflection. 'Put this on and let's go,' he commanded, handing me a helmet.

I dutifully donned it, swung on the back of his bike and threw my arms tightly around him. The motorcycle growled menacingly and then Robert raced off down the darkening streets of the deserted City, past empty office buildings, flashing lights, darkening silhouettes of monuments and those cast-iron statues of dragon guards on eternal patrol of the great financial district.

'London Bridge!' Robert shouted over his shoulder and I tightened my grip on him before we flew down a lit tunnel to emerge right at the station where a flood of people were hurrying back to London from a weekend in the country.

Catching my breath at the traffic lights, we flew on until we reached an unremarkable grey office building. We easily found a parking spot in the almost deserted parking lot while Robert took off his helmet and beamed a warm smile at me: 'Here at last!'

He stretched out his hand helping me to regain a balance after the speedy ride. As I had the first time we met I intuitively felt a great tide of strength emanating from him.

On the way to the office Rob encouraged me with a real-life dental tale '. . . and then we tied his tooth with a rope to the door of an ashram, and on the count of three I kicked the door open, pulling the sick tooth out, and shattering the door. He was lucky that his tooth was reeling. Have you got a reeling one?' he joked, finishing the episode from his Indian travels, where the only doctor lived a hundred kilometres away from their village, but still managed to cure all diseases and deliver babies. . .

We took a lift to the fifth floor where a friendly female nurse told us that Mr Simpson was already expecting me. I threw a puzzled glance at Rob thinking: *How did he manage to arrange that?*

'Fingers crossed! I'll wait here,' said Rob with a reassuring smile.

I had no choice but to follow the nurse into the dentist's chair where the dentist confirmed my suspicion of an acute pulpitis and prescribed antibiotics, adding, 'I'll see you again tomorrow, young lady. If you'd come a little later, I might not have been able to save your tooth. . . As it is, you'll do!'

'Are you alive?' asked Robert compassionately, rising from his chair in the waiting room at my appearance.

'For sure!' I smiled at him for the first time that day.

'You do look happier!' Indeed, the medicine had already started its analgesic effect, and life no longer seemed half as bleak as before.

'And tomorrow I can be your personal driver and bring you back,' Rob offered on the way back to our campus. Overcome with gratitude I gladly accepted his offer – Rob had proven himself to be a true friend! – adding, 'And Russian lessons are on me!'

'Agreed!'

The first thing I did when I got back to the Halls of Residence was to call Quentin to tell him that I was OK. It turned out that he had met Robert on the way to the station, and when he had asked how I was, Quentin had mentioned my tooth.

'He's a good enough guy,' Quentin admitted grudgingly, when I told him about our visit to the dentist. 'And I probably shouldn't have said all those silly things about him,' he added, through his teeth. 'But I'm also worried about you; I'm your boyfriend after all.'

'OK, see you next weekend, boyfriend!'

Following our obligatory parting 'Love you and miss you' I hung up, already missing him and looking forward to the weekend.

On Monday morning Robert briefly joined me for breakfast down in the canteen. As always he was in good spirits: 'Hey, Sasha! How are you doing today? Is your tooth better?'

'Much better, thank you! Quentin was so unlucky to be stuck with me this Sunday. We even had to postpone our trip to the Temple Church until his next visit.'

Robert opened his lips but then stopped himself from commenting, instead telling me, 'Your boyfriend is a real male supermodel.'

'Are there male supermodels?'

'Loads, but you must know that. You must like the type.'

He raised his eyebrow and studied my face with mocking eyes before breaking into a good-natured grin.

Well, it's not like you have anything to complain about, I thought but said nothing, regretting that Robert and Quentin had 'got off on the wrong foot' from the moment they had met. Perhaps I ought to do something about it…

CHAPTER 26

The beginning of Michaelmas term, which Quentin had been looking forward to for an entire year, somehow disappointed him. His College, which swarmed with middle-class grammar school students just like himself, was definitely not the coolest at the University. It wasn't that he had anything against people like himself, but somehow it just didn't fit into his romantic image of an elite educational establishment known for its famous alumni – influential leaders and thinkers, bohemian artists, Nobel prize-winners, the well-born . . .

After meeting some students from his College, Quentin found them to be rather dull, studious, narrow-minded geeks: he couldn't quite understand what Oxford saw in them. Having expected that every student would be the most glittering representative of his generation, he was naturally doomed to disappointment, and he soon started missing his old friends from Wiltshire who – while not especially clever – were somehow better company. The Oxford upper echelon was mostly studying at more prestigious colleges and thus walled off from the rest. 'And why even bother trying to reach them?' thought Quentin gloomily, 'I could never be one of them anyway.'

Quentin had never particularly dreamed about the world of cigars, champagne and Charvet silk ties to which those aristocrats nurtured by Eton, Harrow and similar institutions belonged. Personally, he rated intelligence and personal qualities more highly, considering many Marlborough students, for example, to be little more than spoiled brats. Still, he almost felt a pang of regret about not having applied to Christ Church or Trinity College.

In his mind he vividly recalled the welcoming words that the College President addressing the 'freshers': 'You chose Oxford, and the College chose you.'

Three years of his life would be spent here, after all; he should try to ensure that it was the best time of his life that it was supposed to be. As Quentin glanced around his room he attempted to cheer himself, thinking: *Who cares if the carpet is threadbare and stained, and the sink cracked in the middle, when there's such a view outside?*

And he went to the window to admire the view of the quad, surrounded on four sides by a neo-Gothic church, Grade I listed buildings and an old library featuring steep spiral stairs. In the distance were sinuous outlines of lusciously well-tended gardens and the bronze bust of some eminent personage: he made a mental note to walk in that direction the next day and to look at it more closely.

At first he couldn't quite believe the extent to which drinking and partying featured as an integral part of university life – something seemingly welcomed, not only by the students themselves, but even by the dons.

'You shouldn't get drunk every night,' they lectured the freshers, with an emphasis on 'every,' as if utterly resigned to the fact that most of the students' time at Oxford would be spent indulging in the thoughtless enjoyment of youth. Wine flew like water from Oxford cellars at black-tie dinners, balls and parties, as well as at events held by those secret and not-so-secret societies for which Oxford was famous. Personally, Quentin didn't gain much pleasure from heavy drinking, Evelyn Waugh-style. It didn't even come close to the pleasure he took in drugs – but this hobby he kept to himself.

Quentin coped with his studies with relative ease, and particularly relished his weekly tutorials, often a one-to-one session with a don. A great part of Oxford's unique appeal was the privilege of regularly spending an hour alone with one of the sharpest minds in Oxford – probably, in the entire country.

Quentin disliked intellectual snobbery, of which many of his fellow students seemed full, especially those studying classics or philosophy. Naturally brilliant, he shone even amongst his colleagues in politics, as his intellect was not only remarkably wide-ranging but also naturally curious - he longed to know something about everything and he soon gained a reputation as a thoughtful all-rounder.

Quentin was bewitched by Oxford, the beauty of its 'dreaming spires,' its languid air of supremacy, its arcane rituals and ancient traditions. Each morning he woke up eagerly anticipating the start of a new day, and the feeling of being privileged and fortunate never left him. Yet sometimes it still seemed that the 'real' Oxford remained closed to him, and that life was somehow passing him by. A month had passed, but no one had yet invited him to any secret society, or to any of Oxford's famous drinking or 'foodie' clubs. He still seemed to be skating over the surface of Oxford life.

He cultivated an attitude that was slightly aloof but still friendly. Of course, he effortlessly won attention for his stunning looks, as even next to the most handsome athletes he remained in his own league, but unfortunately some ambitious Oxford males out of jealousy rather shunned his company, while the more geeky types were of no particular interest to him.

During Freshers' Week, Quentin had met many of his classmates along with his neighbours from the Halls of Residence – and had also made a long-lasting impression on every female at the Fresher's Dinner, simply by appearing in his black DJ and bowtie. The DJ, bought by his mother in a John Lewis sale, draped his tall, broad-shouldered figure as elegantly as if it had been made to order on Savile Row.

'Who's that? He looks like James Bond,' the admiring groans of girls had rung across the tables.

However, completely unaware of this social triumph, Quentin still hadn't found any kindred spirits and was moving around in a social vacuum, still wondering what – outside of the intellectual stimulation, of course – Oxford was all about.

A month later, Quentin went to hear a visiting Harvard professor speak about globalization at an annual lecture held in the honour of Isaiah Berlin. Slightly late, he slipped into a seat in the last row. The hall was humming with anticipation as a tall, gaunt professor strode to the rostrum. Suddenly, there was a loud creak from the chair next to Quentin's, and someone noisily fell into it. Surprised by the odour of expensive cologne, Quentin turned his head to see a blond, handsome profile. His neighbour locked his gaze with his, and awarded him a dazzling smile.

'Hate American accents,' he whispered conspiratorially, nodding towards the speaker. 'Hugo Devlin. And you are?'

'Quentin Taylor.'

Hugo squeezed his hand lightly before turning to listen. Quentin didn't find the lecture particularly outstanding, but still enjoyed its spirit and the skills of the speaker. A question and answer session followed, which turned out to be rather dominated by his neighbour, who seemed to have had any number of questions to raise. . . Had it not been for his innocent look and disarming smile, one would have thought that he wanted to call the speaker on something. He definitely drew the attention of the room; even the dons in the first rows craned their heads to get a better look at Hugo, which Quentin supposed to be the purpose of his attendance. He rather wished he had himself something of the same confidence. . .

After the lecture Quentin was heading for the door, when suddenly Hugo called him back. 'Listen, if you're free tomorrow night, why don't you join some friends and me for a small dinner party? It might amuse you.'

As Quentin didn't have any plans for the evening, he said, 'All right, where?'

'You'll be informed,' smiled his new contact. 'See you tomorrow, then.'

His Hollywood smile flashed once again before he moved off to join a tall guy wearing spectacles, who had climbed over a row of seats to reach him.

The invitation intrigued Quentin.

'I smell secrecy. He didn't even mention the venue: I wonder if they belong to some society. And who *is* this Hugo Devlin after all?' thought Quentin on his way back to the Halls of Residence.

In the morning, he found a note under his door - copperplate writing, black ink and all.

CHAPTER 26

Come to the Codrington Library before twelve. Find Plato's Symposium. Inside you'll find the time and place for tonight. There was no signature.

It was probably Hugo's writing – its elegance matched his appearance. Although he wasn't very tall: about Sasha's height, when she was wearing heels, Quentin smiled to himself, as he always did when thinking of Sasha. He thought: *I bet he's reading classics. Judging by his choice of book, secret societies take themselves very seriously here.*

Quentin was already imagining his future secret initiation, almost like the knights of some ancient order, and he also looked forward to seeing his old friends' astonishment when he shared this colourful story with them.

Eager to know more, immediately after breakfast he headed straight to the library. He had to make a large detour, but there was still time enough before class. As it turned out, there were three copies of Plato's *Symposium* in the library, and Quentin had to search them all until he found the note with the time and place of the evening's event. To his disappointment, it was only the Silver Horseshoe, a gastro-pub in town.

Before replacing the book back on its shelf, he thumbed through a few pages, which failed to raise his interest.

'Eros, Alcestis, Achilees, Patroklos - what bollocks! How can anyone choose to study something like this for three whole years? Now politics – that's a different matter altogether!'

With these thoughts he hurried to his political economy lecture. In class Quentin failed to concentrate, listening absentmindedly to the wheezy professor, while worrying about the upcoming dinner. What did one wear to such an event? – the invitation had been silent on this point. He had heard that the most elite Oxford societies had their own uniforms of distinct colours and cut, made by the best tailors in town.

He paused to think. If everyone was wearing black tie, he would look like a pleb in jeans. And if, as it happened, it was the other way around, he'd feel like a young idiot trying too hard to impress. Still, Quentin did want to make an impression.

'I should really talk to someone in the group, but of course I only know Hugo, and I didn't think to ask for his college or his year,' he thought. It was obvious that Hugo was not a fresher – he was far too confident for that, and seemed to know everyone, as well. Then again, was one supposed to ask members such questions? He thought: *What if the dress issue is a test, and, by even asking the question, I fail it?*

There was no point talking to other freshers, he thought glumly. Suddenly, he recalled Charlie Nosie, the College President's nephew, whom he had met at the Freshers' Dinner. Although a fellow newcomer, he already belonged to the Oxford Boat Club and seemed to know lots of people, including some senior year students.

Straight after the lecture, he joined his classmates for lunch in the canteen. Luckily he spotted Charlie at once, seated chatting to some broad-shouldered guys. Quentin loaded his tray with food and hurried off to join them.

'Hello, mate. How's it going?' he greeted him, taking a seat next to him. You could always count on Charlie to know the latest gossip in College.

'Not too bad. We're giving marks to the College female population and we don't have a single A-grade yet. In fact, it's mostly C-minus,' he nodded towards two homely girls in baggy jumpers who were looking meekly around for a free table.

His boat club friends roared with laughter. 'And that one,' the guy next to Quentin gestured towards a very large girl with greasy hair and glasses, 'is only if you're completely desperate.'

'And have had five pints of beer,' joked a hefty rower sitting opposite.

Finally, a tall blonde got an A. Having noticed their approval however, she gave them rather a haughty look, causing her A to go down to a B.

'She looked pretty cross,' they laughed, and Quentin forced himself to laugh too, though wincing inside at their rudeness and chauvinism. He was still hoping for the chance to speak to Charlie, however, and he finally managed to steer the conversation in the right direction. Having heard about Hugo's dinner invitation, Charlie and his friends sniggered, exchanging meaningful looks.

'Hugo's a well-known poof, a second-year law student. He and Tom here were at Eton together,' Charlie nodded at one of the rowers.

'I heard that he and his ex-boyfriend, Alex Willington, belong to some secret society. I can only imagine what they do there, but it's hardly a big secret,' smirked Tom. 'Well, not in Hugo's case, anyway!'

'So, you thinking of changing your team?' Charlie asked, bursting into laughter.

Quentin felt angry. What an idiot he'd been! – Those poofs had played him well. Plato's Eros – a Greek god, the patron of love – suddenly the choice of literature too clicked into place.

Quentin hadn't much cared for those gays he had met. Having spent his entire life in the country, he'd not encountered many – however, a certain visit with friends to a West End nightclub in London was indelibly etched in his memory. He had been about fourteen or fifteen, although looking a few years older. He and his friends had got pretty drunk beforehand, sharing half a bottle of gin in Green Park. Feeling a little nauseous in the noisy club, Quentin had escaped outside in search of some fresh air, swaying slightly on his way. Seated on the stone steps, he'd been having a smoke when a lanky bloke of at least thirty had joined him, asking for a light. Unceremoniously placing his hand on Quentin's thigh, the old pervert had started hitting on him, his breath sour and reeking of booze. Quentin vividly remembered the disgusted horror that had instantly seized him . . . He had sprinted back inside the club, heart pounding with fear, and had rushed to the bathroom, where he'd been violently sick. . . From that moment, neither gays nor London itself had been in Quentin's good books.

Following his chat with Charlie, Quentin had decided to ignore Hugo's invitation, but curiosity and good manners combined were too much for him – and besides, what if Charlie had got the wrong end of the stick and the club had nothing to do with sexual orientation? – so that evening he headed to the Silver Horseshoe in good time, as he hated running late.

The ground floor of the Victorian pub was filled with locals; their drunken uproar drowning the 80s disco music pounding furiously from a tattered jukebox.

'Not the best place for a secret society meeting,' thought Quentin, inhaling the cigarette-fumed air and glancing around for a sign to the restaurant upstairs.

Having mounted the steep stairs, however, he found himself in a smart dining room with a snug country feel. All the tables were free, apart from a round table in the middle taken by a rowdy group of four, beautifully dressed in dinner jackets and bow ties. Their aristocratic accents and exaggerated laughter rang loud enough to shame a much more numerous party, while the table was loaded with bottles. A young waiter, of about their own age, was on standby near them, casting curious glances at the company.

Quentin wished he'd worn his DJ instead of his jeans, but it was too late now.

'Here he is at last!' greeted Hugo, rising from his seat. 'We've just been talking about you. Well, isn't he absolutely delicious?' he said, turning triumphantly to his dinner companions. 'Now, Quentin, let me introduce my dearest friends. The Honourable Lord Alexander Willington, President of the Club, a keen hunter and an excellent shot,' he nodded towards a rather stuffy-looking fellow with well-styled hair.

'Call me Alex, please,' said their President, not troubling to rise, and giving Quentin a condescending look softened by a closed-lip smile.

'And this is Gordon McDouglas. Born in Switzerland, he still hasn't made it to the land of his most prominent ancestors, where they own a great pile. A champion skier and a connoisseur of the best wines and women.'

The 'champion' was short and stocky with a hatchet-shaped face. He squeezed Quentin's hand while patronisingly patting him on the back – much to Quentin's amusement, as Gordon's head barely reached his own shoulder.

CHAPTER 26

'And this is Fernandes de Lopez-Pennaloza – passionate polo player and promising actor. Also the only member of his family not into politics.'

'As of now,' Freddy amended, raising his glass in acknowledgement of Quentin's presence. 'I'm still young and wish to enjoy life free of the burden of duty. Once I've had my fun, I might decide to follow into my grandfather's footsteps, but definitely not before I'm 30.'

'His grandfather was the President of Argentina,' explained Hugo to Quentin in an undertone. Quentin took the vacant seat next to Hugo, who – jumping ahead of the waiter – filled his glass to the brim with wine the colour of overripe pomegranate, shimmering in the light.

'Welcome to our world!' he said, raising his glass to Quentin with a mischievous twinkle in his blue eyes.

'You have lots of catching up to do,' observed Alex, casting an eloquent glance at the row of empty bottles on the table. Then Hugo friends' immediate interest in Quentin waned and they carried on with their rowdy behaviour, laughing and talking over each other, though never omitting to empty the glasses filled up by the waiter.

Soon everyone realised they were hungry.

'Fuck! Where's our food?' shouted Lord Alex, as Quentin had secretly nicknamed him, loudly drumming on the table with two forks. . . However, it turned out that, while drinking and waiting for Quentin, no one had bothered to order.

'Well, what the hell are you waiting for?' Alex summoned the waiter with a grimace and ordered for everyone, without glancing at a menu. 'And three more bottles of red!' he shouted after him.

Quentin was already inwardly counting how much his participation in this banquet would cost, but by this point the alcohol had kicked in, and, forgetting all about it, he started enjoying his first experience of dining with toffs. It was fun watching them, as they behaved like spoilt kids without boundaries.

Finally the food arrived. It was simple but extremely good: fresh-baked bread and soft butter, tender lamb from a local farm, chicken pie with a golden crust, with garlic gravy and crispy chunky chips on the side, followed by a plate of famous cheeses to finish. As soon as the dinner was over, the noise at the table went up by several decibels. Quentin then learned that Hugo, at least, could handle his drink and he had soon engaged Quentin in conversation.

Apparently he had met all of his friends at Eton – except for Freddy. His own father was a well-known QC, which explained his choice of faculty, while his mother was a well-connected interior designer. His family occupied a terraced house at one of the most prestigious corners of Kensington, to which he immediately invited Quentin to spend a weekend. Clearly, Hugo was a typical member of the upper-middle class, but he would have never settled for such a vulgar definition of his own status, regarding himself as more than equal to his aristocratic friends.

It turned out that the group had made thorough inquiries about Quentin's background, and had done their homework well, having learned about Sasha too.

To Quentin's surprise, Hugo was not only open about his sexual orientation, but proud of it. More than anything he enjoyed a good gossip, which, after partying, seemed to be his favourite pastime. Alex had been his lover since Eton, when, according to Hugo, they had been madly infatuated with one another. Unfortunately, Alex loved women as well, cruelly cheating on Hugo – especially during the summer holidays – though he had always pathetically confessed afterwards, and begged Hugo for forgiveness. . . After multiple dramas, they had settled for an open relationship, which eased Hugo's jealous sufferings and in some ways had even made their friendship stronger.

Gordon had a steady girlfriend, but this hadn't prevented him from taking part in some kinky outdoor activities at the Fire Festival last year – a group orgy some society held quarterly in secret places, including abandoned barns, remote fields and – if all else failed – someone's country house.

'I wasn't invited, for well-known reasons,' sighed Hugo, 'but they'll all be queuing up to get you, beautiful. Watch out, you'll soon be wanted everywhere!' Hugo had warned, rather embarrassing Quentin.

Freddy, who according to Hugo, lived to play polo, was only interested in horses and boozing. 'But I keep hoping,' Hugo sighed theatrically, casting a languishing look at the olive-skinned Argentinian.

With the waiter's disappearance, a food fight broke out. Gordon and Freddy, roaring with laughter, started racing between the tables, throwing chicken bones at each other. Meanwhile Alex had positioned himself on top of the table from where he aimed to 'shoot them down' with bread dipped in gravy, before they both ganged up on him.

Hugo winced, watching this, adding to Quentin, 'This is the reason why we have to book the entire restaurant. . . '

Meanwhile, Freddy had managed to leap onto Alex's back, and was making him race across the restaurant, overturning tables and chairs until they both fell exhausted on the floor, accompanied by the dismal sound of broken dishes and fallen cutlery.

'Fancy a line, before the pub owner turns up?' Hugo inquired of Quentin.

They went to the gents and locked themselves in a cubicle. Quentin had never tried cocaine before - it was a costly pleasure, unlike mushrooms - but it was easy to pretend he'd done it many times before.

Hugo fastidiously spread a handkerchief on the toilet seat lid to accommodate the paraphernalia from the inside of his pockets: a white powder package, a credit card and a crisp fifty-pound banknote, which he rolled up and offered to Quentin. Then he crouched by the seat to expertly form two perfectly straight lines of coke with his MasterCard.

Following his example, Quentin closed one nostril with a finger and inhaled the line deep into his lungs, just as he'd seen it done in films. However, trying a bit too hard, he almost blew the other line off of the toilet seat.

'Try to inhale a little deeper,' advised Hugo, as the second line disappeared.

For a moment Quentin felt numb, as he had heard resulted from anaesthesia, but there was no other effect yet, and he felt a little disappointed. Having checked themselves in the mirror for any tell-tale traces of powder, they decided that it was safe to go out.

They returned to find the restaurant in ruins: chairs and tables upside down, broken dishes and shards of glass scrunching and clinging to the soles of their shoes while a single scarlet puddle of wine, like evidence of a murder, adorned the floor. Worse still, the pub owner was there.

'Get the hell out of here! All of you! I'm calling the police!' His voice rang across the restaurant. Lord Alex casually tossed a bundle of crumpled bank notes onto one, still-upright, table.

'Should be enough for you,' he grumbled, his speech slurred and thick with wine. The entire company then hurried to the door, getting ready to sprint. 'Fucking peasants,' raged Alex, as he half-stumbled and had to stop himself from falling headlong down the stairs.

'Let's get out of here before the police show up,' Hugo whispered to Quentin, and they bolted, leaving their drunk friends laughing and pushing each other along the way.

Soon they were safely on the streets with no police in sight. Bursting with an incredible surge of energy Quentin felt powerful, almost invincible... *This is thrilling* he thought, and as he half-raced Hugo down the road, he felt inside himself a craving for new adventures...

CHAPTER 27

A frowning sky mutated into big fluffy waves of dark grey clouds, like the hair of some grumpy old person . . .

Having taken a vacant seat by the window, I enjoyed the idyllic rural landscape spread out before me: baby lambs, like springy balls of cotton wool balls, gamboled joyfully along grass-carpeted fields, spotted cows studded a flowery meadow, while two chestnut horses grazed the lush autumn pasture.

After the buzzy, crowded but oddly empty streets of London such scenery rested my eyes. I caught myself thinking that lately I'd been looking at London through Quentin's perspective: it was he who saw it tainted with grey tinge of bustling anonymity, whilst I had always envisaged London as wearing a vivid, rainbow-hued palette... I wondered: what else had I learned to perceive through Quentin's eyes? Or was it possible that my own perspective had simply altered as a result of recent family events?

From my bag I retrieved an open envelope with an Oxford postmark. Quentin's most recent letter to me, which I already knew by heart, definitely stood out amongst all his previous letters from university. An enthusiastic cheerfulness leaped from every line as if he, like the tiny lambs through the train window, was suddenly keen to remember how to play.

Secret society . . . my new pastime . . . Roman Gods. . . . Greek mythology. . . It was all very unclear to me: however, whatever it all meant, it certainly seemed to have made him feel happier.

His letter warned me that the society's real name was a secret known only to its members; as far as the rest of us were concerned, it was simply Club A. The oath of allegiance, which Quentin had apparently sworn after being dragged out of his window in his pajamas and half-drowned in some ice-cold lake, mentioned something about 'shining sons' but only the founder of the Club held the key to the mystery, which he had selfishly taken with him to the grave over a hundred years before. (I had not been impressed by what I'd heard about the initiation ceremony for Club A recruits, finding it rather disturbing, to say the least.)

And that unconventional new friend of his, Hugo Devlin, will I be equally impressed by him? I wondered whilst rereading that section of the letter: *Hugo is by far the most intelligent of all the people I've met here. He certainly has the edge, and not only because of his scintillating mind . . . it has more to do with his rich and varied life experience. In fact, I was surprised to find that we have a lot in common, despite his being queer and from such a privileged background. Unlike some people here, I really don't care what someone's sexual preferences are – that's their own business, as far as I'm concerned. In fact, I now think that I used to be somewhat narrow-minded in this respect. This is probably because I'm really only a small-town kind of a guy, but I know you love me, in spite of this!*

PS Before I forget: on Friday night we've been invited to a 70s-theme house party, so bring something 70s to wear, although you'd look hot in anything! It's going to be held in some old mansion house, not far from the Students Union, which Hugo shares with a couple of his mates from Eton. It has a reputation as the venue for the most infamous parties at Oxford, so don't be too shocked, please! I don't really know myself what we are in for, but I'm certain it'll be fun! All of my friends, and especially Hugo, are really looking forward to meeting you at last. I've told everyone about you and I can't wait to see you! – I'm sure you'll really like Hugo, by the way. He's so genuine and generous. You'll see that for yourself on Friday....

Slowing steadily, the train hissed and trundled along the remaining track towards the platform. I hastily returned the letter to its envelope and, not bothering to wait for the conductor to announce the station, headed for the exit, my heart racing. At the last moment I was suddenly seized with panic, for no apparent reason. I worried *How will Oxford receive me? What if Quentin's friends don't like me? What if coming here at all was a big mistake?* I couldn't understand why such intrusive negative thoughts were flooding my mind.

The train pulled into the platform, where Quentin was waiting for me, like a well-bred, leggy hound, preparing to jump into the nearest lap, his eyes searching for me anxiously. Seeing him made me feel short of breath: even in a worn jumper and torn Levis, he was so handsome! He soon spotted me climbing out of the last carriage and hurried towards me, his eyes locked on mine. As soon as I found myself in his arms, all my stupid worries dissipated: Quentin was just as much in love with me as ever – in fact, our meetings and partings only gave a unique kaleidoscope of bliss to our relationship . . .

In the taxi, driven by a local Sikh and redolent with a heavy pine of a cheap air freshener, we could barely preserve appearances under the unnerving gaze of those even black eyes beneath his turban. As if in a dream, breathtaking images of the 'city of dreaming spires' rushed by my window: domed cathedrals, ancient roof turrets, ornate clock towers. . . It was a different world to mine, but one to which I also belonged, as Quentin belonged to me.

'Tomorrow I'll take you on a tour of the campus and on Sunday we can find a nice lunch somewhere in town,' said Quentin, as he paid the driver.

The rest of the afternoon we spent naked in bed, having completely forgotten any previous plan, until the onset of darkness reminded us both that we were starving. Only then did Quentin recall Hugo's party invitation.

'Let's get ready, there should be plenty of food there!' Quentin assured me, and I willingly agreed.

A rising tide of pop music was the first clue that we were approaching the venue, and, having passed a row of terraced houses with immaculate gardens we soon approached a fence behind which the mounting flood of 70s disco music came spilling out.

The wooden gate blended so perfectly with the fence that it was signposted by a bunch of colorful balloons tied to a copper handle. The gate creaked opened quite easily, disclosing a steep stony staircase. At the foot of the stairs, shielded by thick shrubs and dense foliage stood a lovely old mansion with wide bay windows overlooking a dimly-lit garden. From the building we heard screams of laughter and voices half-drowned in the blaring boom of the 70s music.

'We're definitely in the right place,' said Quentin with authority, as if someone had contested it. Closing the gate behind us, we started our descent down the steps, hand in hand. Some of the stones shifted under our feet, and I instantly regretted giving in to the temptation of wearing high platforms (in true 70s style) instead of my usual, more sensible, footwear. Seeing that I was struggling, Quentin easily picked me up and carried me, all the way to the lawn, where he carefully put me down.

'Don't tell me that I don't look after you!' he teased, wrapping his arm around my waist and pressing the doorbell.

It seemed that no one had heard, but the door turned out to be open and we entered. I hadn't even had time to glance around when I saw a good-looking blond guy wearing a pearly white smile, almost matching the color of his bell-bottomed suit, heading towards us, champagne glass in hand. I instantly guessed that this miniature John Travolta was Hugo Devlin.

'This is Sasha,' Quentin introduced me to our glamorous host.

'Hello, darling!' drawled Hugo taking a step towards me with open arms and a smile which could have charmed the pants off a boa constrictor. We hugged and gave each other light kisses on both cheeks like dear old friends. 'Where have you been hiding her all this time? She's absolutely lovely, just as I expected!' he complimented me.

'I told you!' said Quentin, seemingly delighted. It was obvious that Hugo's opinion really mattered to him.

'What'd you like to drink?' Hugo nodded to a passing waiter carrying a tray full of drinks. We accepted two glasses of champagne and followed Hugo into the living room, just managing to squeeze inside, for the party was already in full swing. Two guys in funny wigs and dark shades waved to us from across

CHAPTER 27

the room and we started plowing through the crowd towards them, losing Hugo on the way.

'Hi!' Quentin greeted them warmly. 'There isn't room enough to swing a cat! Is all of Oxford here?'

'Only its coolest representatives,' said a big guy with fake whiskers and a thick cigar, glancing in my direction.

'Oh, yeah, this is my girlfriend, Sasha. Sasha, this is Gordon.'

'Gordon McDouglas,' the guy added, tickling my cheeks with his itchy whiskers.

A swarthy fellow almost a head shorter than Gordon was beside him, wearing a Hawaiian shirt unbuttoned to his navel, displaying a chest adorned with massive gold chains.

'Hi, Sasha! Don't you recognize me?' he said, lifting his shades.

'Freddy! You were in C3, right? So great to see you! How's Oxford treating you?'

'Very well indeed. Quentin told me you were in London.'

Fernandes de Lopez-Pennaloza and I had never really spoken at College, but in such a small school everyone knew each other's faces – especially a face as good-looking as the very popular Freddy's.

Over small talk, Quentin and I helped ourselves to delicious canapés and champagne supplied by an entourage of waiters. Without doubt such party must have cost a pretty penny. 'Oxford students do live well,' I observed aloud.

'Oh, well, Hugo and his friends enjoy living in a grand style. Hey, look at that!' Quentin pointed with his champagne glass.

Only then did I notice a huge bamboo cage with two, scantily clad, Latin-type male dancers inside, their bare skins glittering under a mirrored disco ball.

'My dessert for tonight,' Hugo told Quentin gleefully. 'Ordered from a club in Soho, which saved me a trip to Milan. . . Anyway, after the official party I'm having a private gathering. You're both very welcome to join in, of course.'

'Hmm, no thanks,' grinned Quentin, pulling me closer.

'Well, just as you please . . . In any case, you're welcome to stay over tonight. There's plenty of room, especially since Alex'll be spending the night with his new girlfriend from Balliol,' said Hugo, indicating a rowdy mixed group in bell-bottomed trousers and 70s mini-skirts.

'That's Alex in the big Afro wig,' Quentin added, to me.

A pretty blond girl in a gold off-the-shoulder mini kept glancing in our direction. 'And that's Lulu! She's such a darling!' Hugo sang out, blowing her a kiss before turning back to us. 'In fact, Alex is terribly envious of me,' he added, glancing meaningfully towards the caged dancers. 'He'd never admit it, though, not even if tortured. This term he's profoundly into women and not merely because he suddenly remembered his Catholic upbringing. The old Duke somehow managed to find out about his grandson's being bisexual and threatened to disinherit him if he didn't get married and produce an heir quite snappily. And we're talking hundreds of millions!' His eyes grew round in a rather feigned manner.

'Really? Wow!' Quentin whistled, impressed.

'Well, of course, for that kind of money Alex would be prepared to fall in love with a bearded goat,' concluded Hugo. 'But I cherish my freedom too highly.'

Suddenly, with a slick move he freed himself from his white jacket, tossing it casually to the floor. Then he pulled up his shirtsleeves and, grooving to the music, swaggered over to his two caged birds.

'Riccardo!' We heard him murmur before he slammed the cage door open with his foot and wrapped his arms around the muscular torso of one of the Italian stallions. They merged in a lustful parody of the lambada, to the amusement of the passers-by.

'So that's Hugo!' I laughed, turning to Quentin, who seemed to be closely watching the action in the cage.

'Not really, he's just showing off. In fact, he's completely different. You just don't know him like I do.'

'Hey, Quentin! Come and play charades,' implored the blonde in the gold dress.

'Hi, Lulu,' and, to my dismay, Quentin hugged her, and then kissed her on both cheeks. 'Sasha, this is Lulu. Sasha's my girlfriend, up from London.'

I smiled politely, but the blonde, who had barely spared me a glance, immediately clung onto Quentin's arm.

'You simply must come to my birthday party next Friday,' she cooed, shamelessly making eyes at him, despite being right in front of me. 'It'll be so fab that it'll rival one of Hugo's! First we'll have a black-tie dinner in one of the 16th-century halls – Daddy's already arranged this with the Dean, in gratitude for all he's done for the University. After that we'll – '

'Sounds great but actually I'll be in London with Sasha next weekend,' Quentin told her, for which I secretly covered him with affectionate kisses. But then he added, 'Although we could always change our plans and join you if Sasha was willing to come to Oxford instead.' I shrugged ambiguously, as if to reinforce the fact that it was up to me whether 'to execute or to pardon.'

The blonde pursed her needle-thin lips and threw a resentful glance at me from under her glued-on, spider-leg lashes. 'Actually places are limited, and there are just too many girls already. I've even had to turn down some of my own friends. I simply can't allow them to have seats at dinner without a pair and then there's the dancing as well, of course… Well, if you change your mind, you're most welcome to come.' And with this she smiled coquettishly at Quentin and touched his arm, again ignoring my existence.

After getting acquainted with Lulu I lost any desire to play charades and, in a covert attempt to pull Quentin away from the lecherous debutante, I suggested a walk in the garden.

By this time the guests had spread out, moving to dance in the garden or simply wandering, enjoying the warm September night. After taking a lungful of fresh autumn air, I said as casually as I could: 'I don't remember you mentioning Lulu in your letters.'

'She's just some Chelsea debutante Hugo introduced me to. She seems to have got it into her head that there could be something between us,' said Quentin casually, but then, upon meeting my intent gaze, added, 'but you have nothing to worry about. You know how much I love you… You're the only one I need!'

'Oh, I'm not worried,' I said, feigning indifference.

'Anyway, she's not my type: I don't really like stocky girls, even ones with pretty faces. But even if she had the body of a supermodel, she still couldn't come anywhere near you.' And to drive his point home, Quentin took me in his arms and gave me a reassuring hug.

I flushed with pleasure. It seemed that there was really no reason to worry. Anyway, what was the big deal with some self-proclaimed debutante!

In the garden, we joined a colourful bunch of guys in checked jackets dancing with girls decked out in platform shoes and miniskirts. Quentin was whirling me around when Hugo squeezed between us, grasping us both by the shoulders and murmuring: 'Can I tempt you with some "disco biscuits" or may be a popper, you know, for later? I mean, what kind of a 70s party is it without the stuff?'

Quentin looked uncertainly at me, and when I frowned he said hastily, 'Really, Sasha's keen on a healthy lifestyle. I'll give it a miss too - we have plans for tomorrow morning, as I want to show her around Oxford. But thanks anyway, my friend,' and with this he slapped Hugo on the shoulder.

Soon afterwards I felt fatigue flooding over me, along with the pleasant warmth of intoxication and so, having arranged to meet Hugo for lunch the following day, we wrapped up our night out.

'Let's make it a late lunch, as I'm planning a wild night and won't get out of bed before midday,' he suggested, and with that, bidding our farewells, we headed back to Quentin's Hall of Residence.

'Well, what do you think of Hugo? He's quite a character, isn't he?' said Quentin.

CHAPTER 27

'I did like him,' I admitted honestly.

As soon as I reached his bed, I fell deeply asleep. That night, oddly enough, I dreamed of Hugo. Wiggling his narrow hips in a womanly manner, he was twirling seductively in a cage to the Bee Gees' 'Night Fever', but, instead of his white Travolta suit, he was sporting Lulu's gold dress. He was also spinning round and round, like a golden top, faster and faster, his dress whipping up to expose his hairy legs, until all of a sudden he turned into Lulu. . .

The next morning, Quentin took me on a tour of the campus and I instantly fell in love with Oxford University, which seemed to me so close in its spirit and traditions to Marlborough College – although some might contest this point. Its inimitable beauty and natural superiority were breathtaking, and I suddenly realized that Quentin belonged to Oxford and Oxford to him, almost as if they had been made for each another. . . I was even seized with a wild desire never to leave this place, especially since my Quentin was there.

Around 2:00 p.m. we reached the Silver Horseshoe pub, where we found Hugo waiting for us in the upstairs restaurant. He was wearing a blue cashmere V-neck jumper, which matched the color of his eyes, with a fresh white shirt underneath. Compared to the previous night he looked a bit weary, but his face instantly brightened upon seeing us, with any trace of fatigue dissolving into that delightful smile – along with that sense of his being a society host welcoming long-awaited guests.

'Hello, lovebirds! Did you sleep well?' He greeted us, rising politely from his chair. 'I do envy you your fresh looks. I have absolutely the worst hangover after being up all night. Riccardo and Fabrice, no, Riccardo and Pascal, no – ' he struggled to remember his lover's name, 'No, Paris! That was it! Well, it doesn't really matter, as they both buggered off to London about an hour ago, after insisting on a hundred quid for a taxi plus a decent bonus above the agreed fee - for their "special efforts," which I thought was rather cheeky, but also rather cute. . . But then, just after they left, I discovered that my diamond cufflinks, a gift from my stinky rich ex, which I keep in the top drawer of my bedroom chest, had disappeared right along with them. These pathetic thieves probably stole them whilst I was in the shower!'

'How awful! Are you going to the police?' Quentin suggested, while I nodded sympathetically, in solidarity with such a misfortune.

'The police? That wouldn't work. It won't help in the least if my father or the Dean find out about it!'

Hugo's annoyance, though not altogether phony, nevertheless concealed a certain amount of boasting; sympathetic admiration was what he was after from his audience: admiration for owning diamond cufflinks, and sympathy for their loss.

'And, to crown it all, I feel so utterly battered after everything I drank last night – while the ill-fated, if rather glorious, ménage à trois only proved once again that money can't buy hearts. Though, Riccardo is so divinely well-endowed…'

He seemed keen to share some juicy details: however, Quentin hastily interrupted him with a sudden cough, probably thanks to my presence.

'Oh, of course!' Hugo checked himself and, half-covering Quentin's hand, squeezed it lightly.

I noticed that his nails were impeccably manicured and, glancing at my own, was embarrassed to realize that they left much to be desired in comparison.

'Anyway, enough about me! Tell me how you spent your morning. And let's order some food, as well, as I'm starved!' he added, calling a waiter over.

We ordered hastily, and I was relieved to see that they were no longer holding hands. While Quentin was entertainingly relating our morning's activities, I couldn't resist furtively watching Hugo.

If it weren't for his frankly immodest stories, I would never have guessed that he was gay. Despite his lack of inches, Hugo didn't give the impression of a gentle dandelion, easily blown away by a gust of wind. He owned a proud, sturdy, upright presence with strong shoulders and an excellent posture which, combined with his confident voice and easy manners, made him appear to be a blonde version of a modern macho

CHAPTER 27

Napoleon. His chin, so often slightly lifted, might have given him rather an arrogant expression, except for that utterly disarming smile. He seemed always bursting with energy and vitality – even today, when clearly not on top form, he seemed in constant motion: his elegant hands gesticulating, his facial expressions echoing his lively body language, and his voice vibrant and self-assured, almost as if he was speaking in court. (I believed his father was a QC.)

I also noticed the way he looked at Quentin, In fact, I instantly recognised that look, of which I've been so often guilty myself - his eyes firmly fixed on Quentin's face, as if almost drinking him in, entranced, full of admiration and full too of something else, which I refused to recognize, even in the most secret recesses of my mind.

After a hearty lunch, we ordered coffee. The conversation returned to Oxford, to something about the next Club A meeting and to a recent Student Union debate. I tried to appear interested, but I began to feel bored. Hugo and Quentin, utterly absorbed, were sitting with their elbows on the table, as if playing an invisible game, the rules of which I did not know. Looking at them, I suddenly felt like an outsider in some cozy tête-à-tête. Catching my attentive gaze, Hugo suddenly reached out and gently tucked a stray strand of Quentin's hair behind his ear, whilst my boyfriend, without a slightest confusion, continued with his political argument.

The previously amorphous sense of some vague homosexual threat had turned into a flaring red danger signal, and I said, in a zealous attempt to mark my territory, 'Isn't it time for us to be going, my love? After all, we wanted . . . wanted to. . .'

I didn't know how to finish my thought, as we'd made no particular plans for the rest of our time. I caught a rather contemptuous look on Hugo's handsome face and finished, rather fiercely, '. . . we wanted to make love.'

Quentin pulled me close, his hand caressing my thigh under my skirt, while I flashed Hugo a victorious smile.

'So we did!' said Quentin instantly, adding, 'So sorry, Hugo, must run!'

'I'll not detain you, my dear, as women can suffer from neurosis due to lack of sex,' quipped Hugo.

I longed to put out my tongue at him but instead we hugged each other and graciously air-kissed, while I promised to return to Oxford the next weekend. And, after thanking Hugo for the lunch, we hurried back to the Halls of Residence to fulfill our new plans before my departure time.

It seems as if Hugo and I are likely to be seeing quite a lot of each other from now on. Good! – one should keep a close eye on both rivals and enemies I thought – but at the same time I decided not to share any of my latest observations with Quentin.

CHAPTER 28

Every day at 6:30 a.m. Robert took a jog along the Embankment, a delightful route stretching along the south bank of the Thames. He loved this time of day, when the exhausted roads were resting from the roar of constant traffic, when the autumn air was free of fumes and when far fewer people were around – when, even if you cried aloud, it was unlikely that anyone would hear you. Goose-down morning fog hugged the misty Thames; and suddenly Arthur Conan Doyle's Sherlock Holmes crossed his mind. It represented his earliest childhood acquaintance with England – where there was always a thick fog, in Holmes' case, inevitably hiding something sinister. . .

At the same time, jogging along the Thames certainly pales in comparison with the Californian shoreline thought Robert, although without much regret, for he had become accustomed to frequent changes of location. Leaving Westminster Bridge behind, he glanced at his wrist stopwatch, speeding up along the south bank before slowing slightly along the Albert Embankment. There he was level with the newly-built, glass, juggernaut-like fortress of MI6, popularly nicknamed (at least by its employees) Babylon-on-Thames – or Legoland. He stopped for a moment to catch his breath, observing the filtered rays of the morning sun reflected in its dark green-tinted windows, unsure whether to admire or to loathe the view.

Much to his disappointment, the Emerald City of the firm – the British Secret Intelligence Service (SIS) – was a grey, dull, unassuming building featuring bare walls, endless corridors marked only with Fire Exit signs, and standardized, open-plan offices with acronyms on their doors – along with anonymous conference rooms featuring the most up-to-date equipment.

What Robert would have really loved to check out were the many underground levels, which included secret laboratories and classified documents, not to mention the control center itself . . . In his imagination it combined images from the latest Hollywood blockbuster with those of aliens and wild genetic experiments . . . Unfortunately, only a select few could access all areas without special clearance from the top, and a mere CIA agent certainly didn't qualify.

One Serbian colleague had nicknamed Robert the Maestro, a nickname which had stuck, owing to his exceptional ability to build up complex combinations and to unerringly manipulate situations in order to achieve his objectives. His charisma and quick-witted humour camouflaged a cold and calculating mind, combined with an iron self-discipline and a strong nervous system.

Robert wasn't in London by chance. London was his reward, so to speak, for a successful mission in Peshawar, on the borders of Pakistan and Afghanistan, where he attended a secret meeting with the leaders of the Afghan Mujahidin, covering the featureless mountain range on horseback in a *shalwar kameez* in order to bypass the highway of death that the Khyber Pass had become.

Robert still couldn't quite believe his luck at having been ordered to 'become' an ordinary university student again. He wouldn't have missed the chance of returning to that happy era – and in the capital of England of all places! Moreover, on top of his usual remuneration package, the Company paid his tuition fees and living expenses, as well as providing him with a smart one-bedroom apartment in the City.

'Pick a Master's in whichever subject takes your fancy, as long as you leave time enough for work,' he had been told. 'As always, you'll have a lot of travelling to do, so your cover is that you're working on a project for your sponsor, the Royal Institute of International Affairs. The supporting documentation should be on the Dean's desk by tomorrow. The rest is just as

CHAPTER 28

usual: blend in with the crowd, don't arouse suspicion . . . Well, I don't have to tell you. You'll know much better than I what to do - it's been decades since I was a student . . . Your main task is to get along with our 'Big Brother' – the Firm has asked for our help – yet again – in order to manage the Colombians' drug trafficking ring, so don't forget to arrange a formal handover meeting with the liaison officer…I somehow doubt you'll be in London for very long, so enjoy it while it lasts!'

Which was exactly what Robert was intent upon doing.

He had been recruited whilst still a student. After graduating in Toronto with distinction, he'd been awarded a prestigious Kennedy scholarship to read biological engineering at one of California's top engineering institutes. Apart from the course itself, California had attracted Rob with the promise of year-round sunshine, sandy beaches and those tanned Californian blondes: the latter being admittedly a weighty factor in his decision-making.

California had more than met his expectations. Charismatic and popular, he had adopted his preferred role as the life and soul of the party, attracting girls like a magnet, without causing undue hostility from his rivals - everything had seemed to come to him effortlessly, as if by chance. Rob had also succeeded in his studies, and in his second year he'd won a tough contest for a scholarship from the McKinsey Fund to attend a university in the country of his choice for the year following his graduation.

By this time, Rob had already travelled around the world; his father had worked for the Department of External Affairs of Canada (as it was known during that period when Canada's foreign policy had still been controlled by the U.K.), which had meant that their family had moved around a good deal.

As a boy, Robert had only just managed to get settled into some school and begun to feel that he was really fitting in before he'd have to move again – leaving behind not just his friends and his school, but also yet another country, so he found nothing unusual in the fact that the pictures and the people in his life were constantly changing, or that nothing ever felt truly permanent. As a result, he had learned not to get attached to anyone or anything, despite getting along with people extremely easily and making friends almost on the spot. He'd almost lost count of the places he'd lived while his father was moving up the career ladder.

When his parents had first got married, his father had been posted to London, Vienna, and finally Paris. Then came a period in the Eastern Bloc: Czechoslovakia, Yugoslavia, and East Germany, as they'd used to be known - followed by a colorful year in Cuba – where the brutal contrast between poverty and wealth became as imprinted in Robert's memory as that of his first love . . .

Having visited or resided in half of the globe, his father was by then approaching retirement. For his remaining years of service he was called home to the headquarters of his native Toronto, where his family had settled in the large country mansion once owned by his wife's parents, and where Jenny and Robert attended a local school.

Robert had been fond of sports from his earliest years: running and athletics had been followed by judo, in which he won every possible 'belt' – and while living in Cuba he had enjoyed scuba-diving. However, upon his return to Toronto, Rob had immediately fallen in love with ice hockey. He had soon begun to make serious progress and had eventually been chosen as a forward for the Junior National Hockey Team. Despite his parents' growing concern that he wouldn't be able to fully focus on his studies during his senior year, Robert had secretly set his sights upon becoming a professional ice hockey player. With his gifts, which included tenacity and stubbornness, he would almost certainly have achieved this goal – however, an unlucky accident had ruined his plans: during a training session he'd fallen and broken his ankle. Surgery had followed, but for some reason the bone had failed to fuse and follow-up surgery had to be scheduled.

The recovery process had proved to be long and painful. Robert was told that he would never be able to play again and new players were chosen in his place. However, this had failed to discourage him; determined to prove that he

CHAPTER 28

shouldn't have been written off so easily, he'd started training in secret, putting severe pressure on the injured leg and upsetting his parents, who had not been able to stop him.

Then family tragedy had intervened: his sister Jenny had fallen to her death on Whistler Mountain while on a skiing holiday. His sister's death had stunned Robert: he just couldn't believe that someone so young, precious and beautiful could have been ripped away from them so unfairly. He'd done his best to remain strong and to support his inconsolable parents, for the first time in his life feeling the weight of responsibility on his teenage shoulders. His hockey ambitions had ended with Jenny - along with his childhood.

Robert had been contemplating which exotic part of the world he wanted to move to after California when an unexpected encounter had radically changed his course of direction.

One of his lecturers, Bill Wayne, happened to have been his father's friend from their days together at Princeton. As Robert was packing for university in California, Robert's father had recommended Bill, mentioning that if his son ever ran into some kind of trouble, or simply needed advice, he could always depend upon his old friend. Rob had instantly hit it off with Bill, who had once played ice hockey for Princeton. Their friendship had grown even stronger after the slow death of Rob's father from cancer, as Bill had become the last link in the chain of people who had once been close to his dad.

Bill lived in a small, cluttered bachelor apartment only a short walk from the campus, and Rob had often dropped by for a cold beer and a chat, or to catch a televised game of ice hockey. One day Bill had invited him over for dinner to meet his friend Doug, with whom he had served in Vietnam. Doug was a grey-haired man of formidable height, with a strong chin and an upright posture. The look in his steely eyes was intense and penetrating. Over dinner he'd casually enquired about Robert's plans for the future.

'I always wanted to be like my father,' said Robert, without hesitation.

'In which case, you should consider working for the Company,' said Doug.

Does he mean the CIA? Did my father really work for them all these years? thought Robert, in utter astonishment.

'Yes, your father was one of us, and a true hero to boot,' confirmed Doug, as if reading his mind. 'Anyway, think about it. I'll drop by to see you when I'm next in L.A. and we'll have a long chat.'

As it happened, Robert didn't have to think twice and the next time they'd met he gladly accepted Doug's offer.

'First, you'll spend some time on what we call the "farm,"' Doug had told him, referring to Camp Peary, 'That's for paramilitary and tradecraft training. Hope you don't suffer from agoraphobia, by the way – you'll need to learn how to jump out of a plane.'

'With a parachute, I hope,' Robert had added cheerfully.

'You'll probably enjoy it. And in the summer you'll go to a military camp for new recruits on the border of Arizona. Later, after your graduation, you'll be sent to one of our special schools,' continued Doug, effectively mapping out Robert's future on the back of an envelope.

'What about my McKinsey Scholarship?'

'Decline it. For now we have other plans for you, but I don't exclude the possibility that you might get a chance to be a student again, in some country or other. When recruits are young, it often happens.

From that moment Robert had no longer belonged to himself: his life followed a script written by others. Following his extensive training, Robert had been selected for a mission to Turkey - the 'Company' already entrusting him with important tasks. Then had come his first, but by no means last, trip to Pakistan. In the early 90s the Balkans had been riven by civil wars, which had given the Company a huge amount of new projects and Robert, as an agent in a special division, was briefly posted to a military base in the region, resulting in his first promotion. He disliked recollecting his period in the Balkans and all that he'd seen there, but had eventually come to the conclusion that the relations between the two 'brother' nations could be appalling when their interests didn't coincide. . .

CHAPTER 28

After his training, Robert had found that he could easily control most people by exploiting their weaknesses, in order to forward the Company's objectives. Having mastered the art of conversation, he was not only silver-tongued, which in fact had come to him naturally, but was also an exceptionally good listener, capable of appearing absorbed in the problems of others, even when bored. He had a genuine interest in people, and in accordance with the universal law of attraction, most people were drawn to him in return.

Even as a new recruit he'd been the only one in their group to cope with the training task of securing the names and social security numbers of ten random passers-by in L.A., within three hours. Using the business cards of a fake Hollywood talent agent along with oversized shades and a false mustache, he'd wandered along Hollywood Boulevard, offering movie castings to women he'd liked the look of, taking care to avoid foreign tourists. The number of female wannabes had far exceeded his wildest expectations – everyone had been willing to provide their personal details and some had even offered something still more personal . . .

An hour later, Rob had returned with the names and social security numbers of over fifty women. His flabbergasted group trainer, despite his 20 years of teaching, had never witnessed such a result.

'Women are such charmingly credulous creatures. They were so happy to be deceived, that I don't even feel the need to apologize...' Rob had told him, with that innocent smile.

As a strong personality himself he had always tended to avoid pushy women at all costs, the type that weaker men call 'headstrong' yet are subconsciously drawn towards all the same. Instead, Robert had always preferred lovely, feminine creatures who at least looked as if they might need his support and protection. Such women were as rare as gold dust in the Company - concealed under the disguise of a feminine charm was a core of robotic 'honey traps.' He had already once burned his fingers with a young female agent he had accompanied to Pakistan. (He'd even considered the relationship serious, until he'd learned that this heartless careerist had slept, not only with him, but also with a 60-year-old director, as well as his perspiring deputy.) Rob had sedulously avoided combining work with romance ever since.

He still regarded the student years before he was recruited as the happiest of his life: back then he hadn't needed to worry about a sexual partner possibly turning into a double agent. Life had been so easy and carefree! Sometimes he wished to be able to forget who he really was, to blend in with the innocent student crowd, to chase pretty women, to fall in love or even to simply be able get drunk in a bar. . .

He had appreciated Sasha at first sight, it had been hard to miss her in that crowd: statuesque and slender, with that thick hair woven into a single golden plait. As if sensing his glance, she had turned her head, meeting his eyes with her captivatingly restless, doe-eyed gaze. He'd even thought that there might be something familiar about her face, or as if some irresistible force was pulling him towards her. To his surprise, she'd turned out to be Russian. Robert had always been interested in Russia and the CIS countries and, encouraged by his mentor, had even completed an advanced Russian language course. However, with the recent collapse of the Soviet Union, Russia was no longer of quite as much interest for the Company as it had been: other, more pressing, projects required more immediate attention.

Robert had only previously met Russians while in Israel, in one of the special training camps. These had been Soviet Jews attempting to make ends meet in the nearby village. Robert had soon made friends with them, treated them to cigarettes, and told them about America, where most of them had still dreamed of going, while meanwhile practising his Russian, which had certainly improved greatly over those months . . .

So now, with a Russian-speaking 'object' at hand, he hoped to learn more about the Russian mentality and that mysterious 'Slavic soul.' Besides, the object herself was rather attractive.

CHAPTER 28

Realizing that an easy victory was not possible and that the position of Sasha's boyfriend was not vacant, he took the decision to wait, preferring a long and drawn-out siege to his usual, more direct, attack.

'It'll also be more fun, as easy victories are so easily forgotten,' he had mused.

From the time they'd met he had tried to get to know her better and had soon come to the conclusion that Sasha was modest and wholesome as well as kind by nature, completely devoid of any falseness or propensity for showing off–naturally, he'd have spotted that at once; he'd met enough pretty mannequins in his life.

He had also formed a certain opinion of Quentin who - in his, possibly prejudiced, view - so longed to win everyone over, to lead and to impress that his very vanity made him susceptible and easy to manipulate.

Her boyfriend could do with a firm hand to keep him in line. Any female employee of the Company could have had him eating out of her hand within two days, but Sasha was too soft, too gentle and too inexperienced to do it... What she needs is a real man by her side thought Robert. *Her relationship is unlikely to last and then I simply have to be there for her. I'd love to move things on a little faster, but it seems that Sasha is really in love with him...*

Despite the harsh and in-depth training Robert had endured, he was no cynic – not only thanks to the innate optimism of youth but also because of his strong moral compass. He thought: *I can wait, when I think someone's worth waiting for – and I think she is...*

CHAPTER 29

I awoke to dull morning rain drumming on my window. Since my first class wasn't due to start for another hour, I'd just decided to stay snugly in bed for a little longer when an insistent knocking on my door made me reluctantly abandon my cozy retreat.

'Who's there?' I asked drowsily.

'You have a phone call, someone who doesn't speak English properly,' grumbled the irritated voice of our porter.

Something to do with my mother I thought instantly, suddenly feeling scared. Blood pounded in my temples, and my hands felt cold and sweaty. I threw a coat over my pajamas and sped down the stairs to the public phone, losing my slippers along the way.

'Sasha, is that you?' It was Nina, our Moscow neighbour, speaking in Russian. 'Sasha, I'm sorry but your mother has passed away. You have to come home and arrange her funeral.'

I couldn't breathe. Dizzied with helpless anger and disbelief I sank down on the ice-cold floor:

It can't be! It just can't be!

'Sasha, can you still hear me?' cried Nina, panicking.

'Yes, yes, I hear you. I'll be on the first flight,' I whispered back.

Sooner than seemed possible I was sitting on the plane, my forehead pressed against the window. Tears were running down my cheeks and I didn't even bother wiping them off, as they instantly reappeared - everything around me seemed to be in some kind of a blur. I kept hoping that I was involved in a nightmare, from which I would awake with my mother hugging me and gently smoothing my forehead, the way she had always done when I had been a child. . .

Dad missed the funeral, and, although I didn't wish to admit it, I secretly still hoped – until the very last moment – that he would come. I visualized him, overcome with grief beside mother's grave, passionately repenting of all that he had done to her. In my imagination we were silently holding hands, united in grief, whilst my mother was watching down on us from her place in heaven, solaced, finally knowing how much she was loved . . .

Needless to say, none of this fantasy occurred. In fact, my father couldn't have cared less – he was deliriously happy with his new, 'pure' love, whilst I was merely an inconvenient obstacle, unwished-for bAlast from his past. He got away with a telegram addressed to our house in Moscow: 'Truly sorry, but unable to come due to some urgent business. Made a bank transfer to pay for the funeral. See you in London. Love, Dad.'

'No way!' I furiously tore the telegram into tiny pieces.

Returning afterwards, I took the Piccadilly line from Heathrow and, lost in thought, nearly missed the station change-over for the university campus. In the Halls of Residence the porter told me that Quentin had left several messages requesting that I call him back; there was also a card from his mother Debbie, who had sent her condolences and promised to see me in London soon.

I went up to my room. Everything looked as if I had never left: files and books lay spread-eagled on the desk, and clothes were strewn over the bed, where I'd left them while hastily packing . . . Dead tulip petals scattered on the windowsill reminded me of the fragility of life. I resolutely binned the pot of the wilted flowers and hurried down to the phone in order to call Quentin. I was patiently holding the line while they were looking for him in his Halls of Residence – in fact, I'd almost lost hope – when I finally heard his familiar voice: 'Sasha, it's me! Are you back?'

'Oh, I'm so glad to hear your voice!' I sighed, more with relief than with any other feeling.

I didn't want to talk about the funeral, which stood bleakly before my eyes, as if – in my mind at least – I was still standing in the deserted Moscow cemetery beside my mother's grave. As much as I wanted to return to my life,

CHAPTER 29

I knew that it would never be the same again. So instead I said impulsively, 'Come and see me this weekend. I've missed you so much!'

However, Quentin stayed silent. 'Are you still there?' I questioned.

'I'd have loved to. I want to see you more than anything else,' he said, rather guiltily, 'but unfortunately we have mid-term exams and I really need to study the whole weekend. I just can't manage it, I'm afraid.'

I was taken aback: although I'd heard about the Oxford academic race and how difficult it was to stay afloat, surely that concerned the usual kinds of students, those diligent swotters who had gotten into Oxford due to hard work rather than those, like Quentin, who were naturally brilliant at everything. Why should he be so worried about mid-term exams? They'd be a piece of cake for him! However, I hastened to say, 'OK, then I can come to you. Don't worry, I won't get on the way of your studying!'

There was an awkward pause. Afterwards I could tell by Quentin's tone of voice that he was frowning. He said: 'No, no, you mustn't think of it. You'll get bored by yourself, and besides I'd want to be with you all the time and wouldn't be able to study. . . I really wanted us to be able to spend the entire weekend together. Why don't we just postpone our meeting until next Friday instead?'

'Fine, I guess I'll see you next Friday then,' I said, resigned. I was hoping he'd notice my tone and change his mind, but this didn't happen.

'Great. I'll call you tomorrow, after my lecture,' Quentin promised. 'Will be thinking about you. Love you!'

Taken together with all the days that had passed since our last meeting, by the time next Friday came I wouldn't have seen Quentin for almost a month. Sighing, I trudged to my room, feeling disappointed and let down.

Despite his promise, Quentin failed to call the next day. Having waited around in vain, I still refused to call him myself: much as I wished to, I also didn't want to appear desperate. I was at a loss to understand his recent behaviour: it was all so unlike Quentin - he had always been so thoughtful and punctual in every circumstance.

He must simply be stressed out about his exams I thought, trying to explain his silence to myself - I knew how important it was for Quentin to succeed at Oxford: getting in was only the beginning. . .

A few days later, he finally called. To my relief there had been a simple explanation - he was indeed plunged, neck-deep, in his studies.

'So sorry, Sasha, but with all the hours I've had to put in, I didn't even have time to get to the phone . . . But I really can't wait to see you on the weekend!' he apologised.

For the next period of my life I lived like a zombie on autopilot, the days crawling dully along, then rushed past, and then started crawling along again. At night however, everything seemed vivid and horrible. I suffered from insomnia, while thoughts about my mother and our last meeting refused to leave me.

It's all my fault! It was I who brought Alka into our family I thought one night, and cried until almost dawn, when I finally fell into a disturbed sleep. In my dreams my mother was always young and beautiful, as she had been when I was a child, however, I occasionally had nightmares featuring a huge black cat, which smiled at me maliciously, baring razor-sharp teeth that it seemed intent upon sinking into my flesh . . . Waking in an icy sweat from dreams such as these, I turned on the light, made some tea and read a book. In the morning I'd often find that I'd been asleep for only an hour or two, and awoken by my alarm clock just in time for class. Even getting out of bed required a huge effort, which seemed completely pointless; and sometimes all I longed to do was to dive back under my blanket, never to wake up again.

I suddenly stopped caring about the world around me - my entire existence seemed fragile, injured and painful. Yellow stickers randomly stuck around my room reminded me of basic things, as I could no longer rely on myself and didn't really want to: *'Brush your teeth'* and *'Shower'* belonged in the bathroom, *'Comb your hair and dress'* was on the dressing mirror in the hall, whilst *'Eat'* was glued to the door I ignored the most.

CHAPTER 29

I had completely lost my appetite, becoming indifferent to food despite continual efforts to make myself eat. Besides, the food in our canteen left much to be desired and I often settled for fresh oranges, which were given away for free in the Halls of Residence, as if in an attempt to compensate for the poor cuisine. Soon I began skipping classes and spending more and more time feeling sorry for myself, hiding from life in the wounded safety of my room.

In the beginning Jill and my fellow students had visited me regularly, being concerned for my wellbeing and attempting to cheer me. They'd been sincerely sympathetic, and tried their best to persuade me to join them for lunch in the canteen or to make at least some short appearance at some student party. I'd always forced a smile, promising to keep them company next time, but in fact, had always secretly hoped that they'd leave as soon as possible, so that I could be left alone with my grief. They soon enough had become resigned to leaving me alone, only occasionally querying if there was anything that I needed.

One day I was yet again skipping a morning lecture in the quietness of my room, lost in my thoughts, when I suddenly heard a dog barking behind the door. I put down the textbook, upon which I'd been absentmindedly trying to focus all morning, and peeked in the corridor. Outside stood a good-natured sand-colored Labrador wagging his tail. I glanced around in confusion. The corridor was empty; it seemed that all of the other students were in lectures.

'Where did you come from?' I asked him, bewildered. 'You'll be in great trouble if our porter finds you here!'

In response, the dog promptly sneaked past me and stretched out on my floor, his expression a wide cheerful grin, pink tongue hanging out. He was looking at me as inquisitively as an A student and I had no choice but to follow the intruder inside, despite misgivings.

'Where's your owner?' I tried to start up a conversation, reaching down to pat him on the head. 'You must feel thirsty, breathing so hard!' I added, noting his leather collar: obviously, this was no stray. I poured some cold water from the tap into a bowl, which he lapped up, while I puzzled over future actions regarding my unexpected guest.

A little later, I heard a whistle in the corridor. Perking up his ears, the Labrador jumped up, waving his tail wildly and ran to the door, whining with impatience to be let out.

'Nobody's holding you back!' I muttered, opening the door and the dog bolted into the corridor, barking joyfully along the way.

'Buddha! Where you been, buddy? I've been looking for you all over!' Robert's lively voice resounded along the corridor. Canadian good cheer being about the last thing I felt equal to, I was about to shut the door and retreat into my shell when Robert called, 'Sasha, hang on, wait a minute!'

He headed towards me accompanied by the dog and I reluctantly invited them both in. The mess was vaguely embarrassing, but, in my current state, I couldn't have cared much less. Buddha too seemed entirely satisfied and started eagerly running around the room, sniffing various jeans scattered on the floor, at least one of which I suspected had a chocolate chunk in its pocket.

'Buddha, down!' Robert ordered and the dog rushed to lie obediently at his feet. 'Don't you have any classes today, Sasha?'

'Why should you care?' I grumbled ungraciously.

'Because, if not, I'd like to invite you for a walk,' said Robert, kindly ignoring my rudeness. 'Look what a glorious day it is!' He moved to the window and opened the blinds, the first time they'd been opened in weeks. The clear blue sky seemed to know nothing about grief. I hesitated for a second, considering how to refuse his offer without seeming ungrateful, while Rob immediately took advantage of my confusion: 'We'll go for a stroll along the river and then grab a meal somewhere. C'mon, get yourself dressed. It's nearly lunchtime – as Buddha knows pretty well.'

Hearing his name and the word 'lunch' in close conjunction Buddha pricked up his ears, jumped to his feet, and ran to me, looking pleadingly into my eyes and wriggling his entire body in delight.

CHAPTER 29

'OK, the two of you have talked me into it,' I decided, at last giving in to their charm.

Leaving the campus behind, we went for a walk along the Embankment, following Buddha, who was partly running far ahead, and partly falling well behind, diverting his attention to those smells or trees that he particularly liked.

As we walked, Rob explained that Buddha belonged to one of his friends, who had rescued the puppy in Bangkok the previous winter. After becoming lost the poor dog had been found begging food from tourists and scavenging a living from rubbish dumps in a dog pack. Had Rob's friend failed to save him, Buddha could have suffered the sad fate of so many strays in Thailand - to be caught by dog-meat traders and transported to the black market in neighbouring Vietnam. As he told me, 'The poor thing could've been long since cooked.'

Leaving Victoria Embankment we headed west and soon merged with a crowd of Chinese tourists searching for Trafalgar Square.

'Follow me!' Rob nodded in the direction of Whitehall and Buddha and I, leaving the Chinese contingent behind, followed after him, bearing left. After about a hundred metres we came to a narrow cobbled street, down which was hidden The Queen's Head, an ancient pub. As Robert went inside to search for a waiter Buddha and I commandeered a large table in the courtyard, relishing the historic Whitehall views.

For lunch Buddha enjoyed a 'butcher's plate' with smoked ham and sausages, whilst both Robert and I chose the duck with braised red cabbage and mashed potatoes. It was the first time since my return from Moscow that I'd left an empty plate, much to Buddha's dismay.

Later, Robert fancied making an excursion to Scotland Yard, where, to his astonishment, we weren't allowed inside. 'I've always wanted to see it, ever since I was a kid,' Rob lamented. 'In Washington even the FBI building allows tourists in.'

'In my opinion, we haven't missed much,' I comforted him, casting a critical glance at the ugly, sixties-era building. 'And we'd have had to leave Buddha in the street. He wouldn't have liked that much.'

'You're right, let's go get some ice cream instead,' decided Robert, and we headed towards Trafalgar Square.

That evening, having escorted me right to the door of the Halls of Residence before taking Buddha home, Robert closed his warm hands around mine and said, very gently: 'Sasha, believe me, I know how hard it is to lose someone you love. . . I'm truly sorry that you've lost your mother so early… But in spite of everything, you must live on. Promise me that you'll try not to skip lessons again.'

I nodded silently.

'Buddha and I will drop by tomorrow,' he added, sounding much more like himself, as we parted. I headed upstairs to my room, thinking in passing that I should pay Jill a visit tomorrow and find out the latest news.

CHAPTER 30

The following day, intent upon keeping my promise to Robert, I headed to class straight after breakfast. In the new teaching building I came across a group of girls, Jill amongst them, who were enjoying an animated discussion, their heads conspiratorially bowed over something. When they spotted me, they exchanged glances and seemed to hold an urgent, whispered consultation. I greeted them and was about to pass by, when Jill called after me. She separated herself from the group and came up to me, a glossy magazine in her hands and a mixture of commiseration and sorrow in her eyes.

'Sasha, have you seen the latest issue of *Hello* magazine?' The weekly illustrated bible of the rich and famous was the last thing on my mind, and I stared at her in confusion, wondering what this might portend.

Jill hesitated before continuing. 'I only mentioned it because there's a bit in it about your dad. Here!' She hastily opened the magazine at the right page and handed it to me.

I could hardly believe the sickening trash that met my eyes: a double-spread featuring a new bride and groom. Alka, in a fitted tiered wedding dress like a towering, multi-layered cake, was featured holding a huge bouquet, her smile – outlined in vivid red lipstick – like the bloody grin of a feline predator who had just devoured its prey. Beside her stood my father, holding her hard by the waist, wearing the stupendously happy grin of a lovesick teenager above the sycophantic tag-line: *'well-known Russian businessman and personal adviser to the Russian President.'*

Under the heading *'Russian Love Affair in Grand Old English Style'* large colorful type drew the reader's attention to the following paragraph: *'Anatoly Emelyanov married Ala Gromova, the love of his life, in an emotional ceremony* amongst close friends and relatives.' The words *'love of his life'* and *'emotional ceremony'* were highlighted in pink, presumably so *Hello* readers might take at face value the 'true' love of an eighteen-year-old beauty for a forty-five-year-old millionaire. The fact that the groom had remarried almost immediately after the tragic death of his first wife, with whom he had lived for almost twenty years, remained discreetly unmentioned.

Some of the guests were Russians, so far as could be deduced from their names, and there were several photos of respectable-looking men of my father's age with their wives, some of whom appeared young enough to be their daughters. Their gaudy designer outfits and troweled-on make-up suggested that they had only recently tasted money. I noticed that no relatives on either side appeared to be present, despite the headline – not even Alka's mother. Instead of the youthful college crowd, which I half-expected to see as Alka's attendants, there seemed to have been plenty of guests looking even older than my dad, none of whom I could recall having seen before. I also found some of their names truly bizarre, for example 'Higgis' – I'd never seen such a name before. I didn't want to read on – I wanted to thrust it from me – but somehow I read on:

'The happy couple celebrated their wedding in the Oldland-on-Grove, a stunning 19th-century manor house in rural Wiltshire in Italian Renaissance style, with landscaped grounds, a labyrinth and a deer park, as well as seven hundred acres of woodland and farmland, which the groom presented as a wedding gift to his beautiful bride. The happy bride also prepared a return surprise - the planting of a birch grove that, as she movingly said, "will always remind us of our beloved Russia."

'At the wedding banquet to honour the stunning young wife, all 365 windows of Oldland-on-Grove, equal in number to the days of the year, were illuminated throughout the night until at dawn the newly-weds flew on their honeymoon to the Maldives.'

I felt like vomiting but I couldn't stop reading. *Hello* further gushingly reported that the bride had fallen in love with Wiltshire after studying there at an exclusive boarding school with the groom's only child, Sasha Emelyanova, who was unfortunately unable to attend the wedding. The article had clearly been commissioned, and it didn't take me long to guess who had been the initiator of this paid-for PR.

'What a truly horrible person Ala turned out to be!' Jill said, probably reading my stormy reaction in my expression. 'Oh Sasha, I'm so sorry!' And with this she hugged me warmly.

Her sympathy was terrible: it made me long to burst into tears of self-pity, but I checked myself and, having freed myself from her arms, hurried on to my lecture. I might as well not have bothered, except for having promised Robert that I would go, because I hardly heard a single word. Apart from the hurt and the slow-burning anger, other thoughts were also racing through my head: *Who is she, this Alka? After all, I don't know her at all… I never did know her! It was all a lie!*

After class, I was surprised and overjoyed to find Quentin in my room – I'd completely forgotten that, some time ago, I'd had given him my spare set of keys. He was lying on my bed, reading.

'At last!' he exclaimed, tossing the book aside and leaping to his feet. 'I've been waiting for you for nearly two hours!' We hugged each other hard. It was so good to see him again!

'Aren't you eating anymore?' he joked, though giving me a worried look. 'If you don't watch out, you'll disappear!'

After the month-long separation, he seemed almost a stranger: I needed time to get used to him again. I stared at his handsome face: nothing appeared to have changed, except that he'd grown a slight stubble, but it suited him, making him look somewhat older, more dashing and more experienced . . . Anyway, nothing could diminish looks as stunning as Quentin's.

'Designer stubble, do you like it?' Quentin questioned, noticing my inspection. I ran my hand along the strong contours of his chin; the bristle was soft. 'Yes, it suits you!' I approved his new look.

'That's what everyone says.'

Quentin pulled me to him and I kissed him cautiously and almost shyly, as if needing to get reacquainted again. He said, 'By the way, these are for you,' and with this he nodded at a huge bouquet of white lilies in the sink. 'I couldn't find a vase here: you need to get one.'

'What for? It's not like I'm often showered with flowers,' I said, surprised.

'Hint taken! You know, when I was walking here with the flowers, all the girls were looking at me with such envy! They were probably thinking how lucky my girlfriend was, some even followed me with their eyes...'

'And the rest of them ran after you, did they?' I quipped.

'You'll see,' Quentin continued, ignoring my mockery, 'from now on I promise to give you flowers more often. It's definitely worth it!' he concluded, glancing at his reflection in the mirror above the sink.

'So you're going to give me flowers, only in order to attract the admiration of other girls when you're striding around flourishing them, like a peacock displaying his tail, huh?' I inquired.

'Why are you so moody today? You don't even like the flowers.' Quentin sounded hurt.

The heady scent of lilies suddenly seemed to fill the entire room. Suddenly feeling both suffocated and guilty I rushed to open the window. I thought: *My boyfriend really tried his best to please me; he got me these wonderful flowers and all I can do is snipe at him!* I kissed him on the cheek saying, 'I like them very much!'

'I can see that,' commented Quentin grimly.

'And to prove it I'm going to find a vase,' I said, going out into the corridor.

There I bumped into Robert and Buddha, the latter of whom leapt all over me, full of affectionate canine exuberance.

'Sasha! We were just coming to ask you out for a walk,' said Robert.

I had completely forgotten that they were due to come by. The *Hello* spread had put it right out of my head – and Quentin, of course.

CHAPTER 30

'Sorry, some other time. I have to dash, as I have Quentin waiting,' and with this I waved good-bye and went on with my search... I soon discovered that I wasn't the only student not to own a vase. Finally, I managed to borrow a cracked glass wine decanter from the porter, who had himself inherited it from some former resident.

Returning to the room with my new acquisition, I found Quentin in a far happier mood - he was playing some new rock music that he'd brought and half-dancing around the room, singing along to it.

'Let's rewind and start all over again,' he suggested. He was eager to tell recount his successes at Oxford during my absence in Moscow, launching into some long-winded tale about some clandestine party for the A Club followed by a star-studded London ball, where his political acumen had impressed one of Hugo's friends – a Liberal Democrat and a runner-up in the Politician of the Year Award.

'Such a pity you weren't around, as we could've gone to the ball together. Although, to be honest, I'm not sure it would have been entirely your cup of tea...' he added.

As if I cared about his silly balls, considering everything that had been going on in my life! I thought fiercely. For the first time he seemed to me to be entirely self-absorbed – his recent successes had really gone to his head.

'Come here, darling, I really missed you,' he finished, opening his arms to me at last. I went to him obediently, gazing into his eyes, which had a strange, almost glassy, look and which seemed almost jet-black, with their dilated pupils. Catching me looking searchingly at him, he closed his eyes and kissed me. However, we kissed slowly and cautiously, as if we both felt a little unsure. None of the usual eroticism followed this kiss: instead Quentin pulled away and carelessly asked: 'Well, what are we going to do today? How are you going to entertain me?' He instantly registered my hurt look. 'What's wrong now?' he half-groaned.

'Well, to start with, you haven't even bothered to ask how I am. We haven't seen each other for nearly a month – during which time I buried my mother! I don't think I'm hugely unreasonable in expecting a bit more sympathy from you.'

I heard the bitter and vehement reproach in my voice but I couldn't help it.

'Sorry. I'm probably just a cold-hearted moron. So: how are you?' asked Quentin and, without even waiting for my answer, added, as if to justify himself, 'Anyway, I was thinking about you. I called you and I also bought those flowers, which weren't cheap, by the way.' Then he rewarded himself another bonus: 'Besides, I've even been faithful to you all this time in Oxford!'

That last sentence threw me off balance altogether. 'You've *even* been faithful?' I repeated half-mockingly. 'Was that such an effort? Well, thank you very much! You know, probably you shouldn't have come here today, instead you should go straight back to Oxford and stop bothering to make such efforts in the future!'

Quentin, shaken, gaped at me in stunned silence: we'd never quarreled before and we both seemed to be struggling to understand what was happening. What might have happened, had he apologised properly at this point, I'll never know; but instead I threw his jacket at him – causing a packet of white powder to fall out, the contents of which, knowing Quentin, I instantly guessed.

'And don't forget your coke!' I fumed, feeling sickened. 'The last thing I need is to get expelled from university because of you!'

I later realized that, during my absence in quest of a vase, Quentin had found time to sniff coke: no wonder his pupils were the size of a full moon! Stung, he sneered, 'You obviously don't want to go back to Moscow! But your student visa will expire anyway, after your studies, and that'll be the end of you!' As he volleyed this at me he bent down to retrieve his packet, looking relieved to find it still sealed and intact. 'You can be so difficult to love sometimes, Sasha! Anyway, I'd better go.'

Left alone I fumed for a while, moving from feeling furious to being on the brink of tears to masochistically rewinding the whole unpleasant episode in my mind, before I pulled myself together. More than anything I was shocked

CHAPTER 30

by the sudden mutual hostility which had lifted its ugly head during our quarrel. In fact, I felt so shaken by the whole thing that I started considering breaking up with Quentin. However, the very idea of separation was so painful – I had just, after all, been permanently separated from my mother – that I was hugely relieved when, that evening, Quentin called to apologise.

'I'm such an idiot, Sasha! Please forgive me! I know you are thinking of leaving me – ' he seemed to be reading my mind – 'but I still love you very much. And I still need you! I'll come down next weekend and we'll have a great time together to make up for this weekend. Promise me!'

We made it up and I started blissfully counting the days, which remained until next weekend…

CHAPTER 31

On Tuesday Quentin called to tell me that he unfortunately wouldn't be able to make it to London at the weekend: it had completely slipped his mind that he had to revise for an important test on Monday. Clearly, Oxford didn't allow for even a single lapse of effort and concentration! On this occasion, I didn't even try to suggest my visiting him instead, possibly because I had a back-up plan - Jill was having her birthday party in a local pub and I'd been invited. To Jill's great disappointment, Robert seemed to have gone away – and nobody seemed to know his whereabouts, either.

During the week that followed Quentin and I called each other almost daily, but he was still preoccupied with his studies, as his test results continued to fall short of expectations, and he didn't even mention making plans to see me. It appeared that we were growing apart and, having worried about it, I concluded that this was partly my fault. After all, I'd made no effort to strengthen our relationship; instead I was simply letting matters take their own course. I wasn't entirely sure what I was supposed to do in order to turn the situation around, but in the end I decided to take the initiative and to surprise Quentin with a visit.

On Friday afternoon, straight after my last lecture, I boarded a high-speed train from Waterloo station to Oxford, where I already was - in my mind at least - united with Quentin.

Upon arrival I joined the queue for taxis and in about a quarter of an hour I was on the doorstep of his Halls of Residence. Quentin wasn't in his room, which was locked; some time ago we had exchanged spare keys to each other's rooms, but then Quentin had asked for mine back, because he'd lost his somewhere.

I wandered around the building in the vain hope that I might run into him and then went downstairs to locate the porter, who was amusing himself by watching a kettle boil. I waited politely until he'd made his tea but he wasn't very helpful: while he didn't know any more than I about Quentin's whereabouts, he did know that my own whereabouts shouldn't be anywhere near his Halls of Residence.

'Strangers aren't allowed unless accompanied by a resident,' he grumbled, over and over, even though he'd met me on a number of occasions.

I had no choice but to go outside, where I perched myself on a bench in the quad, feeling remorseful about turning up without proper notice. Time itself seemed to be in no hurry, strolling leisurely across the hands of my watch. *My mother's gift,* I recalled with sadness.

Loud ringing laughter suddenly attracted my attention: a group of students wearing black-tie, like a flock of glistening blackbirds, were crossing the quad, arm-in-arm. Everyone else's life seemed in full swing that Friday evening, while I was sitting alone on a cold bench. My eyes filled with tears at such injustice. As the evening descended the weather turned bad: icy fingers of wind fumbled at my collar and the first few drops of rain started to fall. The quad grew empty. Feeling as cold as a well-digger's feet in January, I was about to find a taxi and head back to London, when suddenly a shiny red Porsche pulled up outside the entrance. Someone emerged from the car, and then, with a high-pitched squeal, the Porsche disappeared.

Looking at the tall figure approaching, I struggled to recognize Quentin. He was wearing a leather jacket of dark olive green and black flared trousers - all looking terribly expensive. I stared at him in disbelief.

'Sasha, is it you?' he exclaimed, equally stunned. 'What on earth are you doing here?'

'I don't really know,' I shrugged, examining his new look with frank curiosity.

He didn't look like a student at all, in fact, he looked far more like some metrosexual model who'd just stepped out of the glossy cover of *GQ* or *Esquire*. This newly-coined word was much in-vogue and I certainly couldn't find a better definition in my own vocabulary.

'Do you like my new look?' Quentin asked, regaining his composure.

'I don't know. . . you just look completely different. . . Where did it all come from?'

'The jacket from Calvin Klein and the trousers - Lanvin.'

'Sorry!' I rephrased my question. 'I meant, how did you get the money?' I'd never suspected that he might have even heard of such labels. It made me wonder what else I might not know about him.

'What does it matter? I went shopping!'

'Went shopping?' I dumbly repeated, trying to figure out how much such an outfit might conceivably cost. 'But you always moan that you're broke,' I objected, recalling Quentin's usual line whenever I wanted us to do something which cost money.

'I don't moan!' Quentin protested hotly. 'So what if I don't have money now? I will have, one day. Anyway, I borrowed some money from Hugo.' He sounded extremely irritated by my inquisition.

'What?' I cried.

'And why are we standing here arguing, anyway? Let's go up to my room – and please don't raise your voice, people are already looking at you.' Discontentedly, he nodded at some guys coming out of the Halls of Residence.

'Hey, Quentin! Great outfit!' cried one and, turned to his friend, sniggering. We headed into the Halls of Residence while Quentin muttered, 'To be honest, it's a present from Hugo. I didn't want to tell you, as you can be so judgmental sometimes. . . Everything's black or white with you! Anyway, Hugo really needed a favour – he's got a job interview with a law firm and he wanted to buy a decent suit beforehand. So he asked Lulu and me to shop with him. Afterwards he offered to buy me something, just as a way of thanking me for my trouble – we did go round an awful lot of shops! - though I, of course, refused. So, he lent me some money instead and insisted that I spend it on this outfit. Just feel the leather; see how soft it is!' He stretched out his arm. 'In fact, both Lulu and Hugo thought that I looked like a Hollywood actor, wearing this. What do you reckon? Anyway, I'll pay him back as soon as I get a job. Money's no object for Hugo, so he won't need it to be repaid, not in the near future, anyway.'

'So, whose Porsche was that – Hugo's?'

'Yes. Lucky sod!'

I am just so dumb! This suddenly dawned on me, as I glanced at his white plastic bags from Harvey Nichols. 'You've only just returned from London, haven't you? So this is how you studying hard for your exams!'

I stopped dead in my tracks on the stairs, waiting for his confirmation. Instead he grumbled, 'You always overreact. This is exactly why I didn't want to say anything to you... Really, it was entirely a last-minute thing. I was going to surprise you in London tomorrow anyway, but you've beaten me to it.' I knew he was lying through his teeth.

'No, you were the one to beat me to it - I continue to be surprised with all your secrets. Well, I hope you enjoy your clothes!'

I turned and flew down the stairs, almost running in my eagerness to disappear from view as soon as possible. Tears welled up in my eyes - my feigned self-control was on the verge of a complete meltdown.

'Sasha, wait! Don't leave like this!'

He ran after me, but I kept skipping steps and paying no attention until I almost ran into two girls who were on their way past us and, to save face, Quentin let me go.

On the way back to London, I chose the last carriage of the train and cried wholeheartedly, pitying myself, my face turned resolutely towards the window. Fortunately, the only two other passengers there didn't take a blind bit of notice of me, both being sound asleep.

It looks like Quentin and I've reached a dead-end I secretly concluded, but my inner voice was busy playing devil's advocate: *You're overreacting - the guy simply went shopping and didn't tell you, he probably felt a bit self-conscious. As he said, you can be so disparaging sometimes; Stop making a mountain out of a*

CHAPTER 31

molehill! Then, another, more pragmatic, voice intruded: *He really deceived you: he didn't choose to see you at the weekend (and not for the first time!) and he lied about studying for his exams...I'm not even convinced that he still loves you. I mean, face it; he wasn't exactly thrilled by your unexpected visit, was he? Your boyfriend's leading a secret life!*

I was really unsure which voice to believe...

Before leaving the train, I checked myself in a compact mirror - my tear-stained face was far from perfect; I dabbed some powder under my swollen eyes and headed for the door.

By the time I reach campus I'll look just fine I told myself, trying to instill a little self-confidence. *If only I don't run into anyone I know immediately...* The last thing I wanted was to meet Robert while looking my worst.

The night was pitch-black and I quickened my pace walking across the Waterloo bridge, regaining optimism with every step. Back in London I felt at home again, and I promised myself not to go to Oxford anymore - at least, not for a while.

In the doors of the Halls of Residence I bumped into Robert.

'Hi, Sasha,' he said, giving me a surprised look, but he didn't comment on my puffy face: I was grateful to him for that.

'What are your plans for the evening?' he asked.

I gave him a strained smile. 'To get dead drunk! What else is there to do on a Friday night?'

'We have the same goal then; let's go to the Student Union bar.'

'Why not? I'll see you there,' I agreed straightaway.

Having gone up to my room, I pulled out a red velvet top from my travel bag, which I had planned to wear with Quentin in Oxford, let my hair down, applied some fresh make-up and ended up quite pleased with my appearance: *No worse than a brand like Lanvin, anyway...*

I completed the look with the highest pair of heels that I owned under my flared 501s. I desperately needed to feel attractive and Robert was so...

Suddenly I recalled our dance and the feel of his strong warm arms on my back. *If I wasn't with Quentin, Robert undoubtedly has everything to make a woman go weak in the knees* I thought, disloyally. And I knew – didn't I? – that he liked me… Keeping this in mind, I headed to the Student Union bar and the thought of Quentin left me for a time.

As always on a Friday the bar was packed with students, yet I still wasn't allowed to pass unnoticed: some guys smiled and nodded at me, or followed me with appreciative glances – dressing up can do wonders for the morale!

Just when I was peering into the crowd, absentmindedly looking for Robert, someone took me by the arm, just above the elbow. Turning around, I met his smiling luminous eyes.

'You made it, great! I got us a table over there.' He nodded to some students who thanked him for the beer and moved me towards a table. 'What'd you like to drink?' he asked.

'White wine, a large glass.'

'I see. The situation is serious, but not hopeless – it would've been a vodka, otherwise.'

'No, it wouldn't. I loathe vodka,' I winced. 'I know I'm Russian, and should be full of national pride, but. . .'

'Don't worry, I'd never allow myself to offer vodka to a lady. Only pure alcohol.'

'I love Bulgakov's *The Master and Margarita*!' I admitted.

'Well, I did try something pretty close to that once in Bolivia, made from sugarcane and coconut – lethal stuff! Look, don't go anywhere, I'll be right back,' said Rob, heading to the bar.

Once left alone my thoughts inevitably returned to Quentin. Everyone around me seemed to be having fun; they probably didn't have to worry about their handsome boyfriend being taken shopping by his gay friend. I felt down in the dumps again; it seemed that alcohol was the only remedy. *Maybe I should've gone for vodka after all. . .*

CHAPTER 31

Robert interrupted my thoughts, returning with a bottle and a couple of glasses. 'Here, Chilean white – the best of a bad lot here!'

After the first glass he asked me nonchalantly: 'So, what happened? Although I think I can guess – it's Quentin, right?'

I nodded, raising my glass: 'Let's not talk about that. За здоровье! Cheers!'

'За здоровье!' Rob caught up with me. His Russian was almost without accent. We then exchanged a few phrases in Russian, Rob had been far too modest: he spoke my language really well.

'Hi! Mind if we join you?' It was Jill, with one of her girlfriends.

'Sure, you're very welcome,' I said and Robert immediately pulled two spare chairs over.

'Weren't you supposed to be down in Oxford with Quentin this weekend?' Jill queried and I evasively replied that the plans for my evening had changed. However, once Robert went to the bar, I briefly filled Jill in about my unfortunate trip to Oxford.

'You two will work it out, Sasha, I'm sure,' she said, only half-listening. Instead, she was eyeing up Robert, by then on his way back with their drinks.

Whilst Robert was engaged in animated conversation, accompanied by Jill's tinkling laughter, in order to let him know how incredibly entertaining she found him, I somberly reflected about my recent meeting with Quentin, until the contents of even the second wine bottle were barely still visible.

Rob gave me a concerned look. He had been drinking too, but he could certainly hold his liquor. 'Take it easy, Sasha, it's not lemonade,' he advised.

'Why are you so boring today, anyway? Let's order another bottle and then go dancing!' I said tripping over my tongue and hearing my Russian accent rising under the Chilean influence.

'Great plan! Where can we dance salsa in London, Robert?' Jill had immediately picked up my idea. 'I heard about one place not too far away. . . '

'I'll make sure to organize it some other time,' Rob promised her. 'As for you, miss,' and here he turned to me with one of those lethally charming smiles, 'You've had enough for tonight, I think. Come on, I'll walk you home. Good night, ladies.'

Despite my feeble protests, he took my hand and escorted me out of the bar. On the way to the Halls of Residence I had a shameful attack of drunken talkativeness: 'See, the problem is . . . he doesn't need me. Not like before! Now Hugo and Calvin Klein are both his friends!' I was looking for a captive audience to which to ramble on endlessly on the stairs, but Robert threw me over his shoulder and carried me to my room. On the way, I recall telling something to his back, but nobody seemed to hear me anymore. At the door of my room Rob carefully put me down. It took us quite a while to find my key, which to my surprise turned up in the back pocket of my jeans.

'Come on in,' I invited Robert welcomingly, trying without success to get the key into the keyhole.

'Okay, I will, but only to put you to sleep,' he said, taking my key from me.

Robert opened the door, and I clung to him in the dark, wrapping my arms around his neck and trying to pull him towards the bed. He gently disengaged himself from my embrace and turned on the light.

'It's not going to happen this way,' he said, lightly stroking my cheek. Then, he took off my shoes, covered me with a blanket and kissed my... forehead.

What does it mean? Doesn't he like me after all? Confused thoughts crossed my dazed mind.

'Sweet dreams.' I heard, along with the click of the light switch as Robert left, shutting the door behind him.

The next morning someone's loud banging on my door forced me to wake up. Grudgingly I half-opened my eyes only to shut them tightly again and cover my ears with a pillow, hoping to pretend that I wasn't there, but to my irritation the knocking persisted.

'Go away!' I muttered.

A buzzing sensation in my head, as if someone inside it was maliciously hitting it with tiny hammers, made me vaguely recall the previous night in the bar.

CHAPTER 31

'Sasha! Open up! It's me, Quentin!'

I groaned as I sat up in bed; the clock hands showed nine, and as far as I could figure out, it was Saturday.

What's brought him here so early? I thought, puzzled, but I said, 'Coming!' Rising from the bed, I went to the mirror. *I look like a disheveled panda, with smeared mascara and tousled hair, and besides, why did I sleep in my clothes?* I wandered about, dismayed, splashing cold water over my face and desperately trying to recall the sequence of Friday night's events. Then I remembered.

Robert! I made a drunken pass at him, I thought, feeling utterly ashamed. And: *No wonder he ran away if I'd looked like this!*

Hurriedly I smoothed my hair and removed the remaining traces of the previous day's make-up before opening the door to let Quentin in. He had his new leather jacket on, almost matching the color of the cashmere scarf which I'd given him at Christmas, but instead of his fancy Lanvin trousers he wore his old black Levi's.

To my astonishment he instantly took me in his arms, pressing his body into mine. He held me tightly, not saying a single word and I could feel his body quivering but whether it was from a rush of some overwhelming emotion or simply from the chill, I couldn't tell. He finally released me, saying imploringly, 'I'm such a fool! Please forgive me, Sasha!'

I thought: I've heard those words quite often lately. . .

That thick glossy hair that he usually swept back to open up his beautiful high forehead, fell with a flat fringe just above his eyes, making him look like a seventeen-year-old schoolboy. He pleaded, 'I was so cross with myself for letting you escape from me so easily. Please, never do this again!'

As if my behaviour was merely the whim of some weird girlfriend, who simply loved to drive her boyfriend crazy or else got some kind of a kick out of simply taking a train from London to Oxford and back . . . And I was about to retort, which would have probably started us quarrelling again but Quentin, anticipating my likely response, silenced me with a passionate kiss, meanwhile strategically maneuvering us both towards my bed. My outrage instantly evaporated, and my thoughts took another direction entirely.

'Oh, I've missed you so much!' I whispered, feeling my pulse speeding and my body responding to his immaculate control. I thought *This is pure heaven! Why can't we always be like this?* And: *Thank God nothing happened with Robert last night!*

Following our tumultuous reconciliation, we fell asleep in each other's arms and slept past noon. The rest of the weekend raced by: Quentin was so profoundly tender – more than he'd been for ages – and so passionate that I secretly wondered what I'd done to deserve such an astonishing lover. . . All my concerns and misgivings evaporated like mist in bright sunlight and every disappointment and misunderstanding between us seemed simply water under the bridge.

Unfortunately, on Sunday night Quentin had to return to Oxford. Having grown so attached to the old Quentin, who had so wonderfully returned to me, I felt an overwhelming sadness at this parting. I wrapped my arms around his neck, gazing into his velvety dark eyes, feeling utterly unwilling to let him go.

'Sasha, I really must catch that train. . . If you keep looking at me like that, I'll get upset too. Is that what you really want? Anyway, there are only five days until Friday. You might even get bored if you see me too often. . .'

'Never!' I protested, and, reluctantly, I let him go.

CHAPTER 32

The following Friday I was wondering how to spend my evening: Quentin wasn't coming, as Club A had a secret party demanding his presence.

'Just the usual boys' night-out,' he'd assured me on the telephone. 'I'd far rather be with you, of course! But I must attend. I've only just fitted in here and don't want them thinking that I'm turning them down because of you. By the way, Alex and Gordon have girlfriends too, but, unlike you, they also realise that male friendship is sacred. I'll definitely see you next weekend, darling,' he added, in a rather pleading voice, sensing my displeasure. 'Kiss you!'

I heard a loud smack in my ear.

'Me, too,' I said lamely.

'Enjoy your weekend!' was the last thing I heard before the click from the telephone receiver and a long beep.

I found his new way of addressing me ('darling') mildly annoying: somehow it didn't make me feel special anymore. *Probably copied that from Hugo who calls everybody 'darling'* I thought. *Well, have fun at your stupid boys' party. I don't care!*

Then Jill invited me to check out a trendy West End club with Stuart and Alex, the third-year students we'd met during the Fresher's Week.

'If you come, maybe Robert might join us too. I saw him in the canteen; he was off to play football. I'd love to see those muscles under his football shirt. He's just so fit! Phwoar!' she'd told me.

However, I wasn't in the mood for a disco; instead I was tempted to commit that deadliest sin for a university student - to stay home alone on a Friday night. *Why not? I'll get myself a supply of chocolate and read a novel in bed, whilst listening to some music. . .*

The main thing was to keep it under wraps, in order to avoid being blacklisted as a university outcast and so - with a vaguely mysterious look - I simply told Jill that I had other plans for that evening.

After class, while on the way to the Halls of Residence, I suddenly ran into Robert. He was walking with a soccer ball under his arm, and, seeing me, smiled that broad, infectious smile; I guessed that his match had been a success.

Yes, Jill was right, I thought, involuntarily eyeing him. 'So, who won?' I inquired lightly.

'Who do you think? Three to one in our favour!' Rob pressed the ball against his chest. 'What about you, all alone this weekend?'

'Yep.'

'Then how about a pizza and a glass of wine later?'

I gave him a closer look: *Was he making a move on me?*

'We'll watch a movie,' he said, with chaste and serious eyes.

I considered, and decided that a Friday night with Robert was even more tempting: 'All right, I'll come round at seven.'

'Great! Till seven then,' and with this he cheerfully waved me goodbye and disappeared through the doors of the Halls of Residence.

I was curious to pay Robert a visit - we had been friends for some time but I'd never seen his room. Jill, of course, kept dreaming of finding herself there, but every time she came to visit him – generally under the pretext of needing help with some emergency or another -Robert was never in.

'I wonder if he even sleeps there at all… Somehow I suspect he has a busy love life!' she had moaned to me, more than once.

Indeed, he was often seen around campus accompanied by pretty female students, but that didn't mean anything - Robert loved women's company and, wrapped in his easy charm, each of his female friends probably imagined that his attention was drawn to her alone. . . Once Jill had even got quite upset over the sight of some brassy blonde leaving his room in the early morning, but it still seemed obvious that he didn't have a steady girlfriend. Even a few months

CHAPTER 32

into our studies, when most people had a pretty good idea about each other's intimate business, his personal life remained mysterious, and, as much as Jill tried to collect some gossip about him, no one ever seemed to add anything new. I secretly thought that perhaps Robert was a true gentleman and didn't care to boast about his amorous conquests. . . In any case, he clearly had a life and unlike us, he was not only studying but working too, being engaged in some important project for his sponsor, an independent policy institute.

I wonder if his space would tell me anything new about him at all? I wondered, approaching his room at some minutes past seven.

Robert opened the door just before I had the chance to knock. He was freshly shaven, wearing a white shirt and dark jeans, his bright eyes sparkled, and an irresistible smile played in the corners of his mouth. He looked so good that for a moment I felt awkward under his gaze. *I should've at least applied some mascara* I thought fleetingly before indignantly rejecting the idea: *It's not like we're on a date! Just two friends spending a free evening together. . . it's not the same thing at all.*

Robert's room looked different from how I'd imagined it: although perfect order and immaculacy reigned (no surprise there) it also wore a rather uninhabited, cold look - bare walls, not a single photo of friends or family, no sports trophies – not even a tiny houseplant, to give it a lived-in feel. On the plus side, the room featured a new television set with a VCR in the corner opposite the bed.

It doesn't look like I'll find out anything new about him, I thought, rather disappointed, glancing at his carefully made-up bed featuring a toy Mickey Mouse in those large yellow shoes.

'Make yourself comfortable,' Rob nodded towards the bed. He opened a bottle of red wine and filled two glasses.

'Let's order pizza straightaway, I'm starving after the game,' he said, handing me a takeaway menu from the local pizzeria. Having decided on my order, I picked up the Mickey Mouse: 'Well, which movie are we going to watch?'

'Do you like cartoons?'

I gave him a sceptical look.

'No, I'm serious. I love Disney! Why don't you look through the cassettes on the shelf and see if there's anything you might like, while I go down to the phone to place our order?'

Once he was gone, I started browsing his Disney selection, lined up in alphabetical order.

'*Bambi, Duck Tales, Sleeping Beauty...*' I read the titles aloud. *Despite all his maturity Robert was still a child at heart!* I thought fondly.

'The pizza will be delivered in half an hour. Well, is there anything you might fancy? How about *The Little Mermaid*? Do you know what it's about?'

'Hmm...a mermaid, perhaps?'

'About love facing obstacles,' he said, seriously looking me in the eye, and then added, laughing: 'They ran into problems because of her tail!'

Is this some obscure allusion to Quentin? I wondered. Then I said, 'Well, as far as I remember they all have a happy ending...'

'Let's find out,' said Robert. He inserted the tape into the VCR and settled down on the bed next to me with his glass of wine.

As much as I tried to ignore it, the atmosphere around us was electric - you could cut the sexual tension with a knife. Each cell of my body felt acutely aware of his proximity and his strong energy currents, seemingly directed at me. Being alone with him was so profoundly unsettling that it probably wasn't a good idea, but that evening, for whatever reason, I felt like taking risks.

Soon my back got stiff from sitting upright on the edge of the bed: I decided to get more comfortable. I took off my shoes and hoisted my body up onto the bed, curling my feet underneath me. Forgetting myself, I finally let myself relax in his presence, half-leaning on his strong shoulder, while he gently embraced me, playing with my long curls, then running his fingers slowly down my neck and drifting lightly over my breasts, barely brushing the nipples... My breathing grew faster; I couldn't endure this torture any longer.

CHAPTER 32

'Sha la la la la Kiss the girl… kiss the girl…' The *Little Mermaid* soundtrack was perfectly timed!

Robert gently took my glass of wine, put it on the floor and pulled me down onto the bed in a long kiss. I pressed my lips to his, for a moment succumbing to a long pent-up desire that I could feel throughout my entire body – when suddenly I remembered Quentin. It hadn't been supposed to go this far, and, fearing that I would get too carried away, I pushed my hands hard against Robert's chest, feeling the firmness of his muscles under his shirt. He broke off our kiss and pulled away, gazing at me with an inquiring look.

Only a fool would interrupt something like this! I cursed myself in my mind, sitting up on the bed, my breathing still far too fast.

'I can't, I just – you know that I'm with Quentin. . .'

'Then why aren't you with him now?' Robert muttered, almost roughly. 'He doesn't deserve you. . .'

Seeing my hurt look, he stopped in his tracks, softening. 'Sasha, it's very difficult for me to be just friends with you. You must know how much I – like you.'

'If you can't be with me as a friend, we shouldn't see each other anymore,' I told him honestly – though as I said it I felt my heart skip a beat. Suddenly I was very afraid, afraid of losing him.

For a split second something flashed in his bright eyes as if my words had stung, but his facial expression remained unaltered. Then he gave me one of his full-blown smiles and I decided that I had simply imagined it.

'Not a chance! You won't be able to get rid of me that easily,' he joked, sitting down beside me. He put his arm around my shoulder and kissed me on the cheek.

I was relieved: the old Robert was back. I probably hadn't realised until that moment how much I depended on him.

'So, what's going on with the Little Mermaid?' he asked, returning my unfinished glass of red wine.

Then there was a knock on the door, it was our long-awaited pizza: hot chili and pepperoni for Robert and mozzarella with tomatoes for me.

'I'm even prepared to give up my pizza to kiss you again like that,' Robert joked, flirting with me.

'You're mad, just smell how delicious it is!' I teased him back, taking a piece of juicy pizza out of its box and wafting it under his nose. And then, getting comfortable on the bed with our dinner we watched the rest of the film as if nothing had happened between us.

Glancing at him out of the corner of my eye I unexpectedly caught myself thinking: *But what about me, will I be able to be just friends with him?* It was odd but, prior to our unexpected kiss, I hadn't even realised how much I'd fancied him. Robert was an amazing kisser, but, after all, I'd always suspected this. . .

The cartoon ended and I prepared to go back to my room. He didn't try to prevent me, but he did wrap his arms around my shoulders and look into my eyes with that straightforward gaze, saying, 'Sasha, you must know that I'm always here for you.'

Having returned to my room, I couldn't get the evening out of my head, recalling the taste of his mouth on my lips and his parting words. For a moment I imagined what it would be like to make love to Robert and immediately realized that it would be almost impossible for us to remain just friends after such a thing, if it ever happened . . . Then my thoughts returned to Quentin, seemingly so absorbed in his new life that he didn't care at all about what was happening in mine. I conjured up the image of his astonishingly handsome but somehow distant face - I thought that I still loved him, but, if this was true, then why did my love bring me more sadness than joy?

CHAPTER 33

I didn't even notice how it all happened, although only an idiot could have failed to have seen the change in Quentin. After all, it hadn't been a thinly veiled process, the effect of which could only be felt by some highly sensitive person; on the contrary, it was so blatantly obvious that only a love-sick fool like myself could have turned a blind eye to all the signs and signals.

Before my next visit, to my delight, Quentin invited me to accompany him to one of the University of Oxford's famous black-tie balls. With plenty of time left before the dinner which preceded it, I was fixing my hair in front of a mirror while Quentin was restlessly pacing around the room, occasionally throwing impatient glances in my direction. He looked absolutely stunning in his tuxedo - James Bond would have looked like nothing in comparison - but I felt anxious about partnering someone quite so amazing.

'Darling, how much more time do you need? You always look beautiful, anyway,' he said irritably.

'Almost ready,' I said, ignoring his tone and blowing him a kiss.

Since Quentin had entered Oxford, we hadn't discussed our future plans, so I was really surprised when, for no apparent reason, he suddenly said, 'When we get married, everyone will be so jealous of your getting a husband like me.'

I laughed. 'Of course they will! Well, let them envy me!'

When we get married certainly sounded promising! I thought, intending to forgive him his obvious narcissism – until I heard this addition: 'On the other hand, marrying a Russian might get on the way of my becoming Prime Minister.'

I gave him a puzzled look in the mirror, trying to realise whether or not he was joking, but his face was completely impassive. Only the fact that around half of all British Prime Ministers had graduated from Oxford made his statement not entirely ridiculous.

He squinted, glancing in the mirror in order to smooth down a stray hair before continuing: 'And then, of course, my occasional drug use might come out, but, as is now widely known, many of today's politicians took drugs when they were young. People are fairly tolerant about that sort of thing. I'd just have to confess all to the media. In fact, a colourful past is rather like the dark halo of a once-fallen, now redeemed angel - all very in-vogue - the main thing is not to overdo it. It might even attract young voters; they might even identify with me, as far as that's possible, of course. But a Russian wife. . .' Then Quentin shook his head, as if recalling himself to the present, and looked over in my direction. 'Anyway, are you finally ready?'

I felt as if turned to stone, utterly stunned by his monologue. I recalled that the Romanovs had married British royalty, but Emelianova was hardly Romanova, so I attempted nothing by way of rebuttal to his hurtful remarks, and we left in silence. My evening was utterly spoiled, but Quentin seemed pleased with himself; his goal was achieved – I no longer wanted to marry him.

During the dinner, I felt really down, which lately had become my usual state whenever I was with Quentin, though he rarely seemed to notice, preferring to ignore me. I pushed my food around the plate, having lost my appetite after our earlier interaction, but the wine was relaxing and soothing.

As luck would have it, we were seated directly opposite Lulu, who was impudently flirting with Quentin, appearing to hang onto his every word. A couple of times I caught them exchanging a long look: when this happened I called the waiter to top up my glass.

Meanwhile I listened with half an ear to the conversation around the table. Quentin was enjoying a heated discussion with his bespectacled neighbor, occasionally glancing over to ensure that the girls opposite were still hanging on his every word, basking in the furore that his presence was causing amongst them.

CHAPTER 33

'. . . People generally can't handle the truth: it's easier for them to believe in a 'noble lie,' as Plato termed it,' I heard him say. 'All successful politicians are guided by the teachings of Machiavelli in preference to bizarre or abstract moral principles: it is impossible for them to be honest and virtuous in the name of the public good - not if they wish to stay in power, at any rate.'

'I think it was Nietzsche who said that morality is nothing more than the herd instinct in the individual,' suggested Lulu, making eyes at him . . . I suddenly wondered: *Is he applying Machiavelli's principles in our relationship?*

As if confirming my thought, Quentin gave me a complacent look before returning his attention to his opponent.

'I still think Machiavelli is not as profound as Rousseau, the true ideologist of the French Revolution,' persisted the guy in spectacles.

'Well, I wouldn't be so sure – *The Prince* is still widely read by most politicians, unlike Rousseau's *The Social Contract*.'

'If everyone followed Machiavelli's principles, the world would be full of Stalins,' I barged in, but no one seemed to hear me. *He neither sees nor hears me anymore!* I thought resentfully. Suddenly, I felt a strong urge to act out or at least cut in on the conversation of these Oxford bright sparks. 'So, what I'd like to know is how a lie can ever be noble?' I interrupted defiantly.

Quentin turned towards me in disbelief; it seemed that he had completely forgotten that I was there. He smiled at me with closed lips, his eyes sardonic. 'Well, for example, so as not to hurt someone with the cruel truth, darling . . . '

'Actually, I'd prefer the cruel truth.'

He winced, but said nothing.

What if one lies silently? flashed across my mind.

His condescending look and fancy talk sent shivers down my spine; I could feel my heart quivering, overcome by some dark presentiment, which I desperately tried to drown with wine.

Quentin, however, continued his Orwellian monologue. 'Only simpletons see the world in terms of black and white. They can easily be persuaded that black is white, war is peace and freedom is slavery; and those who manage to persuade them are the real masters of life.'

'How could they?' I asked, genuinely surprised. 'Who could make people believe that evil is good or ugliness is beauty?'

'Darling, you are so naïve! Everything is so simple in that pretty head of yours! Well, to take a basic example, your former Soviet Union's version of Communism – really a smokescreen of Marxist ideology supposedly dedicated to championing the working class and the poor - actually worked to concentrate all power and wealth in the hands of the few.'

He went on but I hardly listened. I could hardly disagree with him; really I was but a poor match to his brilliant mind. . . *Quentin is a born politician*, I thought, though I couldn't help suspecting that someone might have been educating him to some extent. *Most likely, his friend Hugo* I concluded . . . However, feeling courageous after a few more glasses of wine, I felt like kicking up a row.

'Listen, why do you always call me "darling?" now? Have you forgotten my name?' I rudely interrupted, secretly stunned by my vexed tone. The wine seemed to have brought out all the resentment which had been building up in me.

For a moment silence reigned over the table, as everyone's attention was drawn to us.

'Certainly, because you are dear to me!' Quentin's voice was filled with sarcasm as he scorned me. 'By the way, I don't know how things are done in Russia, but surely you know the reason why an English husband always calls his wife "darling?" It's simply in order to avoid confusing her name with that of his mistress - darling!'

I watched Lulu burst out laughing, exchanging thrilled glances with her sniggering girlfriends. *It's official: I've turned into an emotional masochist*, I thought, silently swallowing my humiliation, along with more wine.

Our relationship was crashing down as remorselessly as the force of gravity on an engineless plane, but, in spite of everything I still naively believed that somehow we would tumble through the clouds, maybe breaking a wing in the storm, but ultimately surviving against all odds.

Quentin grew increasingly annoyed with me that weekend: no matter what I did or didn't do, it was always wrong. His constant criticism and growing indifference, occasionally diluted by fake flattery when he needed something from me, was slowly killing my spirit, which he seemed to have noticed too: 'You've become so boring, not to mention crying at every trifle. In fact, you're perpetually sad! And you're even managing to pull me down with you. . . I'm ashamed to take you anywhere; I don't want everyone around to see how insecure you are. When I first met you, you were so strong, and now. . . well, just look at yourself!' he finished scornfully.

I gave him a puzzled look, trying desperately to remember what I had been like before. *I'd been happy*, I recalled *and probably never cried. . .In fact I'd never cried so much in my life, as I had recently, when with Quentin… I've turned into a pathetic whimpering creature, repugnant not only to Quentin but even to myself,* I thought, feeling to my horror that I was about to burst into tears again.

Soon my nerves resembled a tightly stretched bow-string, propelling poisonous arrows in Quentin's direction, whether to attack him or else to defend myself; although our frequent arguments were always followed by deep remorse – on my side, at least. Sometimes there would be a brief spell of serenity while we would recuperate before our next fight.

My looks revealed the pain of my inner sufferings: a pale haggard shadow of my former self looked listlessly at me from the mirror – which I now tried to avoid looking into as much as I could.

Once, in Oxford, I'd unexpectedly run into some acquaintances from my former College, who at first had failed to recognize me. When I read astonishment mixed with pity on their faces, I realized that I couldn't go on like this, but having lost my foothold in the treacherous quicksand of our relationship I had no strength left to emerge from it: instead, I seemed intent on sinking deeper and deeper until we reached our nadir.

One day after making love we had been lying in bed half-watching some Hollywood blockbuster on TV, although its predictability had bored us both right from the start.

Quentin left the bed and went to the window overlooking the quad to enjoy his usual post-coital Marlboro Light. He often tried to give up smoking, but always reverted to his old habits, blaming it on the stress of our relationship: I silently agreed with him.

He lightly turned his intelligent supermodel face in my direction and asked casually: 'Would you be very upset if we broke up and then you suddenly saw me on the Hollywood screen? I think former partners of celebrities must really struggle with this. Such a constant reminder of the love one once lost. . . on billboards, on buses even. It must be torture!'

'Well, I'll try to survive somehow. Do you really intend to become an actor? But what about leading the country, are you done with that now?' I joked, thinking that a small dose of self-deprecating humour wouldn't go amiss.

As it turned out, at one of the Hugo's parties, Quentin had met a famous gay producer, who had supposedly seen a new Matt Dillon in him and insisted on his auditioning.

'What's so special about this Dillon, anyway? Everyone says that, of the two of us, I'm much the better-looking. . . By the way, do you remember I once met him in Camden market, that time I bought my leather jacket for ten pounds? You know, the one I painted with Megadeth,' he reminded me, looking irritated at the rather blank look on my face 'We almost ran into each other, but he just gave me this cold stare and passed by.'

'What, did you think that he'd ask you for your autograph?' I sniggered. 'It's usual to study acting, anyway. Not every handsome person can act!'

Quentin went on as if I hadn't spoken: 'In any case, I've decided to audition.'

I said doubtfully, 'Have you checked out this director? What if he works in the porn business?'

CHAPTER 33

'Are you an idiot or just pretending to be? He was awarded a BAFTA for his last film *The Prickly Weeds*. Haven't you even heard of it?'

I shook my head.

'He's also invited me to this party in London, where I'll meet the whole bohemian in-crowd. You know, the same people we see on the screen, year in and year out.'

I had no idea why he was even telling me all this, except perhaps to boast – or else to torment me by making me feel insecure, which he had been enjoying doing lately. I suspected it might have been a combination of both. . . Sometimes it seemed that my tears gave him the perverse pleasure of feeling validated and superior – the very qualities that he had started aspiring to - and I generously indulged him with this. His pathetic manipulation amused him – until he started to grow bored with it.

'I assume you're going alone,' I said, referring to myself, at the same time sadly realising that there was less and less space for me in Quentin's life.

'No, with Hugo, of course! But, don't you want me to be famous and rich, darling? After all, I'm auditioning for us!'

'For us? Is there still an "us"?' I questioned.

'Just look at yourself! You are about to burst into tears again - your upper lip is trembling!' Quentin rewarded me with a scornful look. 'Why is it always so hard with women?'

Is he implying that there are other women, who also don't make his life any easier? I wondered. I didn't really know anymore – and I probably didn't really want to know. I suspected that I didn't have enough strength to face the truth. *Maybe Quentin was right after all - maybe it was easier to live a lie...*

Back in London, I tried to plunge into my studies, but any inner peace I had left had by then had been replaced with a dreadful feeling of some evil sense of foreboding, which, as hard as I tried, I couldn't shake off.

CHAPTER 34

In my dream I was in a magnificent palace ballroom with soaring white marble columns and stained-glass windows, where, accompanied by some invisible orchestra, anonymous couples in monastic black and white habits and black, Venetian-style masks were twirling across a parquet floor.

I was suddenly mortified to realise that I had come to the ball naked, except for my own black mask, but, to my intense relief, it seemed that nobody noticed me at all – indeed, they seemed to see through me. Suddenly an ancient monk appeared from nowhere, his face hidden in shadow of his hood. The old fellow, almost a hunchback, graciously wrapped me in a long white robe; and then, putting his finger to his lips, gestured for me to follow him before slipping from view behind a marble column. Intrigued, I then saw him in the near distance stepping on a blood-red carpet laid along a very grand staircase. I sped after him, trying to catch him up, and once I reached the top of the long staircase I glanced down to see that the figures had grown small and disrobed, blending into a cream-colored mass, like a freshly homemade *smetana* smudged on the distant ballroom floor.

Turning, I saw the monk's hunched back hobbling along the corridor, moving further and further away until he suddenly shapeshifted into a huge black cat and nimbly sprang through one of the doors. For some reason terrified of losing him, I hurried through the same door, which - to my astonishment - led into Hugo's house. There, waiters wearing only black swimming briefs and bow ties were offering trays full of drinks and scrumptious ring doughnuts. Strangely enough, all the guests were in their birthday suits, except for their masks, and somehow I knew that they were the same 'monks' and 'nuns' I'd observed dancing in the ballroom earlier. I was wandering around the house, utterly at a loss amongst so many intertwined bodies, but - just as before - nobody seemed to see that I was there... Somewhere in the distance relaxing piano sounds resonated and I wandered towards the sound, sensing that it was Hugo playing, and thinking feverishly that Quentin must also be somewhere nearby. I kept thinking *I have to find him and take away from here...*

I approached a group of nude figures, their bodies obscuring my view of the pianist. The crowd parted before me and I then saw that there was no pianist: the keys of the piano were playing themselves... Suddenly I met with those yellow cat's eyes and in the same instant was transferred into a dimly-lit bedroom, where bodies of every possible size, shape and colour were copulating on an enormous bed. The glimmer of candles projected giant shadows of their silhouettes, like some squirming, monstrous chimera, onto the bare bedroom walls.

Quentin was the only one without a mask, his handsome face twisted in a grimace of carnal pleasure. As before, I seemed utterly invisible - until Quentin and I locked eyes, but he hastily turned his face away, pretending he hadn't seen me.

My blood running cold, I longed to rush as far away as I could, but - as so often happens in nightmares - I remained paralysed, as if rooted to the spot.

Suddenly the enormous black cat appeared. With one paw he held a ring sugar doughnut up to his right eye, like the monocle of some refined Victorian dandy, whilst his cat's mouth was stretched in a vicious human grin – not feline in the least. In a split second the doughnut was transformed into a bright yellow eye, right in the center of the creature's forehead. It seemed to be staring wrathfully into my very soul, making me long to scream – indeed, I think I *did* scream, voicelessly – for my throat felt so dry that, no matter how hard I tried, I seemed incapable of producing a sound... Finally, I succeeded in releasing a loud, hysterical scream. The three-eyed cat disappeared and I awoke, my eyes wide with terror, my heart thumping wildly in my chest. This dawned upon me in that same moment: *I've lost Quentin. He is no longer faithful to me...*

It was then just past 3:00 a.m. I tried to get back to sleep but in vain, as I couldn't help reliving my horrible dream, over and over again. I spent the rest of the night restlessly tossing and turning, desperate for dawn to come.

When Quentin called me the following day, I instantly knew, with sinking heart, that his call could portend nothing good.

'I need to tell you something,' he said, coming straight to the point. With trembling voice and unusual seriousness of tone, he continued, 'I've been unfaithful to you and can no longer be with you. Therefore, you'll have to leave me,' he finished, almost pathetically.

It almost seemed as if there had been some psychic connection between us: he had either read my mind or else had truly seen me – as I had so vividly imagined - in that dream, and, although both versions were impossible, I could find no other explanation for the timing of his call.

Whilst he was talking, lurid fragments from the orgy flashed before my eyes. They seemed so closely intertwined with reality that I struggled to distinguish which images pertained to the dream and which might have been real. . . In a daze I overheard snatches of mundane phrases, as if from some enormous distance: 'We haven't been with enough other people . . . it's far too early for either of us . . . something so serious and so long-term. . .'

Somehow I had never foreseen that our parting would take place over the phone, but as he was speaking I decided that this method was easier, and therefore more merciful.

Also to my astonishment, after the initial shock, I felt an almost tidal sense of relief, as if someone had at last put me out of my misery, and a moment later, nausea rising towards my throat - as if the truth had finally been made clear to me.

'Are you still listening? You have to leave me!' Quentin said querulously.

He's breaking up with me but I'm the one supposed to say that I'm leaving him? - What kind of a sick game is this? He probably thinks I'm retarded. . . Or maybe it's simply some etiquette that I don't understand. . .

'Yes, of course, it's over,' I said automatically, and I thought I heard almost a sigh of relief . . . Perhaps Quentin had feared a fit of hysterics, or dreaded some dramatic scene, or even anticipated that I'd refuse to release him . . . Confused, I was preparing to hang up when I heard him add, 'There's just one other thing.'

This is the moment when he tells me how sorry he is I thought, feeling numbed to the extent of almost not caring . . . But Quentin had something rather more prosaic on his mind: 'Remember, I loaned you £40 last weekend? I'd appreciate it if you could please send me a cheque. I'm almost broke!'

His tactless sense of priorities absolutely infuriated me. I said passionately, 'Don't worry, you'll get your cheque and I hope you choke on it!' And with that I slammed down the receiver, utterly humiliated at the thought that I loved someone capable of thinking about something so sordid at such a time.

Later that evening his mother Debbie called. She didn't have much to say, although she certainly seemed to be genuinely sorry. Having expressed her sympathy she mentioned that Quentin had come home and had asked her to tell me that he was no longer in love with me.

As if I hadn't got the message the first time! I thought, feeling traitorous tears springing into my eyes. . . Debbie patiently listened to all the sniffling that followed, probably secretly wishing that I had a handkerchief. 'I'm so sorry,' she kept saying, although, taking advantage of a pause when I wasn't weeping, she casually asked: 'And how is your dad, Sasha? Have you made it up yet?'

Upon hearing my answer, she appeared rather more satisfied: Quentin clearly hadn't lost anything worth fussing about; I might be still a Russian oligarch's daughter, but only a very much out-of-favour daughter . . . After that we both seemed to wish to wrap up the conversation as swiftly as possible.

'Keep us informed about how you are. We all still really worry and care about you,' she cooed. In similar vein, I falsely assured her that I would write, though we probably both knew that this was highly unlikely to happen.

Over the next few days, conscientiously, like a diligent doctor with a sick patient, I carefully monitored my own condition: listening intently to my thoughts, analyzing my inner state, and assessing my daily moods, while

CHAPTER 34

waiting tensely for the onset of depression or even despair arising from my self-pity, longing and loss.

To my astonishment, nothing like this occurred. Instead I started sleeping peacefully at night, no longer enduring horrible nightmares. In the mornings I woke up energized, with that, long-forgotten, joyful anticipation of a new day. I picked up my tennis racquet again and often enjoyed an early morning game before my first class. I regained my healthy appetite and my scales no longer shamed me, as they had when I'd been with Quentin. I gulped greedily at the air of emotional freedom: a new, more positive life seemed to stretch out ahead of me, a life which I felt I was already starting to enjoy.

At first, this all seemed very strange. *Surely this isn't how a dumped and cheated girlfriend is supposed to feel?* I wondered, almost anticipating some unforeseen 'catch'. Sometimes I even suspected my weirdly joyful condition might be due to some abnormality, even to a psychiatric disorder. I really couldn't understand: I'd been so in love with Quentin!

But all the power Quentin had held over me had flowed off like water, freeing me from the bondage of loving him. And under that dreamlike mask, so suddenly torn away, a strangely empty face was looking at me with pure hostility - while the person I'd once adored seemed to have dissolved in the far distant past.

For a while I continued to count the days, and then the weeks, that had passed since our parting - all the while tuning into my inner self to detect symptoms of a broken heart, but - as hard as I tried - I failed to discover any. I didn't miss Quentin; I didn't care where he was (or with whom) and even the CDs which he had left behind evoked no nostalgia in me.

My astonishment was mixed with a vague disappointment, yet I felt at the same time relieved to learn that I'd fallen out of love. Exactly when this had happened, I was unable to tell. Perhaps it was simply that, with each quarrel and each stabbing hurt my love had melted a little - and that, with his betrayal, the last bit had evaporated into thinnest air.

Once I realised this, I was able to enjoy my new freedom with a clear conscience. I wasn't angry with Quentin; lately he had brought me nothing but heartache. It seemed that our relationship had outlasted its meaning - and that Quentin had proved to be the bolder, having taken the initiative to end it . . .

Sometimes thoughts of Robert and that moment in his bedroom did slip into my mind. After our first, and - thanks to me - probably last kiss, he seemed to have disappeared. There were rumours that he'd been sent to India by the Institute, but no one knew for sure: Robert seemed accountable to no one.

I decided not to tell anyone about breaking up with Quentin – the last thing I wanted was to have our relationship mulled over in public, to be endlessly comforted by Jill, or to wind up, however briefly, headlining university gossip.

So I brought forward Quentin's Oxford exams, and then his grandmother's unexpected illness, regularly inventing plausible excuses for my being single every weekend. I wasn't sure how long I'd be able to continue lying before someone's suspicions would become aroused, but luck was on my side: Jill was so completely absorbed in her new relationship with Alex, a third-year maths student, that she hardly seemed to notice.

Robert was the only person whose opinion I really cared about, but – luckily or unluckily - he wasn't around. More than anything I couldn't bear the thought of seeing pity in his eyes: Robert had always looked at me so differently.

I'll never be a victim again; I decided, and repeated my new motto aloud. It sounded fairly convincing, and I was starting to believe in it, when an even better idea came to my mind: *And I won't fall in love again, either. Never again.*

At this moment the image of Robert somehow sprang back into my mind, but I pushed it away. *No he's a great guy but just a friend. No special feelings, I've had enough of that!*

CHAPTER 35

Time flew by, when one day I returned to my room after my final lecture of the day to find a message that Quentin had called and had asked me to call him back. I stared at the wall calendar in a daze – 31 days had gone by since that memorable parting over the telephone.

Thirty-one carefree precious days without arguments, fighting or tears… I thought, feeling my body tensing at the recollection of our stormy relationship. In the end I listened to my body, and ignored the message.

Quentin called me again, but I didn't pick up the phone. After our last conversation I had no desire to hear his voice, ever again. *If there's something he needs to say he can do so in person*, I decided, but as far as I was concerned, we had nothing to talk about.

I was relieved when Quentin didn't come and when the calls stopped. However, I soon received an unexpected letter from his mother Debbie. She wrote that Quentin had realised that he'd made a huge mistake in leaving me, which he terribly regretted. He had called to tell me this himself, but I had never bothered to call him back.

'You shouldn't be so cold-hearted, Sasha,' Debbie had written disapprovingly. 'After all, anyone can make a mistake.'

Why hadn't Quentin written to me himself? I thought, very puzzled, having finished the letter. But another question seemed far more intriguing. *Now that he wanted me back and I had a choice, what did I really want?* Though deep in my heart I knew the answer to this question, I decided to take time over my reply and put the letter away in my desk drawer.

The following morning, as always on Wednesdays, I was on my way to the new university building for a lecture in commercial law, when I suddenly heard someone calling my name. Turning, I saw Robert heading towards me. He looked bronzed, lean and toned, as if he had been in training for the Olympics; his face looked slightly tanned but his eyes seemed to have become still brighter.

'Hi, Sasha! How's life? I hope you've been bored to death without me,' he said taking me in his arms.

For a moment I felt breathless, pressed against his strong chest. Before I could reply, Robert took something out of his jacket pocket and placed it inside my palm, closing his hand around my own. It was a carved miniature palace of white and pink marble, decorated with blue turquoise, clear pearls, green malachite and other stunning jewels, glowing in the sunlight with every colour of the rainbow. I'd never held anything more beautiful in all my life.

'This is for you, from the Taj Mahal.'

'For me?' I was gazing in utter astonishment at the amazing palace on my palm. *So it wasn't simply gossip: Robert had been to India!*

I suddenly felt his intent gaze upon me and glanced up. Seemingly uncomfortable that he had been caught off-guard, he quickly lowered his eyes and instantly the old Robert was back – that confident male gaze and that familiar ironic smile. 'You look great, almost like you've had a nice long break,' he said.

Yeah, a break from Quentin I thought, and couldn't help smiling back.

'Well, what did I miss during my absence?'

'Hmm, not much. . . All first-year law students are moaning about our new lecturer in criminal law - a real bulldog. Apparently only 10% passed his exams in his last university. And Jill has a new boyfriend, a third-year mathematician.' I decided not to share my own news. 'But what about you? How was India?'

'The heat was unbearable despite the monsoon rains, but the wildlife was incredible. By the way, what are you doing after class?'

I shrugged my shoulders - I really had no plans.

CHAPTER 35

'Then, how about we get out of here for a breath of fresh air? I can fill you in properly then.'

I needed very little persuasion and readily agreed.

After classes I headed back to my room to drop off my files, locate a prominent place for the Taj Mahal on my bookshelf, grab a scarf and rush back outside, where Robert was waiting for me on his motorcycle. I swung my leg over the low-slung seat and wrapped my arms tightly around Robert's waist, clinging to his back and breathing in the masculine smell of his worn-out leather jacket mixed with the odour of gasoline fumes.

So great that he's back!

The silver stallion let out a guttural thunderous roar in sync with my speeding heartbeat and raced off; I closed my eyes, feeling the fresh autumn wind caressing my face and playing with my hair, which flew out behind me from under my helmet.

We slipped through the city streets, lane-splitting the crawling traffic and had soon left London behind, racing along the motorway, overtaking passing cars with a breathtaking speed. With bated breath I pressed my body into his back; Robert slowed down.

'Hold tight, we'll be there soon,' he shouted, slipping down an exit leading south towards Surrey. Dropping speed, we drove more gently through the drowsy streets of some provincial town before finding ourselves back on the road, this time deep in the countryside.

Leaning forward, Rob followed a winding, shady road framed by thick pine forests until he slowed down before a right turn signposted 'The Old Forrest Club' - which we had nearly missed.

'We've arrived,' said Robert, smoothly driving through the wide-open gates of the country club.

Acres of golf courses seemed to stretch in every direction towards the horizon, where over green hillocks, once we had driven closer, we could see a beautiful country mansion surrounded by lusciously green gardens and a picturesque lake. We found a parking spot and immediately set off to explore the area.

'Come on, let's go choose some horses to ride,' said Robert, taking my hand. Skirting around the hotel we headed down a path towards the Equestrian Club, relishing the smell of fresh-cut grass.

'Can you ride or do you need lessons?' asked Rob, his arm around my shoulders.

'I can manage,' I assured him, secretly hoping not to fall off, which had happened the last time I'd ridden, while spending a weekend in Scotland with my Marlborough College friend Catherine.

At the stables a red-haired groom was putting tack onto a jet-black horse with three white socks, which appeared to be stamping in irritation whilst worrying the bit between its teeth.

'Othello, boy!' Robert patted the horse. The latter neighed happily in recognition, briefly releasing the bit.

'He's been waiting for you, poor thing! Not much action for him, I am afraid. But it's his own fault - even most experienced riders avoid his temper,' the man told him, nodding politely to me. . . At this Othello tossed his head and we all burst out laughing at his evident impatience.

'Let me show you around,' offered the stable manager, but I'd already noticed a light chestnut in the corner. The manager approved my choice. 'Angelina is calm and responsible! Good for beginners,' he said, opening the gate and leading her out into the yard.

'I'll be right back. I think Othello needs to stretch his muscles,' said Robert. They soon disappeared out of sight. Soon, dressed in borrowed jodhpurs and lost in thought I was enjoying stroking Angelina's long elegant nose, while the groom put on her tack for me.

So, this isn't the first time Robert's been here. I wonder whom he brought last time? I caught myself feeling jealous of some imaginary female stranger. About ten minutes later the approaching clatter of Othello's hooves interrupted my thoughts. Their shapes seemed so kneaded together that from a distance they looked like a centaur - Rob was definitely at home in the saddle. *I wonder if there is anything he can't do?* I thought admiringly.

The groom assisted me in mounting: Angelina and I were both ready for heading out with our gentlemen. After an hour's quiet ride in the woods surrounding the club, we were both starving and wandered back to the hotel to find something to eat in one of its restaurants. My thighs felt a little sore from the unusual exertion, but I didn't mention it.

'What would you like for an aperitif, sir? Your usual?' the waiter inquired.

'Yes, that would be great.'

I raised my eyebrow: 'Shaken not stirred?'

'How did you guess?'

Robert looked amused, shaking the ice in a glass of gin and tonic.

'I thought you only drank extra dry martini,' I said, feigning disappointment while sipping an orange juice through a straw.

'Only when at work,' he said with a smile.

'Tell me about your work. It must be great traveling around the world.'

'Why would I want to talk about something as mundane as work when I'm lucky enough to be with a beautiful girl in a romantic place?' And with these words Robert took my hand and locked eyes with mine. . . I felt as if transfixed with his piercing gaze and, lowering my eyes, smiled weakly, mentally cursing my lack of confidence.

'Have you decided on your order?' The waiter arrived just in time to rescue me. Having ordered, we continued our conversation.

'Sorry, I always forget when I'm with you that we're condemned only to be friends,' Rob sighed, but he still held my hand and his gaze was still fixed upon me.

Flirt with him, Sasha! Flirt! Why just sit there like a bump on a log? My inner voice sounded extremely annoyed with me. For a split second I imagined Alka in my place, she'd be on fire!

But I am not Alka. (I scarcely needed to remind myself of this.) We were brought some delicious fresh olives.

Tell him that you don't see him just as a friend. Admit that you like him and that you're finally free! That voice in my head gently encouraged me, but instead of listening, I said, in a somewhat whimsical tone:

'I'm still waiting to hear all about India.'

Robert tilted his head with an engaging smile, reluctantly released my hand and started retelling the legend of the Dudhsagar Falls, the magnificent 'sea of milk', followed by the sad love story of the Taj Mahal. . . Over the main course we were jointly discovering the hidden gems of Goa, cooling down after a wild rush through the jungle, swimming naked in the pristine azure Pichola Lake and weaving a beautiful alpine flower wreath in West Himalaya while thinking of me. Listening to him, utterly spellbound, I could almost imagine that I too had only just returned from India. . .

After leaving the restaurant, we continued our evening in a cozy Irish pub, where we settled into big leather armchairs next to a crackling log fire. The weather had deteriorated; the sky was covered with heavy, navy blue clouds. Suddenly a strong wind appeared out of nowhere, violently twisting the branches of the century-old trees.

Robert frowned. 'Looks like a real storm's headed this way. We need to get back before dark.' As we left the pub he put his arm around my shoulders, pulling me tightly to him in a vain attempt to shield me from the howling wind as we headed to the car park.

We weren't even halfway there when his prophecy came true: suddenly lightning cracked the blackening sky, accompanied by roar of a thunder like an untamed lion under the crack of a trainer's whip. The heavy rain that followed almost instantly turned into a near-tropical downpour. Hand in hand, we turned and raced back to the pub, chased by enraged clouds spewing lightning like the tongues of an enormous dragon.

Soaked to the bone, we ran inside, laughing with relief, shaking water off

CHAPTER 35

from our hair and clothes alike. Luckily our former table by the fireplace was still free and we hurried to reclaim it. We were dripping, leaving puddles on the floor and wet prints on the leather seats, whilst my soaked clothing stuck to me like a second skin. My hair felt iced and my teeth kept chattering.

'Don't worry, we'll soon get you warm,' Robert promised, calling a waiter over. While our hot drinks were being prepared, Rob took my chilled hands in his and began to rub them vigorously, warming them with his hot breath until they felt as fiery as my cheeks. The hot grog with cinnamon pleasantly burned my throat and my shivering subsided. I looked out of the window. The storm persisted – it was wilder than ever - and we could forget about returning to campus anytime soon.

'Looks like we'll have to stay overnight, but at least that means we can continue enjoying our evening,' said Robert, adding immediately, 'Don't worry, I won't disturb your privacy. I'll get two rooms.'

I wasn't sure at all that I wanted to be in a room alone when Robert was near, but I tried to seem indifferent: 'OK, that's a deal!'

He immediately went to the reception desk and five minutes later returned with a single key, smiling broadly and not even trying to conceal his pleasure. 'Looks like we're not the only ones needing a last-minute refuge, but we were lucky: I got the last room - a suite by the way. So, there should be enough room for us both,' he said, trying to not look too delighted.

I sensed that we were both secretly thrilled, even though I tried my best not to show it. We hastily finished the remaining grog and, wasting no time, headed straight to our suite. I could only guess what Robert was thinking about. All my thoughts were focused on the fact that soon we'd be alone in a room where there was a bed – for the first time since that memorable kiss.

'If I sleep with him I'd never be able to return to Quentin,' I thought nervously. Then I thought *What nonsense! How could I even contemplate a possible return to Quentin, after everything?*

'We haven't been with enough other people,' he had told me, and those parting words had resounded in my ears. *Well, surely Quentin's number of partners must have grown since then . . . ugh! Why am I even remembering him at all? . . . But Robert was different . . . Robert is so . . . But maybe for Rob too I'd be just another notch on his bedpost?* I fretted over this until suddenly a wild thought crossed my mind. *What do I care? It could be fun! And besides, I've promised myself not to fall in love again!*

My inner monologue lasted until I got completely confused. Robert unlocked the door to our suite and we found ourselves in a cozy one-bedroom apartment with a separate living room and a bathroom with floral wallpaper.

'Not too bad; what do you think?' He turned to me.

Confusion must have been written all over my face. Quentin had always said that he could read me like an open book: however, I couldn't help it.

'You OK?' Robert asked, puzzled. 'If you don't like it or if you just don't want us to share, then….'

'No, no!' I quickly interrupted him. 'Everything's great! Really it is.'

'Yeah, well, there's a decent chesterfield, a TV, and, most importantly, a mini-bar,' said Rob checking out the small fridge. 'The bedroom's yours, but if I were you I'd jump in the shower first after a wetting like that,' he said, helping to rid me of my cardigan and kissing the back of my head.

I entered the bathroom and turned on a hot shower. Two white robes with inscriptions 'for him' and 'for her' embroidered on their breast pockets were dangling from the door hook. For some reason I imagined Quentin and Hugo in them. . . *Why has he been creeping into my head the whole evening?* I fumed, and, throwing off the rest of my wet clothes, headed for the shower.

The hot stream of water was bliss after all that cold and chill. For a while I stood there, squinting, my face blasted beneath the fall of water, my mind completely blank. Then I unhurriedly washed my hair and leaving the shower, dived into the bathrobe 'for her' in which I seemed almost submerged, as it was too big for me. Finally, I hastily roughdried my hair and gave myself an appraising look in the mirror: I had a fresh, if slightly ruddy, appearance; my hair was shining, my skin was glowing and my eyes sparkled (although I couldn't take credit for that last attribute, which I suspected was down to Robert).

I haven't looked so well for a long time, I thought with pleasure, recalling my pathetic appearance during the last stage of my relationship with Quentin. Feeling content, I left the bathroom.

'We seem to have lost all the channels, thanks to the storm,' Robert told me, from the living room. He was standing there, wearing only his jeans, busying himself with the TV. The shirt he'd been wearing was drying on the radiator.

I couldn't take my eyes off of his magnificent torso (its perfection reminding me of that Roman statue cliché) drifting to his broad, well-defined shoulders and to those strong masculine arms, both adorned with a sword piercing a skull tattoo.

Robert looked up.

'The bathroom's free,' I stammered, recovering my senses.

'Oh, you look so cute in that huge robe!'

He came up and embraced me, kissing me on the nose and giving me that familiar, immediately affectionate look which he didn't even try to hide.

'I'm going to take a quick shower. Enjoy yourself looking at the rain!' I went to the dark window: the rain was still pouring down, loudly pounding on the windowpane. *Let it all go and be washed away with the rain,* I thought, thinking about my past. I instantly felt my worries dissipating and my mood turning light-hearted and carefree.

From the bathroom I heard a cheerful tune being whistled, which made me smile. After a while the singing stopped and I heard him leaving the bathroom. I turned back to the rain.

'In my humble opinion, we both look pretty neat in these outfits!' said Rob, appearing in the living room in the snow-white bathrobe inscribed 'for him'. . . He looked so damn desirable: the white color set off his tan, his damp hair carelessly swept back and this intense male gaze of those luminous eyes. . . I felt as if an electrical charge had just shot through me.

'So, what do you think?' Robert interrupted. Looking at him, I really couldn't agree more, admitting again how much I fancied him - I wasn't going to deceive myself any longer.

I couldn't tell him, but Robert could read the language of my eyes. He came close and pulled me to him, his lips fervently pressed to mine; our tongues tangoing, reigniting the memory of our first kiss and every pent-up sense of unconsummated longing that had followed it. Although this time it also felt different – I could sense his urgency and barely restrained passion and I knew that - even had I wanted to - I wouldn't be able to get away. However, getting away from Robert on this occasion was the last thing on my mind. . .

His warm hands were travelling down my back, for a moment lingering on the belt of my bathrobe - willing to waive the white flag at once – briefly resting on my buttocks, before smoothly getting under my terrycloth and teasingly moving higher. . . I felt both scorching hot and disturbingly wet, neither of which he seemed to mind. His breathing grew faster and more uneven. Suddenly, pulling himself away from me for an instant, he gazed into my eyes: we understood each other without words; Robert scooped me into his arms and carried into the bedroom. With my arms tightly wrapped around his neck I carried on kissing him until he gently put me down on the bed with a muffled groan.

'No rush, we've got the whole night ahead of us,' he whispered, running his fingers through my hair. 'Oh, Sasha!' He smiled at the pleasure I took in undressing him, at the unlocking of my own hunger and our joint desire.

I fell asleep sometime around dawn, pillowed in Robert's strong arms, feeling the warmth of his body melding into mine. It must have been late morning when I woke – perhaps eleven or so - but I'd been caught up in some engaging dream featuring us both, the end of which I really wanted to see, when I stirred, half-opening my eyes, and saw his real face looking back at me with a smile. *I wonder how long he's been watching me like that* I thought self-consciously, waking entirely at once.

CHAPTER 35

'Good morning,' he beamed.

My head was still resting on his arm; it seemed that I had slept in his embrace for several hours. I sat up and glanced at my watch: 'Good afternoon, is more like it.'

Robert reached out to me and gently touched my lips to his: 'What a night!' And with those words he pulled slightly away and looked intently at me. While I recalled dizzily all that had happened, how I'd never felt anything like it before. . . I gave Robert a meaningful and – with luck - seductive glance from beneath my lashes, as a sign of a strong consensus on my part.

'I suggest that we don't go back at all and stay here forever instead,' he said exuberantly.

'Forever?'

'Well, at least for another day.' He pulled me towards him in a lingering kiss.

The sun was shining through the chintz curtains, and the birds' chirping promised a great day. Robert jumped out of the bed, giving me another chance to admire the almost sculptured perfection of his body, and crossed to the window. He moved the curtains away and flung open the shutters. I closed my eyes for a moment, almost blinded by the brightness instantly flooding the entire bedroom. There seemed no trace of the previous night's torrential rain, other than dampness on the drenched pavements across the way.

'Look, a rainbow! Can you see it, Sasha?'

I sat up in bed and followed his gaze out of the window: a magnificent rainbow spread its vibrantly colored arch across a pallid blue sky. It looked so close that it almost seemed that we could reach out and touch it.

'Have you ever thought about . . .' he said dreamily. I drifted my gaze back towards him and felt desire rising in me.

'Come to me,' I pleaded in a low voice, throwing the duvet on the floor.

'Sasha, look what you are doing to me!' he said with a half-mocking reproach, before getting back to bed.

Later, wearing our dried clothes and Wellington boots borrowed from reception we headed for lunch in a local pub, making it just in time before the kitchen closed to order its signature dish, a crusty shepherd's pie.

On the way back we decided to stroll through the woods, where only occasional puddles and the acres of mud sticking to our boots reminded us of yesterday's rainstorm. The forest air was filled with lung-piercing ozone, almost making me dizzy from the shock to my system, which had been anesthetized by London's air pollution assault. We walked arm in arm, chatting about nothing and I kept thinking how happy and peaceful I felt with Robert.

I continued to relish our romantic idyll, when he stopped in his tracks and turned to face me. His face suddenly grew serious and his bright eyes darkened, which made me a little concerned. 'Sasha, I have to tell you. I can't share you with anyone. You have to leave him.'

It was only then I realized that he meant Quentin: I had completely forgotten that I still hadn't told him about my drama. And now that I could it all seemed so hugely unimportant. . . I said quietly, 'That's all right. We'd already broken up. For good.'

'Do you want to talk about it?' he asked.

I shook my head. Robert wrapped his arms around me and pulled me close, pressing his body into mine. He said, 'I only wish I could've been there for you when you needed me.'

'It's OK. What matters is that you're here now,' I assured him.

He lightly traced my lower lip with his finger:

'You have such beautiful lips.'

He kissed me slowly, taking his time, and then harder - almost fiercely - making my mind blissfully sink into oblivion. I was still overwhelmed by that kiss when he picked me up and headed back to the hotel with his cargo.

'You can put me down,' I joked. 'Really, I know how to walk.'

'You're like a feather; I can carry you forever!'

I had agreed not to fall in love again, I reminded myself – although, taking

CHAPTER 35

Robert's hand in mine I was already feeling that conviction slipping. We returned to the campus the following morning, intoxicated with each other, and having acquired a new and still unaccustomed status as a couple.

I dropped into my room to change and then to rush to a lecture in criminal law read by Mr. Thompson, a former Crown prosecutor, desperate not to be late. During the lecture, however, my head remained in the clouds. I smiled wistfully, thinking of Robert: my imagination drew again on our first kiss on the night of the rainstorm, then I mentally blushed, remembering what had happened afterwards, my breath quickening even in retrospect.

Robert I repeated in my mind, twirling a lock of hair around my finger, my lips parted.

'Emelyanova!'

Mr. Thompson's sharp tone voice brought me back to reality. 'Can you tell us why you are smiling whilst constantly looking out of the window during my lecture? Kindly repeat what I've just said.'

I blushed and looked down, frantically trying to pull myself together, while feeling the eyes of everyone in class upon me. 'Um,' I said, reading from my neighbour's proferred notes, 'The main features of a subjective Mens Rea in a crime are: the defendant's guilt, motive, and. . .and . . . ' I struggled to make out my neighbour's clumsy writing at the end of the sentence.

Mr Thompson snapped, 'And the emotional state - which is extremely important, remember that! I'd suggest you pay closer attention next time – your first exam is coming up. And that applies to each one of you!'

After class, back in the privacy of my room, I got Debbie's letter out of the drawer - it would have been rude to leave it unanswered. So I wrote that I understood everything and felt really sorry, but that I could never return – Quentin and I had broken up for good.

Then I put the pen down and mentally turned the page – I had no desire to think about the extinct volcano of my first love. Besides, tonight I was seeing

Robert and, recalling Mr Thompson's earlier words, I really wanted him finding me in my best emotional state.

CHAPTER 36

Robert had announced that he was cooking us dinner. 'Perhaps I could help?' I said, daring to offer my culinary abilities, though painfully aware that they left much to be desired. . .

'No, no, leave everything to me. All I need is for you to be free around eight.'

I was curious as to what Robert could possibly manage to summon forth from the appalling upstairs kitchen, using a cooker and microwave generally used for nothing more sophisticated than baked beans or macaroni and cheese - the usual affordable student treats grabbed between regular trips to the communal dining room.

At 8:00 p.m. sharp I heard the long-awaited knock: it was Robert smiling enigmatically on my doorstep.

'Ready? You look so appetizing!' he said, pulling me close for a kiss, his hands squeezing my bottom through my snug jeans. Then he swept my jacket off its hanger and ushered me out of the room, slamming the door behind us.

'Why are you going downstairs and not to your room?' I asked, confused.

'I just thought we might take a short walk before dinner,' said Robert, assisting me with my jacket while wrapping his own scarf around my neck.

Soon we'd left the campus behind and were wandering along the Strand, stopping only long enough to admire the stunning Gothic architecture of the Royal Courts of Justice before carrying on along a subdued Fleet Street. There we crossed the road and walked down the narrow Middle Temple Lane, continuing to the paved streets of the historic Middle Temple.

'Maybe this is where you'll wind up working after you graduate, Sasha,' said Robert, nodding towards the barristers' chambers, all in red brick, with their symmetrical sash windows.

'What are you talking about?' I protested. 'I could never be a barrister - they need to speak in court. With my English that would be just impossible!'

'If I were a judge, you'd win every trial with your accent alone!'

With this Robert brought my hand to his lips and kissed it, adding more seriously, 'Sasha, you can become anyone you want to be. Nothing is impossible if you really try.'

He makes me feel so great! I gushed, feeling my self-confidence soar and squeezing his hand more tightly. We walked across the wide lawns of the Inner Temple Garden, surrounded by the grand terraced barristers' chambers and soon arrived at Temple tube station, leaving the tranquility of the Inns of Court behind.

'Can't you tell me where we're going?' I asked.

'You'll find out soon enough. Nearly there, I promise,' he said, hugging me round my shoulders.

The night was sharpened with the November chill as we walked along the Victoria Embankment, glowing as ever with the million lights of the city. It didn't have the feel of a random wander: Robert seemed absolutely certain as to where he was striding, at the same time adjusting to my own pace. *We even walk in harmony,* I thought, *and yet, where are we going?*

At the next traffic lights we crossed over the road and soon approached a private gated development with CCTV security outside the entrance. Through the metal bars I could see a tall white building surrounded by dense bushes and trees, mysteriously illuminated. With a conspiratorial wink Robert pressed some digits on the security keypad: the gates gave way and we entered. We then cut across a small square, which included a fountain, towards an elegant residential building, which, although a new build, didn't look in the least out of character beside the neighbouring Inns of Court.

In the communal entrance Robert exchanged greetings with a stern middle-aged concierge: he was obviously no stranger here. In the lift he continued to impersonate the strong, silent type, a version of Rob complete new to me, as he could generally talk anyone under the table. . . We emerged on the second floor, where he led me along a corridor featuring numbered apartments, stopping outside number 13. He unlocked the door, and switched on the lights, saying, 'Welcome!'

I followed him inside, glancing around curiously whilst getting a whiff of some mouth-watering smells coming from the kitchen. The flat's modern design resembled that of a brand new four-star hotel: beige carpeting, modernist furniture, canvas wall art and a white marble table set for two in the corner.

'So, where are we?'

'This is my aunt's apartment. She's moved to New Zealand for a year to help out with the grandchildren.'

Somehow it just doesn't feel like a lonely aunt's flat I thought, rather doubtfully. There was nothing suggesting that this minimalistic bachelor pad might be the family home of Robert's aunt - or of any other female, for that matter.

'She bought it as an investment. Never lived here herself, so I'm looking after it for her, along with her house in Essex. We'll go there some other time,' he added. 'I do hope you're hungry, though!'

Robert headed towards a large, open-plan kitchen.

'Moroccan chicken in mango sauce – I stole the recipe from a Moroccan when I was there.'

'A Moroccan lady, of course?' I mocked.

'A very elderly Moroccan lady,' Rob agreed with a smile, appearing with a tray of juicy, golden chicken. Having dished out the food, he then opened a bottle of red wine and filled both of our glasses to the brim. 'To us!' He raised the toast and we tucked into our plates of food.

'Yum, it's delicious. . . You're a great cook! So, this is where you bring all your Moroccan girls!' I teased.

His look was reproachful. 'Now that I have a lovely Russian girl, I don't need Moroccans or Americans or girls of any other nationality at all!'

'Yeah, they all say that - at first,' I muttered, giving him a doubtful look.

'I'm serious. And, as I want you to truly feel at home, I'll even give you the spare key. You can even move in - if you'd like . . . At least, think about it. It'd beat where we're living at the moment, anyway!'

I stared at him in astonishment. We had only just become an item and Robert was already suggesting that I move in with him? What did this mean? I wasn't sure, but I didn't refuse the key, all the same. It certainly eased my mind about any female Moroccans he might be tempted to invite back of an evening. . .

'And what about the dessert?' I asked, savouring his response in advance.

It turned out that my favorite Häagen-Dazs strawberry and cream was on the menu. Seizing both bowls, Robert headed to the bedroom. 'I never know where I'll finish my evening when I'm with you,' I murmured, looking around.

His fingers were deftly unbuttoning my blouse, whilst his hot lips brushed against the skin just above my breasts. I was melting under his hands, very like the Häagen-Dazs - which was lying abandoned on the bedside table - and was about to surrender entirely when my eyes happened to fix on a family photograph on the chest of drawers.

There, a young Robert in a paper crown was smiling happily at a festive table next to some girl whose long, honey-coloured locks framed a slender, delicate face. Beside them were two older people.

'Are these your parents?' I asked, my curiosity getting the better of me.

His hands froze for a second and he straightened up, though his face remained both sad and calm. 'Yes. This was our last real family photo. Shortly after it was taken, my sister Jenny died in a skiing accident - and my dad also died, as you know.'

I wrapped my arms tightly around him. 'I'm so sorry. Your sister looks so young. . . You must still miss her!'

'Yes,' Robert sighed. 'I do miss her. I miss her all the time. . . And my father too, of course.' Suddenly he reached for the photograph and picked it up, glancing at it intently. 'Look, why haven't I noticed this before? You're so like Jenny!'

CHAPTER 36

I glanced at the girl in the photograph more closely; and I had to admit that indeed we looked very similar: both fair and slim with large eyes and long eyelashes. . . I briefly wondered if she'd been good at tennis.

Hmm, I don't feel exactly thrilled if Robert only likes me because I remind him of his dead sister I thought, rather dubiously. Robert carefully put the photo back and, turning to me with that damnably sexy grin, switched back to playful mood: 'But you'd better beware! I have no brotherly feelings for you – none at all!'

He pulled me towards him by the waist, the immediate evidence of his arousal dispelling any worries I might have had with regard to my desirability.

Wow, he wants me that much! I thought, overjoyed.

His hands traced the contours of my waist, almost fitting his grip around it, and then moved down to my thighs before undoing the zip of my Levy's and pushing warmly towards my buttocks.

'Mmm, an absolute hourglass,' he murmured. Working up an appetite, I hastily helped to rid him of his clothes, hungering after my dessert.

'Oh, Robert,' I breathed, my hands all over him.

He's perfect, just what I need right now, I thought, enjoying his body whilst thinking that Robert was, without any doubt, the best lover I'd ever have.

CHAPTER 37

It was so cool to feel grown-up, to have a love nest in London, a microcosm of our own, where we belonged only to each other. As often as Robert had suggested it, I hadn't moved in with him - although in fact most of our time together had been spent in his flat in Temple Mansions.

'Now that you're with me, I don't need to hang around the Halls of Residence. In fact, next week I'll be moving back to Temple Mansions altogether. It's just so much nicer there! Sashenka, you can do so too - why would you want to stay on the campus, anyway?'

Sashenka . . .

I was melting, at simply hearing my name roll off his tongue in that uniquely Russian, uniquely affectionate, diminutive – no man in the UK had ever called me by this name before. As for the accent: whenever Robert spoke Russian to me, it was pure aphrodisiac.

Certainly, his offer was tempting, but I was determined to demonstrate my independence. Also, I so cherished our happiness that I was almost afraid that living together might destroy the idyll. . . *Why should we change anything, when everything is already perfect?* I said to myself. Which was why I told him that I wasn't ready for such a serious step.

In addition, I didn't want to bore him with my permanent presence, though I could probably have spared myself this particular fear: Robert had been so busy with work that we saw each other mainly in the evenings. Sometimes he had to travel, but in his absence I never stayed in his apartment by myself, believing that, having refused his offer to move in, I had no right to usurp his territory. . . Besides, I really wanted to show him that, despite my experience with Quentin, which Robert had probably guessed, I trusted him and wasn't entirely neurotic. . .

Occasionally, I used to escape from the wild noise of the student crowd to Temple Mansions, but the apartment always felt empty without him there and, having wandered about, I always returned to the campus. In the evenings we shared, we either cooked dinner at home – I was gradually growing to enjoy cooking – or else we chose some cozy restaurant in Covent Garden nearby. From time to time we attended some student parties, but mostly preferred our own company.

Despite my firm intention never again to fall in love, I was aware that I was breaking my resolution. My affection grew stronger each day, and soon I couldn't imagine my life without Robert. Sometimes the intensity of such feelings really scared me - the thought of losing him made my heart feel as if it was about to split into millions of tiny pieces. I was so afraid that he would notice that I tried to hide my feelings under the guise of self-sufficiency, which at times drove him crazy.

'Sasha, when will you stop trying to prove things to me?' Robert once moaned, watching me unnecessarily demonstrate my independence once again – that independence which Quentin had so often told me that I lacked – 'I get it, I really get it! – You don't have to move in with me if you don't want to, but - since you're spending most of the nights here anyway - why don't we at least move some of your stuff?'

It makes sense, but how would a strong independent woman act in my place? I considered, but finally decided that this halfway type of move wouldn't threaten my budding self-respect . . .

I tended to consult this mythical internal super-woman every time I was in doubt or feeling lost, but unfortunately she didn't always have the answers.

'Don't make me laugh! If you insist, you can buy me a coffee,' Robert would say, brushing aside yet another attempt of mine to pay for our dinner, sometimes adding in a growl, 'When will you finally relax and stop protecting yourself from me? I'm not Quentin, you know!'

Robert was indignant, but it was my survival instinct that forced me to be so constantly on the alert. However, despite my best efforts, I finally

CHAPTER 37

decided that it was silly to continually erect artificial barriers in the path of our relationship. Moreover, by then Robert had grown to know me pretty well and was also too intelligent: he could spot any touch of falseness almost instantly.

I liked the fact that Robert never pried into my mind but, if I longed to share my problems, he was not only ready to listen, but also ready to come up with possible solutions - nothing ever seemed unsolvable for him.

I soon learned that, thanks to Jill, Robert had known about Dad and Alka all along, but had tactfully decided not to ask me about it, thinking that, had I wished to discuss it, I'd have told him myself.

One evening, after returning to Temple Mansions, Robert found me sitting in the living room in the dark. He turned on the light and inquisitively peered into my gloomy face.

'Are you OK? Has something happened?'

I silently handed him the current *Standard*, featuring a photo of my father and his 'stunning young wife' surrounded by glamorous celebrities at Elton John's black-and-white ball. Tossing the newspaper aside, Robert folded me in his strong arms: 'Sashenka – красавица, don't be sad! We'll think of something! You'll see - everything will be fine!'

'How? What can we possibly do?' I sighed, although - still - his unshakable confidence did give me a glimmer of hope. Simply with his presence Robert could always lift my spirits; with him by my side I had even started to believe in my own strength.

'Leave it to me; I'll think it over. Why don't we have dinner in town and then go dancing?' he said, gently stroking my cheek.

I agreed without hesitation: by this time I'd learned to dance salsa really well and had also fallen head over heels for it - just as I had for Robert.

***

A week later, having made some inquiries through reliable channels, Robert had gathered some very interesting information about Anatoliy Emelyanov, a high-risk politically-exposed person, who had recently emerged onto the radar of several international intelligence agencies. As it turned out, he had got himself involved in some occult organization – one in which his new wife, despite her youth, was believed to play a significant role.

'Stay out of it, some powerful people are behind this,' he was advised. He was even warned: 'The Company will neither encourage nor countenance any personal initiatives on this.'

Rob had long known that it was dangerous to cross swords with cults or sects, some of which wielded tremendous power. These people were said to be above the law or any sense of justice, but very few knew exactly who they were. His first thought was that he had to think how to tell Sasha about all this in the best possible way - after all how could an ordinary student (such as he was supposed to be) have access to such secret information? And also: why should she believe him?

I need to figure out a story, he decided.

He didn't want to sugar the pill, as he knew pretty well that it was never an easy task to free anyone from the tentacles of any influential cult – in fact, quite often it was simply impossible.

He thought *By this time, they'd probably reduced Emelyanov to a near-zombie, using such methods of mind control as torture, hypnosis, drugs or the latest medical technology in order to split his mind into differently structured alter-egos, with each one programmed as a human computer under separate code numbers and colors. He would almost certainly be suffering from memory lapses, amnesia and loss of perspective – while - in order to defend against deprogramming – a programme for self-destruction would probably have been placed somewhere in the deepest recesses of his mind, something that would naturally remain under control of his handler.*

From what Robert had been briefly told about Emelyanov's talented young wife, it was likely that she herself was overseeing him and from time to time reinforcing the inbuilt programmes through access codes, triggers and cryptic keys, all of which would effectively prevent him from realising that the cult was probably by this time in control of his entire fortune, including his financial empire.

The truth was that Emelyanov would serve them as long as they needed him, but if he made the slightest attempt to rebel he would be reprogrammed – and, when he had served his purpose, either an accident or some 'natural' death would almost certainly be arranged for him. But Robert simply couldn't paint such a hopeless picture to Sasha. *She really doesn't need to know everything* he determined.

With this on his mind he hurried to Temple Mansions, where they had agreed to meet for dinner before catching a West End musical. On the way he didn't stop thinking about Sasha.

At first, he hadn't given much thought to his feelings for her. She had certainly made his heart race from the moment he'd met her; and once he'd grown to know her he had wanted her - wanted her badly - her desirability only intensified by her innocence and her unavailability. However desire itself was nothing new to him, unlike these other feelings, which he'd never experienced before, feelings he couldn't quite put his finger on - feelings he probably wouldn't even be able to describe coherently, even had he been asked to do so. . .

He pushed this thought away. Anyway, they were good together and that was surely all that mattered. Why complicate things? Despite all her recent misfortunes, their relationship had evolved much more easily than he had ever anticipated: she didn't demand a constant emotional response from him, neither did she ever seem to wish to plunge into any analysis of her family problems. She was in fact far stronger – and therefore far most interesting – than she'd seemed at first glance. Before he knew it his own feelings were running deep. . . *Probably, it couldn't have been any other way, with her,* he thought.

He wanted to wake up with her every morning, to look out for her and to protect her from everything: a tremendous tenderness threatened to almost overwhelm him. She had also grown passionately attached to him, which moved but at the same time alarmed him.

Perhaps if his life was simpler, Sasha could be 'the one.' Why not? . . . There was always the possibility that his current project in London might turn out to be long-term he thought, approaching Temple Mansions. And yet, as a general rule Robert didn't like to plan ahead, believing that life would show him the way.

Something smelled good in the kitchen. Sasha, beautifully flushed from the heat of the oven, must have heard the click of his key in the lock, as she ran out to meet him. 'Robert! Perfect timing! Dinner is just ready. Come and sit down, while it's still hot.' He could tell she relished her new role as hostess, which she had adopted perfectly.

I could so easily get used to this! he thought, locking Sasha in his arms and inhaling her scent.

'I probably reek of kitchen,' she said self-consciously.

'No, you smell of warm apple pie!'

'Actually we have beef stroganoff on the menu. Go wash your hands,' she said, freeing herself from his embrace in order to set the table. 'How was your day? What's new in your institute?'

'Oh, busy as usual. You'd better tell me what you were up to today.'

Robert listened to her with half an ear, mentally steeling himself for the upcoming encounter. He opened a bottle of red wine and lit candles on the table - a softened atmosphere contributed to a relaxing and trusting environment. He truly hated to upset her, especially today, when she was in such high spirits in anticipation of their trip to the theatre. . . Robert even considered delaying such an unpleasant conversation, but, having decided that it was inevitable, preferred to get it off of his chest. He gently raised the subject during dinner.

'Sashenka, look, I've made some inquiries through my father's good friend – he works in intelligence, so his sources can be trusted. Anyway, he's gathered some information about your former friend, Ala Gromova.'

She turned her doe-like eyes questioningly towards him. He felt like an assassin.

'Turns out that she now belongs to some weird, quasi-religious sect. Nobody seems to know much about this organization, but somebody powerful is assuredly behind it all, as I was strongly advised to forget all about it. In short, your dad seems to be in a tough spot.'

Robert hesitated for a moment, considering how to soften the blow, but still make Sasha understand what could happen to a victim of mind control, when she exclaimed: 'I knew it! Alka's a witch! Quentin accidentally witnessed her initiation in the woods last December, but I didn't believe him, thinking it was just some drug-induced hallucination. . . Well, he used to say that drugs like LSD, expanded his mind,' she added, in response to his inquisitive look.

Yeah, a healthy dose of psilocybin can come handy in interrogations, which the Company knows only too well thought Robert grimly.

'The expanded mind combined with a suppressed willpower is easy to control,' he observed, but she wasn't listening.

'Quentin even wrote the name of the group in that letter he sent me in Moscow last Christmas. I remember it - the Circle of Georgina. He said that they'd initiated Alka as Lilith – or maybe Lilian, I'm not sure – that night – and after the Christmas holidays she even returned to college with an owl tattoo on her shoulder! . . . By the way, I always wanted to ask you about your sword and skull tattoo. Is there any special meaning to it?'

'Well, it is symbolic – one interpretation is that you must never allow your mind to rule over you.' He kissed her gently on the forehead. 'By the way, Sasha, did you keep that letter, the one Quentin sent you last Christmas?'

'No, I have none of his letters now. Quentin asked for them back last summer and I returned them. I think he was a little worried that evidence about his drug use could get out, having decided to go into politics.'

Robert thought gloomily *Probably Quentin had simply imagined the name of the Circle of Georgina, as well as perhaps some other details of that night. . . Though, there did seem to be a few too many coincidences for it to have been simply some fantasy, or a drug trip. In any case, they didn't have much choice. In the absence of any facts, they had to clutch at what straws they had . . .* To cheer Sasha, he said reassuringly: 'Well, it's a start! We already have something to dig deeper into.'

'How it all fits together,' she marveled, her chin in her hand. 'Alka really did bewitch my dad, somehow. But he's never going to believe it – he's a scientist and a materialist. My grandma told me that they fell out badly when she had me secretly baptised into the Russian Orthodox Church.'

'Really?'

'Absolutely. He refused to speak to her for ages until eventually my mother forced him to become reconciled - I believe by threatening him with divorce. I was still too young to remember anything about it. My dad was a committed atheist, but as you know, in Soviet times atheism was official state policy, while religion was persecuted and suppressed. Perhaps Dad was afraid that his career might suffer; also he could've been expelled from the Party.'

'Yes, of course,' said Robert, listening intently.

'Still, I find it hard to believe that my dad would let some cult brainwash him. He's a firm, strong-willed person, but. . .' and here she grew thoughtful, 'I suppose it's fair to say that this didn't prevent him from falling into Alka's clutches.'

Robert said, 'I'm afraid the rich and powerful can easily fall prey to groups like this, as they have the financial resources and the power to manipulate – which makes them a target. Also, these kinds of groups can find the ideal methods for everyone: vices to be indulged, and then, well, possibly blackmail for the highly-placed, perhaps the promise of power for narcissists. . . even love can be twisted into a merciless weapon in their hands, as it was in the case of your father. The most horrible part is that, once they get their grip on you, you become their brainwashed slave – someone no longer able to think independently, especially if the slavery is reinforced chemically. Breaking free from such cults is extremely difficult, but not impossible.'

'What should we do?' Sasha asked mournfully. *Oh, God! Not that look in her eyes, like a wounded deer* he thought, with a vague sense of guilt, suddenly

CHAPTER 37

feeling outside of his comfort-zone . . . In fact, this was what he'd been afraid of from the beginning.

'Don't worry: no-win situations don't exist!' Robert assured her, wrapping his arms around her slim shoulders. 'There are specialists in these matters – doctors, therapists - they assist victims of mind control. They've helped thousands of people in these kinds of cases. The problem, of course, is that he's not even aware that he has been programmed.'

'Bewitched,' Sasha corrected him.

'Call it whatever you like, but in order to be helped he must first realise that something's gone very wrong. As long as he's in love and utterly content with everything, we can't force him towards the help he needs. . . Besides, the mind control can be simply too strong to enable him to be able to see clearly. . . But don't despair! Just give me a little time and we'll figure something out,' he promised reassuringly.

A touching hope and gratitude warmed her eyes: she clearly believed him, which made Robert inwardly sigh with relief. Now that the conversation was over and had gone so much better than he'd feared, they could go to the theatre and forget about it all. . .

However, the fact that he couldn't offer any real solution to her father's situation still tormented him - and this was really all he could think of during the musical and the rest of the evening. He knew that he wouldn't be able to rest until he'd figured something out. He had always been able to find a solution in any situation, no matter how hopeless it had seemed at first glance: and, after all, he had to live up to his name - Robert the Maestro, even if it was not a name Sasha would ever know . . . *It won't be any different on this occasion,* he secretly determined. *For Sasha's sake I'm prepared to override the Company's warning and risk everything, regardless of consequences . . .*

As he established pretty soon, the Circle of Georgina was unknown and unheard-of, almost as if it had never existed - nor did it feature in any reference book or official register. He spent hours reviewing press cuttings at the British

Library, but as expected, he found nothing even remotely relevant. However, the concept of Lilith was surprisingly popular: according to various myths and legends, the lady was a goddess of the night, a winged serpent, a seductress demon-queen and even the mythological first wife of Adam. Robert pondered longest over a translated ancient Hebrew poem of the Sumerian legend of Lilith (Lilitu in Sumerian) next to a black-and-white picture of the Babylonian Lilith depicted with an owl in the Encyclopedia of Ancient Myths.

'Lilitu knew she could never love….Her tears brought life, but her kiss brought death …' he read, a strange sense of dread creeping over him. . .

Utter nonsense, he concluded, rubbing his weary eyes. He shut the book and plunged into his own thoughts. He needed to start his investigation in Wiltshire, where the organisation in question carried out some of its activities, whatever these might be, under the name of the Circle of Georgina (the name meant nothing to him and he had concluded was probably a fake).

From Sasha's story, he'd secretly decided that those people were wizards, or else druids, possibly worshipping pagan gods, and perhaps holding strange rituals in the woods. Robert had never faced anything like this before and right from the start it provoked in him both scepticism and distrust. He thought *Why is all this provincial mumbo-jumbo so intriguing to some people! Who the **** needs it?*

Then, Robert suddenly remembered his old friend, Bill Wayne, former lecturer at his previous alma mater, in California. Perhaps Bill's connections in Princeton could help him to reach some academic who specialised in the study of pagan cults – someone who might be able to put him on the right track?

As soon as he got back to Temple Mansions he dialed California, relieved to find that Bill hadn't changed his number following his recent, well-deserved retirement. Robert briefly outlined the essence of the matter, and, as usual, Bill promised to help if he could, without asking questions, a quality that Rob had always appreciated. Then he decided to make a swift trip to Wiltshire.

The name of the Emelyanov's Wiltshire estate featured regularly and heavily in the glossy celebrity magazines – so finding it, he assumed, should be a piece of cake. . . On his way towards it Robert suddenly remembered that only a few days ago he had seen an article in financial press about a forthcoming sale of Emelyanov's Metallurgical Plant in the Urals to some Saudi consortium. He thought *It's possible that we don't have much time – it might be that those people wouldn't still need Emelyanov after the sell-off. However, best not tell Sasha anything, not at least until I find out more.*

On Sunday, having told Sasha that he had to go down to Essex as his aunt's house had been broken into, Robert drove his motorcycle to Wiltshire instead. Even without a map he easily found Oldland-on-Grove: every local knew the way perfectly. He soon found himself on a country road running along a dense forest surrounded by a high brick wall neatly fitted with metal tridents entwined with barbed wire, through which the dark peaks of pine trees could be seen. The extensive grounds lay behind this impregnable wall, which stood around five metres in height and had obviously been erected only recently, despite suiting neither the architecture nor the landscape.

Such electric fencing installations are definitely prohibited in this area, Robert recalled with surprise - he had only ever seen similar structures at such top-security sites as prisons, military bases or intelligence facilities.

He had driven around another mile, when he saw a warning sign stating that he was bordering private property accessible only by its residents: a view confirmed by the locked wrought-iron gates he propped his motorcycle against as he eyed the alley, framed by ancient oaks and maples, disappearing into the distance. The coat of arms of Oldland-on-Grove's former owners, including a Latin inscription, decorated the handles of the heavy gates. Out of the corner of his eye Robert saw a barrage of CCTV cameras so, in order to avoid arising suspicion, he turned and rode thoughtfully away.

Having hidden his motorcycle in public woodland across the road, Robert decided to wander around before it grew quite dark and to attempt to work out how he could conceivably gain access to the grounds of Oldland-on-Grove.

The pine-needle-strewn pedestrian path stretched for miles along the road, with only occasional cars passing, at least on a lazy Sunday afternoon. Robert ran an expert hand along the new yellow bricks of the fence. With a rope and a grappling hook, he could easily climb over it at night; the only problem being the electrical current on the top. He was familiar with this type of installation and knew that if he were to attack any part of the wall, the alarm would go off immediately, signaling his location to the security guards. . . *There has to be a better way,* thought Robert, continuing his walk.

It was getting dark when he stumbled across a few pieces of broken brick scattered on the ground: in places the new wall's foundation was actually missing cement between the bricks.

With a sudden surge of hope he crouched down to shift the loose bricks, which gave way without much effort, exposing a cavity just wide enough for an adult to get through. In fact, he wondered if someone – a poacher, even a burglar? – had been there before him. Robert replaced the loose bricks and returned to the forest to wait for onset of darkness.

He didn't have to wait long. As soon as night fell Robert, equipped with night-vision goggles, ran across the deserted road and headed towards the secret hole. *Good thing the police don't patrol the area,* he thought.

Once he'd wriggled through to the other side of the wall he found himself in the earthy green darkness of the dark forest that seemed to surround the mansion. He proceeded further in, accidentally terrifying a few sleeping deer, who leapt, panic-stricken, into the darkness. He froze to illuminate the area before carrying on, while carefully tuning in to the forest sounds. After a while the dense trees began to thin out and he emerged along a broad well-trodden path, his trained, near-photographic memory recording the trail.

Somewhere in the distance a lake glinted silver. The moon was reflected in its still, liquid surface, like an alluring phantom or naiad – but Robert's intuition told him not to approach the lake. He obeyed, turning into a narrow track tacking along the water's edge. Leaving the lake behind, he came to a grove of slender birch seedlings. ('Our piece of Russia in England,' he recalled Ala Gromova's words in *Hello* magazine, which Sasha had shown him. How upset she'd been – and no wonder!)

Can't imagine what Oldland-on-Grove is like on the inside, must be magnificent! thought Robert, recalling that, according to *Hello*, it had as many windows as there are days in a year. . .

The screech of an owl disturbed the night silence, but it didn't startle him as much as it would usually have done. Instead Robert felt strangely and suddenly drowsy, as if his legs were almost ready to give way beneath him. . . In fact, all he longed to do was to lie down somewhere –anywhere – and to close his eyes. (Could there have been some drug laid shrewdly along his path?) However, he forced himself to move on, stifling his yawns until he emerged from the forest, when his head seemed to clear.

He found himself in a barely-lit park with artificial rocks, plunging waterfalls and caged wild animals: he spotted tigers, sleeping wolves and something that might have been the form of a panther neighbouring what he supposed, from the inscription outside, to be a reptile house. His drowsiness vanished as if by magic.

That's the scale, a real safari! he thought, moving stealthily onward while still keeping a safe distance, so as to run no risk of awakening the animals. On the way, he almost ran into a patrolling guard, having just enough time to dive behind a rock-ledge and to wait, with beating heart, for the guard to pass by before continuing along his way. After leaving the park, he slipped across a bridge over a pond which appeared to feature farmed sturgeon and soon found himself in a landscaped garden adorned with marble sculptures, ornamental fountains and a maze.

Ahead of him lay the flood-lit outlines of Oldland-on-Grove, partly shielded behind the border of the maze, Robert was heading towards it when he suddenly heard a couple of dogs barking in the distance. He thought, with foreboding, *they might have caught my scent on a breath of wind. . .* With every second the barking grew louder. Then suddenly the garden was flooded with harsh weaving spotlights and Rob heard the alarmed shouts of security guards, presumably following the dogs. Could they be armed?

Robert jumped out of the bushes and started running; the wind whistling in his ears, his feet scorching the ground. It was crucially important to reach the fence before the dogs caught up with him. Judging by what looked like triangular horns but which were really their ears flying in the wind, they were Dobermans, known for both elegance and ferocity. . . If he didn't make it to the fence first, his fate might be sealed.

Promising himself not to glance again over his shoulder, he skirted round the now-buzzing zoo, which had been awakened by some fearsome feline roar, and, taking a running jump across the bridge, sprinted towards the grove. The dogs were of course catching up: *Whatever you do, just don't trip over,* he instructed himself grimly.

Just as he was running into the grove the smell of burned meat hit his nostrils. Without slowing down, Robert ran on. To his surprise, the dogs' furious barking seemed to ebb away into the distance: were they no longer after him? – It seemed unlikely. And what about the guards?

He was still running when bright fire flames silhouetting someone in a hooded robe seemed to rear up beside the slim birch trees. The figure must have seen him, without a doubt, but that hardly mattered. Rushing past the grove, he ran surefooted through the woods to his secret entry in the wall, its location imprinted in a memory that had never yet failed him. . . Once safe on the far side of the wall, he raced across the road to retrieve the motorcycle hidden amongst the pine branches. His breathing gradually recovering, Robert leaped on his bike and drove back to London, analysing his Sunday evening in Wiltshire along the way.

What a strange night picnic! Could it have been some bizarre ritual? Unfortunately, he'd not had a chance to take it all in, but – on the plus side – he was extremely lucky to have escaped unharmed. Most likely the guards

CHAPTER 37

would speedily locate the secret break in the wall: he'd have to come up with a better idea next time. At least he was now more familiar with the grounds.

He certainly hadn't liked what he'd seen – in fact, in retrospect it made his skin crawl. Though Robert never liked dealing with anything he didn't understand.

Returning to Temple Mansions late that night, he found a voicemail from Bill asking to call back, as he immediately did - in California, of course, it was still only early evening.

'You need to contact an Oxford don, a history professor. His name's Hayes: he's a member of the board and specializes in the study of pagan traditions and British folklore. Please pass him kindest regards from Trevor Erickson. . . . And Rob, you will take care, won't you?'

'Of course,' Robert assured him, though rather unsettled by something in his old acquaintance's tone.

He made a mental note first thing in the morning to call the Oxford don and arrange a meeting.

CHAPTER 38

The professor lived in a prestigious northern corner of Oxford, about half a mile from the town centre and around twenty minutes from his own college.

Professor Hayes, or 'the don' as Robert secretly thought of him upon meeting this intriguing breed for the first time, turned out to be an elderly man with a short grey beard and a liveliness remarkable for his age - it seemed obvious that he'd never lost interest in life. Robert thought: *He looks like some ancient wizard - all he needs is to swap those corduroy trousers for a long, white robe!*

'Mr. Lambert? What a pleasure! Please, do come in,' he said, running a distracted hand through his still plentiful hair. 'You're just in time for afternoon tea!'

Robert, who had assumed the institution of afternoon tea long since abandoned, followed him into a shabby living-room with a fire crackling cozily away in the grate and a wicker chair still swaying next to it, where the professor had probably been warming his bones before Rob's arrival. The cluttered air of a bachelor's residence, devoid of even a single feminine touch, seemed to confirm that Professor Hayes lived alone.

'Earl Grey tea? Or perhaps you might like something slightly stronger?' With this, Professor Hayes reached for a dusty bottle on the mantelpiece, adding, 'Sherry has a certain historic affinity with afternoon tea, at least as conceived by the Victorians. . .'

'No, sorry; I came by motorcycle.'

'Yes, I observed how you rather boldly rode straight into the drive. . . One could tell at once that such a dashing rider came from fields afar, as we generally favour quieter means of transport here . . . Why don't we go into my study? That's where I hold my student tutorials; I find the atmosphere

here almost too tranquil for serious discussion,' the professor suggested, not forgetting to take a bottle of sherry along with him.

The dimly-lit study had the feel of a library; the sheer volume and rich abundance of books piled up everywhere filled Rob with awe at their owner's presumed brilliance. Meanwhile, Professor Hayes was saying, 'So you're from Toronto, how marvelous! One of our Rhodes Scholars was originally from Montreal. What's the weather like there now?'

The professor continued the flow of small talk, while sinking in a stuffed leather armchair and cheerily waving Robert into one of the shabby chairs opposite. Robert was fidgeting by the time Professor Hayes finally checked himself: 'But, how rude of me – I'd almost forgotten our tea!' and here he bustled towards the doorway.

Left alone, Robert glanced around, breathing in the distinctive musty smell of ancient books along with floating dust motes. It made him long to sneeze - it seemed that the windows here were opened very rarely, if ever. The desk was buried beneath scattered layers of essays, while heaps of paper had been moved to the floor where, arranged in seemingly random stacks, they appeared to be resting against the wall. Rob idly wondered how many years it would take someone to read all the books which filled the cobwebbed bookcases drifting towards the ceiling - not to mention various valuable editions bound in shabby red leather and encased behind glass shelves, as if marked with an invisible sign 'Do not touch'. . .

His thoughts were interrupted by the professor. He was balancing a heavy tray rather precariously and Robert jumped up from his chair to help him.

'It's fine, young man. Believe it or not, I still have the élan vital,' he protested, rather crustily. He placed the tray on the desk atop the pyramid of papers. Following Rob's eyes he added rather defensively, 'I'm the only one who knows where everything is, so I don't let my cleaning lady in here – she'll only create chaos. . . Although, out of chaos comes order, don't you find, Mr. Lambert?'

CHAPTER 38

The professor carefully stirred strong black tea into chipped cups; poured himself a generous portion of sherry and, placing a tin box of biscuits and milk beside Robert, gave him a sharply inquisitive look: 'Now I'm all yours!'

Rob took a deep breath.

'Professor, I'm here on a personal matter concerning some people I care about a good deal. Unfortunately, I'm not in a position to disclose much more than that: although I can say that I'm investigating a possible cult – something about which I know very little. I understand that you've researched pretty much everything about historical paganism. So, what can you tell me about Druids?'

'The Druids! – I've been studying the ancient Druids for the past thirty years! While I can assure you that they certainly existed, perhaps from the time of ancient Babylonian and Sumerian culture, very little can be said definitively. . . They've become a legend, along with Merlin himself, leaving us no written legacy of their existence, so ultimately we have to rely on the Greco-Roman historians and Julius Caesar. Those sources seem to suggest that the Druids were once an elite class, as honoured in their culture as the ancient priests of Egypt, whose magical arts were passed down orally, from one generation to the next. They possessed secret Kabbalistic knowledge, were particularly concerned with astrology, astronomy and divination, and were regarded as guardians of profound wisdom. Now almost nothing seems to be left of their teachings – '

'Did the ancient Druids practice sacrifice? And whom did they worship?' interrupted Robert rather impatiently, recalling the strange figure in the mansion garden.

'You may well ask! We know very little about their rites, as unfortunately there is a dearth of sacred texts – perhaps these never even existed. They mainly worshipped the sun god, but also the moon and the stars, along with rocks, trees, rivers and other pagan deities, to whom they did supposedly offer sacrifices. Despite the fact that ancient sources mention human sacrifice, no firm evidence exists on the basis of the available facts, including archaeological evidence, which is also questionable. Some scholars seem to impress the literary record of Druidism upon archeological evidence - conveniently forgetting the bias of Roman literary sources, of course.'

But Robert wasn't particularly interested in ancient Druidism. He said intently, 'What can you tell me about these rituals?'

'As far as we can ascertain, their rituals were carried out during eight special festivals during the year, the timings – unsurprisingly – being directly related to the changes in the sun cycle and moon phases. Yule – the winter solstice - was one of the important dates in their calendar, celebrating the rebirth of the sun. As you're probably aware, to this day, on the 21st of December, people with sympathies in these directions descend in astonishing numbers upon Stonehenge, in order to watch the stones become aligned with the sunlight on the solstice.'

'The rebirth of the sun?'

'Precisely. Just so. To them it's the seed time of year - the rebirth of the sun god. It was the sun, as you recall, that the early civilizations worshipped in ancient times, viewing it as the source of plant and animal life. Despite failing to understand the science underpinning its cycles, they still prayed each day for the sun to rise . . . In ancient Babylon, erected on the plain of Shinar - the primeval source of idolatry and the most ancient of such religious systems - the sun god was called Nimrod; in Egypt Osiris; in Greece Apollo; while the Canaanites called him Baal, as is evidenced – '

'Forgive me for interrupting, Professor, but I wondered if you might have ever heard of something called The Circle of Georgina?'

The professor, frowning slightly, said, 'No, never. To which historical period might it relate?'

'Actually, to the present day. We're talking strange rituals in the woods, possible sacrifices, perhaps imitations of some pagan practices.' Here Rob lifted an eyebrow skeptically, as if to signify that they would never believe in such nonsense back in Canada.

The professor took a rather deliberate sip of his tea, saying, 'As a historian I don't concern myself with modern paganism; it's not my area of expertise.

CHAPTER 38

Although, as they say, history has a tendency to repeat itself... It's certainly possible that there may indeed, conceivably, be various contemporary movements loosely based on historical pagan beliefs, even though Druid teachings themselves died out centuries ago. I'm afraid I really can't tell you anything about your Circle of... um, what was it called again?'

'Georgina.'

In a sudden, clumsy movement Don knocked over the rest of his tea. Robert rushed to help him rescue the soaked papers beneath.

'No, no, please don't trouble yourself, I can manage... Dear me, what a clumsy old idiot I am!' the professor protested, wiping the papers vaguely with the patched elbow of his cardigan. 'You must forgive me, I'd thought that you'd said "Georgiana" before – not that there's any research of which I am aware on either...' He then glanced over at the old clock, adding, 'If you'd like to learn more about the ancient Druids, I'd be delighted to give you a copy of my latest book, which the Oxford Press so kindly published last year... I only wish that I could have been of greater help! But unfortunately, I now must head off to college for a board meeting. No rest for the wicked, as they say!'

Leaving his unfinished tea without much regret, Robert warmly thanked the professor and hurried back to London carrying a signed copy of *Pagan Practices within a Historical and Sociological Context*, reflecting: *He clearly wanted to get rid of me, which is entirely understandable – I'd already taken up quite a lot of his time. But he also seemed rather anxious at the mention of the Circle. Is it possible that Professor Hayes knows something that he's decided – for whatever reason – he didn't want to share with me? Or is this just my imagination working overtime?*

Although his trip hadn't resulted in anything substantial, Robert decided that a negative result was still a result. Once back in Temple Mansions, he replayed the conversation in his mind: ('... *very little is known about their rituals...*')

Somehow, he simply had to get into the grounds of Oldland-on-Grove on December 21st, and find out what was really concealed behind all this mumbo-jumbo . . . Had he been a betting person, he would have bet that something interesting would be happening at Oldland-on-Grove in ten days' time. . .

Finally he allowed himself the luxury of looking forward to the Christmas holidays, when he and Sasha had planned a skiing trip to Cloisters. He thought: *A change of scenery - especially some skiing - would do her good, by which time – with any luck - he might even have some good news for her to celebrate. . .*

CHAPTER 39

In three days following Robert's visit to Oxford a thick envelope postmarked Wiltshire came in the morning mail. Intrigued, he hastened to open it – and there, to his utter astonishment, was an invitation to The Sol Invictus Masquerade Ball at Oldland-on-Grove at midnight on December 21st.

Lost in thought he fingered the watermarks along the edges of antique gilt paper, the brocades and damasks shaped like a dahlia, though the sharp, multi-layered petals looked far more like the tentacles of an octopus than the petals of a flower. He reasoned: *So they know who the intruder was - and dare to invite him to return! Most likely they want to find out what it is that he wanted, threaten him, intimidate him or even teach him a lesson. Although, they could've done this anyway...*

It didn't even cross his mind to refuse the invitation. He'd been already racking his brain about how he could possibly get into Oldland-on-Grove on the date in question when fate had dealt him this trump card. His intuition told him that he was playing a dangerous game, but the gambler in him secretly craved the thrill.

On the day, around 11:00 p.m., his black dinner jacket, concealing his Walther P99 in a leather belt-holster, Robert left Temple Mansions and was about to head to the parking lot to fetch his motorcycle when a chauffeur in a red-and-gold uniform sprang out of a shiny black Bentley parked across the way, opening the back door for him.

'ID?' inquired Rob. The chauffeur half-bowed, and displayed a driver's license that passed the firm's click-check.

Well, that is very gracious of them. I very much doubt any others of their guests would arrive on a motorbike, thought Robert, accepting the invitation.

On the way he tried to strike up a conversation with the chauffer, but despite of his best efforts the latter remained deaf and mute. However, upon their driving up to the gates of Oldland-on-Grove, he graced him with a faintly disgusted look and a golden Venetian mask, which Robert accepted.

Upon the twelfth strike of the clock from an ancient tower on the grounds, they drove into the wide-open gates to join the end of a long queue of posh cars – these four-wheeled poseurs reduced to crawling along a spacious alley lit with flaming torches between magnificent oak trees. Passing the security check halfway through, upon producing the encrypted invitation, they continued to the end of the drive, where, in the wake of a Rolls Royce Phantom, they took a gravel road leading towards the dramatically illuminated facade surrounded by the now-familiar landscaped gardens, with sculptures and fountains, where only recently Rob had been chased by the Dobermans.

Into the jaws of the devil, he thought at the sight of the approaching manor house, which was in the romantic French Chateau style of dirty-gray stone, complete with soaring towers and gables decorated with gilded suns.

Sol Invictus . . . the Invincible Sun. . .. there must be something behind the imagery, but what? he wondered, recalling what Professor Hayes had said about the pagan worship of the sun god.

The Bentley slowly drove up to the arch marking the entrance to the house and having adjusted his mask Robert left the car, without waiting for the chauffeur to open the door for him. Joining a party of other newly-arrived guests wearing identical gold masks, he followed them up the stone steps of the grand staircase, between serried ranks of motionless servants holding blazing torches.

Upstairs more servants ushered them into a long dark corridor; the light from the torches occasionally illuminating ancient portraits of some long-dead nobles, some of whom appeared to be watching them from the walls. Baroque violin music played, its lament rising at ornate gilded doors with heavy wrought iron handles. Butlers in blue eighteenth-century livery and white wigs threw open the heavy gilded doors: then Robert and his chance companions found themselves in a grand banqueting hall where a chamber orchestra of superior quality was playing in eighteenth-century dress. The only bizarre part of the scene was fractured antique dolls' heads and body parts were scattered artistically around the edges of the stage.

The masked guests were sitting at round tables exquisitely set with white embroidered linen, silver cutlery and fresh bouquets of red dahlias in Venetian vases. The tables were arranged in a peculiar formation: five circles with five tables in each, lit by the burning candles, like a constellation of stars on a dark night. At the far end of the hall was a magnificent Christmas tree almost attaining the height of the sumptuous ceiling and wearing an inverted five pointed gold star at its peak, which for some reason made Robert think of the Medal of Honour.

'Please, follow me, sir!' An elderly butler emerged as if from nowhere to accompany Robert to his table at the back.

There he found a vacant seat next to four seated guests: a rather elderly lady (judging by the withered skin of her neck under the black-and-white scarf and a mesh of fine wrinkles around her mouth); two pretty brunette twins in identical black lace who seemed easily young enough to be her granddaughters; a fat fellow with a massive build and a triple chin and a middle-aged man with a neat goatee.

'Good evening,' Robert said, politely greeting his table companions, and they barely acknowledged his presence as he took his place. *Hmm. It doesn't seem appropriate to introduce oneself here. I must find out where the Emelyanovs are sitting. Perhaps in the ring closest to the stage?*

He glanced around the faceless crowd, noting that there were no vacant seats left at the tables.

Butlers in white gloves were silently moving among the tables, topping up crystal glasses with fine wine and champagne. A mountain of hot buttered pancakes under a high gilded lid and caviar were delivered to their table and the large man unilaterally decided to make a start. The old lady refused pancakes, but helped herself luxuriously to the caviar – perhaps she was Russian? - smacking her lips in approval and licking the spoon. Her 'granddaughters' prickled Robert with appraising glances from under their masks, put a pancake on each of their plates, but then forgot all about food, whispering between themselves.

'It's the first time I've tasted caviar! In some countries they say you should make a wish if you taste a dish for the first time,' said Robert with a charming smile, attempting to encourage some small talk.

'Be careful with what you wish for, young man, because you might just get it,' said the old lady in a soft Scottish accent.

I wonder if her 'granddaughters' are also from Scotland? Thought Robert, glancing in the direction of the serious twins.

'Well, it'd be great if it was true! Then, to the beautiful ladies!' Robert raised his glass and the two gentlemen (who seemed to be in the middle of a private conversation) courteously followed his example. He tried to strike up a conversation again, but no one seemed to be disposed and he soon gave up.

Meanwhile, the fat man was saying something to his goatee-bearded neighbour in Russian, pausing from time to time to adjust his tight mask with an annoyed grunt. Listening carefully, Robert distinguished some Russian words:

'Emelyanov has gone completely nuts. He told me, *"I am linked to the cosmos. The Sun is my god and the Earth is my temple."* Or cathedral - I can't remember which.'

By the tone Robert guessed that he had known his confidante well for some time. The man with the goatee added, shaking his head, 'Yeah, the thunderstorm is my brother and God in every tree and pebble. Worse than the evangelicals in the States!'

'Tolik should never have left Russia: he's lost his entire identity here. To crown it all, he goes and falls, head over heels, in love with someone his daughter's age, in fact her former best friend, if the rumour I heard was true. . . By the way, which is the delightful Mrs. Emelyanova? They say she's well worth a second glance!'

CHAPTER 39

'Careful, someone may overhear. . . '

They cautiously looked around, while Robert pretended to be completely absorbed in the ballet, which had replaced the chamber orchestra on stage. Despite the fact that he'd never been a big ballet fan, it was simply impossible to remain indifferent by dancers from the Bolshoi . . . For dinner there was sturgeon soup followed by a jellied meat delicacy, 'The Tsar's Kholodets' with horseradish sauce on the side, which was hugely appreciated by his Russian neighbours. To his secret amusement, they seemed much relieved by hearing his Canadian accent, and continued to comment in undertones, not wasting much energy on the ladies on their table. The ladies were most intrigued by the show, occasionally whispering amongst themselves, though less impressed than the Russians when some female Estrada performer in a bombastic sparkly outfit with a tousled mane of hair appeared on stage and wailed hoarsely in Russian. Following the performance of the Crazy Horse *corps de ballet* from Moulin Rouge, the programme ended with a famous Italian tenor, who rightly earned tumultuous applause for his interpretation of 'Nessun Dorma'. Then the bells chimed outside and the clock struck three times. Robert checked his watch; it was indeed three in the morning.

A tall figure in a gold mask and a red robe appeared on the stage:

'Dear guests! Let us honor our Angel of Light by lighting a thousand points of light!' And with this – oohs and ahs - the Christmas tree suddenly became illuminated with countless miniature lights.

'A service will soon commence in the amphitheater, following which all guests are invited back to the house for a masquerade ball. Horse-drawn carriages are waiting for you outside . . . However, if any of you wish to first visit the medieval dungeon, might I ask you to be so good as to remain seated.'

The figure disappeared and most guests, including the ladies at their table, left their seats and headed for the doors.

'Shall we?' The fat man turned to neighbour, rising from his seat.

'Not I,' he retorted, in Russian. 'You can swan around your Moscow dacha in a horse-drawn carriage as much as you like, but when will either of us get another chance to visit a medieval dungeon? We'll live to tell the tale, don't you worry!'

'Are you still really looking for adventure at your age? All right, I'm game, I suppose,' the fat man muttered, sinking back in his chair. 'Ah! It seems Emelyanov himself is also going underground!'

Robert instantly followed his gaze towards the main table in the upper ring.

Which of them is Emelyanov? He wondered, looking at the identical masked faces. In the secretive atmosphere, he realized that he was unlikely to get the answer, but nevertheless made an attempt.

'Do you know which of these is our gracious host?' he asked the fat man, who seemed rather chattier than his friend.

'It's impossible to recognize anyone with these damn masks on, but I'm pretty sure he's the one leaning backwards at the main table, just over there,' he nodded towards several people with their golden faces turned to the stage. 'Are you going to the dungeon too?'

Robert nodded, noting that the Emelyanovs also remained in their places. He already had a reasonable plan of the grounds and couldn't wait to explore how to get out of the house through the underground passage. . . Also, he simply had to find some way of speaking to Sasha's father: only then would he be able to decide what to do next. Of course, it was difficult to predict where their conversation might go - especially if Emelyanov had really been driven mad. In which case it might well be necessary to get him out of here . . .

Meanwhile, servants equipped with burning torches escorted the remaining guests to the wide-open doors past the blindingly-lit Christmas tree. With tenacious gaze Robert's eye followed the Emelyanovs, determined not to lose them in the crowd, but having merged with the flow of guests, they soon disappeared. Once they were out of sight, the people remaining from the second ring of tables followed them ceremoniously. Finally it was their turn, and Robert headed for the exit together with his Russian neighbours, at the tail-end of the sightseeing party.

CHAPTER 39

After leaving the banqueting hall, they found themselves in a long corridor adorned with classical sculptures; its windows opening onto landscaped gardens from where the serene trickle of a water fountain could just be discerned. On the other side, private drawing rooms could be glimpsed sported gilded ornaments, antique objects of luxury, blood-red tapestries, and exquisite carpets in warm gold tones. The corridor ended in a right turn curving into the East Wing gallery of Renaissance masterpieces.

'In the Hermitage they still think they have the originals,' Robert overheard the larger Russian snigger, just as their procession came to a sudden halt.

Two of the servants lifted the edges of stunning Gobelins wall tapestries, revealing a low mahogany door. Their group lined up in a queue, and soon those who happened to be at the front crouched down and disappeared behind the door, one after another, accompanied at intervals by servants lighting their way. When his turn came, Robert followed the others behind the door.

Inside, the dungeon smelled of the damp mold covering its stone walls. The deeper under the ground they walked down the steep stone stairs, the lower the temperature fell. An English lady about ten people ahead wished to turn back but the people behind, including the fat Russian, barred the way.

Upon reaching the end of the stairs they found themselves in a spacious stone dungeon with a high ceiling, as Robert was surprised to find straightening up to his full height and touching moss-covered stones above his head with his hand. The floor seemed to have only recently been paved with brick of the same yellow color as the walls surrounding the castle – suggesting, to him at least, that the new owners made regular use of the tunnel. The light of torches revealed wall cavities branching out from the cellar, hinting at extensive underground pathways under the house.

'Damned mask! I can't be doing with it anymore, I'm taking it off,' said the fat Russian, breathing heavily from the stairway descent.

'We were warned not to do so! Be patient a little longer,' another Russian voice whispered.

'I don't care for these warnings, or for their Yule, either. Phew, that's so much better!'

Turning round, Robert saw the fat guy's face for the first time, his nose fleshy in the torchlight. The golden masks nearer the front had also turned around to face him briefly, but their replica faces, of course, did not alter, and no one said anything. They were continuing along a rising path when suddenly a bloodcurdling scream broke the silence, unnerving the servant besides Robert into dropping his torch, plunging their section of the party into comparative darkness.

'What's going on there?' asked Robert, his question was followed by some Russian obscenities from his companions. While the servant was falteringly fumbling with his flame, Robert quickly switched on a battery torch which he'd brought along, but failed to see anything suspicious.

'The dungeon is teeming with ghosts,' explained the servant, raising the re-lit torch. 'Probably they scared someone in front of us.'

Nobody contested this assumption, and without further adventures they emerged from the tunnel, finding themselves near the top steps of the amphitheatre. It was a dramatic setting, surrounded by a semi-ruined stone wall from the arches of which they could see the birch grove.

'How extraordinary!' said an English lady, 'When was it discovered?'

'It was excavated by the previous owner during the construction of defensive ditches last century. It's amazing how well the amphitheatre has been preserved since Roman times,' the servant replied, leading them down the stairs towards the stage.

In the middle a wooden structure made from birch, resembling a pyre, towered, encircled by a black iron fence with trident spears from under which straw sheaves stuck out. A tall moss-covered statue of a naked woman with an owl on her shoulder stood behind the fence, facing the pyre, as if overseeing it. The owl's eye sockets were ominously lit, like burning hot coals, casting part of the shadow in an eerie red glow.

CHAPTER 39

'The eternal flame of her eyes will not go out, either in night or day,' the servant whispered, as if the owl could overhear them.

'Who is she?' asked Robert, feeling chills down his spine. His question remained unanswered, but he suddenly felt that he knew the answer already:

Lilith!

The statute looked almost exactly like the Babylonian Lilith he had spotted in one of the books in the British Library.

The rows of seats with black velvet cushions were filling up quickly with the arriving guests, all gossiping amongst themselves, as if with relief that the underground ordeal was over. . . To Robert's relief he spotted the Emelyanovs in the red velvet seats in the front row, which seemed to have been designated for important guests yet to arrive, as the remaining seats were still empty. He might still get his chance to speak to Sasha's father. . .

Only a row of chairs and the trident iron spears of the fence separated his hosts from the pyre. However, Rob didn't have much time to look around, as hoof-beats and the creak of the carriage wheels announced the arrival of the remaining guests. The servants ushered them to vacant seats before swiftly disappearing back into the tunnel. Everyone fixed their glances upon the stage in anticipation of the upcoming performance: only most of the front-row seats remained empty.

Suddenly, a funeral march began, as every eye was fastened on six powerful male figures wearing hooded red robes and masks approaching, between them carrying something resembling a very large human body wrapped in black fabric. Marching down to the macabre music they walked solemnly up to the pyre onto which they lowered their heavy cargo before lining up facing it. The funeral march stopped to the sound of loud sobbing, which appeared to be coming from the figure on the pyre.

'Please! Have mercy! I haven't done anything,' begged a distraught male voice, choking in sobs.

What the ****! Robert winced inwardly. There was disquiet among the audience, with several people assuring others that it 'was just another show.'

But at the same time, Robert noticed how they had all been drawn in, watching the stage spellbound along with the rest of the audience, feeling almost a participant in some bizarre ceremony.

Accompanied by the resurrected funeral march a hunched old man in a silver hooded robe appeared on the stage carrying an unlit torch in one hand. All six figures bowed low at his appearance. Moving softly he walked towards the statue. In a moment two red-and-gold figures silently left the line of six and followed him, keeping a respectful distance.

A high Priest, Robert guessed, unable to take his eyes off the stage.

The High Priest stopped by the statute and the two red-garbed figures, as if on a signal, leveled with him. He handed the torch to one of them and the red figure instantly started climbing up the steep staircase towards the statute, until just high enough to reach the burning eyes of the owl with the torch. Having lit it, he then carefully carried it to the ground, where he returned it to the High Priest, who, walked back towards the pyre in a snail's pace, muttering something under his breath.

'The pyre, illuminating the shadows,' was all Robert heard, along with the rest of the crowd.

'Have mercy! Please!' Suddenly came from the bound body, loud over the Priest's barely audible mutterings.

But the High Priest was already by the pyre. Ignoring the victim's pleas, he lit the funeral pyre, and greedy flames almost reaching the sky swallowed the blood-curdling cries. A few more words rose to Robert on the breeze as the implacable voice continued: 'We praise you, black birds, pecking the carrion. . .'

The screams gradually subsided, turned into faint moaning until silenced altogether, while the insatiable flames continued to rage, appearing to inflame the trident spears with a ring of fire. The High Priest and the six red-hooded figures then silently took their places in the front row on the red-velveted armchairs.

Robert caught a strong odor of something that reminded him of rotten eggs: even the smoking of the fire couldn't drown it out: suddenly a dull

CHAPTER 39

hissing was heard behind him. Turning around, he saw several monstrous slimy reptiles, which looked rather like enormous lizards sitting amongst the guests and staring at the fire with ravenous, yellow, bulging eyes. Their human neighbours stayed calmly in their places without even flinching, almost as if hypnotized into not realising what was happening. And then, as he blinked, the lizards turned back into well-dressed, masked guests.

Could it be that their dinner had been laced with some drug and this strange hallucinations was the result? He thought, trying to have recourse to logic, but immediately rejected the idea, unable to doubt the reality of what he had seen.

The rest of the 'service' was incomprehensible to anyone, as far as Robert could tell: incantations, some rather odd singing, and finally inoffensive excerpts from Mozart's *Magic Flute*. The guests - seemingly in high spirits at the conclusion of this part of the event – then hurried to the horse-drawn carriages waiting to bring them back to the house to dress for the ball.

But where is Emelyanov? thought Robert, glancing around. He walked through the masked crowd, but couldn't see his hostess' distinctive pair of shoulders anywhere.

I must find him at the ball. It's my last, best chance. . .

Still overwhelmed by what he had just witnessed, Robert decided to walk instead of queuing for a carriage, and think about it all on the way. . . Several of the others appeared to agree with him: there was an English couple just in from of him asking eager questions of a torch-carrying servant.

Was all that had happened on stage a masterful acting? He pondered. *Most likely it was, but what if it hadn't been? In that case all those in attendance of that disturbingly weird night 'service' had unwillingly became accomplices to a murder.*

And there had been something oddly familiar in the tones of the victim . . . *what if it had been Sasha's own father?* He thought, in a rush of horror. But then he thought: no, the pair of shoulders and her husband had been in the front row, assuming everyone else had been correct. So: what other tones might he have half-recognised? Then he remembered that he had failed to spot his table companions in the amphitheatre, even though they had definitely come out of the tunnel with him - the fat man swiftly fixing his mask back on. Robert couldn't really tell where they had disappeared to in the crowd of guests afterwards.

What if that was the fat guy who had been sacrificed to the stone woman? Suddenly it dawned on him. *He had clearly violated their rules by revealing his face and scorning their precious Yule. Even if no one else in the tunnel spoke Russian his attitude had been blatantly obvious. (Perhaps one of the servants had informed on him?) And yet was it possible, to haul him off and kill him, just like that? Judging by their conversation at the table, both Russian knew Emelyanov well. They even called him Tolik, with the familiarity of old acquaintances. Or maybe the fat man was some business partner who had been in Emelyanov's way? – that might explain their comparatively lowly table, as well. . . At any rate, if the big one doesn't show up at the ball. . .*

Robert, lost in thought, wandered down the gravel alley towards the house behind the English couple, occasionally overtaken by horse-drawn carriages.

CHAPTER 40

With dawn approaching the mansion seemed to have metamorphosed: its windows were illuminated, as if brushed with fire, so bright that it seemed almost like daylight; the gilded suns on its towers and gables razor-sharp and the house itself far more glowing and also far less sinister than when Rob had seen it.

In the banqueting hall the masquerade was in full swing: formally dressed, golden-faced couples swept past Robert, almost knocking him off his feet, and everyone, even the eldest of the guests, seemed full of gleaming energy, as if they had been plugged into a mega-power supply overnight. There was not even a trace of the off-hand superiority that had prevailed during dinner or the bewilderment and mystification that had greeted the bizarre 'service': the crowd seemed rowdy and even playful, like young children, giving off a highly-charged vibe: a group of ladies were laughing madly, a couple in the corner seemed to be enjoying a private brawl, while two distinguished-looking middle-aged gentlemen were awkwardly running around with outstretched arms, trying in vain to catch three giggling dwarves who were darting in and out among the dancing couples emitting high-pitched squeals.

Robert searched the crowd from one end to the other, but without spotting Emelyanov or his missus anywhere. His new Russian acquaintances, whether embellished with several chins or with a neat goatee, were also nowhere to be seen. He would, he thought, have really liked to have spotted the pudgy one . . . Rob was about to leave the banqueting hall in quest of Sasha's father, when suddenly a curvaceous young woman with golden hair down her waist rushed up to him. Wearing, like several others, a short Roman tunic barely covering her hips, she seemed both distressed and rather unsteady on her feet –

unsurprisingly, given the height of her stilettoes - and Rob had to grasp her arm to prevent her from falling over.

Her eyes blazed beseechingly at him from a face, which, although stamped by the inevitable golden mask, couldn't hide the real terror beneath.

'Dance with me; we're being watched,' she whispered, saying out loud, 'Sorry! Just lost my balance for a second.' Obeying, he put his arm around her waist and whirled her into a waltz, instantly merging with the crowd. She danced brilliantly, he couldn't help observing, more like a professional than an amateur.

'Where are you from?' he asked, having recognised a distinct Eastern European accent. She drew closer.

'Help me! They want to kill me. But don't stop dancing, in case we draw their attention, please!' she whispered, ignoring his question. They continued to waltz until the smooth flowing melody changed to the unmistakable rhythm of a tango. Then she spun them off to one side.

'Please, come with me! – If we're stopped, just say that you've chosen me.'

'Just that? I've chosen you?'

'Yes, that only,' she said tensely.

They moved through the double doors and found themselves in an empty, darkened corridor leading to the East Wing. The woman glanced around fearfully to ensure that no one could hear before she began speaking rapidly and nervously, hardly pausing for breath.

'I am from Latvia. A man in Riga promised me a really good job in London, earning lots of money by dancing in an exclusive nightclub and - like an idiot - I gladly accepted, even though I had to leave my two-year-old Dmitri with my mother.

'Upon arriving at Heathrow with four others, our passports were taken from us and we were beaten and brought here. Then we were imprisoned in a dungeon – a real dungeon, I do not exaggerate, there is one here! – Then one day a girl from Hungary overheard the guards saying that we were being kept alive only to be sacrificed on the night of the ball. That is why we were

CHAPTER 40

brought to this accursed place! And those girls chosen by the guests are "lucky, so lucky!"' At this she smiled bitterly. 'Before being killed, we are to satisfy any perverted desire a guest might name - only to be killed afterwards!'

She nodded towards closed doors from where muffled screams, interrupted by macabre laughter, cries, wails, moans and unintelligible voices could just be discerned.

'They don't know that we know. If you're truly human - if you still have a heart – please help me to escape from this hell!'

Robert considered: *Sounds like a typical sex-trafficking tale, except for the threat to kill . . . and really, why would they choose to kill her? A human commodity – especially one still so young and attractive - could be sold many times over, bringing in steady profits. Her intended murderers must have paid extremely highly for the chance to screw her and then murder her . . . unless it was some perverted voodoo thing like the 'service' had been, with human sacrifice at its heart? Either way, of course, I can't just leave her to die. . .* He recalled the secret tunnel leading to the amphitheatre and resolutely took her hand: 'Let's go!'

They were hurrying towards the East Wing when one of the closed doors swung open and the fat Russian emerged, contentedly puffing on a cigar and vaguely adjusting his tight mask.

'Ah, my Canadian friend!' he joked. 'Great party, isn't it? Very unlike the grim show they put on for us earlier. And as for the girls, they are all top-notch! I see you've got yourself a beauty!' and here he leered at Robert's golden-haired companion, who shrank fearfully from him.

'Have fun, my friend,' said Robert, grimly continuing in the same direction.

So, the great fatso is still alive! Of course, everything that had seemed to have happened at the amphitheatre had been simply a show. They wouldn't dare to kill someone in front of all those guests, he thought, at the same time greatly relieved.

At the end of the corridor they were about to turn the corner when the woman suddenly stopped dead in her tracks and anxiously squeezed his hand, whispering, 'Oh God, I'm dead – it's one of the guards!' . . . Some muscleman in a dark suit was strolling along the gallery: his back to them, the gun in his holster very obvious.

I'll have to take him on and then hide his body in the dungeon. I should still have enough time to return to the ball and find Emelyanov, thought Robert, his right hand reaching for his gun. He was interrupted by her anxious voice in his ear: 'We must go back – quickly! - before he sees us!' She insistently tugged the sleeve of his jacket, pulling him round the corner, adding, 'We need to hide: they're bound to start looking for me soon!'

She glanced around in utter terror. Fortunately, with the Russian gone, the corridor was empty again, but even then the music and discourse emanating from banqueting hall couldn't entirely obliterate the sounds or orgies arising from behind almost every closed door. Rob chose one at random and listened intently, but couldn't hear a thing: they were in luck - the room was empty. Robert pulled the gilded door handle, but the door seemed to be locked. He was about to pick the lock, when his companion pushed the opposite left side of the door, which gave way with ease.

'Here, nothing is the way it is supposed to be,' she said bitterly. Robert closed and locked the door behind them. Before them lay a barely-lit smoking room decorated in Moorish style: its crimson velvet curtains and draperies rich with motifs of the Middle East exuded a faint echo of Cuban cigars. On the ebonized round table embellished with marquetry he spotted two empty brandy glasses.

Robert thought: *Hmm, it's useless to stay here; someone might come in at any moment! The tunnel is probably the only way to bypass the security guards* . . .

Suddenly he heard the girl gasp and saw her falling into a secret doorway buried in some paneling, which she must have leaned against. . . In a flash he had caught her and pulled her to him, picking up the subtle and distinctive scent of her skin, which reminded him of a tropical forest after rain, or of the sea with a wind blowing over it . . . Her fathomless eyes swept him like a plunging wave and before he knew it, he was dragged into the ocean, sinking down like a stone.

CHAPTER 40

I'm drowning...

This thought flashed through his deep subconscious; while his mind registered, with a detached surprise, that drowning was easy and even enjoyable. He didn't even wish to resist, feeling lethargic yet strangely ethereal with everything swimming before his eyes. Then he heard someone calling him. Turning round, he saw a Cuban girl with a white mariposa flower between her black braids. The apparition, from a long-buried childhood memory, was standing on a shoreline in a colorful Bata Cubana, waving to him.

'Robert, come here!' she cried joyfully.

Without thinking he rushed towards her, to the sound of waves caressing the beach, plunging deeper and deeper into the sea's rhythm until his thoughts, being washed away, were drowned in the depths of the limitless ocean. . .

'Wake up! You must hurry!'

He heard the faint voice of his long-long Cuban sweetheart as if from a great distance; yet at the same time she seemed to be leaning over him, insistently shaking him by the shoulder, forcing Robert to open his eyes. Once this happened his vision of her burst like a soap bubble. Instead, he was still holding the Latvian stranger in his arms, but how long they had been standing like this, he couldn't have said - a minute, an hour - time itself seemed to have ceased to exist. Gently freeing herself from his embrace, she took off her mask. Her face was a striking blend of the delicate freshness of youth and a robust sexuality; her wide-open eyes both disarmed with their innocence and burned with urgency.

How can anyone even consider destroying a creature of such gleaming beauty? Robert wondered, unable to take his eyes off of her. He followed her example, gladly removing his mask and loosening his bow-tie. Meanwhile she was saying, 'How I long to get back to my little Dmitri! . . . My mother must be going crazy, not knowing whether I am alive or else dead. . . Will you really help me? You have such a noble face!' Fighting back the tears, she looked at him, transfigured with hope.

'I'll do all that I can,' Rob promised recklessly. 'I'd love to get you to London - then you'd be able to see for yourself what a great city it is, full of normal, decent people. It's unacceptable for this damned house and its freakish residents to be your only memories of England! I should be able to find a way to get you home; I have contacts…they can probably help. With luck your nightmare will soon be over – but first we have to get you out of here. Hang on to me tight, otherwise you won't get far, especially on those stilts of yours!'

By this point Robert had completely forgotten the main purpose of his visit. All that mattered was to save this Latvian girl at any price, so that he could be with her - he felt as if all the years of his life had only existed in preparation for this fateful meeting, while the thought that his mission was predestined was growing more and more embedded in his mind.

They slipped through the secret door she had accidentally located, which slammed behind them, and were instantly swallowed up by complete darkness. Robert swiftly turned on his torch. In response, a bright light suddenly blinded him; someone flashed past in the dark and with lightning speed pulled out a gun almost before Robert had enough time to point his Walther - which he instantly lowered, in that split-second that it took his brain to accept that his own reflection was facing him in a mirror opposite. Then his fingers located the light switch within the ice-cold glass of the wall.

Instead of a secret passage – which he'd hoped might lead to the tunnel - they had found themselves in a confined space of some strange, square room. Paneled, and with mirrors everywhere, it was empty and appeared to have neither windows nor doors, except for its secret link to the smoking room. From the countless mirrors which stretched from floor to the ceiling hundreds of his twins indulged Rob in a childish outstaring game, and the longer he looked, lost in the mirrored infinity, the more it seemed to him that he himself was merely their reflected image, some anonymous creature lacking both heart and soul.

'Desire is love. Love is desire,' he heard.

Her voice brought him out of his trance.

CHAPTER 40

'What did you say?'

'Nothing. I don't want to die,' the Latvian whispered, pressing her body into his, and making him acutely aware of the warm nakedness under her short silk tunic.

'Don't worry! I won't let anyone hurt you,' he told her, as she buried her face in his chest.

He felt himself becoming very hard with a burning, almost aching, sensation deep inside his groin. The mirror floor treacherously betrayed her tantalizing availability while the spaghetti straps of her tunic seemed ready to slip off her shoulders, beneath the heavy gold of her hair. A scorching desire awakened, stirring his blood. Sensing this, she slowly lifted her head, her eyes burning deep into his being, and bit into his lip. The silk garment fell to her feet, revealing the limitless beauty of her flesh to the lecherous gaze of a thousand mirrors. Robert was lost long before, with an involuntary groan, he acknowledged the virtuosity of her fingers. Greedily drinking her scent, forgetting their danger, forgetting everything, he caressed the scalding nakedness of her body. She lowered herself to her knees, caressing his swollen member with her sensual lips, winging him nearer and nearer to purest rapture, until, at the last moment, straddling him on the floor and merging with him in wave after wave of ecstasy, while at the same time catching an admiring glimpse of her multiple reflections in all the mirrors . . . while leaving him limp with pleasure.

Eventually, she rose and casually slipped back into her silk tunic, as if nothing had happened, tossing back her golden hair and rewarding Robert with a curiously mocking look. Rob rose from the floor with a strange sensation that he had been used, which he fiercely tried to shake off, but this, not altogether unpleasant, feeling for some reason failed to let go of him.

He was still watching her, still half-hypnotised, when his eyes alighted upon an owl tattoo on her right shoulder . . . In that second Robert felt as if plunged into an icy shower, dumbstruck at his own blindness.

'So! Do you know who I am yet? – or need I introduce myself?' teased Lilith, releasing masses of lustrous black curls from under her wig with a contemptuous flick of her fingers.

He straightened up. 'First tell me this: were the sex slaves and their planned murder a mere trick, like the one in the amphitheatre?'

He couldn't stop staring at her, but this time in disbelief, noting that her eyes popped slightly, rather like a frog's. She no longer seemed either beautiful or particularly desirable; in fact she looked repulsively reptilian: he shivered at the thought that he had, only minutes ago. . .

She shrugged.

'All the world's a stage, and all the men and women merely players. . . Of course, what Shakespeare couldn't reveal was that a few of us write the script, which all the "players" blindly follow!'

'Well, I certainly failed to recognize *your* part under that damned mask! Otherwise, I'd have never touched you!'

'How sweet. But as long as it wasn't really me, but was instead some random Latvian whore then that would have been fine . . . As for Sasha – that *is* your girlfriend's name, if I'm not mistaken? – I can just imagine her face, had she seen us!' And with that Lilith burst out laughing, until her merry, insolent eyes met his stony gaze. 'Oh, for fuck's sake, just chill out! Only idiots or complete losers are entirely faithful. For the rest, it's simply too boring!' She faked a yawn. 'What were you doing here last Sunday, anyway? I suppose you came to save my husband? I'm betting sweet little Sashka doesn't even know that you're here – am I right?'

'I heard you'd driven him crazy – is it true? What have you done to him?'

'Many men go crazy for me. There's not much I can do about that situation,' she shrugged, with a coquettish smile – but then, her mood suddenly altering, she added: 'No one can help him where he is now, but your own skin is still salvageable - if you're a good boy, of course!'

Robert froze as a terrible guess crossed his mind.

CHAPTER 40

'You *should* have been able to see precisely what happened to him,' said Lilith lightly, confirming his grimmest conjectures. 'You were only a few rows behind . . . However, his fate had long since been sealed. Now we'll send his "double" to sell factories in the Urals, where, according to the official version, poor Mr Emelyanov will disappear for good . . . '

'You witch!' Robert lunged towards her, upon which he felt suddenly pulled back, as if unseen hands were attempting to half-choke him.

Alka was much amused. 'Ha ha! Don't you realise that it was I who had you invited here, for you to see everything with your own eyes? After all, you so longed to learn about us! . . . Yet what you failed to realise was, in reality, so simple, so very simple! Listen then, and learn . . . The whole world belongs to us, the inheritors of ancient wisdom and the true servants of our Angel of Light, the sun god – Lucifer, Lucifer himself! He is our voice, our true god, the god of reason who has chosen to reveal to us - and to us alone - the deep knowledge, the one who illuminated our paths when we were wandering in the darkness of ignorance, the one who grants to his true believers enormous power, riches and glory! You can have no idea who graced us with their presences earlier!'

Robert remembered the huge reptiles in the amphitheatre and said, through gritted teeth, 'I think I might just have some vague idea.'

But the exultant Lilith paid him no attention. 'Since ancient times all kings and emperors served him, and him alone, worshipping their lord through mysterious symbols. Times have changed, but our faith has prevailed, becoming a secret religion hidden from the vast majority, just as the faces of those present here are hidden behind gold masks. This is something you won't find out from your Oxford professors! . . . A double face conceals a double faith with its double mind, which truly doubles the pleasure of our deceit, but only because it's all for the universal good, so that we can fulfill our sacred duty to institute that true order which the world so desperately needs. Soon we'll no longer need to wear masks. We'll rule freely and openly, just as in ancient Babylon, worshipping our lord, the light-bearer!'

'No one will ever pray to your Satan, however you disguise him!' Robert rasped back, wondering sickly if the invisible fist around his vocal cords would finish him off.

'Ha! They only need to know what we required them to know – a half-truth, which is still a lie. Only the truly elect are aware of our plan. We'll enslave the rest, confuse their minds, re-interpret history, play with the scripture and mask the agenda using compulsory "education" to bring up a young generation already advanced in witchcraft,' she smiled mischievously at him, adding, 'Yes, you are really rather handsome, aren't you? Far too good for someone like her . . . At any rate, with the help of our global PR we'll lead a trend of "spiritual awakening" for all people to worship the rocks and the trees, mother earth and the stars – thankfully, the Angel of Light, may he be blessed, has provided his own teachings. These people will consider themselves spiritual, progressive and even enlightened, since, by rejecting their true creator, they'll believe in pretty much anything - much to Lucifer's delight! Our rich, successful and beautiful representatives will convince people that rebellion against God is, in fact, progress towards liberty by giving it all a glamorous and even revolutionary coating, so that most people - as usual! – will strive to blindly imitate us. And we'll finally win the battle for the soul of humanity, allowing our own beloved Angel of Light to rejoice in the Heaven of his own choosing . . . In the new age of the late 21st and 22nd centuries the churches will universally preach the religion of ancient Babylon, singing Hallelujahs to the Egyptian Trinity, while monuments to Osiris, Horus and Isis will tower everywhere, right in front of your noses. . .

'Of course, while we're busy achieving our goals, the "sheep" will still need to be distracted and entertained. The media, which has always been one of our many tools, and also so-called "education" will hypnotise and dumb down the masses to such extent that, even if they're accidentally exposed to the truth,

CHAPTER 40

they will never believe it.' At this, Lilith laughed out loud. 'The whole world will be deceived!'

'Hey, you're one crazy witch!' gasped Robert, pretending admiration. His hand was just moving towards the gun in his belt, when he felt the invisible hands upon him reinforce their grips, half-strangling him as he pulled ineffectually against them, hacking with cough.

Alka continued, paying not the slightest attention to his convulsions, 'Open your eyes, fool, and you'll see that Lucifer was ever with us: on banknotes, on secret signs: his symbols are everywhere! As the saying goes, if you want to hide a tree, plant it in the forest. His phallic towers and Egyptian obelisks rise towards our beloved sun in every capital of the world; his upside-down pentagram is formatted into the streets of the federal city itself and, as an ardent student of maths, I could read you an entire lecture on his sacred numerics (personally I rather like number five – a top mark in Russia and also the number associated with Mars, the Babylonian God of War) . . . He is loved and idolized throughout all the Earth, which belongs to him. I could tell you much more, but I simply can't be bothered, since you'll forget it all anyway . . . you must forget it all. . . ' Here Lilith finally paused, as if lost in thought

'As for you, ramrod, you'll always obey someone else's orders. We command armies composed of the likes of you! And you'll never be free because all you are is just a small cog within our perfect master-machine. . . In short, I believe that your – ha! – mission here is now over. Goodbye. I doubt we'll ever meet again.'

He realized that he was no longer being choked, but the bloody picture of the horrible murder in the amphitheatre was still flickering before his eyes, mixed with the mirror images, images he longed to break into thousands of tiny pieces. He was hardly aware that Lilith was now intoning: 'MIRROR MIRROR ALL AROUND, ON THE CEILING, ON THE GROUND, SPINNING FASTER ROUND AND ROUND! Mavr!' Here Lilith rather impatiently clapped her hands, and a huge black cat, easily the size of a panther, appeared in the room. Robert was surprised to note that there was no reflection of him in any of the mirrors.

'Please see our guest out,' she ordered the cat, before turning her back on Robert, making it humiliatingly clear that his audience with her was now over.

He could never recall what happened next, or how he found himself on the soft leather backseat of the same Bentley, speeding on the M4 towards London, except that, this time, the chauffeur in a red and gold uniform vaguely reminded him of that monstrous black cat.

Was it all real or was he in the middle of some surreal dream? He thought, falling as steeply into unconsciousness as if into a pit. . .

When Robert opened his eyes, he was back in Temple Mansions. Obviously utterly exhausted, he had dropped onto the bed without even bothering to take his shoes off, and instantly fallen asleep.

He couldn't tell how long he had been sleeping when the persistent ringing of a phone woke him, but as soon as he reached for the receiver it stopped ringing. His whole body felt sore and aching, as if he'd been plowing a field: he even struggled to untie his shoelaces, feeling a sharp pain in his lower back at any attempt to bend down.

Robert lifted the wrist of his weighted arm and stared at the watch, trying to focus. It showed 8:00 p.m.

But why am I wearing my dinner jacket? Did I go somewhere? But if so, where? He struggled to find an answer, but his brain felt like an over-squeezed lemon, an aching sensation gripped his head, and everything swam sickly before his eyes.

Finally, with a huge effort, he got up and staggered into the kitchen, half-holding onto the walls, in order to look for something to eat. The fridge was empty, except a few cans of beer. Holding an icy can beside his aching head he turned on the TV in the living room and, stared almost blankly at the Sky Sports' ice hockey: normally his favourite. A sudden phone ringing startled him, but this time he managed to answer in time:

CHAPTER 40

'Robert Lambert.'

'Finally! Where have you been? We couldn't get hold of you for days!' The voice barked on the line and without waiting for an answer, commanded in the tone that brooked no argument: 'See you at midnight, sharp. We need to have an urgent conversation. Agreed?'

'Agreed,' said Rob, his ear buzzing unpleasantly. Robert put the phone down and glanced at the TV screen - he had exactly an hour before his meeting. He headed under a tepid shower, beginning to gradually feel more alert, although his body still ached and his lips felt strangely sore. He seemed to have had nightmares all night . . .

Dressed in jeans and a fresh shirt he was on his way out when his eyes fell on the gold Venetian mask left on the marble table in the living room. He paused, his brain working overtime in a desperate attempt to make the connection, but all that emerged was a splitting headache, as if an alien force had mercilessly seized his head in a grip of iron. . . *Perhaps Sasha and I have been invited to some masquerade party?* he wondered. The mask certainly had a familiar look . . .

Anyway, he couldn't be late. Robert picked up his jacket, slammed the door behind him and, without waiting for the elevator, hurried down the stairs to fetch his motorcycle, deciding to drop by the nearest petrol station for an M&S bacon-and-cheese puff pastry on his way.

At 12:00 a.m. sharp he was already in rendezvous 17, having automatically used his usual series of measures in order to ensure that he hadn't been followed, finishing by slipping his motorcycle along the side of a building with the red-glazed terracotta façade.

CHAPTER 41

'Incredible! To survive a fall like that with only a few cuts and bruises! She must have nine lives,' I heard a stunned male voice through a vague haze.

'I wonder if we could sell this one to a newspaper? I could snap her on my phone,' some female suggested nearby.

'You never know. I'd Google her. Cool name, anyway – probably Russkie - and rather a looker as well,' agreed the male nurse.

Subconsciously I felt them gazing at me and kept my eyes shut, hearing the woman add, 'Remember that size 0, forty-something Hollywood overdose case? Sam got around 5000 for that from the *Mail on Sunday* . . . think I'll go back to the nurse station and take a shuftie at the computer just in case!' Her voice buzzed unpleasantly in my ear.

I must have fallen somewhere . . . that would explain the strangely drained feeling I had, as if all energy had been sapped away from me. . .

As this realisation dawned, without opening my eyes, I immediately tried to wriggle my toes under the blanket, which to my great relief, I was able to do. My arms seemed to be all right too, though I felt subtly bruised inside, and utterly exhausted, as if I hadn't slept in a hundred years. Once the nurses moved on I tried opening my eyes, but it felt as if someone had suspended some free weights on my eyelids.

What happened to me? I tried to remember whilst struggling in vain with an overwhelming desire to sleep. Then a bright light, almost like a laser, speared my eyes illuminating the blood vessels.

Lights! I muttered, fearing that I was going blind, but no one seemed to hear me.

'The injection will take quite a while to wear off,' I thought I heard from a distance in deeper tones, before drifting back to sleep.

In my dream I was transported to some student party with torches glowing in the dark and people drinking alcohol straight from the bottles. *Brompton Road* read the inscription in cream and green on the tiled wall in front of me. I heard some guys talking nearby.

'My granddad told me that this place was a secret command center was during the war. Then, the building was transferred to some ministry or other and the station never opened again.'

'Hello, Miss South Kensington. Enjoying the party?' Another guy in a gray T-shirt with 'The Waterloo' inscribed across it smiled at me. 'I am Marcel.'

'Hi, I'm Sasha.'

Only then did I take much notice of my own peculiar outfit –green jeans along with a yellow top with a glued-on paper compass, its arrow pointing south. Along with other students I was also holding a torch, as well as some invitation on the back of the London Tube map, which read: *'On 22 December you are invited to the midnight Underground party - THE super-secret Party of the Year. Location to be disclosed by word of mouth.'*

Meanwhile, Marcel's friend was saying: 'Only Timokha could arrange a party in a ghost station! What a party animal! Remember his 21st?'

I then recalled that Tim, or Timokha, as he liked to be called, had invited me to come along, as a fellow Russian. (Timokha ostentatiously claimed Russian origins through a great-grandfather from Odessa.)

What a pity Robert's not here, I thought, aware that he would hardly have encouraged me to attend such a social event on my own. . . Still, I'd jumped at the opportunity for at least one evening not to be left alone with the gloomy thoughts which have been haunting me ever since Robert's most recent departure. Recently, some notion of inevitable and impending disaster has been haunting me relentlessly. Worse still, I've caught myself feeling certain that someone has been constantly watching me, often feeling a piercing gaze upon my back - but every time I turned around, I couldn't see anyone.

CHAPTER 41

It's so mean to send someone away on a business trip right before Christmas! And as usual, he didn't even tell me where he was going! I felt equally angry with Rob and with his mysterious Institute.

However, such behavior was nothing new: Robert rarely talked about his work and never considered it necessary to report his movements. He simply presented another departure or sudden arrival, never asking my opinion on the matter, and making it perfectly clear that - within our relationship, at least - I had to be fully prepared to accept him on his own terms.

'Sasha! We're here!' Jill and her boyfriend Alex waved at me from the crowd and I hurried to join them along with the 'Waterloo' guy, Marcel.

'We've already been here for hours; everyone's wasted, and there's no return train for another two hours! I can't believe I was so stupid as to come,' Jill rattled on, without taking time out in order to say hello. She was wearing a tweed jacket with a dark knee-length skirt and a short string of pearls around her neck.

'I'm a Sloane,' she explained, upon registering my bewildered expression. Meanwhile, Marcel – who had been checking the Tube map – said, 'There's no such Tube station.'

'It's slang for upper-class girls living in a very posh area of Chelsea,' I explained.

'Aha! Like "Rich bitch!"'

Marcel looked Jill over with a renewed interest whilst Alex pulled his girlfriend closer, much to Jill's delight, adding, 'Anyway, there must be an exit somewhere. And if we're quick, we should still be in plenty of time to get to my mate's party near Earl's Court. I suggest that we go on a tour of the station right now,' he said, taking the lead.

'I only hope we don't meet any rats on the way,' said Jill to me, in an undertone, and we both shivered at the thought.

We jumped off the stub platform and started walking, following the shabby 'Way Out' signs along the tunnel walls. To our surprise, the tunnel was lit by a series of yellowish lamps and it was hard to imagine that for the past 50 years it had been entirely empty. After a hundred metres, we encountered several partition walls (probably built during the war) each with a small doorway. We went through one of them and then ascended a short, narrow staircase ending up in a crossover area - which to our disappointment only led to the opposite track.

'Wow, look at this layer of dust: it's like sand! My shoes are completely ruined! Let's just just go back and wait for the train with the others,' Jill moaned. However, Alex remained reluctant to give up on his idea.

'Let's carry on down towards the platform. We just need to locate the "Way Out" sign leading to the exit,' he said.

We carried on along the green-tiled corridor until eventually we came to a wide staircase with a thick yellow stripe down the middle.

Alex was exultant. 'This must be where the lift shafts used to be!' Inspired, we started climbing up the stairs, holding onto walls covered with a thick layer of dust, so as not to stumble in the dark.

'I feel like a chimneysweep! I just want to go home!' Jill whimpered.

'I just want a hot shower,' I moaned.

'Girls, please stop whining! We'll get you home safely,' Marcel promised, and we had no choice but to continue.

Upstairs we eventually found ourselves at a dead-end – a short corridor blocked by a locked gate with iron bars featuring a frightening skull and crossbones sign inscribed: *Danger! High Voltage. Authorized entry only. In emergency the door can be opened with key №13.*

'13? Hardly a lucky number, especially in emergency,' noted Marcel sardonically.

However, there seemed to be no point in hanging about and we all turned round to head back.

Number 13... I suddenly paused on the stairs, my memory vigorously pummeling me: though I didn't know what it was on about.

CHAPTER 41

Then, it dawned on me. *Robert!* He'd often said that thirteen was his lucky number - not only did he live in apartment 13, but even made an effort to book plane seats with 13 in their numbers. I marveled: why had I suddenly recollected this, out of the blue?

For whatever reason I suddenly had a strange impulse to return to that door: I didn't know why, it just seemed important, even urgent.

'Sasha, don't leg behind! We *must* catch this train; otherwise we'll be stuck here till morning. I still can't believe what an idiot I was to agree to come to this party at all!' Jill's fretful voice resounded from below.

I called: 'I'll catch up with you shortly! I've lost a pendant, my mother's gift. . . '

'Well, for God's sake hurry or you'll miss the train,' I heard Jill respond.

'No worries, I remember exactly where I dropped it,' I shouted over my shoulder, unsure if anyone heard me and hurried back up the stairs.

Feeling nervy and out of breath, I returned to the door covered with grey dust. What if it wasn't locked after all? Uncertain about why I was even there, instead of forming a combined front against any rats, I pushed hard against it, but – no surprise – the door was locked. I then tried peeking through the iron bars, but the metallic danger sign prevented me from seeing anything. Resigned, I was about to turn around and go back, when I heard a distinct click from behind the door.

Key №13, I remembered, crouching down in front of the keyhole with a light shining through.

In that moment I couldn't believe my eyes! There, leaning on the fireproof safe stood a silver motorcycle at which I stared, gobsmacked. As I watched, two men entered. I recognized Robert at once and almost recoiled in shock. I only saw the other fellow's heavy middle-aged back, encased in his long black coat. They both immediately disappeared from my sight but didn't leave the room, since I could hear heels clattering against the concrete floor, as one of them – I guessed Robert's companion – was pacing about the room.

I pressed my ear to the door, hurting it in my anxiety to overhear something of their conversation.

'So, where have you been lately?' inquired a voice with a North American accent and without waiting for an answer continued: 'Anyway, I have some news for you: you're to go to Bogota. There's something urgent to do.'

'No probs,' said Rob tensely.

'You'll be going in your McKensey persona, of course: I know it takes a few hours to get that right.'

'McKensey is also OK. When will I be back?'

'Actually, Rob, it turns out that you have no further business here in London.'

Rob took his time responding, while my heart almost stopped beating.

'What, you mean I'm not coming back?'

'Certainly not in the short or medium-term. There was some problem – I'm not privy to the whole story, but they said you'd understand – something to do with a house in Wiltshire. Your current identity is reckoned compromised. . . Ring a bell, does it?'

'Look,' said Rob urgently, 'Bogota is not a problem, the McKensey disguise is no problem. But I need a little time, a day, even half a day. . . '

'You haven't got it, have you? The flight's booked and the snow's already falling, so we have to hurry. In Bogota one of our men will introduce you to the DEA attaché, with whom you can go over the logistics. The Colombians behaved precisely according to our expectations. As you know, we had to sweat fucking buckets in order to wriggle back into favour . . . Now all that's left is to make sure that everything goes smoothly at the customs. Everything's under control at the D.C. end . . . Your ticket's waiting in the usual place at Heathrow and you should still have a few hours to pack.'

'But I need to say goodbye,' Robert's voice expressed unusual hesitancy.

'What for?' The owner of the other voice sounded genuinely surprised. 'You've always been so good at cutting off private connections! But do whatever

CHAPTER 41

you like,' the voice grew indifferent, clearly losing interest. 'Whatever happens, you've got to make that flight.'

The sound of retreating footsteps and the clatter of heels on metal followed; I could hear no more.

Leaning against the door, I felt completely crushed by what I'd just heard - in a single instant, my entire world had collapsed like a house of cards. And yet, at the same time, suddenly it all made sense: Robert's frequent 'work trips' – I almost wished it had been a case of another woman instead! – his secure strength, and his worldliness about so many things I didn't have a clue about. A click of the light switch brought me out of my stupor, leaving me thinking *What if they find me here spying on spies?*

Recoiling from the door in a sudden panic, I ran towards the stairs and instantly stumbled over something soft, which silently leapt from under my feet into darkness. I screamed in shock, dropping my torch, which immediately went out, along with any hope of ever finding it and found myself in near-total darkness.

It must have been a cat, I tried to console myself, moving ahead in search of the staircase. It was too big to be a rat, surely... With a sudden gust of draught a door slammed nearby, accompanied by that long sarcastic laugh I had known ever since my childhood, but which now made my skin crawl. Startled, I'd half-turned, when I suddenly felt a strong push in the middle of my back. Losing my balance I felt myself rushing screaming down a lift shaft, snatching in passing at some hoisting ropes in which I seemed to have become partly entangled, as if suspended in a free-floating cocoon.

'Somebody, help me!' I screamed at the top of my lungs.

I thought I heard somebody shout back and in a surge of hope screamed again as loudly as I could, when I realized it was only a mocking echo thrown back by the chill walls. It felt as if I was most of the way down a well.

My friends must have caught the train back by now. I thought whilst desperately trying to find a ledge on the wall to get a foothold.

I stretched out my arm, grasping at some wire cable instead and suddenly felt myself being jerked high in the air by a vibrant shock accompanied by a furious electric pain juddering right through my body, removing even the breath from my lungs. *I'm falling. . . falling. . . I'm about to die. . .*

When I came to I felt as if my insides had been scooped out. Then I thought *Am I dead? If so, I disappointedly failed to get into heaven . . .*

I knew this because Alka herself – it was she who had laughed, of course – was standing before me, arrowed by a narrow ray of sickly yellow underground light. Her arms were folded and she was attired in long navy or black velvet, its plunging neckline adorned with some strange and lurid symbols in blood red.

'Alka? It was you! You pushed me! I knew it!

'You are sharp; I'll give you that,' she sniggered, though simultaneously wrinkling her nose in disgust. 'Yet so righteous and pure! Yuck! By the way, my name is Lilith now; remember! Perhaps you're even smart enough to guess why I'm here? On second thoughts, please don't strain yourself; your head must be like jelly after a nasty fall like that, ha ha!'

I was still too shocked or groggy to respond: Alka surveyed me contemptuously.

'Well, I'm here to do you a favour really. Think about it, what's the point of your whole existence, anyway? You've never known how to enjoy life – you never wanted anything and even if you *had* got your precious daddy's fortune you'd assuredly have wasted it!. . . He's dead, by the way – had a heart attack somewhere in the Urals this afternoon, what a surprise *that* was!' She chuckled then – or at least I thought she did – and, in a blind uprush of fury and sudden sorrow I lunged towards her, longing to dig my nails into the lovely face. . .

I might as well have spared myself the trouble. A strange orange-red glow briefly illuminated her eyeballs and I was as frozen in place as if I'd been tasered.

'So, a little filial loyalty at the last, eh? Don't worry, you lost him a long time ago! . . . Now where was I? Right, well, unlike you, I always wanted everything because I have ambition and drive, along with a few other notable

CHAPTER 41

talents. . . Not to mention that everyone simply adores me, including your precious Robert. Oh, yes! Just ask him who he's been with – in *every* sense, believe me – '

Of course, I didn't believe *that*, not for a moment. Instead it was obvious that she was purely intent upon tormenting me – though I still couldn't see why. After all, she'd already had taken my father, effectively killed my poor mother and absconded with most of my inheritance. . . I thought, bewildered: *Why did I never see this before? – she hates me. She must have always hated me!* Meanwhile, Alka leaned back against a hot water pipe and examined her perfect fingernails.

'See, I was simply destined to get everything in this life. While you… Well, let's face it; nobody's going to miss an orphan, especially one without much money. . . I guess it will have to be up to me to grieve for you all!. . . Oh, all right, you may as well speak, for the last time!' And with this she murmured something under her breath and I found that I could move my face again, though the rest of me was still grasped by – by whatever it was that held me.

I burst out rashly, 'I'm not afraid of you! You can deceive everyone else but I know exactly who you are! You're just Alka – a stray cat who has been homed and treated with kindness only to turn into a vicious creature capable of scratching and biting even those who had wished to help it! I don't believe a single word you say. You're simply treacherous, vain, selfish, greedy and arrogant Alka, a fake charmer who'd clamber over any number of dead bodies just in order to get what she wants! You may rise very high – I wouldn't put anything past you now – but to me you'll only ever be a Nobody from Nowhere, as we both know all too well!'

To my astonishment I registered a furious bewilderment on Alka's face. She half-spat at me: 'Alka? I am Lilith! Lilith! You have no notion how powerful I am! She hissed, absolutely stamping her foot.

I've found your weak spot now, I thought with satisfaction, adding fiercely, 'Powers? I don't care about your silly powers! All you are is an imagination, an evil spirit, which craves the thought of instilling fear into hearts and blindness into minds! If you *are* Lilith – and I really don't care what fancy names you use nowadays – then Alka must be the lost human body, some carcass left sleeping at home, whilst you're sent here to do her dirty work! Why, you don't even have the guts to face me in person!'

Alka looked at me, stunned, eyes wide with horror. 'What are you talking about?' she snarled.

From somewhere I heard the sound of sirens. The police? An ambulance?

I must have guessed part of her secret! I thought triumphantly, and carried on: 'But I am not going to be your victim! You've killed both my parents, but you'll live to regret it, Alka! You shall not suffer a witch to live!'

Just as these words – and I still don't know where they came from – were coming out of my mouth, I heard approaching footsteps, commands, even shouting. *They've found me,* I thought utterly relieved. The vision of Alka wavered, shivered and disappeared, releasing the rest of my body to surge back to life. The duel was over and I had won it, although I instinctively knew it was only a first round. . .

Only in the ambulance, still lifted and subtly exhilarated with the discovery of new purpose and power, did I remember what I'd overheard in the passageway.

Robert, I thought, for a moment utterly desolate. Then somebody gave me an injection and I lost consciousness.

***

'It's Friday and Jane will probably wear red underwear for our date. She seems to think red turns me on, not that I mind, of course. . . And now look, Katie, as if by chance, forgot to do up her top button! Bend forward like that again, beauty!' I heard a lustful male voice through my dream.

Wakening, I purposely kept my eyes half-closed, looking through my eyelashes. I spotted two female nurses in light blue uniforms tagging along behind a bespectacled doctor, clipboard in hand. I couldn't hear their conversation, however, as the level of noise was astonishing. There were rows of beds opposite complete with female patients of every decade, almost all of whom seemed to be talking incessantly and loudly over each other, despite the doctor's presence, and yet the doctor didn't even seem aware of it...

Why is the hospital so horribly noisy?

I tried to turn down the sound in my mind, and to my surprise, the tumult died down. Then I remembered.

I had some really bizarre dream...with Alka in it...No, wait it wasn't a dream... I had to fight for my life – and I won - but why am I here, wasting time? It's up to me to revenge the deaths of my parents... In my anxiety I opened my eyes and locked gaze with one of the nurses, who immediately leaned over me and inquired compassionately:

'Are you awake? How do you feel?'

Must be Katie, I thought spotting the missing top button on her uniform.

But then, before I could even reply, the multitude of voices flooded in again, seemingly from everywhere. After the initial shock I caught words, sentences and even snatches of phrases:

'The food here is disgusting!'

'Home! I can't wait to go home . . . but will I ever go home?'

'If he doesn't come to see me soon, I'll exclude him from my will!'

The last voice seemed to be coming from a nearby bed belonging to an elderly lady with a chignon, but her lips didn't move and her eyes remained closed.

'He was such a good boy until that tart made him marry her!' I heard her say, again without moving her mouth.

The voices grew louder bickering, moaning and chatting incessantly amongst themselves. In desperation I gripped my head: *Am I going mad?* This was the moment when I realized: *Thoughts! I can hear other people's thoughts!* I froze then almost as fully as when Alka had 'frozen' me, trying to fathom what this might mean. *Had she done it, out of malevolence, or accidentally? Was it a stage in her efforts to kill me too? Had my own father. . . And how was I supposed to live with something like this? I can't even handle my own thoughts!* I kept thinking, in full disarray, whilst the nurses were anxiously fussing over me.

***

A business-class flight attendant with an air of superiority drew the curtain, walling the privileged few off from the economy travelers, and began serving lunch. Robert glanced at the food blankly. He had no appetite, but it was a long-haul flight to Bogota.

'I'll come back,' he promised himself, just as he did every time it hurt. . . . It had hurt before, in Japan, in California, but this time was so much worse.

Robert leaned back in his seat and closed his eyes, longing to drift away into a doze. This time, he vowed to himself, he really would come back. . .

Sashenka…

In his thoughts he was already feeling light and free somewhere 'over the rainbow where skies are blue and the dreams that you dare to dream really do come true…'

About the Author

E.L. Gogh grew up in Ukraine, but at the age of 16 she came to England to study at Marlborough College. After graduating she qualified as a lawyer and practised law in London, where she is presently based. The Secrets of One Marlborough College Girl is her debut novel.

Printed in Great Britain
by Amazon